Kerryn Higgs was born in Sale, Victoria in 1946 and was educated at the Universities of Melbourne and Tasmania. She has written poetry and plays and does freelance environmental research and writing. She divides her time between the bush in northern NSW and Brooklyn, New York.

ALL THAT FALSE
INSTRUCTION

Kerryn Higgs

Spinifex Press Pty Ltd
504 Queensberry Street
North Melbourne, Vic. 3051
Australia
women@spinifexpress.com.au
http://www.spinifexpress.com.au

First published 1975 by Angus & Robertson (Sydney, London)
Also published in Sirius Paperback 1981 by Angus and Robertson
And 1979 by Fraüenoffensive, Munchen
2nd edition 2001 by Spinifex Press

Cover design by Deb Snibson
Typeset in Garamond by Palmer Higgs Pty Ltd
Printed and bound by McPhersons Printing Group

National Library of Australia
Cataloguing-in-publication data:
Higgs, Kerryn, 1946– .
    All that false instruction.

    2nd ed. (corr.)
    ISBN 1 876756 14 4.

I. Title

A823.3

"This publication has been assisted as part of a joint
initiative by the Commonwealth Government through
the Australia Council, its Arts Funding and Advisory
Body, and the National Council for the Centenary of
Federation."

to Penny and Robert
for all their true friendship,
especially
in the years at Montrose Road

For permission to use the following copyright material the author and the publishers wish to thank: The Estate of W.B.Yeats for the quotation from 'A Dialogue of Self and Soul' from *The Collected Poems of W.B. Yeats* on p.96; The Harville Press for the quotation from 'Autumn' by Boris Pasternak on p.100; Bronwen Levy for the quotation from 'Different Views, Longer Prospects', her address at *Women Writing: Views and Prospects 1975–1995* on p.241; Sue Higgins (Sheridan) for the quotation from 'Breaking the Rules: New Fiction by Australian Women', published in *Meanjin*, on p.242; Suzanne Bellamy for the quotations from 'Fucking Men is for Saints', published in *Refractory Girl*, on p.243; and Germaine Greer for the quotations from *The Female Eunuch* (1970) on p.243.

Acknowledgments

Thanks are due to many people who contributed to the original edition of this book back in the seventies. To Penny and Robert Gay, who intermittently spent their Sunday afternoons over two years reading the emerging draft and providing fine critical comment as well as endless encouragement. To Toni Pollard who brought home the news of the Angus and Robertson Fellowship, to A&R who awarded it to me, enabling me to write without interruption in 1972, and to John Ferguson and the staff at A&R London for their enthusiasm and warmth. Thanks, too, to Dave Kerrigan and Sandy Buchan who lived with me at Powerscroft Road through the intensive part of the writing and provided evenings of Neil Young, great food and riveting conversation. Thanks to Carl Harrison-Ford, my 1973 editor, who did a very good job with the first draft and to Jenny Pausacker for her comments on the London draft in 1972 and for trawling her memory, more recently, to shed light on events from that era.

Thanks to Susan Hawthorne at Spinifex for her enthusiasm for both the book itself and the idea of returning it to its original setting.

Thanks also to my brother Shane who first raised the idea of reviving the novel for what he hoped would be the wider audience he felt it deserved. Special thanks to Sandy Fitts for the preservation and copying of my letters during my years in Europe and for her un-flagging and indispensable research, lexical and advisory work during the revision of the novel and the writing of the Afterword. And profound thanks to Harriet Malinowitz, for her acute and affectionate reading of the book, for seeking me out to write her article about it, inspiring me to take action to revive it—and exerting gentle but unremitting pressure in the direction of returning to my own name—as well as for her astute and unstinting editorial assistance.

Contents

Introduction

It's 1989, and the St Marks Bookshop, a beloved independent bookstore in New York City's East Village, has announced a dire-straits, crisis-averting booksale. Only too happy to conflate my book-buying addiction with my devotion to the cause, I go in, browse zealously among the fiction shelves. Soon, I notice a lone volume whose compact size, stiff cardboard cover, and cramped Victorian-era typeface flag it as clearly *not* a product of the US publishing industry. I am attracted, most of all, to its title—*All That False Instruction*—which I am convinced (without any evidence of authorial intention) refers to a long-term preoccupation of mine, the dearth of education in youth applicable to the many sorts of lives a person might actually go on to live.

On the cover is an illustration of a tough, auburn-haired young woman who has halted on her bicycle to stare purposefully at a blonde in a whimsical, Jane Austenish outfit on a balcony; the latter gazes back, transfixed and alarmed. Yet something in the picture is ambiguous; at one moment, the women's eyes seem locked in portentous exchange; observed again, they seem to be missing eye contact altogether, their respective intense expressions simply, sadly, not hooking up. On the back cover, a short blurb advises that this is 'an extraordinary first novel' about a young lesbian in Australia who painfully confronts 'the pressures of an outraged society'. No information is given about Elizabeth Riley, the author. A modern-day *Well of Loneliness?* I buy it.

Reading, I'm immediately charmed by a particular fusion of humour and pathos I haven't encountered in other lesbian novels I've read. Riley's narrator-protagonist Maureen Craig couches her confessions in wry self-deprecation, exposing herself as a Woody Allenish, Charlie Chaplinesque schlemiel whose intelligence and sensitivity saturate her with an excruciating consciousness of her failed attempts to garner love. Her voice is also strikingly female as it lays bare Maureen's hunger for warmth and belonging.

Beginning with her rural, working-class childhood—in which her spirit is nearly overpowered by her sadistic mother, her favoured younger brother, and her social isolation (all of which are offset by prodigious academic achievement, affording the classic scholarship kid's way out)—the narrative traces her development through, and just beyond, her college years in stiflingly conformist mid-1960s Australia. *All That False Instruction* is, in many ways, an archetypal outsider's Bildungsroman. Like prior fictions of loneliness refracted through the permeability of mistreated waifs (David Copperfield, Sara Crewe, Alice Walker's Celie), the bitterly honed vision of marginals or outcasts (Shylock, Hester Prynne, Fanny Price), or the agonising sentience of highly charged intellects (Agnes Smedley's Marie Rogers, Jane Eyre, Hamlet), Riley's is one in which feeling and desire, transgressive and suppressed, are ultimately resurrected as moral imperatives of their own.

Leaving her volatile home for university, the gifted but vulnerable and needy Maureen finds intellectual companionship and a succession of lovers, each of whom promptly withers in the face of social pressure (from parents, peers, college officials) to go straight. Maureen is, on the one hand, a fool for love; she will compromise almost anything—her pride, her backbone, her reputation, her sense of self—for immersion in another woman. She is disturbingly malleable, so eager to please that she irritates and makes herself an easy object of exploitation. Yet her compulsion to love and be loved is so powerful that it becomes a radicalising force. With no women's movement, no gay liberation movement, no bohemian culture to fortify her, Maureen is nonetheless galvanised by her growing conviction that pleasure, desire, and warm human connection have an integrity of their own that supersedes that of the Law, whether religious, state, bourgeois, or patriarchal.

The slavishly smitten teenager who will turn up late at night in her glib and callous ex-lover's room, hopefully brandishing mugs of coffee (making the reader cringe and cry out, 'No, go back!' as if to Janet Leigh driving towards the Bates Motel) is the embryonic form of the mythic hero, the one who ventures beyond the putatively safe walls of the town in search of a higher redemptive truth in the great unknown. By the end of the novel, Maureen hasn't quite found a new mythos which will help her to live, but she has set out in quest of one. She is ready to grapple with her fundamental difference from most of the society in which she is ensconced; this means choosing self-exile from the pervasive conservatism of Australia, at least for a time.

For Maureen, this quest is more realistic than it is for most; unfettered by the frosty nurturance that drives the parents of her peers to sever their offspring's same-sex ties and secure their marital prospects 'for their own good', she is free to go. Indeed, it appears that freedom's just another word for nothing left to lose.

When the scandal of Maureen's affair with another student breaks in her college residence—resulting in Maureen's cruel rejection by her lover, a threatened expulsion, and a tidal wave of social ostracism—she is left to wrestle alone with the inflicted image of herself as monstrous, predatory lesbian. Despairing, she finds in a Yeats poem 'a little sense of solidarity': 'How in the name of heaven can I escape/ That defiling and disfigured shape/The mirror of malicious eyes/Casts upon my eyes until at last/I think that shape must be my shape?'

'That shape is not my shape, even though they have nearly persuaded me that it is,' Maureen reflects. But self-determination, for the outsider, often comes at the expense of intimate human connection—a conundrum especially painful for the female hero. There is no Nietzschean or Emersonian smugness in Maureen Craig's alienation; she is no Hermann Hesse character, no aloof nonconformist striding resolutely apart from the herd. 'I desperately want acceptance entirely on my terms—it isn't to be had; if I can't generate it myself I won't get it at all. This is a burden I cannot, easily, carry,' she agonises.

Near the end of the book, just before she leaves the country, she briefly meets an American feminist at a party who disgorges early-1970s oracular wisdom about male violence and drudgy housewifery and allusions to the power of separatism. (Maureen absorbs it all with fascination, reporting, 'I was not at all sure what she meant, but she spoke with a serene conviction that could not be gainsaid.') This exchange furnishes a perplexing departure from the trajectory of the book; Jody's justification of lesbianism has nothing to do with desire, but rather with a rational solution to gender oppression and inequity. In a strange sense, she (like many lesbian-feminists of that era) invokes the same liberal Western ideal that 'rational men' have agreed, since the Enlightenment, legitimates a good society: the entitlement of the downtrodden to an equal share of justice. With a rhetorical appeal to the potentially hostile reader based on women's 'rights' and long-endured 'wrongs', she manages to elide the sticky question of whether human passions carry any valid claims of their own. Maureen seems sufficiently roused by Jody's exposé to leave one fearing that the helplessly affection-driven invert that we've come to love will suddenly come out as a political lesbian (an ephemeral species which, 'sleeping-with-the-enemy' politics and all, always seemed ineluctably heterosexual).

Still, looking back at this strange turn in the narrative more than three decades after it ostensibly transpired, one is struck by its historical richness: lesbianism and feminism *were* beginning to coalesce ideologically at precisely that moment, with the guiding premise that a common enemy—the patriarchy—rendered them virtually synonymous. Maureen Craig would naturally have been captivated by an argument that seemed unimpeachable in a way that the story of her own frustrated needs did not. And in hindsight it is also heartening to know, even if Maureen doesn't, that Jody's speech is a harbinger of real liberatory movements which are at hand, and which will even infiltrate the stodginess Down Under. Their shape will be her shape.

Despite her frequent slides into the slough of despond, Maureen remains an appealing character/narrator because of her wit and edge, regularly aimed at herself. Especially engaging is her ability to portray feigned emotions and acknowledge a parallel track of acute perceptions at the same time (a two-pronged state of consciousness that has often served as the modus operandi of the closet). Ignored at a party, she explains, 'I keep moving, not for myself so much as to foster the illusion of a sought-after Craig breezing from one expectant group to the next.' After the breakup with Julia, her first lover, Maureen is offered 'tea and sympathy' by Libby, a self-professed liberal heterosexual who grills her intently:

> 'Isn't it hard if you find yourself looking at girls with a sort of sexual interest?' Her blue eyes wide open with a studied innocence. I felt curiously unnerved and babbled, 'Well no, not so much. I mean. I don't really.' That's not the point, I thought, but couldn't sound convincing ...
>
> '... I would have thought, once you've had a relationship with a girl, it'd remain a perpetual possibility ...'
>
> 'Only in a world of speculation,' I countered in her style. We laughed ...
>
> 'But what if the friend were willing? What if she wanted it too?'
>
> 'There's a difference. Like Julia. I don't know.' But I was quite aware of what she might be driving at.

Some of the most poignantly comic scenes in the novel are those which portray the trials of a young lesbian earnestly and rigorously working at being heterosexual. In her romance with the gallant, quixotic Andy, Maureen—bent on losing her virginity, but defeated by Andy's chivalry at every turn—finds herself at a loss for a language in which to communicate her actual desires:

> I was terrified of blunder, almost convinced that there existed a body of precise rules governing the minutest details, something which couldn't possibly be in print, yet something which everyone but myself appeared to be in command of ...

To adhere to 'rules' which are not 'in print' anywhere but which are nonetheless universally in force is an imperative that continually stumps Maureen. Each of her attempts to conform to 'the rules' brings either failure or, at best, renewed stupefaction as to why such hollow, anhedonic rules carry such clout at all. The central conundrum of her life—the impossibility of listening to her own voice without losing the acceptance of others—is neatly expressed in Maureen's wry observation to Cleo before setting off on her travels:

[A]lways, always without fail, I'd do anything for anyone if they'd like me for it. Terribly untenable for someone who usually wanted to do the things people never like.

Riley's handling of Maureen's relationship with Cleo—and its seemingly inevitable demise—is remarkable for its sensitivity to the plight of good people who cannot help making cowardly choices. Had Cleo been damned for her choice, the novel might have descended into a polemic in which Jody and her 'correct instruction' would have enjoyed a shallow triumph. But Cleo is portrayed sympathetically—not as a villain, not as a betrayer nor even as someone inordinately weak, but simply as a fairly typical human casualty of stultifyingly rigid cultural mores. Maureen is the 'hero' of the story, the maverick outsider capable of undertaking a journey beyond the bounds of civilisation as we know it. If a fundamental component of the mythic hero's story is a voyage to the underworld, Maureen's decision to leave home is spurred by the realisation that the world in which she has come of age *is* that underworld; she has performed exceedingly difficult tasks there, negotiated with the gods (who in this case appear in the earthly guise of parents and school administrators), and has emerged by discovering the capacity within herself *not* to compromise, the fortitude to seek fulfilment somewhere beyond the pale.

Cleo, on the other hand, is an ordinary person who has to live without heroic visions or abilities. Though she briefly managed to stand at a philosophic remove from the world of her peers during her university years, she hasn't ultimately unearthed any inner resources to counteract the pain and isolation which almost always trail in the wake of social disapproval. For her, conformity brings comfort; there is companionable solace in blending into the blur of everyone else. It is a humble version of a Faustian bargain—to sell one's soul for very little in return. That this is an all too familiar bargain in which many women have been cheated of their lives is clear to Maureen as well as to the reader. Maureen and Cleo recognise and accept one another across the divide which separates them; there is resignation, but not rancour, in the knowledge that their paths will run in precisely opposite directions.

Finishing the book in 1989, I am enchanted with it. Among other things, Riley has induced me to heave with sobs—always, for me, the high watermark of sublime literature. The ending has been as fulfilling as the last moments of *Casablanca*. There is, too, something about the novel's frank emotional intensity that lends it the immediacy of memoir. Certainly, novelistic structure and keeping the reader fully cognisant of the chronology of events at all times are of less paramount importance here than immersion in the endearingly sardonic, self-exposing subjectivity of Maureen. The telegraphic prose style sounds less like modernist stream-of-consciousness than like a surge of turbulent water that's broken through a dam. Maureen Craig is often too preoccupied with life's meatier issues to adequately introduce minor characters who waltz into—and then out of—her narrative, or to bother explaining what anyone looks like. But the colloquial dialogue she reproduces, peppered with Aussie slang, brings individuals into focus as vividly as the beer bottles piled in the backyard of her student digs evoke the exuberance of undomesticated youth.

Putting the book down, I find myself fervently hoping that Maureen goes on to have a good life. But then she can't, can she? She's a fictional character. Her story is over. *She's* over.

Elizabeth Riley's apparently over, too. The book, published fourteen years prior to my reading it, is out of print; no literary or book-industry people in the US have heard of it, not even feminists; no print source that I can locate mentions it; and no Australian I meet knows more than that it exists, Riley's unknown, doesn't seem to have produced anything else.

It's the fall of 1999, and promotional messages from an 'independent feminist press' in Melbourne called Spinifex are appearing sporadically in my email. About to delete one, I change my mind and impulsively click on 'Reply', writing, 'Since you are such a self-described press from Australia, I was wondering if you'd have the answer to something I've been wondering about for a long time ...' A friendly editor responds with what at this point feels like a cornucopia of information: 'Elizabeth Riley' is a pseudonym, her real name is Kerryn Higgs, she's living in northern New South Wales, and the editor would be happy to forward a letter to her if I'd like to send one.

Of course I would! Only, what will I say? I'm struck by shyness in the unexpected face of opportunity. After all these years, I can't bring myself to simply send a gushing fan's 'I loved your book' (to which she will, most likely, reply graciously yet deflatingly, 'Thank you'). So I rapidly hatch the idea of proposing to write an article about her book and what's happened to her in the years since she published *All That False Instruction*. My plan is, fortunately, supported by my editor at *The Women's Review of Books,* an American monthly to which I contribute. Armed with a legitimate *raison d'être*, I send an email to my long-sought author via the friendly editor in Melbourne. I get a reply. (She's cautiously interested in my proposal.) To which I reply (with reassuring details). To which she replies. (She has to decide whether it's time to finally 'jump off the cliff' and shed her pseudonym.) It is, after all, the Electronic Age, and very soon I'm in a voluminous daily correspondence with Riley/Higgs (/Craig?).

We write about writing, language, politics, parental loss, Jane Campion films, feminism, cricket, Prozac, class, Reconciliation, rainforest ecology, Australian shiraz. But most importantly, she unravels for me, at last, the mysteries of *All That False Instruction*'s publishing history and 'Riley's' unaccountable obscurity. The book, I learn, had been awarded a major literary prize in its development stage in the early 1970s. Publisher, media, and family members had trumpeted the news of the incipient novel before becoming apprised of its lesbian content. When the novel's subject matter was revealed and libel suits were threatened, Higgs and her publishers heeded hastily-sought legal advice to release the book under a pseudonym. Higgs retreated to the shelter of anonymity with (as she confessed in one email to me) some relief, while her publishers grimly tried to market a novel severed from both its prize-winning glory and a live author to promote it.

Despite these setbacks, there was good word of mouth and much appreciation for the work among Australian feminists; and the critics who weren't inflamed by what they perceived to be the 'anti-male' standpoint of Australia's first patently lesbian novel received it with interest and praise. *All That False Instruction* sold well for a first novel, eventually coming out in paperback and in a German edition. It probably would have achieved wider recognition had it been reissued in 1989, when the publisher wanted to include it in a new paperback series of Australian fiction, asserting that the time had come to 'get this notable work the attention that it deserves.' But with both of her parents still alive, Higgs once again baulked at the use of her real name, and the plan was abandoned. Apart from the used copies and remainders which still occasionally circulated, and a stack of musty hardcovers propping up a mattress in a spare room, the book—and the furore which had surrounded it—faded from view.

The university at which I teach generously supports my work on the planned article, and in April 2000 I fly to Australia to interview Kerryn in person. Outside customs at the airport in Sydney, she is, as promised, easy to recognise: a very small, slight woman with an explosion of bright red hair. At 53, her swift, jaunty movements radiate energy and competence. We drive out of Sydney, across the Harbour Bridge, and head north up the coast. We stop for lunch at the Karuah River, where pelicans fly overhead. My host, I discover, always travels with a gas burner, a billy, and complete tea-making supplies.

As I munch my first Vegemite sandwich and ask questions with the uninhibited abandon of the truly jetlagged, she tells me more about the last three decades of her life. While living in London in the early 1970s, she'd read a couple of key texts published by eminent scientists hoping to persuade the rest of western civilisation that an environmental crisis was imminent and could yet be averted. The first Club of Rome report and *Blueprint for Survival* were enormously persuasive to her, and she returned to Australia 'with the absolutely explicit intention of getting a four-wheel drive, finding a very remote place at the end of a road somewhere, and creating a self-sufficient agriculture.' She laughs. 'I've been at it for 27 years, and there's no sign of it yet!'

In the attempt, she did found a rural community that continues to exist as a part-time retreat for a number of urban women. But not all members shared her sense of imminent ecological disaster or her mania for self-sufficiency. Perhaps it was just as well. 'By the 1980s,' she says, 'I realised that even if the world was going to collapse at some future time, I had definitely got the timing wrong.'

Along the way, she'd taught women's studies, creative writing, and environmental studies at the University of New South Wales. Later, while working for the public service, she also taught herself building, chainsaw mechanics, solar electrics, irrigation, botany, and geology out in the bush, and over the course of twenty years built herself a stone and timber hexagonal-shaped cabin. In the mid-1990s, she went to Tasmania and earned a diploma in environmental studies, with a thesis on beetles. 'Fleetingly,' she says, 'I was the southern hemisphere's only expert on predatory beetles of the rainforest leaf litter.' Urged and funded to go on for a Ph.D. happily pursuing her study of 'invertebrates in all their mind-boggling variety—very good work for an obsessive, taxonomic sort of person'—she suddenly, for the first time since 1972, received a literary grant. She left the beetles and set out for 18 months in her remote 'hex', working on an unwieldy, uncompleted novel which in resignation she came to simply call The Unmanageable Manuscript.

As we continue our journey up to the lush river valley where Kerryn lives, she gives me a synopsis of The Unmanageable—a story of intrigue in which a tribe of wild women face off against rapacious landowners ready to destroy stands of fragile rainforest. I'm a bit startled at how radically the fanciful, adventure-charged plot of this later work departs from the passionate inner landscape of *All That False Instruction* that I have so taken to heart, but I don't want to be like the Kathy Bates character in the film *Misery,* the 'Number One Fan' who tortures the author who thwarts her readerly wishes. Besides, I'm impressed at her scope; not one to be stuck in a strictly personal, psychological viewpoint, and unlike the nervous arty types who took 'Physics for Poets' to satisfy their science requirements at American universities, this person has the guts to branch out, to amalgamate far-flung experiences and interests. 'Anyway,' she reassures me, 'I'm still interested in the humour of human relations.'

Her house, a beautiful old converted timber church, is nestled among jacaranda trees. On the verandah, I read chunks of The Unmanageable and watch parrots, magpies, ibis, currawongs, mudlarks, and kookaburras flutter among the branches. In preparation for my visit, I'd asked Kerryn to gather together any critical writing that had appeared on *All That False Instruction*. Internet and database searches had disentombed references she'd never known existed. Now, as maggies sing and kookas cackle, I burrow into my chair and eagerly plough through the pile of clippings, many of which had—amazingly to me—long eluded the author as well as myself.

The articles were published—in both Australian and British periodicals—beginning in the mid-1970s (when *ATFI* first appeared) and throughout the 1980s. Whether laudatory or dismissive, critics were riveted on the novel's bold subject matter and forthright language. In many cases, the dividing line of appraisal appears to have been drawn based on gender, with women generally sympathetic to Maureen Craig's despair of finding heterosexual satisfaction and full humanity as a woman, and men frequently (though not always) angry at what they perceived to be a polemic supported by a stacked deck of sorry male specimens.

Sue Higgins, writing in *Meanjin Quarterly* ('Breaking the Rules: New Fiction by Australian Women', Summer 1975) argued that Riley's novel affirmed a view of

love as Eros, passion and energy, that refuses to romanticise, and so avoids both idealism and its correlative cynicism.

In a *Birmingham Post* review (22 November 1975), Elizabeth Harvey located the novel within a tradition of gay writing:

All That False Instruction ... is an honest effort to deal with one aspect of love. Havelock Ellis would have welcomed such evidence.

Meanwhile, in a *Nation Review* piece (6–12 February 1976), Carole Ferrier saw *All That False Instruction* within a tradition of Australian women's writing:

The novel is in many ways a rewriting, 30 years later, of Stead's *For Love Alone*—except that, rather than pursuing an ideal of heterosexual love, the heroine has a concept of herself as a person worthy of being loved, if social conditions could allow this on her terms.

A scholarly survey called *The New Diversity: Australian Fiction*

1970–88 (Ken Gelder and Paul Salzman, McPhee Gribble Publishers, 1989) placed Riley within the 'realist' tradition, noting that at the same time 'the novel's progamme is uniquely radical: it wishes to make a place in the world for the lesbian woman and for sexual frankness.'

Other critics agreed. Mary Lord wrote in the *Australian Book Review* ('A good bundle of early goodies,' October 1981):

> This is a powerful first novel, psychologically persuasive and, at times, painfully explicit. It is shocking in its realism, its cool description of scenes many of us would prefer not to know about, and in its unselfconscious use of language unfit for the drawing-room ...

Margaret Smith, writing on 'Novelists of the 1970s' in Carole Ferrier's collection *Gender, Politics, and Fiction: Twentieth Century Australian Women's Novels* (UQP, 1985), lauded the 'breadth' of *All That False Instruction,* and observed:

> Many reviewers still seem surprised that Elizabeth Riley's work is so competent and far-reaching; it was largely overlooked in 1975 because of the nature of its material ... [It] also deals with a wide range of human relationships, not only lesbian ones.

Marsaili Cameron, in *Gay News, London* back in 1975, was one of the few to have early-on reached the same conclusion: 'It's a pity, in a way, about the subtitle,' she wrote. (*A Novel of Lesbian Love* had been appended by the publisher to the title on the original hardcover edition, over Kerryn's protests. At the time of my visit, this crass act of pandering to sensationalism still rankles the author.) 'The heroine of this novel is looking for many things, not just love, lesbian or otherwise. One of the things she's pretty concerned about, for example, is her desire to live a fully human life.'

The novel's 'frankness', remarked upon in almost all accounts, was assessed by various critics in strikingly diverse ways. 'Elizabeth Riley, in *All That False Instruction,* shows a strong talent for language. The dialogue is racy and fluent,' wrote Sue Ross in *Campaign* (April 1976, 44). Olaf Ruhen, writing in the Melbourne *Age* (21 February 1976), was less impressed. Finding the novel to be 'overstated' and a socially superfluous artifact (Radclyffe Hall had already 'invoked sympathy if not respectability for the daughters of Lesbos' in her 'rather stuffy book' *The Well of Loneliness* almost fifty years earlier; what more needed to be said on the subject?), Ruhen considered *All That False Instruction* to be mainly about the exercises and frustrations of tribadism, with a few hetero experiences thrown in for contrast ... That the lady can write well is abundantly apparent in many places, but in others a deliberate predilection for gutter language makes much of the communication repugnant.

John Lapsley, writing in *The Australian* in 1975, praised Riley for, among other things, her 'level-headed' and 'sensitive, illuminating account' of a lesbian's coming-of-age. But he took umbrage at her depiction of men:

Not one to be accused of inadequate research, Craig experiments generously with heterosexuality. But always without satisfaction. The men she meets are, almost without exception, emotionally incompetent and, without exception, sexually incompetent ... One is forced to quibble with Elizabeth Riley's presentation of the male of the species. (If you're brave and bent enough to say to hell with the feminist mafia.)

In a 1976 *Southerly* review essay on four new novels ('Sensitives and Insensitives'), R. K. Wallace disparaged Maureen Craig's 'aggressiveness' and what he felt to be the novel's 'special pleading of a rather skimpy psychoanalytical kind'. Asserting that the narration's 'defensiveness rapidly shifts to open attack', he argued that the protagonist's depiction of parents and men emerged from an over-reaction to her disappointments, and that they 'blasted away' whatever compassion one might have had for her:

There is considerable cause for anger, but not such all-inclusive contempt. Eight (recorded) promiscuous disasters in heterosexual intercourse are perhaps enough to convince any lesbian to stick with her own, but hardly a justification for dismissing all men as clumsy, insensitive, exploiting blunderers.

Jeremy Brooks, on the other hand, writing in *The London Times* (Sunday 26 October 1975), seemed quite taken with Maureen Craig and evinced an altogether different response to the same material:

[T]his is not an easy book for a man to review without reacting in a 'typical' way ... Meeting a lesbian (if at all personable), most men feel: what a waste! There's no dodging that. Reading this book I felt: Ah, if only she'd met *me,* instead of all those selfish rednecks ... An intolerable reaction from the author's point of view.

Suzanne Bellamy in *Refractory Girl* ('Fucking Men is For Saints', June 1976), conversely imagines that she *shares* the author's point of view:

> In spite of myself, I find the descriptions of the encounters with men really funny. I suspect Riley does too, now.

Sitting on the verandah, I read some of these excerpts out loud to Kerryn, who reacts with neither extreme elation at the praise nor defensiveness at the digs. In fact, she often speaks of the novel as if it were written by someone else. She refers to it not as 'her' book, nor by its title, but simply as 'Riley'. ('You can take home a few Rileys from under the bed, if you'd like,' she offers, gesturing broadly toward them, as if my doing so will make her spring cleaning a little easier.) Shortly before my arrival, she had reread *All That False Instruction* for the first time in many years. Now she cites passages that made her laugh—the way a friend would who shared my enthusiasm for a book I'd recommended.

Over the next two weeks we make several trips, including an overnight visit to the 'hex' in the mountains. In the afternoon, when the sun finally comes out, Kerryn leads me slogging through the muddy rainforest, cutting the viny tangles which block our path, explaining the dynamic balance in which rainforest interacts with wet sclerophyll, and giving an impassioned account of the politics of logging.

She is clearly still absorbed, as she has been for more than thirty years, by humans' calamitous indifference to the natural world. During the late 1970s, she was a founding member of WANE (Women Against Nuclear Energy), which worked with the Movement Against Uranium Mining (MAUM). She also produced and appeared (as lecturer) in a short documentary film, *The Nuclear Fuel Cycle,* which was broadcast on one of the major networks. In the 1980s, she helped stop the Forestry Department from logging old growth rainforest which has since been included in the wilderness area of the Werrikimbe National Park. In the 1990s, Kerryn wrote plays about climate change and water quality which were performed at regional theatre festivals. These days, she takes on ad hoc writing projects which address issues ranging from 'rubbish rescue' for the arts to sustainable development.

It is the northern hemisphere's spring of 2001, a year after my visit. My article on Kerryn has appeared in the US and many readers have asked where they might obtain a copy of *All That False Instruction.* 'Nowhere at present,' I tell them, though I cautiously lend out the 'Rileys' retrieved from under the bed at Kerryn's house. Kerryn has got the rights to her book back, and it is about to be republished by a new press. (Appropriately, the press is Spinifex, the facilitator of our serendipitous acquaintance.) She has also made the decision—long overdue, she feels—to reclaim authorship of the novel under her own name. Her parents are both dead now, the old pretexts for remaining anonymous are gone, and anyway she's tired, she says, of being a wimp.

The resurrection of her first novel has spurred her, too, to start thinking once again about writing another. She's concluded that her current manuscript—The Unmanageable—is, for the time being, Unworkable. She imagines a story that will link her passion for geology and natural history with a psychological narrative.

I feel confident that the scorching, vigorously honest, eclectically-fashioned intelligence I've come to know through Kerryn's work, her correspondence, and her conversation will be put to excellent use by such a project. Meanwhile, I hope that presses outside of Australia will take notice of *All That False Instruction* so that it achieves the broad international readership it abundantly deserves. I suspect that I won't be the last seeker of exquisitely gripping novels who writes to Kerryn—as I did in the final line of my first letter to her—'Thanks for producing one of the literary treasures of my own life.'

Harriet Malinowitz
Brooklyn, New York
May, 2001

Acknowledgments

A shorter version of this 'Introduction' appeared previously in *The Women's Review of Books,* Vol. XVII, Nos. 10–11/July 2000. I would like to thank the Research Released Time Committee, the Trustees, Dean David Cohen, and Dr Michael Arons of Long Island University, New York, for making this project possible. I am especially grateful to Provost Gale Stevens Haynes and Dr Bonnie Borenstein for their characteristic generosity of spirit as well as their material support.

Part One

In which Maureen comes into the world,
her brother hot on her heels

The first thing I remember. I was running in the long summer grass above my grandmother's house with the red dog. The red dog was much bigger than I was; he leapt over me, rolled me, licked my face. Up through the paddocks I scrambled to say hello to my father perched on the scaffolding of our growing house. He was up there in his always khaki overalls, nails between his teeth and arm swinging the hammer through the blue. He smiled from way up there, brown eyes and reddish hair, his bare back hunched brown and an army hat cocked on his forehead. On the brown of his skin were freckles and darker blots arranged across his shoulders from arm to arm.

When I was just three years old I sat one evening in the dining alcove of the house my father had built. He was serving out custard, smooth yellow stuff more distinct in my memory than is his face. He sat under the window opposite me, and if I say I was glad that we were alone together, I'm probably not making it up. My mother had gone off to collect an extra child, something for which I saw no need at all. If I didn't understand why it took a week to bring Ken home, I did, on this peaceful custard-eating night, wonder whether his advent was any cause for rejoicing.

The sofa used to stand slantwise in one corner of the lounge; a puffy affair covered in large blue blooms which seem to have been faded from the beginning. They were fighting again. My mother had fled behind the sofa and now my father stood over it, gripping her wrist to drag her into the open. She clung to the webbing. I wondered if he wanted to kill her, and why. The noise was deafening. They screamed their insults so loud they couldn't hear each other; you just heard tangled anger. That day, fortunately, they weren't throwing things, though Father once hurled a bowl of peaches the length of the kitchen, covering the walls and floor with syrup and china-chips. Cornflakes were stuck to the ceiling above the alcove. When he dragged her out from hiding they stood flailing each other, the yelling now punctuated by my mother's sobs. She kicked his ankle suddenly

1

and, breaking his hold, ran out into the road and down to my grandmother's house. My father let her go. Cursing under his breath he made coffee and sat down moodily.

Combat was constant. Later on I identified Saturday morning as chief row-day. Shopping occurred on Saturdays; with weekly regularity the wages were found to be inadequate. Mother would sit by the wood-stove warming her feet in the oven and complaining to the world at large of our poverty and my father's irresponsible purloining of two bob for tobacco.

I thought that it was all a matter of giving in and decided that when I grew up I would be willing to say I was wrong, able to give in and make peace quickly. To live at war struck me as incomprehensible— surely one could choose not to? It was strange that they never appeared to make a truce. Sometimes they laughed and even hugged each other but it didn't seem to make any difference once they got annoyed. Why were they so angry, I wondered. What was wrong with the world?

There were two photographs in the photo-box, perhaps so strongly memorable because they didn't seem to fit. In one my father looked buoyantly boyish, with his airforce cap at a rakish angle, a soft mischievous face with a grin. The photograph was torn and battered; my mother had carried it with her when she fled the big bushfire, the only possession she'd saved. She lost it in the frantic attempt to get through the boxthorn hedges, but found it again when they came back from the river. It was spiked in a tiny patch of surviving thorn; the fire hadn't touched it. Maybe she took it as a sign; maybe that's why she married him. The other was of her, leaning against a rustic post-and-rail fence in a drapish ankle-length dress. Her face too was soft, even calm, strikingly elegant. There was another picture of the four of us—baby Ken was in Mother's arms. The parents look worried, now, but have mustered abnormal smiles. The little girl in the overcoat, short and stocky, scowls under tight curls. Her whole face is sulks and distemper.

I disliked Ken from the beginning. He was a brown-eyed chubby boy with delicate tendrils of chestnut hair curling around his ears. Ken was placid and a winner of all hearts. His early talk consisted of pointing his thumb at his chest and lisping: Kennyboy, Curlyboy, bigboy and goodboy. To which stunned friends and relations responded with charmed laughter. To my mother I seem to have been the proverbial difficult child and Ken increased the difficulties a thousand times. As a child he knew his advantage. One evening at tea-time my mother called for one of us to run down the lane with Granny's meal. Ken went. After tea she discovered that the lid with which she covered my grandmother's food was missing.

'Maureen, where's the lid?'

'What?'

'Where's the lid?'

'What lid?'

'The lid off Granny's tea.'

'I don't know. Ken went.'

Ken broke in. 'No I didn't. She did.'

'I didn't.'

'Yes she did, Mum.'

'Now I don't want any more of these bloody lies out of you again, Maureen, or I'll belt the bloody hide off you. Where did you leave the lid?'

Trapped. Granny was no valid witness even if she had bothered to investigate, for she recognised that the old woman's love was fixed on me. My voice became shrill with the knowledge of impending punishment and angry with the frustration of my helplessness. The more vehemently I accused Ken of lying to get me into trouble, the more sin was heaped up on the pile, the more expiation required. Not only had I lost the lid, but I'd lied about it and was now attacking poor little Ken.

The southern paddocks beyond my grandmother's house were covered with stark dead trees. In winter the fields were dazzling green with sheets of water in the hollows, in summer shrivelled brown, in spring vibrant with the luxuriant yellow daisy of the cape-weed. Old gravel pits were here and there, overgrown years back, full of the sweetness of summer blackberries. It was my grandmother who took me there. Every weekend I escaped to the open fields with the wiry old woman who still crawled through fences and trotted to keep up with my careering across the paddocks. She'd get a picnic together, sweet things forbidden down on the Home Front, orange-cream biscuits and little rocky cakes. On rainy days I'd sit in the kitchen while she built her fire wigwam-fashion, bending intensely over the smoke, blowing and blowing in the cinders. We took tea together like adults.

But the best time was summer. She sat on a mound shading her eyes from the glare, peering through her glasses. She was as interested as I to see the rings of brightness spread out from the stones I threw in the muddy pools; the delicate ripples from the pebbles growing imperceptibly calm however closely one gazed; the waves I could make with rocks. I'd line up my ammunition along the edge and hurl it into every corner of the water creating a multitude of warring backwashes, which always returned to stillness under the still sky. She laughed. We joined hands and danced in a circle over the stubble between the white skeletons of dead trees.

In her garden were strange flowers, bird-shaped orange blooms, morning glory struggling under the broom tree, the small blue flowers she called soldiers, purple statice with its white eye, growing wild and profuse, the orange fists of the red hot pokers. We cut the tiny round lawn with big scissors; or I chipped away at the weeds along the gravel while she painted her bricks out of a magical pot of yellow ochre and poured water onto the parched earth. In the old sleepout, covered in with flywire, she tended a jungle of ferns. I loved to go into the damp cool place among the mossy greenness, to hear her inside blowing at the fire or clattering the cups. Strawberries choked in the wiry couch-grass under the nectarine tree. At the end of the house stood the dowdy drooping peppercorn and the lucerne tree, a child-climber's dream, knotty and angular, with one long branch resting on the woodshed roof. Here, on a carpet of dry lucerne pods, I could lie down and chart the clouds through the branches. I was quite old before Ken got the size and courage to pursue me into my private retreat.

This place was my refuge from the Home Front when I took flight from the thick canvas belt with its brass buckles. I dreamed of running away, a change of singlets knotted up in a red polka-dot handkerchief at the end of a pole. I would see myself, momentarily, striding out across the daisy paddocks towards the Cockatoo Ranges. From Granny's front verandah we could see a road on one hill which seemed to run straight up at a great rate. That was my road. But somehow I realised that food doesn't always grow on trees and that I'd be in for the canvas thrashing of all time if they caught up with me. Better to wait until I'm grown up, I thought. I looked forward to that.

Mother hit on the idea that Granny was spoiling me and made her house out-of-bounds. Naturally I wasn't permitted to go to the paddocks alone. She kept the order in force for countless miserable months. I invented excuses to visit the old woman—she thrust them aside. One afternoon, while she was safely out of the way 'lying down', I slipped out with the nominal justification of a new puzzle-book to show my grandmother. I was just crawling through the wire fence when I heard her screaming from the window. No amount of tiptoe quiet was enough to elude her detective instincts.

'Maureen,' she yelled. 'What are you up to?'

'Nothing,' I screamed back, struggling with the fence and getting hopelessly hooked by the barbed-wire in my panic. She had sprinted out and seized me round the neck before I could free myself and escape. Another unforgettable thrashing.

At first I thought it grand when Mother was accepted as craft-mistress in the little State School up the hill. A cut above the ordinary. I was about six and proud of her. The children I disliked without exception. No-one wanted to play with me. Being crafty and small I was often the last left at hide-and-seek; they ignored me and started a new round. When the kids were led to suppose that it's all one big competition, it's not surprising that they detested little Maureen who took out the spelling-prize for the entire school at the age of seven. I hovered on the edges of their games.

Mother might have become a respected teacher if she'd been born male or to richer parents. As it was she had left school early, convinced, despite her own good record, that there was no point in her getting an education. So she had no qualifications and this meant no promotion, of course. She even had to pretend that she'd got Leaving.

She made a good fist of craft-instruction anyway, and Mr Crackhard had her hired as temporary infant mistress a few years later when the school got bigger. She must have been a remarkable find for Crackhard—the District Inspectors usually awarded her the rare distinction of an 'A', complimenting her on imaginative teaching. She'd glow with pride, and we thought it was pretty good to have a mother classed 'A' when even Crackhard had his share of 'B's. By this time, though, pride was alloyed with something else. The arrangement was a double-edged blade. Kids always got nastier with the teacher's children. Crackhard himself set the example of steel impartiality by strapping his own children for the most trifling offences and my mother, anxious to show no favouritism, ended by blaming me for other kids' chattering and giggling.

There were sixty of us in the school, all in one long draughty room, each column of desks comprising a class. The building must have threatened to collapse at some stage because it was supported all along the east side with monstrous flying-buttresses in weatherboard. In front was the gravel courtyard where we were encouraged to folk-dance and forced, each day, to assemble military-fashion and 'march in' to Mr Crackhard's massed bands records. On Mondays, Anzac Day, Queen's Birthday, Empire Day and Coral Sea Day the assembly was longer.

'Right hand over your hearts!'

'Together NOW.'

An earnest young chorus.

'I love God and my Country
I will honour the Flag
Serve the Queen
And cheerfully obey my Parents, Teachers and the Law.'

'Maureen Craig! Will you join in next time.'

'Yes sir!' But I had to skip the cheerfully bit—that was asking too much.

'TEN-SHUN!'

Everybody sprang to attention, chests out, hands rigid at their sides. The oldest most trusted boy stood by the flagpole where the flag had been hoisted.

'SAL-UTE THE FLAG!'

Crackhard and the boys came to a swift vibrating salute, froze an instant and slapped their stiff hands back to their sides, the boys delighting in the flurry of smacks as their hands came down. The girls watched mutely.

Once in a while the headmaster went off on school business, leaving Mother in charge of the lot of us. We fourth-graders were doing free painting to ease her vast teaching task. She already had an imposing list of big unruly boys chalked on the blackboard—transgressors ear-marked for the strap, a peculiarly solid band of greasy black leather. When his nibs returned they'd cop it. Diddy Schmuckel, a runt-girl, freckled and mean, jabbed me slyly in the ribs from across the aisle and resumed angelic scribbling as I let out a yowl of pain and fury. As I rose righteously to my tiny feet, arm pumping the air for the teacher's attention, relishing the while the idea of Diddy Schmuckel's name added to the chalk-list, Iron Mother came storming up the floorboards, scowled, and wrote up Maureen Craig.

'Mum!' I yelled. 'It wasn't me.' Forgetting that I was supposed to call her Mrs Craig in school.

'Sit down and keep working.' Her voice colder than ever.

'Mum!' I yelled louder. 'It was Diddy.'

'Sit down and be quiet.' Each word said separately and distinctly through tightly-pursed lips.

'I will not. It was her.'

She wheeled and, was this possible? was this real? chalked up the number two beside my name. I could feel the whimpering coming on. I wanted to strangle Schmuckface. The hatred of it was black enough to gloom the face of the earth.

And I sat down.

Mr Crackhard arrived beaming just as school ended and inquired genially of my mother how had they been? She smiled charmingly and told him good enough, though she'd had to keep a steady eye on them and there were one or two who needed to be shown who was boss. He smiled back his acquiescence, strolled up the room, examined the list. Lips thrust out, he nodded his cumbrous head with a wisdom intended to convey that he'd expected as much from this lot. Sorry lads, he seemed to be smiling, but this is an educational institution, not a free-for-all—a frequent contention of his.

On with his stern face and out with the strap. 'RONNY JONES!' he rasps at the top of his voice. 'Four of the best.' Crack. Crack. Crack. Crack. And Ronny takes it quietly and sourly. Down the list. 'EDDY COOK!' rasps Crackhard. Eddy's a smart little bastard who once whipped my ankles with a plastic skipping-rope. Eddy's got a bit of fight in him. As the strap comes down there's no crack. Eddy's drawn in his hand at the last instant and left Crackhard flailing the air. But the amiable headmaster sees the joke apparently and only chortles gently as he recovers his balance. He raises his affable eyebrows and, taking Eddy's dirty fingertips so gently my stomach turns over, he steadies the boy's extended arm.

'You'd better not do that again, had you? You wouldn't want double now, would you?' Eddy submits.

My name is next. MAUREEN CRAIG. Must be somebody else. I won't be able to stand this. Bad enough when she belts me. Bad enough with canvas. Bad enough when I can just dimly make out why she's doing it. But this?

'Come on, Maureen. Out here.'

I'm terrified and aflame with resentment.

'Please Mr Crackhard, Sir, I didn't do anything. It was Diddy.' I turn to her—hoping for corroboration? She's smirking.

'Maureen!'

'My mother wouldn't listen to me. Please, Sir, I didn't do it.' What it was that either of us had done has by this time entirely evaded me.

'Are you coming, girl? Or will I have to drag you out?'

I stagger up. What a cowed child. Not a split-thought of running. Only hope—to argue them out of it—a vain one. In a flash he's dabbling at my fingertips, straightening my arm. Nausea. Eyes tight shut. The whistle of leather in the hushed air. A report like a rifle. Searing pain from hand to arm to body. I let out a kind of animal groan.

'Quiet!' he orders. I slit my eyes to look at my hand, purple; the welt already swelling.

'Again,' he says. So bloody quiet, this voice of his can be.

'No. Please. No.' Great lumps of water are gathering in my eyes. But he has my fingertips again, a feel like stroking, like gentleness. I am still holding the same breath. Down comes the leather. The crack sounds duller—it's no longer hard flat flesh it connects with, but a purple jelly, thinly held in by transparent skin.

'Back to your desk.'

He gives my rigid frozen body a shove. I sob. I hate my sobs. I want to be able to take this like the boys, to return his slime-smile, to act contemptuous. But it hurts and I cry, crumpled and hating my weakness—a broken little girl—who is enraged at their cruelty and totally unable to fight it.

The Mathers boys spent the afternoon with us while our parents went off together. We were sitting on the earth among the fruit trees, deciding what games to play.

'I bet you don't know the worst word of all,' Denny Mathers exclaimed triumphantly.

'I bet I do.'

'What is it then?'

'Er ... bugger, I suppose.'

'Nah—'s worse 'n that.'

'What then?'

'You won't tell your mother I told you?'

'Nah.'

'It's fuck.'

'Fuck.'

Sounded innocuous, like truck or stuck or muck at the worst—funmuck. I wondered how you used it but didn't like to ask. Like bloody? you fuck bastard; or bugger? you rotten fuck; or damn? like fuck it; or just like shit? I don't give a fuck. It all sounded polite by comparison and I remained sceptical of its awfulness until curiosity got the better of me and I tried it out on Granny. She was so shocked that I regretted it instantly and told her I had no idea what it meant or anything about it—I'd just learnt it from the Mathers boys.

'Tch tch tch,' she clicked. 'That's no way for a girl to be talking. You take care now.'

My father was a failure; my mother had realised this and reminded him continuously. He worked for next to nothing doing maintenance on the petrol depots—had done ever since the war. When she was promoted to full-time infant-mistress Mother would point out that she was bringing more into the home than he was and doing all the housework as well, something no-one could be expected to do. Not that she regarded her money as anything other than utterly her own.

'You may not understand, Maureen, but it's very important for a woman to have a bit of money of her own. Without it she's beaten before she starts.' Finally Dad threw in the dead-end maintenance job and set about making a fast fortune in the insurance business. Her initial radiance at the prospect soon bittered.

'How many policies did you sell today, Joe?'

'Well, I didn't actually sell any, but ...'

'What! You realise we can't live much longer on this pittance.'

'Christ, Lotty, you've got to expect it slow for a while, till I get the hang of the game.'

'That's all bloody well, but you've been saying that for six weeks.'

'Well Jesus, six weeks isn't that long.'

'It wouldn't be either if there was the slightest sign of any improvement.'

'It'll take time.'

He looked jaded, and strange anyway, in a blue suit, as if he was on his way to church. I liked his overalls better, and the dirt under his nails.

'Well you needn't think we'll be dipping into my teaching money much longer. A man's got to support his family. That's not up to me you know.'

'Of course not, Lotty. Just give it a month or so more.'

'We'll be starving by then. I always knew you'd never be any bloody good at this sort of thing—you've got to be sharp. You're too damned soft, never want to hurt anybody's feelings—as long as it's not your own family of course.' She'd forgotten how she'd hounded him out of the depot job and into this racket which he must have known as well as she did was no place for him. He made his cup of black coffee and went out the back.

'You'd better change that suit. We'll never be able to have it cleaned at this rate.'

'I'll just throw on the overalls, Lotty. I have to go back out later, anyway.'

'Back out? Where to?'

'There's a chap out on the Toongabbie road wants a life policy. A really certain prospect—and I might sell him some fire, too.'

'And pigs might fly. I suppose this'll be happening all the time, eh? You having to go out every night of the bloody week? I suppose you expect me to just put up with it?'

'It was your idea, this insurance job. Ask any agent. They all have to work at night. Don't think I get anything out of it.'

He cut out in a hurry, letting the wire-door slam hard behind him. A little later the rhythmic echo of the axe. Out of the window I could see his face lit up by the evening sunshine, an orange glow in the gum trees that only seemed to make his weariness heavier. Mother turned to me from the stove, still looking furious.

'You'll learn,' she said with malice. 'A woman just has to put up with it. Here. Peel those potatoes.'

Her teaching money had paid for our chief luxury, the second-hand Humber, which Father now needed for his work. We could have better afforded something less flash, but Mother hated having the common things that other people had. She liked a bit of style. One morning they'd been fighting since seven to no clear purpose.

'All right, Lotty, don't give me the money for the petrol. I'll get it on credit somewhere.'

'You'll do no such thing, running us into debt all over the countryside.'

'Jesus Christ woman, you want me to earn a bloody wage for you, don't you?'

'Oh, you call it a wage, do you?'

'Well you won't get anything if you don't let me work.'

'You don't expect me to believe you're working do you? Sitting around all day drinking tea or God knows what with some woman or other.'

'For God's sake, Lotty.'

'Well that's all right, Joe; yes that's all right. If that's what you want to do with your life, go ahead. Go ahead and starve your family to death. Go ahead—I always knew you had no pride. Just keep going until we're all in the gutter—but you're not using my car to do it in!'

'FUCKING HELL!' She blenched.

'How dare you say that in front of me and the children. That settles it; you're just not getting the keys. So just clear out of here.'

I was expecting him to pounce on her in the usual way and force the keys from her, but instead he crumpled up over the end of the piano, his fist making a dull bass clang on the keyboard. Covering his face with his other hand he broke into dry rattling sobs. I'd never seen a man cry, much less supposed my Father might so horribly burst. I would have liked to hold his hand, but my mother stood glaring at him. I watched. After a long time he drew in a lot of breath, rasping unevenly; with his face hidden in his hands he staggered down the passage past her to get out into the air. As he passed her she simply muttered, 'You ought to be ashamed of yourself,' and threw the keys hard at his back. They fell to the lino, a muffled clatter, and he lumbered on without noticing.

'Will I take them out to him?' I asked her hopefully.

'Yes, yes, anything to get him out of our hair. Go on.'

He was sitting by the wattle in the cane chair the cats slept in, bits of fur and filth clinging to the back of his precious suit. He was still sobbing a bit and blowing his nose. When I handed him the keys he thanked me tonelessly and I left him alone. Later he drove off, skidding and sliding, taking it out on the car.

We spring-cleaned every holiday, irrespective of the season. Mother was one of those who flinched if a visitor's thumb scored the dust, or an eye caught fluff under the table. The Big Clean involved every square inch of the house. The drawers had to be emptied, all the clothes shaken, folded and replaced symmetrically. I came across a pale blue satiny garment, looking like Mother's corsets, with whalebone ribs, little cotton ties and a solid stiffness.

'What's this, Mum?'

'Put it back, Maureen. It's nothing to do with you.'

'But it's funny.'

'Put it away.'

'Is it yours?'

'It's your father's. Now put it back.'

'Dad's? He never wears anything like this.'

For some reason she was angry and grabbed the pretty thing. It fell out of its folds, a pale rectangle with elaborate strings like a fancy-dress apron.

'It's his lodge apron,' she said shortly. 'That's where he's always going on Fridays.'

'But what does he do with this thing?'

'He wears it of course.'

'Why?'

'I don't know.'

'I'll ask him then.'

'He won't tell you. It's a secret society for men.'

This was unbelievable. All those Cobb men taking off their black suits every Friday and tying pale blue aprons around their middles to indulge in something I would never be allowed to know about.

'Don't you go?'

'Of course not. It's just for the men.'

'What do they do?'

'I don't know dear. I've never been.'

'Well what's wrong with a girl being in it?'

'They're all freemasons—the respectable working-men of the town.'

'But you work—you teach school.'

'They don't take women.'

'Do they take men who teach school—like Mr Crackhard. Is he in it?'

'I imagine he's got too much common sense.'

'What if I was a truck-driver—like Dad?'

'That wouldn't make any difference dear. It's for the men.'

'Why?'

'Shut up, Maureen, and get on with the work. They only gossip I should think, and learn to shake hands so they know each other.' Weirder and weirder. And my poor father mixed up in it.

'It's not fair.'

'No dear.'

There was the incident of the stick. Ken and I were playing by the drainage pit; cowboys and indians or cops and robbers. Something violent at any rate. My weapon, slung furiously through the air, grazed his eyelid, nearly a King Harold job. Blood trickled down his long, dark lashes. He let out a fearsome whoop, a mixture of pain and pique at the direct hit. Mother appeared already armed with the canvas belt; the curly-headed boy buried himself in her apron. Above his head she glared at me.

'You'll suffer for this, Maureen.'

But it wasn't the thrashing, nor even the hours locked up in the bathroom, that worried me that day. Rather the fact that my mother believed I had tried to kill Ken.

Another time I very nearly did kill him. Sunday at Lakes Entrance. I was twelve and he nine. Mother swallowed her fears and allowed us to take out a toy rowing-boat if we stayed inshore in the shallows. She used to do all the worrying or panicking while Dad slept in the sun or read the paper. Ken was hopeless with the oars and kept standing up to turn round when he wanted to row the other way. I thought it easier to jump out and pull the boat around. We got on well enough until I stepped out into fourteen feet of water. Neither of us could swim; as I came up out of the bubbles and greenness for the third time I grabbed onto the hull. Ken kept surfacing and sinking. I dared not let go for my own sake. Dad and some other men came sprinting down the sand and we were rescued. I was as frightened of my mother's wrath as of drowning; being saved was the lesser of the two evils by the narrowest of margins. Fortunately, Ken was unconscious when they carried him ashore and I was able to build up a tale of his fault in the matter since he'd been doing his turning around stunt when I walked overboard. Saved from the belt. For six years I lived as if with a mountainous guilt and told no-one.

I hated housework. I was older of course and expected to bear my proper responsibilities, but it emerged with distressing clarity that I also belonged to the drudging half of the world, the women. I couldn't work out why Ken was not obliged to polish floors and clean stoves while I appeared as some sort of filial abomination if I so much as grumbled over it. From a daughter of my age, whatever it happened to be, Mother had expected help and comfort; what did she get? resentment and lies. Every new conflict provoked the stock accusation. She'd thought I was getting better, but how wrong could she be? Apparently I spent my youth deteriorating at lightning speed, a process which revealed itself nearly every day. This was her carrot: that she had thought I was improving. Approval offered and with-drawn in one breath. Try as I might, crawl, comfort and help as I might, I was never able to confirm these evasive beginnings of it. I simply did not care for the endless boring tasks which normal daughters were meant to enjoy—and didn't see how anyone could.

The dreary duty-hours I passed off with the spinning of stories. I was a prisoner confined to hard labour; I saw our house surrounded by its barbed-wire and board fences grown three times taller, and planned an ultimate escape; I dug tunnels under cover of weeding the garden, prepared incendiary diversions in the cleaning of the fire-place, planned floods in the bathroom, devised weapons out of vacuum-cleaner bits or simply pondered on the best moment to make a valiant all-or-nothing dash through the gates. Sometimes the wraith of a warder approached me and, with sincere apologies for all the hardship and injustice or words of congratulation on my impeccable work, he'd pat me on the back and give me my freedom. I performed the odious tasks and waited to grow up.

I felt sick that morning, a strong oceans-deep nausea. I hadn't got into the green apples, but still my guts hurt bad. The pain was strange to me, very low and intensified by the nausea. I thought I should go and try to shit but our lavatory was a little house way down the yard where the nightman had once caught me with my pants down. It seemed an intolerable distance away. But maybe if I go the pain will stop, I thought. The discovery I made threw me into panic; my underpants were wet and sticky with fresh red blood. It must have come out of me. But where from? and why? Maybe I was sick—or dying. My mother was washing and I could hear the fresh wet clothes flapping cool and loud in the breeze. I stumbled out and made for the house. Somewhere on the path I looked down; all the pebbles and stones were resolving into a pattern like iron filings around a magnet. The pathway designed itself into points, the buttons which hold down upholstery, and the gravel arranged itself about these dark points. Slowly, this pretty earth came up to meet me.

'This is your pain, dear.' More coy, even, than curse. How could I dare to ask her if it would ever stop? ever get less painful? But then the pain would be, by its nature, painful. What a shock that the body, stink and vomit as it had and might, could be so much worse still than it had seemed. What other horrors was I in for as time went on? She admitted that she should have told me about it before it happened and was unusually kind to me, brought soda water, even sat neglecting the washing for a few minutes. But to dress my bleeding body she brought rags folded into rectangles, pinned to a belt stained and no longer elastic. After this began the new unbearable task of washing these rags, soaking them, pouring off the blood-water and scrubbing at the thick pink slime which clung, at the irremovable brown stains. I hated to put my hands amongst all this filth, but she always reminded me that it was my own excrescence and my own responsibility—there was no getting out of it. That Ken would never suffer this degradation made me boundlessly, impotently jealous.

The detestation of blood. Light red, dark red, clotted, black, new blood, dead blood; the wound opening, opening, never healing. Life was to be lived in the shadow of a bloody sickness. I would bleed dishes, barrels, rivers of the stuff, a hopelessly crippled being. Pour it

13

down the drain, reticulate it through the sewers, restore the whiteness up top, an endless pointless struggle.

High School got me relief from Mother in the classroom at least. The first week. Me the shortest Form One kid, and hefty too, ugly. By the end of the week the girls had shuffled into pairs and groups— I was hardly surprised to be left single. I ate lunch alone; found a wattle that grew by the school hedge making a feathery hiding-place where they could not see that I hadn't a friend. I crawled in there for more than a year with Robert Louis Stevenson or Sapper and the mountainous comforting Vegemite sandwiches. The best of the day was the visit to my grandmother on the way to the bus-stop. She'd be up already, the door open, and greet me on the verandah; it faced east and though Cobb Swamp was bleak in the winter, these mornings seem always to have been vibrantly sunny. She'd press sixpence in my hand, however scurrying my haste; she'd give her throaty chuckle and pack me off. I've got this over Ken I thought—still a little boy, still at State School, still running home to Mummy for lunch. I teased him for being little, the only tangible disadvantage he had.

And was I ever good at school work. Natural aptitude maybe, but a kind of desperation about it. One term, when it was in doubt, I lived in terror of not taking the form prize. I got it. Relief. My mother didn't forgive second placings. You've got to come top. Since I was five I'd been learning untold poems for the Cobb Grand Gippsland Annual Eisteddfod—and coming first. It pleased her a while. Adjudicators told her that she had an astonishingly talented daughter; some said I should go on the stage; she liked that, her own talents having been utterly ignored. She got over her pride bloody fast but it did flash on for a day or so, sometimes. Like sunshine. Like love. Surrogate, but good enough. So I tried, thirsted for the teachers' questions, longed for the exams that proved me top, knew damned near everything.

Even when Ken got big enough to join the competition he never equalled my shining record. He was talented, they said, but not astonishingly talented, merely talented. What talented, gifted children you have, Mrs Craig. Ken learned 'The Happy Prince'. Mother stood him at one end of the room to hear his lines. He knew it all, but could never get through it. 'Fly away, fly away, little swallow,' the Prince said for the last time as the snows began to fall. 'Fly away.' Ken cried. Tears rolled down his chubby cheeks. It broke him up. He could recite no more. Standing, weeping. This was a Ken I barely knew, a Ken who, quite probably, didn't survive his childhood.

In the summer the whole school went swimming on Wednesday afternoons. At first Mother made me come home at lunchtime that day on the public bus with the Balts (bolts, I thought, but never saw them bolting) against whom I'd been early warned. People from the migrant camp were understood to be different. I remember them as fat, with warts and pockmarks. How the kids laughed. Maureen Craig's not allowed to go swimming. What a laugh. Finally she consented on the condition that my grandmother come to the Town Baths and spend the whole afternoon watching me. My spindly granny spread out her blanket on the grass slope near the shallow end and peered three hours over the bobbing heads of a hundred small children—doubtless she too knew that my mother would strangle her if anything happened to me. She sat up there, in a long floral dress of green silky cotton with her dark blue hat, the shiny straw sort, full of bundles of cloth-flowers, wire stiffened. And while she watched with the burden of my life on her shoulders (could I imagine her romping down the grass in patent-leather lace-ups, her long drapes billowing in the wind, her hat skew-whiff, to do a rescuer's racing dive amongst dozens of little kids?), the hearty male teachers patrolled the pool in lifesaving caps. I pretended every week that she wasn't there, while the kids, who knew she was, splashed and sniggered in the fake-aqua clarity of the pool.

We took the elocution lessons, which were meant to train us up for the annual eisteddfod, at the girls' college near the water tower. It got unbearable when Miss Sweeting took over the teaching; a willowy, freckly woman of thirty who spoke impeccable English without a grain of fire. Doubtless on purpose, I forgot to go to my lesson one day after school. As the schoolbus lumbered out over the river I remembered it was Thursday. I grabbed my satchel, ran up the aisle and yelled to the driver.

'Stop. I gotta go back to Cobb. I gotta speech lesson.'

The kids screamed with laughter. The bus-driver grinned and nonchalantly ground down the gears to stop. I hurtled down the steps and picked myself up out of a puddle. A wintry afternoon; misting rain; mud caked on my brown shoes; my green blazer spattered all over with slush; my pinafore wet through down one side. Miss Sweeting's neat hand-written manuscripts spilled out onto the roadside and went limp and yellow in the stormwater, the ink running all over the damp paper. Children cheered and waved satirically from the back window as the bus pulled off. I half-ran, half-trotted the mile back to Cobb where Sweeting was waiting in the shadowy front-entrance of Saint Mildred's.

'Whatever became of you?' she inquired sweetly.

I blurted my forgetfulness and my apology. She received it sweetly.

'Please Miss Sweeting, please it won't happen again really it won't, but don't tell my mother, please don't tell her I forgot, she'll belt me, please, please, don't tell her please ...'

'Of course not, Maureen. Calm down. It's only one lesson ... we've plenty of time until the eisteddfod. Calm down now.' I was crying and pleading, clutching shyly and desperately at her arm. 'Now, Maureen, it's perfectly all right dear. We won't bother any more today. How do you usually get home?'

'My Dad collects me up by the signpost at five.'

'Well it's nearly five now, dear, so off you go. See you next week.' She patted me on the shoulder and let me go, my mind relieved beyond belief.

'How was the lesson?' said Dad. 'OK,' I answered. We drove home quietly.

'How was the lesson?' glares my mother as I walk in.

'Oh all right. Miss Sweeting's very pleased with me.'

'Oh is she?'

'Yes.'

'How did you get so wet and dirty?'

I recognise the coldness in her voice. I know she's threatening me. 'I fell over in a puddle,' I reply truthfully.

'Really?' A note of total scepticism. Did she think I'd been rolling with the boys in the schoolyard swamp?

'Yes, I tripped over, but I'll clean my blazer up myself. It's all right.'

'Maureen, it's not all right.' I can see it coming, now. 'I want to know where you've been.'

I frown fakely. 'At my lesson, Mum.'

'Miss Sweeting rang me five minutes ago.' Stone suddenly material- ises in my guts. I can't think of a thing to say.

'Now Maureen,' with that detestable reasonable tone. 'Missing your lesson is bad enough, but lying is worse. Where have you been?' I am about to break down—again. I tell her thickly that I forgot, got half- way home; ran back .

'And you expect me to believe that?'

'It's *true*.'

'Oh yes and I wonder what reminded you so suddenly? Eh?'

I mutter that I don't know. We were crossing the river.

'Really? Then if it's as simple as that why did you try to lie to me? Why did you try to get Miss Sweeting to hide it from me? I'm not a fool, Maureen, and I intend to get to the bottom of this.'

'But I'm telling you the truth.'

'We'll see about that when we belt it out of you.'

'No, no, please, it's TRUE.'

'Get to the bathroom!'

Another canvas thrashing. Deadlock. Like torture to get it out of the spy who doesn't know the answers. 'What were you doing?' as the strap comes down across my backside. 'I told you, I told you, ask the bus-kids ...' between sobs. Deadlock and misery.

My grandmother was, in fact, my only friend. My playmate, my benefactor, my warmth. She even swore black and blue that she'd given me tuppence for chewing-gum, to get me off the hook when I pinched Fat Suzie's chewy back in State School. The time I lost five pounds—a monstrous sum—I was desperate enough to think of hanging myself. I got home in a cold sweat—to the unexpected reprieve of my mother's absence. Granny just wiped off my forehead and beckoned me into her room where she produced a tiny bundle of fivers which she'd saved from her pension now and again and hidden away from my mother under her mattress. I'd never been more grateful to anyone. Mother had no belief in loss or forgetfulness. Lapses were crimes. Saved from the belt.

On my way to the bus one day, Granny's house was quiet, the door still closed, no smoke coming from the chimney. I went in scared and found her in her room which was dark and stank horribly of her stale chamberpot. She was lying on the floor beside her bed, her nightdress askew and blood caked across her forehead. I flinched coming close, terrified at the sudden transformation of that kind alert woman who waited by the door into a helpless bundle of piss-sodden rags. She begged me not to get my mother, swore she'd be all right. As I ran back to fetch my mother I felt an unforgivable betrayer of trust. She didn't want my mother. She wanted me. It was, after all, just we two who ought to rely on one another. If only I was bigger ... grown up ... I got Mother. She sent me to school.

That day was the beginning of endless years of sickness and weary suffering for her, and the end of our freedom. When I got home Father had partitioned off our old lounge, the scene of countless fisticuffs; my grandmother lay in bed, delirious and grey all over. Going to the bus-stop became a bad time—no sixpences, no laughter, no warmth. No playing together at weekends. For weeks the sick woman didn't even know who I was; didn't seem to remember our pacts of solidarity, our *entente cordiale* against the rest of the world. After a long time the worst of her sickness passed, but it was never quite the same again.

With my unblemished elocutionary record I got the plum part in the end-of-year play. My prince was a twelve-year-old too, a thin sandy boy who spoke quietly and never joined in those fistfights the girls watched from the girls' playground. Milling yelling boys linked arms to make a tight cordon around the fighters whom we only saw afterwards when the teachers broke it up, emerging with red faces, bleeding noses, bruised eyes. David was one who stood aside and whom the other boys thought hopelessly sissy. What self-respecting boy would take part in a play?

But we took the school by storm. Prize night. The interminable succession of speeches, good citizenship prizes, recorder bands out of tune, schoolchoir beefing 'Nymphs and Shepherds, Come away.' In rehearsal we'd been coy about the hand-kissing reconciliation of prince and princess at the end of the play; at the end of that loathsome concert (me with my top-of-Form-Two prize safely in Mother's lap down in the audience, he looking resplendent in his paper-tinsel crown and cotton-wool ermine robes) we fell into each other's thin shy arms and kissed full on the mouth and gently, as the curtain rang down and the Cobb Town Hall thundered with clapping, whistling, stamping and yells of encore. Princess Maureen taking bows, sweaty little hand in his. Breathless tawdry happiness.

A few months before, I had won a scholarship to a posh school for young ladies. The day after the concert was my last at Cobb High, and my last with the freckled prince. We sat all day in the corner of Room Four exchanging earnest words and shy protestations of fidelity. He saw me off on the school bus. That Maureen Craig, embryonic tart if you like (mother feared as much), faded out as suddenly as she'd been born.

In which Maureen attends a school for young ladies

During the summer we left the home-town for my start at the flash school on the outskirts of Melbourne. Mother had always entered her gifted children for everything the Cobb Gazette happened to advertise; she liked me to win and softened for a day or so whenever I did. The prize only covered tuition, such as it was, but Mother, with a weather-eye on my astonishing future, thought St Agatha's offered an opportunity to be grasped with both hands. Since they couldn't afford boarding fees the only solution was to live near the school. They rented a farmhouse cheaply enough—a weatherboard relic in a latter stage of decay; the windows rattled, draughts whistled down the corridors and the wind howled in the pines.

I was not allowed to forget the sacrifice—it loomed always larger in the paradigm argument.

'Maureen, will you do this for me?'

'Not just now. I'm going down to the haystack. Get Ken to do it.'

'Now you know I can't ask Ken to polish the bathroom. He's a grown boy, now.'

'But I want to go down to the haystack.'

'It's not much to ask, Maureen, when we've moved all this way away from our friends just for you, and you won't even put a cloth over the bathroom floor.' Always the obligation, always having to repay what I had never asked for. Strings attached to everything.

The scholarship was a mixed blessing. I had no ties in Cobb Swamp apart from my ailing grandmother and Prince David—no friends. Bleak all right, but that loneliness had not disturbed me bitterly. I'd gone my way, read dozens of books, was a regular authority on Sapper and Hornblower.

St Agatha's old red-brick buildings sprawled among pines and gardens—once a country estate. A beautifully-kept playing-field, a host of tennis courts, the school pool, and three or four horse paddocks where the Young Ladies, decked out in creaseless jodhpurs and fox-hunt jackets, used to play with their horses. It was a school with little to its credit but a dazzling sporting record, a school which competed against colleges ten times its size and won astounding success—due doubtless to the bracing country air and the fanaticism of the sports mistress.

Miss Shittleback was small, a ball of muscle and disciplined energy, a die-hard for the try-hard, try-again philosophy. There we'd be, in that hideous sports-uniform with its baggy olive-green shorts, hopping about in the school hall. They were always going to build a gym but Miss Rollande-Clagge, the head, felt a chapel would be more appropriate and neither was built in my time. Unfortunately Shittleback was a believer in the efficacy of jumping. The class lined up. One at a time they pounded down the hall and jumped. Green lumps bursting with Shittleback energy and enthusiasm flew effortlessly over the vaulting-box, were caught firmly by the Shittleback grip and bounced joyously off the mat, eager for the next leap. It wasn't so bad getting over the box—even a fat four-foot-ten could manage under the pressure of twenty hostile spectators and the Shittleback eyes gleaming beyond the obstacle. The trouble began with the lengthwise leaps—the box was not only four feet high but also four feet long. The green line shortened always in front of me; the moment always came. Grit the teeth, stiffen the upper lip, immolate the mind and summon the will. A hectic dash, a ferocious bounce off the springboard, and there I was, flat on my face, full length on top of the box. So much for vaulting ambition. I never broke any ribs, but that was no compensation for the moment when Shittleback would help me off the box amidst suppressed giggles and suggest that I try again.

Softball was little better. I'd always enjoyed our family cricket games, fancied myself as adept with bat and ball; but here I was amongst sporting giants, vocational athletes. They put me in the outfield chasing long-shots without much responsibility. One afternoon I was distracted from my sunny, grassy reverie by a multitude of screams: Craig! A catch! Visions of triumph. Up with the gloves, close the eyes and bring the hands firmly together. Crack. Forehead dented, I collapsed. Through the stars Shittleback's stringy face bent over me, smiling tolerance and sympathy. She hoisted me to the shade of a pine and sped back to the game. Ah, but they were great ones for the game!

Nevertheless, the sporting arena was but a fraction of the trouble. A plump young lady with a brand new uniform for a brand new year, green socks and tan shoes of unimpeachable quality, tackled me in the playground.

'You're the new girl, are you? What does your Daddy do?'

God knows how she would have reacted if he'd been a wharfie or a tram-conductor. The word truck-driver was enough to throw her into horrified amazement.

'Oh, my Daddy's a lawyer in the city. He has his own partnership with Judy's Daddy. Fluke and Potter. I suppose your Daddy has his own firm?'

It appeared that what a girl's Daddy did for a living was the way she was defined. Our mummies were unimportant—and our status in the school had even very little to do with ourselves. I took it for granted along with the others.

I jumped at the chance to be sent home to Cobb Swamp to check up on Granny, see if she was managing and do her springcleaning which, Mother feared, she might neglect altogether without pressure. So they put me on the train armed with sandsoap, scrubbing brushes and a dozen mousetraps. I went home. The winter paddocks stretched boggy and waterlogged, the pools full and muddy, the brambles wet and shiny slapping against legs, tearing at trousers. I felt good back there on the pit-scarred green flatlands with their tree-skeletons thrusting white arms into the wintry sky. Must've been quite a fire to kill them all so dead that not one had ever come to in the spring. Trunks weathered hard as iron, standing naked in the wind. Granny thought the cleaning was 'rot', but we agreed conspiratorially to humour Mother, and do it. I gathered her a mountainous stack of wood from the paddocks, chopped it small for the winter. In the evenings we sat by the fireside in her old faded front room, played euchre and yarned until midnight over our cups of tea.

My mother had been spasmodically ill for as long as I could remember; more and more of her tasks fell to me. Of course, Mother couldn't expect a grown boy to sink to domestic concerns. Ken even baulked at being asked to dry the dishes; whereupon Mother would apologise to him for her being sick and for me not pulling my weight. He blamed me with gusto for any job she gave to him and we rarely spoke to each other without coming to blows. Mother's insides had had it; every month she bled rivers and, in between the floods that left her weak and anaemic, she suffered from headaches, backaches and stomach aches. I never sympathised properly—it meant more work for me. Dad never believed she was sick anyway and, if anything, made more mess than usual. Ken stepped into the breach rarely and timely, made tea, cakes, scones; never enough to build up expectations—just enough for the accolades.

She made any favour—from sixpence to a free Sunday—dependent on what she described as Good Behaviour. This system of outright bribery didn't apply so stringently to Ken—her definition of Good Behaviour was lighter for him anyway. It was her reversals that infuriated me. She made the rules; she broke them; she had the whip hand. For a week you're labouring faultlessly to get Sunday afternoon off—you want to explore the valley over the hill where the power-lines rush down through the scrub. You've scoured, polished, washed, ironed and curbed all the welling nastiness, not saying a hard word to anyone for days. Admittedly you've had to rip up the old telephone directory at night to keep sane under the strain. But Sunday dawns and everything looks set; you've lasted the distance, you can stay out till dark. She will base her counter-attack on anything—the weather, a raised voice, a door slamming, a lack of definition in the bargain.

Having waited patiently I down tools at half-past two and change into denims like a mouse. 'I'll be off now, Mother.'

'Off? Where?'

'To the paddocks over the hill. You said I could go if I was good.'

'Yes. Well I suppose that'll be all right. Don't go near the power-lines.'

'No, Mother.'

'And be back by four.'

'Four? But you said I could stay out all afternoon.'

'Someone has to make the scones and your father's gone out for wood.'

'Ken can do it.'

'Ken's out at the dam with the boy from the next farm.'

'Well he can come in at four, can't he?'

'Maureen, he hasn't made a friend since we left Cobb Swamp. You're being very selfish dear. After all, we came for you.'

'I haven't made any friends either.'

'Well that's your fault, isn't it?'

'It is *not*.'

'Don't you raise your voice to me.'

'Sorry.'

'Now off you go, Maureen, or you'll hardly have any time at all.'

'You should have told me this morning. I could have gone earlier. I want to go right over past the scrub.'

'Well you can do that another time.'

'Then I'll have to be good again.'

'Really Maureen, it's your fault if it's so hard to be good.'

'But I've done everything this week—just so I could go out today and now you won't let me.'

'You shouldn't be doing it just to get out, should you?'

'It's not fair. I'll be back when I'm ready.'

'You'll be back at four.'

'I will *not*. Ken can make the scones.'

'If you don't promise to be back at four, you won't go at all.'

If I run I'll be thrashed when I get back and she'll punish me in other ways for a week. If I stay I won't be allowed to go at all—but it's hardly worth going for an hour. I turn to her, as menacing as a kid can be.

'You are not fair,' I snarl, 'you trick me into working night and day and then you won't give me what I want. I hate you.'

Her eyebrows shoot up.

'Get out to your room you selfish little bitch, and don't expect to go wandering off around power-lines. Your father'll deal with you when he gets home.' Her voice is cold and strident. I do what I'm told. I tear up another old directory and cry my tears of rage.

On one such afternoon I collect three bottles of painkillers from the bathroom cupboard. I wander down the long farmhouse yard to the haystack, sentimentally saying my farewells to the old plough and the bull by the fence. There's been the usual row and, as I climb up in the hay, I see my mother and Ken struggle through the barbed-wire fence and stroll down the valley hand in hand. I'm sniffing audibly but there's no-one to hear. I throw out a half dozen aspros in my hand and gulp them down. Three codeines—taste awful. This is not going to be enough, I know that. I toss out another handful. And stop. Suicide's such a great idea. It will show her—will it ever. I can just see her trying to face Dad and her friends. Just think what people will say! Her favourite moral ploy. She'll suffer for years about what the people will say. But Christ what's the use if I'm not there to enjoy it? There's a sneaky flaw in the logic. I've got to be there too. I'm getting drowsy. But I'm not dying. Have to think quick. I've seen the stomach pumps on TV—I won't mind that—it's just that she'll most probably belt the shit out of me when I come home from hospital. Worse than ever. Kill myself then, really kill myself. That'd show her. That'd change her attitude. But what's the good of that, if I'm dead to the world as well as to her, Dad too, the scrub and the valley, the lot? No bloody use at all.

I wake up a few hours later, glad to be breathing; pretend I've had a headache, get into strife, ditch the whole idea.

The countryside offered its refuge. The barn was full of hay, musty and secure. I constructed tunnels and hideouts, played at forts on the battlements, or sat alone in the dimness nursing the quiet down there. At night the frogs raised their voices around the dam, offering a companionable complaint to the stars. It was worth a row to get out there with them and croak and rail at the way of things. The bull snorted and pawed the clods in his paddock, sheep drowsed and prattled, lambs streaked across the springtime green of the valley. Outside there was none of the heavy freakishness of life in the house. I served indoors to make good my escape to the fields.

One of my mother's dearest hopes was to avoid the poverty she'd known as a child. Her father, a handsome Irish-looking chap in the pictures, with flowing hair and beard, looked too flamboyant for a bootmaker, and probably was—the family saw little of his wages. Father wasn't much of an ally when it came to the heady pursuit of security, but the momentum of Mother's schemes dragged him along. She believed passionately in free enterprise and often warned me that if people like my father had their way no-one would be allowed to have any property at all. That Communist, Evatt, had nearly tricked the country into that sort of thing. One may rise to the dizzy summits of wealth by one's own exertions; the poor deserved to be poor and Father was lucky to have married someone with a bit of ambition.

Why pay rent out when we could, instead, be paying off our own (second) home? With this premise began countless feverish weekends on the Display Home scene. I was glad to stay home, but as often as not the whole family did over a few of these execrable display estates while Mother took notes and Father smiled at everyone but Mother. In the end, after bank managers, architects and builders had cracked their skulls over her designs, construction did begin on a house in Malmsy, not a half-mile from St Agatha's. It was ineffably sweet to her that the nobodies from deep Gippsland had risen out of abject poverty to live amongst the élite of the countryside in the village of Lord Cunningham's country seat. Here indeed was eminence. We moved at the end of the year—the usual picaresque ferrying, Dad's truck stacked with every sort of junk—cots, pots, commodes, cupboards, a spare kitchen sink. The acquisitiveness of the deprived.

It wasn't hard to see why Malmsy had attracted its population of the wealthy and the retired, lying amongst spacious hills between the Dandenongs and the sea. From the quarry hill you could see clear across the flat land to the sea. The bushland of the mountains began on the edge of the town. St Agatha's pool was one of the dozens, tennis courts adjoined countless homes, neatly-decked riders ambled down every street and lane on fine shiny horses. A dry sherry belt and no mistake. Even the day-girls—locals whom the boarders regarded as socially inferior—had the accoutrements of a wealth that left the Craigs in the shade. Mother's decisive move in amongst them had none of the desired effect. Nothing overlaid our accents, our origins and our moderate if no longer straitened circumstances. I took to romancing about our country estate at Cobb Swamp, vast and run by a manager in our absence, but I'd left the fantasy too late and it made no impression on anyone.

When Mother had her wounded womb taken out I visited her in hospital, glad of an excuse to skip Shittleback's sports afternoon. Mother lay weak and purplish-grey against the white sheets, a bottle of clear stuff seeping into her punctured wrist, her veins black against that sick-looking skin.

'You all right, Mum?'

'Yes dear. I'm all right now.'

I felt sorry, troubled by the exhausted look of awful suffering survived. I wanted to kiss her. But we were oceans apart, Mother and me, and I just sat an hour or so while she drowsed; and went away. 'I'm never having children,' I thought. 'Not if it comes to this.'

Malmsy had no High School, so when we moved into the new town, Ken had to leave the quiet farming kids for Rosella High, a prefabricated corrugated jungle on the industrial fringe of Melbourne.

The new High School served the needs of thousands of duplicated slap-up houses cluttered over the industrial estates, between smoke-stacks and factories. The Highway swept down Malmsy Rise with the trees and the coy survivals of replica-English-village, rolled in through two or three wide lush valleys whose years were numbered and, breasting the Rosella Hill, you saw the grey city at a blow. 'We should never have moved. You don't appreciate the opportunities you're getting at St Agatha's. And now Ken has to go to school with factory-workers' children.' And now Ken, poor Ken, has to rough it with the concrete-slum kids. I was all right of course. I was mixing with decent well-brought up children. Snobs and prigs? 'But Maureen, they're decent girls.' And always, always, from here on out: 'We shouldn't've done this for you. You're not even grateful. And we've had to send poor Ken to that terrible school.' Right there, Mother, anyway. No doubt about that—concrete breezeways, glass shacks, not a shred of equipment, kids as tough as nails. Cobb High scuffles had been mild by comparison. 'You know Ken's got a weak heart, Maureen, since the rheumatic fever. In there with all those toughs, you wouldn't care if your brother got beaten to death.' Right again.

Ken started to come home with black eyes, gasping for breath, face white as a sheet. And he started giving cheek to his mum. He stopped chopping wood. He disappeared at weekends and at night without telling her a thing about where he was going—or what he was doing. He started telling her mind your own business you silly bitch. Ken was becoming a man. 'If only we'd stayed in Cobb, Maureen, your brother would have been all right. It's Rosella's done this to him, mixing with those delinquents out there. He was never like this as a child. He was such a placid baby.' Ken wouldn't have any of the canvas belt—he'd got it occasionally before. Now he began to face his mother, grip her wrist, disarm her and slap her across the face if she struggled. 'We should never have moved. You're always complaining about the girls at St Agatha's but what you don't realise is that we did it all for you, for your own good, we've scrimped and saved to do the right thing by you, to give you the things we missed out on, to give you an education. Other girls your age are working in Woolworth's. I was working in Woolworth's at your age. And look what it's done to your brother. You'll have to learn a bit of gratitude if you're ever going to get on in the world. Other people, you know, won't put up with what we do.'

What with the Home Front ever worsening and a daily dose of superiority from the girls, it was a stroke of luck that Mrs Grantly came to teach at the school. The headmistress was the anachronism one might have expected, a waddling grey-haired woman with delusions of educating Young Ladies. It's a puzzle that she should have employed Mrs Grantly at all. Her connections with the Australian

Communist Party, though vague now, had obviously been strong at one time. (Mother regretted that the Party had not been banned—'a disgrace in a free country'.) Mrs Grantly appreciated Calwell—'the most honest man in Australian politics,' she used to say, 'which accounts for his failure'—and she talked more politics than she could ever have got away with in a State-run school. Miss Rollande-Clagge must have guessed that the political mind of St Agatha was inviolably empty.

Mrs Grantly had a craggy unbeatable face, by no means the strength which controls half-witted schoolgirls, but dedicated, the kind of face that would stick to its guns. She had fought in the Spanish Civil War; she talked of the trenches there—the mortars landing, a church blown clean apart with its congregation, flights and narrow escapes—and she talked of the terrible sadness of a battle utterly lost.

'She was fighting with the Communists, I suppose,' was Mother's cool reaction to my enchantment.

'Well that Franco—he was one of Hitler's mates. And *we* fought Hitler.' I thought I had her whipped, but she went on to tell me that I'd understand better when I got older, but that I must remember that General Franco won in Spain, so the Spanish people must have wanted him.

'You reckon the Germans wanted Hitler?'

'Well you can't tell with Germans—it's Dutch people I get along with. And anyway Maureen, you weren't even born then.' That sealed it.

Mother was even less pleased when she discovered that we were doing a course on the Chinese Revolution, one which, as she suspected, had been added to our curriculum by popular vote. On Mrs Grantly's invitation. Mao without malice. One contrast stuck in my mind. Previous leaders, Mrs Grantly told us, wore white collars, kept clean hands; Mao went into the fields, worked with his people, worked with his hands. Sitting amongst the bored well-groomed ladies, I received the information with delight. Fortunately, I refrained from discussing Mao with my mother who regarded Formosa as China and felt that trade with the Reds was another national disgrace. She used to talk about General MacArthur with awe and reverence. 'I will return,' he had promised, and he did. We owed more than the Battle of the Coral Sea to the Americans, more than I would, Mother suspected, ever understand.

Mrs Grantly rarely dictated and encouraged the class to read books and sort it out, an unwelcome task for most of the equestrian ladies who preferred old Clagge's pontifical notes. In 1456 comma the Turks ... captured Constantinople full stop ... Scholars fled comma ... thus causing the Renaissance full stop. Indeed, the headmistress felt that Mrs Grantly was handing out blank cheques for youthful arrogance and shook with fury when I announced that I preferred to study Golding and Hardy on my own than take her lessons on *Pride and Prejudice*. She had made her own selection from the external lists, excluding *Tess*, she hinted, because of the rape and questionable moral code. She warned my mother: 'Maureen is headstrong, Mrs Craig—oh well-behaved of course, exemplary, but ... agin the government, yes, agin the government.'

'Gels,' she warned us—unexpectedly since Mrs Grantly was in charge of all twentieth-century literature—'Gels, *Cry the Beloved Country* is a beautifully-written book, but yoom'st all be careful with the bias in this book. Mr Paton is well known to be Communist and his work must, in cons'quence, be regarded as propaganda of a highly subtle variety. Your education here should, by now, have taught you to take this kind of revolutionary writer with a grain of salt.' She footnoted my article in the Magazine, dissociating herself and the school from its 'leftist' views on South Africa. She implied that giving scholarships to working-class children had its dangers. She need hardly have worried—neither myself nor Mrs Grantly had the slightest impact on the daughters of the prosperous.

St Agatha's wasn't a church school proper, but the daily assembly had its quota of hymns and prayers led by Rollande-Clagge. She'd look up, scanning the rows of green-clad girls, then tilt her glasses forward and bow her unctuous head over the lectern. The Craigs weren't a church family either—Mother limited her worship to Christmas and Easter. Twice a year, with Father more or less in tow, she made her public confessions of faith, and took it seriously. But even after a three-hour dose on a Good Friday afternoon she'd return with the old vitriol boiling out of her. The pair of them would be out only minutes before the nagging recommenced and hit its fistfight crescendo. This god of theirs had scant effect, I thought, but I kept my doubts secret, fully aware of the danger of inviting Mother's wrath, disgust and punitive action. The beginning of the Confirmation classes at school put an end to the clandestine policy.

'Aren't they having Confirmation classes at school, Maureen?'

'I suppose so.'

'You'd better find out when dear. You're old enough to be done this year.'

'I don't think I want to be.'

'Don't want to be? Confirmed?'

'No. I don't think I will.'

'But you're getting on for fifteen. It's certainly time.'

'I don't want to be.'

'Why ever not? You can't take Communion till you're done, you know.'

'I just don't want to.'

'Come on Maureen, there must be some reason. I suppose it's that Communist woman you're always talking about—what's her name? Grantly?'

'Oh hell, no. I just don't want to.'

'But you'll have to. Everyone in your class'll be done this year.'

'I don't mind.'

'You'll have to mind. It's just laziness I suppose.'

'No it is not. I just don't believe all this stuff they tell you. I can't go swearing that I do.'

She looked at me, pale and aghast.

'Just what I'd have expected from you. Won't do a thing you're told, bury yourself in all kinds of weird books and now you tell me you don't believe in God.'

'Well I don't.'

'Well you'll bloody well have to learn. I haven't brought you up to be a heathen or an atheist or whatever you call them and I won't have one in my house.' With that, a burst of tears.

In the end she persuaded me to go to the classes, though I knew that would not be enough, even if I attended the lot and still held on to my guns. This was the beginning of the end as far as avoiding the Confirmation went. My mind did its usual somersaults to please her. I knew a woman, years later, whose Confirmation story got my wide-eyed admiration. Her parents had forced her off to those unholy catechismal lessons, basic theology, dust-dry and contorted, without a grain of wonder in it. She suffered the whole circus with outward good grace, delighting in posing awkward questions. Finally she dressed up in the virginal white garb, shined her patent leather, drew on spotless white socks and went off to church. She simply waited until the whole gang was assembled, purple bishop, black clergy, colourless local dignitaries, and her parents safely inside, to creep out the back and go home. Not so Craig. And certainly the penalties would have lasted for months with the whole fiasco to live through next year. My mother never gave up.

But neither did I seem capable of a conscious and cynical lie. I had just three months to locate God. Strafford Hill looked as likely a place as any, with its ruined Victorian mansion, gnarled trees and lofty lookout—as well as the crater of the old quarry where water lay, a magical spot like the gravel pits at home. I went there whenever I could dodge my mother. I knew every inch of the hillside, every cranny inside the crater itself. With a pencil and notebook I climbed up for the sunset, watched the course of clouds, the coming and going of light and colour, wrote lengthy verse—usually blank: Reveries at Sunset, 1 to 784. Ambitiously one summer, I wrote a play—keenly impressed by one of the Young Ladies who had managed to be having an affair—or so she said. 'You wouldn't understand, Maureen, but the only thing I want in life is to marry and bear the children of the man I love.' Sounded all right. Visions of the sensitive intelligent lad who would fall desperately in love with my mind. The play's narrator fervently extolled the magnificence of love (more blank verse); cerebral romantic situation with animated discussions of music and literature punctuated by passionate sexless embraces.

The frenzied hunt for Faith took me up Strafford Hill more and more often, creeping away behind my mother's back. But God rode up on none of the trailing clouds of sunset glory, nor spoke with tongues in the wind. I had to make do with a far quieter revelation. On a hot still evening, the sun in its last hour and unusually bright, I came down the hill through brown dock-weed and horse-shit to the storm-water drain where the hawthorns grew. There it was quiet, secluded from the road. The rickety old mansion tumbled across the hill, stumbled amongst weed; intensely bright bands of light shot out of the clouded sun striping the sky. The white of the lit clouds was blinding. Saul crossed my mind. I fell down in the grass burbling prayers and had myself convinced in a trice. No other solution would have been tolerable.

Having fixed up the integrity, paste-board and stage make-up, I went through with the ceremony in a spirit of due solemnity and gradually became a regular fiend for church-going, vicar-visiting and mountain-mysticism. The sincerity of it was world-shattering, but the chagrin infinite when Mother was unable to notice the improvements in me which were my guarantee of the reality of it all. Not only did I polish up the floors with the cleanliness next to godliness, but cheerily took on the lawn-mowing and wood-chopping which Ken neglected. I was inspired with a thirst for good works.

Countless Sunday mornings went by—lusty church-choir singing, tearful attentiveness to the sermons, the whispered sentences of everlasting preservation at the altar-rail. I had to convince myself of my sinfulness, not seeing much wrong with my spinelessly well-intentioned life. The preparation book was invaluable with its finicky inventories of fractional misdemeanours. I still had to rack my brains to get together enough sin to make it all worthwhile. I spent hours praying for the strength to tolerate the savages around me, both at home and at school, begging the good lord for a submissive heart and quiet head. Somehow, the anticipated surges of loving-kindness never overcame me in my anger, yet I went on dragooning myself into patience.

My fervour finally led me to make inquiries of the Archbishop about the possibility of entering the ministry. I fancied myself up there in the pulpit drenching my awed congregation in brimstone and tears of penitence. The answer cooled me off, though. No chance of Holy Orders, it appeared, and I had no intention of being a Deaconess, whose duties looked like a combination of social work and back-staging for the men, despite the Archbishop's glowing account of the indispensable role of women in the church. To my daily orisons I added a prayer for acceptance of my woman's lot. Mother naturally opened up the letter the instant it arrived—couldn't wait to know, she said, who could be writing to me from St Paul's Cathedral. She was shocked and provided me with a lecture on arrogance. I took it all quite well—so strong was my pursuit of the Faith. Her meddling embarrassed me but I stifled my anger.

The male didn't exist for me through those years; men might be some irrelevant species from another continent. The ladies of St Agatha rarely deigned to invite me to their parties, and when they did I was left quite alone. My brother was the mortal enemy, but a stranger just the same. While I messed about with God and Golding, withdrawing further and further into myself, Ken was starring in the Rosella High School Scandal, fucking freely in the breezeway. It was many years later that he told me about one desperate afternoon, caught with his pants off somewhere in the schoolyard, running for the cover of Conroy Creek, a sort of gutter denuded of its under-growth which trickled across the Rosella Industrial Estate.

I didn't discover the penis until I was seventeen; certainly there was the hypothetical spermal cord mentioned briefly in the holy hush of The House Not Made With Hands, my mother's 1939 handbook to sex, and there had been a lump of dun-coloured flabby-looking flesh which fell out of my father's pyjamas when he leapt with unusual abandon from bed one Sunday, and which he hastily hid away. But it wasn't until the Christmas Test Match after I'd finished school that the prick took on a more familiar shape. I was alone. On the top tier of the Northern Stand, in brilliant sunshine, I amused myself sorting out the distinctions between short square leg and silly mid-on. Into the idyllic afternoon intruded a snub-nosed, narrow-eyed slip of a fellow. We chatted a little, drinking Coke, and his friendly offer to see me to the train delighted me. When he suggested a stroll in Jolimont Park and finally thought we might 'stretch out' on the grass for a while, I agreed with only a faint suspicion that things were not as they should be. Such a charming afternoon. Shades of *Tess of the D'Urbervilles*. I'd read it, too, but apparently gathered nothing from Tess's signal lesson. So we lay down in the relative privacy of a corner of the park near the railway yards—thin gritty grass. After that introductory spiel which I learned later to recognise, he abruptly took my hand and laid it on some sort of stiff object in his pants ... this was the mythical spermal cord. Hard, unyielding, infinitely unpleasant. With embarrassed words of apology I fled ...

I worked the summer for Incorporated Victorian Life Assurance—calculating vast amounts of interest on their thievish Housing Assistance Loan programme. The idea of the penis obsessed me. Walking in the streets of the city in lunch-hours I stared below male belts, detected the bulge, squirmed, wondered why it had never struck me before. Even in the baggiest of business pants I made out the thing swinging a bit. Boys in tight jeans intrigued and assaulted my mind. Sometimes you could see it resting like a stiff turd across the crutch. At the office Christmas turn I watched a vibrant Italian woman with her slim husband. She dark and Carmenish; he lithe with the bulge. I half-swooned, illicitly contemplating the conjunction of these two ... that in her. Infinitely attractive; infinitely repulsive. I wanted to tell someone these things, shout a confession, but dared not (even on the lonely summit of Strafford Hill) whisper a syllable of it.

With University lined up for me, Mother had conceived a new housing project to get Ken out of Rosella. I deserted one afternoon from a peculiarly boring collection of identical display-homes and made for the railway station. Down bleak Bluff Road a car stopped. A man. Thin in whites. Tennis shoes. Did I want a lift somewhere? Affable. Try it. How lucky, we both agreed, that he was heading out Dandenong Road. Me coy and callow stole a glance at his tennis pants—he had one all right. Was I in a hurry to get home? Snigger. Me in a hurry to get home? Me? Well what about a spin out into the hills—just an hour or so up towards the Dandenongs—he could drop back through Malmsy and leave me right at the door. Why not? He spoke quietly, a fine English-flavoured accent, a gaunt pleasant face. Why not?

In the bush he pulls over. I'm not even faintly afraid—I've been fighting Ken for a decade. But the man doesn't threaten anyway; he takes my hand and says to sit near him. I comply.

'Let me kiss you.'

'OK.'

He puts his mouth on mine. He parts his lips. He forces his tongue through my grinding teeth. My body's like a board.

'You don't like this?'

'No.'

'Why not?'

'I don't feel anything. I don't like it.'

'Are you a lesbian?'

A shock this word, which I scarcely know. But I'm not that.

'No. I just don't like it.'

'You can tell me. Some of my best friends are homosexuals. I'm not going to hurt you.'

'No. No. No. I don't know anything about it.'

He looks puzzled, sceptical. Starts up the motor.

'Can I see you again? Take you to a picture, maybe?'

I can't see why—unless he wants to get that thing in me. I don't even know where the place in me is—though the blood comes from somewhere. I say yes, ring me the week after next, when I've left home. I'm starting at the University, in college. He looks sceptical and drives off.

Part Two

---

*In which the landscape
acquires a population*

I went up to University with unrivalled childish optimism—a rare thing except perhaps in working-class families. The star in the ascendant, a great academic future, a niche even in the civilised comfortable classes. Not to mention the bracing air of free and ranging thought which I anticipated. Hearing the notorious Menshinski, a White Russian philosophy professor of no mean sophistry, I applauded his laudable demolition of the grounds of accepted sexual ethics. What fun!

No wooden-headed headmistress would draw my mother aside and warn her of incipient socialism, revolutionary tendencies, unrealistic idealisms. The atmosphere indulged my dreams, offered exotic stimulation. Everything was dynamic. The sun of late summer poured down on the college gardens, the brickwork pavements, the big stone chapel. My room, narrow and cell-like, was nevertheless my own. I rearranged the furniture around its edge to create a token space on the rug. Outside, the creosoted-wood fire-escape mixed with branches and sky. The college bell rang out the orderly hours; at six-thirty we donned our academic gowns and forgathered in the big dining-room with its polished wood chairs and tables. On these academic and cultivated bagatelles I throve the first months; single-minded, clear-sighted, untrammelled ... The years of St Agatha, claustrophobic years in training as an outcast, ebbed away like a meaningless charade.

Tramping off through the night streets of Carlton with Abigail, a fellow-fresher—a bit amazed that working-class origins left her unperturbed. I'd decided on a hard, honest, fuck-you-jack line for the University. But Abigail, the daughter of a Professor by God, seemed puzzled when I warned her that my father was a mere truck-driver. She became my companion without the slightest patronisation and obviously didn't see my father's job as a vital part of me. That party, the first of countless in the unknown world of terrace houses, where students lived free and (probably) practised free love. A drunk boy fiddling with his guitar; a slender girl swathed in bead-chains, face daubed and patterned; two people locked together twisting and kissing and mauling. I couldn't take my eyes off them, but I was scared someone would notice me watching. Music insistent and deafening—Ken's ready fervour for the 'Top 40' had left Beethoven for me. Anything he liked had to be bad. Some bearded student poured us claret which I sipped most cautiously while another guzzled a half-pint of Fosters at a go, belched and extended his shaky glass for a refill. I took a few gulps of vinegary wine, wishing they had some of that sweet Communion port. A long-haired giant stood, legs wide, with his hand touching the spine of a thin fair boy with rimless glasses. Oh the daring we thought we had, Abigail and me, as we poured our claret into the weirdo's fur-lined boots. An obvious target: little girls, but well-trained withal. He didn't even bother to look down.

A year or so later I fled to a similar party alone. Sitting on the floor drinking too much Cinzano too fast. A student squatted beside me, and was going to speak. I turned to him gratefully and looked into heavy hostile eyes: 'Whatta you doing here? You're just a lesbian.' But I hadn't the composure of the big man. I cleared out like a shot.

A bit amazed to miss out on the lead in the college play, I had stolidly refused to temporise with any bit-parts or backstage work. I managed to get in on the cast-party in the mountains, and rode up in the van to a hillside barbecue after the last night.

Blind drunk for the first time I falter and lumber at deterring a thin youth intent on feeling me, hesitantly insist that it'd be nicer to watch the stars drift and talk about the meaning of life. He laughs heartily, persists, gives up. Intensely aware of the branches of thornbush, the countlessness of stars, the brittle dead leaf by my hand, quite unaware of this boy.

What rampant romances dance in my mind. Dark Steve with the turbulent hair, nonchalant Steve with his shirt-tail always flapping from his jeans, ingenuous black-eyed, wide-mouthed Steve, Steve stammering delightfully, is the object of my asexual attraction. If I just look right at the right moment he will approach chivalrously and kiss my grubby hand. During the bits of the night that are free of those loathsome young men seeking feelies, I lurk around Steve. I try winsome thoughtful poses, carefree joking ploys, even magnetic half-lunatic lures, but shining Steve is thoroughly preoccupied with his beer and a bevy of girls all trying more direct methods.

I envy Erif, who lives next door in college. She goes up to him without a sign of manoeuvring and jokes without a sign of strain. Her long brown hair spills down her shoulders; her small slim body in gingham cut low. Steve inclines his big dark head, laughs. Though I stand near them gazing into the charcoal, though they both know me from college tutorials, though I laugh audibly at their jokes, I go unnoticed, unaddressed. The young gentlemen haul steaks out of the fires and slap them into the bread on their ladies' palms.

'Have you got one?' a boy asks me.

'No.'

'Here.'

Steak without chivalry. I go into the hall to get my own drinks, ashamed to be without a beau to fetch and carry. The senior gentlemen operating the beer-gun are patronising and embarrass the blush into my cheeks. I keep moving, not for myself so much as to foster the illusion of a sought-after Craig breezing from one expectant group to the next. Hours later, with the soles of my feet aching, pints of Black Tulip gurgling around in my gut and not one offer of a dance, I flop down by a tree-stump, finger my glass and close my eyes.

'Is anyone sitting here?' A St Agatha voice. Julia Vernon, the college's intellectual prodigy, reels beside me—the last person I want to talk to.

'Enjoying yourself?' she slurs.

'Oh yeah, all right.'

'I'm not. No-one's been talking to me, and there's nobody interesting anyway.'

'No. I guess not.'

'And I've laddered my best stockings.' She always dresses impeccably—F.J. tailor-made skirts, David Jones fineknits, ten quid pumps.

'You should wear jeans to this sort of turn, Jules.' Everyone calls her Jules—sarcastically somehow.

'I don't like *Ash Wednesday,*' she remarks provocatively, and out of the blue.

'I think it's great.' Eliot's faith-block fascinates me, and I often mutter bits of it.

'Because I do not hope to know again
The infirm glory of the positive hour... .
I rejoice that things are as they are and
I renounce ...'

'Oh come now, it's so fragmentary—worse than *The Wasteland.*'

'I like *The Wasteland* too.'

'But why?'

'Oh shit, I dunno. I've had a lot to drink...'

'None of that early Eliot is really knit together; they both lack essential unity.'

'Oh I don't think so.'

'Where's the unifying factor, then?'

'Oh shit, Jules, I dunno. I understand it. I like it.'

She takes the hint and shuts up. In second year, with a trail of prizes, she was taking the English I honours for fun. Tutorials: she beamed her chisel-intelligence on our fresher-attempts, our unacademic halting comments.

'Do you know that joke about Eliot and Hopkins? I forget who said it. That the Deutschland's a waste and the Wasteland's a wreck.'

I laugh. 'No. That's very nice.'

'Yes.' She pauses only an instant before continuing. 'It's a pity you're not taking Ancient History.' One of Julia's Exhibitions. Is she going to volunteer coaching?

'Why?'

'Oh it's by far the best of the first year courses.'

'I'm interested in the Reformation.' She makes me feel surly.

'That's the trouble. You studied it at school. First years are awfully scared to branch out.'

'I want to learn more about Luther, and the whole crack-up of Catholic Europe.'

'History's not learning facts, you know. It's the discipline. You'd have done better with Dr Fortescue—he's one of the best lecturers in Australia.'

'I guess so but I still like the Reformation. You know—Luther getting to be a revolutionary by default in spite of himself ...'. I've got to get out of this. I detest this woman's overwhelming superiority. I skol the Black Tulip. 'I'm off to get a drink. See you.'

'Oh,' she counters, slurping rapidly and thrusting her glass into my hand, 'get me one too. It's brandy and dry.'

I haven't the presence of mind to say get your own, so I'm trapped for another session until I excuse myself on the grounds of having a piss. Yet I feel sorry. She's as lonely and out of place as I am myself.

I stagger into Erif by the fire. Steve's stretched out on the grass with his glass upturned on his shirtfront—asleep. I can talk to her now.

'Having a good time, Erif?'

'Yes, isn't it lovely up here with the smell of the fires and the leaves.' I like her soft Lancashire accent, agree enthusiastically.

'Isn't Steve gorgeous.' Schoolgirl Maureen.

She looks away. 'Mmmm.'

On the homeward trip at five or so I still can't catch his eye. Jolt down to Melbourne; getting the feel of a hangover, guts churning. Until, just as we're climbing down, he offers me his hand.

'You look p-p-p-p-p-pale Maureen.'

'I'm all right. Had a lot of Black Tulip.'

'The trick's to drink a p-p-p-pint of milk before you go to s-s-s-s sleep.'

'Got no milk.' I speak briefly. Might chuck any minute.

'Water then. It'll d-d-d-dilute the mixture.' He breaks into hilarious laughter and waves as he wanders off. But I treasure the moment. I've been noticed. That's what a girl's got to get to be—noticed.

Emma Brightfort came into college for three weeks while someone was sick. She wanted to read my poetry. I'd been pouring out the sunset reveries on mortality and ephemeral beauty for years and came to Emma with little to show. She inspired the confidence that her judgements were sound and worthwhile. A blonde big-nosed compelling face with every lineament of determination; but something locked up about it, as if will ruled the affections and might have crippled them.

'You've got the gift of the gab,' said Emma.

'Have I?'

'Yes, but you've got to get rid of this self-pity, you know.'

'Have I? But Shelley is just like that.'

'Yes,' said Emma. 'That's exactly right. Shelley is a wallower.

'Oh.'

Emma read so avidly, believed, did she? that she'd found a poet. Glimmerings of self-faith. She told me what she thought was good; again if necessary. Never baulking at reassurance.

She had an unfailing eye and ear. Saw the florid nothings, heard the lagging rhythms. And she was lucid. I began, painfully and nostalgically, to abandon my superstition that the poet's inspired word is immutable, stands. I started to work with words, hack out dead wood and burn it. Emma, who insisted that she was neither poet nor creator—just critic—placed her finger on the strengths of my writing, gave me my poetry. Which, in these next years, would be much the same as giving me my sanity. She was hard on sentimentality, murderous about self-pity; and if detachment had with her the status of a moral imperative, it was not one that I was any the worse for contemplating.

There was, too, a splash of something like hero-worship in Emma's attitude; surprising in a woman so self-assured, so categorical. An illicit attraction for the daring and original. Emma probably didn't know that I went to those dozens of student parties only to sit around in terror of the milling drinking strangers—and I didn't admit it. Rather, I hinted at unspeakable exploits, cracked myself up as something of a seasoned drinker, gay and worldly, a youngster ranging through her experiences with the artist's absorption.

A Parkville party. 'Why don't you come, Emma. It'll be great.' In an upstairs balcony room people tripped over one another, hid their beer in corners or carried it about with them, and a girl who might have been the hostess tried to clear bodies from the centre-floor to start some dancing.

'What would you like to drink, Emma?'

'Oh, lemonade.'

'Come on.'

'A bit of vodka perhaps.'

'I'll see.'

I threaded through the press, found the kitchen, pinched a nip of vodka from an unattended bottle, opened my Cinzano and headed back. On the stairs a boy asked me for a swig. I poured some. He slopped it over and I filled it up again.

'Good grief Maureen, have you drunk all that already?'

I passed it off brilliantly. 'Oh well, feeling pretty thirsty, you know. Here's a vodka and orange—pinched.'

Just as I slumped back with studied ease into the armchair a reeling dancer crashed back into my lap grinding my ankle with his boot. I went white; Emma helped me out into the air and took me back to college. We drank coffee all night, a luminous warmth between us. Finally, fearing the moment she'd get up and leave, I said, falsely, 'I'm tired. Must get to sleep.' Throw her out. Get in first. Yet I'd have liked to spend all my time with this sympathetic, encouraging girl. Which I admitted neither to myself nor to her.

One night, late, after a session on my poems—she didn't get tired of the fantastic output—she climbed into bed and asked to be tucked in. Craig embarrassed. I strode to the bedside and heaved the mattress like some sort of super-muscular nurse, slapped the blankets under and stood back. Not just Craig clumsiness; she wanted me close and I, wanting to be close, recoiled.

'You tuck in like a ditch-digger,' she mumbled, and there was hurt in her voice. For an instant I wanted passionately to lean over and reverently kiss her forehead, but I gave the laconic adolescent grin, said good night and was gone.

After a film the others went back in the tram and I walked up through the city alone. Ripple-soled desert boots creeping along the pavements, crossing at red lights, green lights, amongst many-coloured lights. Cars stopping. 'No. I like the night and walking, thank you.' Tongue whipped across dry lips. A tense heroic figure in the streets. Running the imaginary gauntlet of a neon underworld; feeling tall, muscular, equal to any tough who might slip out of an alley, knife drawn. Across the wide asphalt of the Victoria Street junction, tram lines greasy in the slant-light. All this, but a posture walking it. Playing cool, a game with no rules, one player.

Next Sunday, in chapel. Split second collapse of this whole religion. One instant I seem to be Maureen Craig in the presence of the Lord. The next obliterates me. I feel the tense agonised face-muscles, register the forehead's dented frown and the head's Rollande-Clagge angle of devotion. Straining at the attitudes of sanctity; manifest constipated godliness. Craig shoots up to the chapel vaulting, sees holy-Craig; titters. I look around expecting an audience, observers of holy-Craig. But there are none. The priest is still handing out wafers, the rest of the congregation is praying. And Craig, unobserved, unverified, melts into the wooden pew.

With staggering rapidity I identified dozens of Craigs, each playing its appointed role to perfection—Craig the Moody, Craig the Gay, Craig the Detached, Craig the Witty, Gritty, Lovely. Leaving only a thunderous vacuous consciousness of nobody.

College seemed tomb-empty when Emma left. I borrowed a book I didn't need from Jules Vernon and returned it late one night, happening to be carrying a sheaf of poems (mine) on my clipboard. How to write verse and influence people. Motives hopelessly confused. Loneliness? Solve the enigmatic computer mind? Get even with the oneupmanship which plagues my attempts to star in the Steve tutorials? Make friends with her?—anyone can see she's lonely. Everyone makes excuses for being friends with her, as if it's a minor scandal. Why join her against the rest? Some kind of deep-set fellow-feeling? Or ... someone who'll need me so much I can ask the earth? But I did not ask myself these things.

'Oh, come on in, Maureen, do.' Accent of St Agatha, but I skipped it. 'Stay and have a coffee.'

'OK.'

She fussed with her sugar basin and super-nice chipless mugs, making nervous gestures which were stage-sweeps of the arm, but interrupted, arrested. She dropped it half-way, couldn't carry it through.

We sat down, she sprawled on the bed, me tensed in the armchair, and started sipping the coffee which she made in a stylish china coffee-filter. She grilled me harmlessly about progress in History I.

'You're awful in English tutes, Jules.'

'What?'

'Oh, you know, nasty—clever. It's hard on us real first years.

'Whatever do you mean?'

'Oh I dunno. You admitted you hadn't read that Eliot, but you kept saying my ideas were shit.'

'I didn't agree with you, Maureen.'

'But you hadn't read it.' She pursed her lips and beamed. Then I dropped the bombshell.

'You know Julia, y'shouldn't do that kind of thing. Makes people hate you.'

Shock registered; real horror. 'Who?' came out like an explosion.

'Oh just Abigail and Erif and me.'

'You mean just the girls in that tute?' There was a trace of relief.

'Oh yeah, and everyone else too.' Jesus, her face was starting to crumble. Was I doing this for her? or for me? or why the hell was I doing this? 'Oh yeah, lots of people. Not just classes. Y'do it all the time. Even talking about the bloody weather. Y'always think you know the answers. People hate it ...' I trailed off, but she was tense and said nothing. 'Oh you know, just that you're always right about everything. And shit you are brighter than most of us, probably, but sometimes you could be wrong, y'know.' Floundering here. And the stricken face in front of me wasn't what I expected or even wanted of the confident Jules. 'Oh it's not that bad, Julia, just y'could think before y'say things sometimes and people mightn't put you down as such a smart-alec, such a bloody know-all. You know I think you're all right, I just get hurt when you pick my ideas to pieces and you haven't even read the stuff. That's all really.' Capitulating, but to no visible effect. I was scared she'd start crying any minute, I wouldn't have the first clue about comforting anyone. I didn't touch people.

But she didn't cry—as if it was worse than crying.

'And you? You hate me too?'

Cornered. 'Shit no. I just hate what you do to me in classes. I like you.' A lie. But I had no alternative. The honesty-bit had gone much too far. I escaped after I'd downed the coffee, saying I'd see her tomorrow and show her the poems.

The beginning of those nights we stayed up talking forever until dawn, breakfasting bleary-eyed. Her family was academic and upper class, she the eldest child when old Vernon evidently thought it proper to have a son heading the family; Julia out of step, wrong sex from the start. It crossed my mind that my mother, too, might have preferred an eldest boy. Julia had had to labour hard in every arena to compensate for being female, to fulfil the sky-high expectations of her parents—a first-rank economist and a reader in sociology, both of them straining to the top of their fields with the children in tow. Scarcely knowing, I had hit the weakest link in her confidence. For a long time she dropped her everyday sparring and listened to me. I confessed the story of how-I-nearly-drowned-Ken-and-got-away-with-it. To admit simply, to anybody, that it had been my fault. A mere fact. Dead and harmless. A nothing—eating away my skull for six years. Julia got the lurid, humourless life-story. The patience of her, the warmth, the sheer sympathy; I was believed, good Christ, believed on my own terms. Someone agreed it must have been tough. She sat, nightslong, listening, listening. Finally, and this felt odd to the point of embarrassment, she offered physical comfort, an arm around the shoulder, a hug, a brief clasp of my hand. How could I have seen Julia except as the epitome of goodness.

I was wearing cheap floral pyjamas. I scuttled around the corridors to see Julia before I went to bed, to swap our days. Her existence was priceless. It was cold in her room and she said I might crawl in under the blankets. Shyly I agreed, aware with a flash of misgiving of her huge breasts under flannelette. Her arms around me, I felt the touch of hand on flesh with panic. I stayed there frozen. Gently she stroked my back; gently she moved her hands around my waist and began touching my breasts. Every muscle went as stiff as bone, the flesh across my stomach like a board. The word lesbian flashed through my petrified mind. Why, I wondered, wasn't I beating an instantaneous retreat? But nothing permitted escape. I heard those vehement denials to the man in the car turn antique inside my head. The schoolboy who kissed me at twelve; that prick at the cricket; the driver's bafflement at my non-response. Not that I cared for Julia's rubbing either. My flesh crept with the embarrassment and shame of it. People had much better leave their bodies alone—the body will do its stuff, needs no attention; the stench of thin shit, the ignominious lump of bloodied cotton-wool between the legs—these were the body's perpetual realities. I wanted no dealings with bodies. I said my good nights in a hurry and fled.

I avoided her for three days—three helpless days, knowing I wouldn't be able to do without her much longer. No choice to be made. I simply procrastinated the inevitable. She came one morning before breakfast.

'Hello,' she said, anxious.

'Er. Hullo.'

'I'll make some coffee if you like.'

'Tea?' I was able to suggest.

'If you'd rather.' She sat on the bed and took my hand in both of hers.

'I've been ... er ... working hard on Luther.' An inexact truth.

'Good,' she answered readily. 'I've been busy too.'

As if by common consent we both avoided any reference either to the night in both our minds or to my days in hiding.

After that first-flesh encounter Julia simply waited for me to catch up to her own radical stage of ability to touch naked skin. By hair-breadth degrees we grew accustomed to each other. Without, how-ever, removing our clothes. Fractional reticent lovers—the closed-lips kiss, the audacious fumbling with breast and back, the automatic mutual abstention from any move below the belt. The word—the awful slimy word, lesbian—was a continuous discord at the back of my mind.

'Isn't this a lesbian way to behave?' I asked her a few weeks later.

'I suppose it is,' she said. 'That's what the psychology books would say.'

Two highly intelligent young women gingering in total darkness. Both of us needing desperately a physical warmth which seemed to have nothing to do with such a loaded and nasty idea as lesbianism. Yet the label pushed itself forward. We knew we had to hide though no-one had ever told either of us. Unspoken rules overshadowed the present and threw doubt on the tangible affection between us. How unnatural that neither of us could trust her own feelings.

From the fire-escape came a girl's dulcet voice.

'Do let me in, Maureen.'

Julia sprang up off the bed as if there'd been an almighty thunderclap. I, actor since five, rose from her arms studying calm, my heart thumping, and answered, 'Sure.' I unbolted the fire-exit and let the girl in. She smiled sweetly and asked if I was having Julia to coffee tonight. I couldn't work out how much she'd seen or inferred.

'Yes.'

'Oh well, I'll invite you round another time.' She smiled.

'Great.'

Julia and I said nothing. When her footsteps had gone, I unbolted the exit again and carefully climbed up and down the fire-escape from roof to landing, assessing what range of vision was possible. It was obvious that, if the girl had cared to lean over the railing, my bed with its guilty activities would have been all too visible. It was bad enough that the rooms couldn't be locked—an ancient deterrent to fornication—but neither of us had dreamed of ladies taking nocturnal strolls on the fire-escape. It looked too much like spying for comfort. With the terrorism of letting us know they knew, thrown in. What expectant little group was waiting somewhere for their agent to report?

A week later, just as we were going to sleep, there was a shuffling and sniggering outside my door. A light tap. Would they come in, maybe? Turn on the lights? Expose us? Call the Principal? Someone thundered on the door. Silence. I felt Julia's body tense up. They were still there. Then the sound of running footsteps and giggling. We stayed awake for hours, Julia afraid to go back around the passages to her room, both of us hearing night-noises magnified by fear.

Always an element of terror. Springing apart when the knock came on the door; dread of the girl who might just walk in and catch us at it. A secretive subterranean existence—underpinned by my unremitting shame of the body itself. Surrounded by polite deadly spies, animal nervousness when they dropped the slimy ubiquitous word, consciousness raddled with guilt. Guilt sprouting from their malice. And guilt implicit since earliest memory, guilt over every damned impulse.

Julia went often to chapel, though the formal absolutions of the church proved inadequate. Besides, she intended to repeat the sin. Long tortuous discussions about the form and evil of lust—a poor excuse for lust, our feeble solemn gentleness. We applied the idea of lust, the idea of sin, to everything that involved our bodies. Whatever we said, the fact of our guilt remained, and whatever we said reinforced that anyway. Along the line, we had both acquired a dislike and mistrust of ourselves which made nonsense of the other idea—the idea of love.

Confusion. It felt good, warm, secure—to be able to speak openly to another person; to be able to give; to feel warm and unjudged. Yet all this was just as surely negated.

Julia went out with a spindly hook-nosed biochemist from one of the men's colleges. I resented that she continued to do so, though he used up little of her time. I craved assurance that he wasn't important, and didn't believe her when she gave it. She insisted that she wasn't in love with him, which afforded marginal security, yet she evidently enjoyed his attentions. I wanted exclusive territorial rights. Whenever she spent an evening with him I plunged into a black and well-enacted despondency.

'Why don't we go to the pictures instead?'

'I've promised to go to the dance with him, Maureen. I like him.'

'You'd prefer to go off with him.'

'But you and I spend most of our time together. You said you have to get that essay written anyway.'

'I can't work when I don't know where you are.'

'But you will.'

'Roughly.'

'Come now, Maureen. A college dance is a college dance.'

'Oh shit it's all right. I'll go for a walk down to the park.'

'You shouldn't go over there at night alone. It could be dangerous.'

'Who cares?'

'You know I care.'

'Oh yeah?'

'Of course.'

Patterns of blackmail.

She came home early, her eyes red and her hands shaking. My satisfaction ill-disguised.

'What's wrong?'

'Christopher.'

'What about him?'

'He loves me.' I winced inside, a falling premonition of loss.

'Isn't that what you're after?' A shade of sarcasm.

'No. No. No.' Her voice was tense and her eyes bitterly afraid.

'What happened?'

'I don't know.'

'Did he want to make love to you?' Scared out of a more usual timidity.

'No. Not that. He was very understanding.'

'What then?'

43

'He wants me to love him.'

'Well?'

'I can't.' Buoyancy again. She couldn't be lying in this state.

'You've got me, Julia.'

'It's different.' Doubt crept back.

'How?'

'Oh you know. We've agreed. We'll need men in the end.'

'I dunno.'

Silence.

'He was so good to me, it was awful. Because I couldn't. He even asked if I'd like him to fetch you.'

'Fetch me?'

'Yes. He thought it might be you I was in need of.'

'It wasn't?'

'I couldn't have told him anyway. So I had to stay. I was just afraid. And upset that he should think you're more important than he is.'

'I suppose it'll be all over the college.'

'He's not like that, Maureen, shut up.'

'Why don't you go back to him then?'

'I can't, I can't, I can't.'

I depended with rapacity—as thoroughly as once on my mother, but Julia was complaisant and rarely frustrated me. A visit to her room if she happened to be out landed me in acute depression pointed up by pique. I checked her common resorts in these moods, ferreted for her. Eventually my check on her movements was total. Her consideration for me amounted to reporting departures, arrivals, destinations. Julia liked being so jealously guarded; her strongest need was to lavish, spend, exhaust herself with giving away: 'It is good to see you happy Maureen—so good.' While I leant on her she saw lonely Craig made happy and secure, saw that it was her doing and that it was good—the heavier I leaned the better. She had her proof of indispensability, again and again.

In between the days of sunny security there were slippery times when the inured loneliness of earlier years seemed to have been a lucid pool of freedom and uncomplicated joy.

The end of the year approached bleakly for all the gathering of summer. Still hounded by the compulsion to come top. The exams triggered off a welter of colics, cramps, gastric explosions, splitting headaches and nightmares: a month of giddy nausea which even Julia's company and solicitude couldn't mitigate. I regarded my return home for the long vacation with dread. I could count on my mother's being tractable at first if my marks were sufficiently remarkable, but four months could be a challenge—I hoped for the best.

The Post Office job offered a temporary panacea. Erif was living in

Carlton, Julia and I with our parents, but we all got jobs as mailsorters until Christmas and converged on the Spencer Street GPO every night. Working the nightshift gave me a perfect case for sleeping all day and only spending dinner-time with the family. By then they'd be settling over the TV anyway. Mother complained that I'd taken such an antisocial job as soon as I got back to my family, but took care just the same to make me a meal when I got home at eight in the morning and to keep the house quiet during the day.

The mailsorting barracks occupied a huge near-derelict building, black with the soot of the docks and the railway yards. The Christmas extras went to school first, and indulged in the splendidly mindless activity of learning the postal district for every town and hamlet in the Sovereign State of Victoria—Boinka, Benambra, Bindi, Bundalaguah —an exotic collection. I attacked the task with confident gaiety.

It became evident on the second night, when I'd already got Northern and Western suburbs differentiated, and went out to collect the South-eastern card-stack from the flea-faced supervisor, that my memory for inconsequential minutiae surpassed that of any other trainee, including Julia.

'You can't know them yet,' she complained.

'I do.'

'Show me.'

So I shuffled the pack of replica letters and sifted out the three stacks perfectly, secretly glad to have exceeded her in some area but still puzzled by the intensity of her chagrin. It spoiled her pleasure, unexpectedly and genuinely undermined her. She was only slightly mollified when the English results were published, and she'd beaten me.

When they handed out the Bibles to swear us into the Public Service there weren't enough to go round even the professed Christians. They had to huddle in groups around the tatty volumes and get a right hand to one, while chanting after the supervisor, in the tone of the marriage ceremony, an oath to treat H.M. Mails as secret and inviolate. The straining to get a fingertip to the Good Book modified the solemnity intended. We escaped without singing 'God Save The Queen'. Occasionally they'd round us up and take us down to the threshing-floor, where we'd be placed alongside a vast conveyor belt which fed the franking machine. This gadget devoured letters especially of the frailer sort with regularity. The floor was littered with muddied dog-eared letters—evidently dead.

Early December, and the nights were short. Before five, the sky-lights began to show a deep purple, shallowing out through phosphorescent midnight blue and cobalt to the pale almost colourless sky that preceded the sunrise. At six-thirty we punched our cards and went out into the bleary, drab city, sun's first oblique shafts striking the blackened uprights of the railway yards and the opaque dark windows. At Julia's station, I often got down and strolled around the end of the platform with her, talking nothings, always loath to part.

After our three weeks' training, we were sent up to the sorting machines where we passed seven hours a night flipping letters down slots. Erif, who'd spent her weeks of Post Office school much more profitably than I—dreaming and doodling—sat on one side of me. We were instructed to sort those destinations we didn't remember or recognise into the N.W. slot. Some fulltime cracksman was doubtless employed on the resorting somewhere out in the desert amongst the Mallee hens and saltbush. Erif stuck to the suburbs—she'd flick half her country letters down the N.W. slot and hand the rest to me. I admired her forthright indifference to duty, her nonchalance, was myself obsessed with the perfectibility of the task as if my mother had been standing at my elbow, checking over my shoulder.

Letters to Santa were addressed to Greenland, Iceland, Finland— some even to the North Pole. Her Majesty's Official Secrets obviously debarred us from taking them home. I sorted them into Overseas. Julia thought the N.W. slot a more sensible choice, and argued piquantly for removing the extra clog from the machinery at the earliest opportunity. I preferred to give the kids a chance.

Family Christmas holiday. Ken, who'd been expelled from his new school and now sold suits, didn't have to go this year, but I was still unable to decline the annual holiday. They'd rented a beach-house at Inverloch. I faced two weeks' separation from Julia with gloom, though we promised each other a voluminous correspondence. Mother was quick to observe that my continuous writing couldn't all be poetry.

'Where are you going, Maureen?'

'Walking.'

'Where?'

'Down the beach.'

She pounced on me as soon as I got back.

'Maureen, you went off up the road when you left.'

'You can get to the beach that way.'

'Bloody long way round.'

'I was just posting a letter.'

'Who to?'

'Julia.'

'Again?'

'Why not?'

'That's the fourth in three days.'

'Third.'

'Seems funny to me.'

I shrugged her off the first few times, though her irritation intensified as the days dragged on. After a year away, making only the briefest visits consistent with her notions of proper filial duty, I had grown unaccustomed to such a heady dose of my mother's authority and inquisition. The twilight colour over the sea one night—the black cross-tree telegraph poles lining the horizon. I intended to be good to her, tolerant, slow to anger. My intentions still the old ones. But I no longer expected success. I was beginning to accept that I was unable. Cross-trees. A faulty love.

Saddled less willingly than ever with household slop-work, I was bound to get restive rapidly. I looked for another job—the government scholarship paid a pittance and this was still sliced into by the means test on Dad's income. Tram-conducting looked promising but the officer took one look at me and told me they didn't employ dwarfs on the tramways. The Victorian Railways, however, wasn't cast-iron about willowy waitresses and I got myself a job on the Sydney run. Free food, overtime, danger-money and tips. Mother was all too impressed.

'Well, Maureen, now you've got a job again, you could let us have a little board.'

'A little what?'

'Well we do feed you.'

'I'm out of Melbourne half the time.'

'Well I won't ask much.'

'Look, Mother, I get an allowance of four quid. I pay college, books, fares and everything else. College is six quid alone. I'm not asking you for your filthy money—that's why I'm working. And you, crazy about education you reckon you are, and you ask me for board.'

'Ken pays board.'

'Ken's working.'

'So are you.'

'Jesus Christ. Ken spends his wages on beer and rubbish. I'm trying to study.'

'I can't treat you differently, Maureen. How do you think Ken'd feel?'

'It's got nothing to do with Ken. The reason I get a half-allowance from the Commonwealth is because Dad earns enough to make it up.'

'He does not.'

'They think so.'

'It's not my fault if the means test's so mean. I don't believe in socialism.'

'Look I know it's not your fault and I don't want you to pay me anything. I only want a place to live—and there's a room here anyway. I've got to save two hundred quid.'

'Well a quid or two a week isn't going to make much difference, is it?'

I groaned.

'Well you'd have to pay to live anywhere else. You wouldn't get board any cheaper.'

'I can get a little room in Carlton for two quid. I can even live with Erif for nearly nothing.'

'So you'd rather spend your money on some dingy slum of a place than live with your own flesh and blood and pay us a little to help us out.'

'Yes I bloody well would. If my flesh and blood acted like my flesh and blood I might think twice.'

'All right then, please yourself. You never had much time for us, that's obvious. I thought the University might have done you some good. Evidently you haven't improved a skerrick.'

'You want board, then, do you?'

'Of course I do. It's only fair.'

'I'll be packing my stuff then, you lousy bitch.'

I stormed out to my room, packed everything and came back, suitcase in one hand, guitar in the other.

'Where are you taking that guitar?'

'With me.'

'It's mine, you know.'

'Jesus, Mother, you can't play it. You gave it to me years ago.'

'I lent it to you. And you're not going off with it now.'

'I bloody well am.'

She seized it before I could drop the suitcase or dodge, and she stood away, holding it by the neck.

'Give it back,' I told her through grinding teeth.

'Get out,' she screamed. 'Get out.'

I made for her with murderous stubborn intentness. She lifted the thing high over her head. 'Get away. Get out.'

I jumped towards her. She brought the guitar down with all her force, missing my head and splintering it in pieces on the chair. I broke into violent involuntary sobs.

'You bitch ... you detestable ... destructive ... neurotic bitch.' She said nothing. I looked an instant at the wreckage, grabbed my suit-case, kicked open the back-door and thundered out, kicking the rubbish tin fifteen yards down the back garden.

Maureen at bay

I shrank and withered at these partings in anger and hate. How often, pacing furiously up and down some railway platform, I let remorse and regret drag me back home—one more attempt at harmony. The uncanny guilt, the need to cleanse the mind of all fault, to show an impeccable spirit of goodwill—goodwill towards her, the ostensible oppressor of every second memory. But this time the anger boiled on through the tears, brewed healthily for weeks.

Erif welcomed me to her balcony on Cardigan Street. A big chaotic room which she already shared with another semi-solvent student. He occupied the floor; she let me have half her bed and half her food when she had any. Waitressing down in the city, where the clientele were lascivious businessmen and the rest of the staff compliant, she took pinches, slaps and tickles with an equanimity based on the heavy tips, and fled home by back alleys to dodge the odd fat executive who lingered in wait. She took it for granted that I should share the available bed—a kapok mattress laid out in the corner. A surprise to be treated as non-lethal. Most of the girls who had been in college would have offered me the floor, however tactfully.

The Sydney run didn't, in fact, run to Sydney. The Victorian staff got down at Junee, a half-way mark in the backblocks with nothing to recommend it except a pool, four or five beat-up old pubs and the poker-machines at the RSL Club. The returned soldiers had apparently voted the Buffet-girls into the League, and by common consent opened their doors to the itinerant waitresses. Regularly, perhaps in return, the women blew their wages on poker—a sport banned across the border in Victoria. We spent the night in the Railway Refreshment Rooms, seedy survival of the days when the rail trip to Sydney took two days. A few gilded mirrors ornamented the halls where the travellers had stayed overnight; sluggish propeller-fans hung from the ceiling of the vast polished dining-room, decorated these days with plaster vases of plastic blooms; the bedrooms, built like cells along either side of a long corridor, occupied the top storey of the weatherboard relic catching the maximum force of the Junee sun. We vied endlessly for the shady side; in the windless brown valley it made no difference. Junee seemed to own very little air at all.

I wolfed two or three steaks and mountains of railway mash on each trip out of Junee and survived in between on strong tea thick with sugar. Gertrude, the head of our crew, slipped me leftover fruit from the sleeping cars. A strong, warm German of thirty-five, she made not the slightest play of being boss. I joined the Buffet-girls with pleasure after a year of academic effort. Scots Janet was the cook, rotund mother of a dozen children; Ilse from Hamburg, a pin-sized woman with a squashed Slavic face, delighted in her broken English, called the Buffet Car the buff-et car with superb innocence; Kelly, the second cook, was an Irishwoman, slow and gentle; Jen nattered harmlessly about her boyfriends and make-up. Edith was the odd one out, the only Australian amongst them and a tough, lonely woman. Right eye flickering behind black-rimmed glasses, she bore a grudge against the world for her husband's war-time death—which she took out on everyone else. Gertrude mollified her by constant consultation and the revered responsibility of counting the till at the end of each journey. Edith's sense of her status as the oldest Buffet-girl was overwhelming; only a woman of Gertrude's ready kindness and strength could have made old Edith feel comfortable. Most of the crew bosses wouldn't have her travel with them.

We were talking about the bombing of English cities during the war. Janet had seen Coventry, Kelly had been in London. Edith sat back in the corner of the staff-compartment, blowing her cigarette smoke vengefully and said, 'But we got Dresden, didn't we?' She rose primly, dusting her dirty-green uniform, and went out. Gertrude looked hopelessly sad.

'Did you know Dresden?' I asked.

'Slightly. I was in Berlin.'

'What did you do?'

'Typing.'

The two German women were both nervous about the war, especially under Edith's tacit accusations of their guilt. She'd been on the right side.

Edith cross-examined me frequently on my monstrous appetite. 'Doesn't your mother feed you?' In the end I admitted I didn't live with my family—tantamount to an admission of open immorality in an eighteen-year-old. She lectured me mercilessly on the permissiveness of the times, and doubled my relief that I spent half my time with people who knew nothing of my insupportable deviations. Erif, who must have known, never hinted about it, never made equivocal comments, always spoke neutrally when I mentioned Julia. One afternoon, when the tomcat mounted her male kitten she said, 'More people should take a look at animals.'

'What do you mean?'

'Dirty old Janus doesn't give a shit that the kitten's male. Most people don't even consider what's natural. They just get scared and make rules.'

'Yeah.' Grateful for her unembarrassed tolerance, not nearly so convinced as she of the ignorance of the world at large.

The jockey lingered over his unpalatable steak and kidney mash, called for coffee after coffee and conned a third (illegal) bottle of beer from me with his compliments which, though frankly incredible, were pleasing.

'I'll be riding at Caulfield next Saturday. How about dinner?'

Confusion. 'Oh I can't. I'm working the night-train.' Lucky, that.

'Well Friday then. I'll be down by then.'

'Oh, don't put yourself out.'

'No worries there. Just scribble down your address. I'll pick you up at six.'

'Oh shit,' I thought as I wrote Erif's address, totally unable to refuse.

On Friday afternoon, without telling Erif why, I took out a dress, hemmed it up to the fashionable level at laborious length, borrowed an iron from downstairs and pressed it.

'Going out?' Erif asked casually.

'Yeah.'

Escape to the bathroom for an hour or so. I emerged, nervously, stockinged legs and made-up face. Christ what a farce. Erif showed no amusement or contempt, though I expected it and felt it—my own emanation. I minced about until seven, pretending that I looked my normal self. Purgatorial. His non-arrival itself was a relief. But it left me painted and prim, a stranded being, with no reason to stay decked out and a violent sense of the absurdity of the whole operation. By nine I'd got the courage to scrub my face, change into jeans and suggest fish and chips to Erif who'd gone on reading, ignoring the pantomime.

'Decided not to go?'

'Yeah. Thought I'd rather have some chips and do a bit of writing.'

'Good idea,' she answered easily. 'There's money on the mantelpiece. Why don't you bring back some cold beer? It'd be nice in this heat.'

'Yeah, I will.'

College again, with mixed feelings. The ideal aura had dissipated. The St Agatha sense of being not quite acceptable had grown back— the social terms of it replaced by notions of morality. I went back to be with Julia.

The new first years were a sad lot—hardworking mealticketers dedicated to passing exams and the bright lure of some career. They even looked alike. In March they already talked incessantly about the examinations; the sort who never miss lectures, never learn anything. The only one who stood out at first was a thick-lipped, brown-haired girl whose pungent wit and joke-collection drew notice. Her name was Libby Stace. At afternoon tea she asked for advice on early Eliot. I agreed to help.

'My mother was in college,' she told me proudly.

'Really.'

'Yes, it's a great feeling, following in her footsteps.'
'I wouldn't know. My mother worked in Woolworth's.'
'Because there is something exciting about the idea of wandering in the gardens and corridors just as she did as a young woman.'
'I suppose so.'
'I went to the same school as she did, too. You know—Fintona.'
'Oh yeah. We used to meet them at basketball.'
'What was your school?'
'St Agatha's, unfortunately.'
'How fantastic! I remember going out to a basketball match a few years ago. I might have met you.'
'I shouldn't think so.'
'Beautiful-looking school.'
'If you like that sort of thing.'
'Could I see you about Eliot tonight after dinner? I'm sure you'll have the answers. You got a first, didn't you?'

Checking on my credentials. Enviable self-possession, and a rare ability to stick to her own line of talk in the face of contradiction.

Emma Brightfort was allotted the room next door to mine. A unique experience, to live awhile in a women's hall of residence—or so the legend went. Proximity to the university was the big argument in favour, but the college students, with their meals provided, avoided the campus and were drawn back by the dubious magnetism of their colleges to the familiar corridors and faces. Emma, anyway, was no victim of the prevailing insularity. Having spent two years living at home and having passed her university days in the university, she wasn't so susceptible to the ghetto-mentality of the majority. I, spending most of my time with Julia, was no exception to the climatic rule. I came back like the rest every lunchtime, even between lectures. Many only left to go home to their parents. Bizarre stultification.

I was faintly nervous of Emma. Of course we'd be able to resume those invaluable discussions of my poetry and everyone else's—a mine of stimulus to my reading and writing; but her personal approval was obscurely necessary to me and I shrank from her detecting the Julia affair. The information was at large amongst the students; the curious stare, the voices that dropped when we passed. Somebody would tell Emma—or she might innocently walk in. Julia and I had been placed in the same wing as requested. No fire-escape spy-holes and a readier reason for being in each other's company. But still no locks. Might not Emma, or Libby Stace, or any of the freshers simply knock and enter?

'Perhaps the best thing would be to stop,' Julia suggested.
'What? Stop sleeping together?'
'Stop making love. Just be friends.'

'That's impossible.'

'But it makes you so guilty, Maureen.'

'It also makes me happy.'

'Sometimes. But it can't go on forever, anyway. It's dangerous. It'll have to end somewhere.'

'I don't see why.'

'Because, well, women can't spend their entire lives together.'

'Why not? I like sharing your life.'

'Can't you imagine what it'd be like living your whole life in secret? Always afraid it'll leak out?'

'I'm not going to let other people run my life. Anyway, we could escape.'

'Nonsense, Maureen. You don't want to escape from people like Emma. You're an extrovert.'

'Bullshit. I'm very contemplative.'

She laughed. 'That too of course. But seriously now, you need people. It's silly to go on living in a way that cuts you off from them.'

'It can't be helped, Julia. I'm in love with you. It's you I want.'

'But that's so naïve. The longer you go on like this, the harder it's going to be to branch out, to meet men.'

'I don't like men. And they don't like me. And anyway you talk as if I'm the only one in danger. Aren't you in love with me?'

'No.' Something of a shock.

'What do you mean?'

'I love you—dearly. But no, I'm not in love with you. And I'm thinking of your best interests.'

'You're my best interest, bugger it.'

'You won't always think so.'

'I think so now.'

Julia made it clear that for her this would not be going on much longer, that only her weakness and sinfulness made her unable to take a firm stand. When she talked of our friendship as ruining our lives I understood what to expect. Cut loose, I said to myself each day. Cut loose and stand alone. Before the trouble. Cut loose, I muttered as I looped the day's knots. It seemed that something was quite wrong with me; absence of spine, I defined it. The thought of imminent loneliness hurled me into blank panic. Cut loose, I commanded, bombarding myself with resolutions not to seek Julia out, to get myself used to the idea. I was living all the time with an undertow where I was scared and horrified that this was what love came to. How did I get like this? I asked myself, certain that I must've been better off in my isolation on Strafford Hill, apostrophising the sunset and eulogising the earth. I simply could not understand how I came to be the way I was—I wondered if I'd been born with a fatal flaw.

Nor could I change myself. If I could get to be isolated again, I thought, really cut off from all of them ... so I didn't need them, didn't love them, didn't mind one way or the other about any bloody thing ... If I could only get tough, detached like Emma. I wanted to grow a shell as if that might somehow be the answer but I suspected, vaguely, that it couldn't be. How did it come about that I was almost incapable of doing anything without someone's approval? Mother's or Julia's or whoever? How did I come to have no centre, no certainty, no will of my own? I read a bitter quip somewhere: There is a rat in my bed at night; that rat is me. I was impressed and copied it down on my desk calendar. I am not even as tough as a rat, I thought. Rats are hardy.

Julia was reading in the Library when I dragged her out for company.

'Maureen, I really mustn't stay long. I've got an essay to do.'

'But I'm feeling lonely, miserable.'

'I'm sorry my dear. I'm sorry. But everyone's alone.'

'Oh sure.'

'No, Maureen, don't shrug me off like that. You really don't seem to accept that at all.'

'I didn't say I didn't accept it. It's just I don't like it.'

'And you want it different?'

I scowled.

'Because it's a fundamental of the human condition. We're all born alone; we all die alone; basically we're alone.'

'Yeah, but we can get close to each other.'

'But never identical.'

'Shit, Julia, I don't want to be identical. I just want to be with you.'

'There's a limit.'

'Well why is it so much harder for me, apparently? Why am I so bloody spineless and gutless and helpless?'

'I don't know, Maureen. But you must know I've done my best to help.'

'Oh, sure.'

'Anyway,' I continued after a moment, 'what about marriage? Do you reckon that married people are still utterly alone?'

'In a way.'

'Argh. Sophistry—they've got company, someone to sleep with, someone to talk to, someone who cares.'

'Sometimes.'

'Well, Jesus, it's up to them to make it work, isn't it?'

'Some people are really together, I suppose.'

'All right then. Why not us?'

'Maureen. Two women do not get married.'

'Not formally. But that doesn't matter, does it?'

'It wouldn't work. It couldn't.'

'I just don't see why not. If there's affection, sympathy, communication—I think it'd work.'

'You should try to meet men, Maureen.'

Every exchange with Julia confirmed the panic. Only occasionally would she let me get into bed with her and even then threw me out before morning. Scandal-scare and self-scare. I started thinking about marriage. Obviously the exit from the impasse. I couldn't tolerate the isolation I ought to have embraced; I imagined a husband instead—soulmate and lover. But Julia was the only person I'd ever known who approximated the image. I couldn't see too many husbands in the offing.

In her anguish, expressed as usual as concern for my normality and future, Julia wrote to the Student Counsellor to see if he could help us put a stop to the lesbian bondage.

'Do you want to stop?' he asked us.

'Yes,' said Julia loudly.

'I don't know,' I muttered.

'Why?' he asked.

'We think it's bad for us. It makes things difficult in college, and we are afraid of becoming homosexuals.' She spoke quickly, nervously; and she spoke for both of us. Why, I thought murderously, did she let it all get under way if she was going to back out at this stage? But she insisted to the Counsellor that my welfare was her central concern. My objections to her corrective course seemed churlish, even to me.

When he suggested that we might see less of each other and masturbate instead of making love, I nearly fell off my chair. The word, which had much the same slimy quality as lesbian, was a shocker. And perhaps he was, indeed, only trying to point out the absurdity of Julia's project for purity.

'I wouldn't get anything out of that,' I blurted out.

'No?'

'No.'

'I shouldn't think I would, either,' Julia added quietly.

Evidently he overestimated the sexual content of the whole affair—or wanted to let us know that we did.

Our visits to him must have assuaged Julia's guilt—we drifted on as before, in a spirit of tenuous truce.

The discovery of Shakespeare's sonnets cheered me—a lucky identification.

'Did you know, Emma, that Shakespeare had homosexual tendencies?' Bull at a gate.

'Nonsense. He can't have had.'

'Why not?'

'There's nothing in the plays.'

'I've been reading the sonnets. They're written for a young man.'

'What about the famous dark lady?'

'Oh yeah, there's her, but that's only the last thirty or so.'

She was interested, but sceptical.

'Listen to this—number twenty:

> "And for a woman wert thou first created,
> Till nature as she wrought thee fell a-doting,
> And by addition me of thee defeated
> By adding one thing to my purpose nothing.
> And since she pricked thee out for women's pleasure,
> Mine be thy love, and thy love's use their treasure." '

She took the book and bent over it, frowning.

'There's only one interpretation,' I said. 'And I've just read the rest. It's all intense. He gets jealous of his friend's adventures with women. In one he's waiting up for him. It's a love-affair.'

'I suppose so,' she murmured, thumbing the pages.

'And anyway, people who think they're for a woman read them as love-lyrics.'

'Yes. I've read about the idea somewhere, but I assumed it was crackpot. People are always trying to prove artists are homosexual.'

'Some are, I suppose.' I was taking care to speak casually. With Emma—indeed with everyone—I pretended that the matter had nothing to do with me. A game of tactful silence.

'Undoubtedly.' She let it rest, delicately, without reference back to me, made no sign that I might have an investment in the interpretation—though my love poems could have had no conceivable object but Julia. Emma never asked. What she guessed she kept to herself. We skirted the realities.

Yet, from Shakespeare's apparent passion for a fellow-male, I drew some sort of strength, a fleeting fellowship with the great and the maligned. They might dismiss Wilde as *fin de siècle* and febrile; no one dared blackball the Bard.

Vacations cropped up like rapids—always sudden realities in the relative calm of the terms. Julia went to a conference in Hobart. I went home, once more, to my mother's house. As each vacation began, it struck me that to stay away was bound to breed more bad blood than a new, more intensive attempt at getting on with her. Boundless optimism—unable to admit that nothing I tried could, in the end, make a truce on the Home Front. 'Do come home, Maureen,' she urged me over the phone, 'we're always glad to see you.' And a cryptic precarious gladness it would be.

Days passed dully at first without much of the usual warfare. I put most of her pleasantness down to the current contretemps with Ken, who, according to her, was turning into a delinquent with criminal tendencies. Despite the privilege of Brighton High—a vast improvement on Rosella—he hadn't turned back to her hopeful notions of obedience and educational advancement. She had stood behind him through the expulsion, believed in him, denounced the Head in those daily running commentaries on the state of the world which she conducted whoever the listener. 'The boy only wrote a few blue poems on his maths paper. I saw them, you know, and they were very witty in their way.' If anyone was to blame for Ken's lamentable performance at Brighton it was, of course, not Ken but Willy Smythe. 'Such a dull kid really, not nearly as bright as Ken. I don't know what Ken sees in him. I suppose having a weak heart he feels inferior, feels he has to combine his brains with someone else's brawn—poor kid. But what a choice. Willy's practically a half-wit *and* been in trouble with the police. I tried to tell Ken, but he never listens any more ...'

She had hoped that Ken's switch to the suitshop after he left school would keep him and Willy apart. On the contrary, Willy stayed in the town-centre until five and they joined up as free men with Ken's money to spend. 'After six—he should have been home fifteen minutes ago—I'll bet he's with that Willy Smythe.' By seven Father said he wanted his tea, and she served it up grumbling. 'It wouldn't hurt you to wait a bit longer, Joe.' She covered Ken's meal with a tight aluminium lid to keep it from drying out, and put it in the oven on low heat.

'You're going to waste the gas half the night again, are you Lotty?' he chipped in. Her solicitude over Ken's meal palled as the evening dragged on. During every TV ad she remarked that it wasn't like him and finally begged Father to go out and find the boy.

'Jesus, Lotty, y'get some bloody spectacular ideas in your old age. Where for example would you think I'd start looking? There's a lot of streets in this place, you know.'

'You wouldn't care if your own son had been run over.'

'Run in, more likely—whatever's happened to him's happened. Me driving the streets isn't going to make any bloody difference at all.'

'You never cared for the boy. God you're hard, Joe.'

'There's not a bloody thing I can do about it. And anyway, Lotty, I don't know who you're trying to fool. The boy's been out with Smythe till all hours before. I'm not making a fool of myself chasing the streets when he's probably sitting in some park cracking bottles.'

'What I can't understand is why you don't put a stop to it. You've never even talked to the boy.'

'He's the one who doesn't talk. Just clears out.'

'You've never tried.'

Father lapsed into silence.

By midnight she was frantic and muttered about ringing the police.

'If the cops've got him they'd've rung us,' Father said, summoning his reasonable voice. 'Unless he's given a false name, in which case you ringing up'll only make it worse.'

'Ken wouldn't give a false name.'

'No? That little larrikin'd be stupid enough to do anything.'

'Don't you call my son a larrikin, Joe.'

Father went to bed, followed by her accusations: he was hard, he was indifferent, he was too soft, too selfish. He wasn't even an excuse for a father.

'I've got to leave for work at seven,' he told her.

'Just like you. Put your job before your son.'

She begged me to stay up with her; I read a book while she blazed on, thankful that, for once, I wasn't among her targets. Strange, though, to be sitting at her right hand while she sifted through Ken's misdemeanours—not without the excuse appropriate to each: '... but he shouldn't be drinking at fifteen—not the way he does. If only your father would take him in hand ...'

He reeled up the back steps just after one. She jumped off her chair, her hand to her mouth, her greying hair frowzy and her eyes underlined by deep black creases. Her dressing-gown swept the floor as she ran over to the window. He staggered in. Suit crumpled, tie askew as if he'd been swung by it, lip split open, blind drunk.

'Ken! Whatever happened to you?'

He broke into boisterous hollow laughter. 'Just had a few beers, Ma, just one or two with the boys. Just had a spot of bother, Ma, but she's right, she's right.' He grabbed at the doorway and stayed upright. She made for him.

'You've got to pull yourself together, Ken. You can't go on like this.'

'And why not?'

'Where do you get the beer? You're too young to drink in pubs.' His machine-gun laugh came out again, empty cackling. 'I look pretty grown-up y'know Ma. She'll be right.'

'I won't have you doing this kind of thing. I've been sitting up worried stiff all night.'

'Outa me way or I might just spew on ya.'

He lurched for the sink and bent over it dry-retching.

'Who were you with, Ken?'

'None o' your bloody business, woman. Just one or two of me mates.'

'We'll see whether it's any of my business. Your father'll be dealing with you.'

'I could belt the shit outa that weakling. I'm not scared of him, Ma, don't worry!' The staccato laugh, without humour.

'Why didn't you ring to say you'd be late?'

'Didn't know I would be till I was, did I?' He doubled up over the sink, hysterically amused by his own joke.

'It's not much to ask you to ring when you won't be back for tea.'

'Shut your trap. It's me that's missed me dinner, not you.'

'I've wasted six hours' gas keeping it hot in the oven.'

He laughed wildly. 'More fool you, you idiot bitch.'

'And how did you cut your lip?'

'Tripped over a stamp, Ma.'

'Give me a look.'

'I can look after meself thanks. Outa me way now. I'm off to the cot.'

'You're not going anywhere till you promise me this won't happen again.'

He turned around slowly and smiled broadly. 'All right, Ma. This won't happen again. OK?'

'You don't mean it.'

He kept grinning as she burst into tears, then staggered over to her and said, as if to a spoilt child, 'Off y'go to bed, Ma, Little Kenny's home. No worries. No troubs.' She flailed at him, but he pinned her easily with his arms, smacked a kiss on her forehead and flashed out.

She collapsed with her head on the table and cried. After a little while I asked if she'd like a cup of tea. She shook her head and looked up, face anxious and weary. 'I'd better be getting to bed.' She shrugged and blew her nose, trying desperately to be strong.

Next morning's brawl was earsplitting, but Ken had the gift of leaving her to it, a unique blend of good humour and brutality. Throughout this spate of Ken's alleged delinquency she leaned on me gratefully. Indeed the vacation might have gone off well enough, on the tenterhooks of my best behaviour, if I'd had the sense to receive my voluminous mail at another place—though her hawk-eyed watch on my movements and the tiniest reason for each might have found me out anyway. By the time Julia's fourth fat letter arrived her suspicious curiosity could no longer be contained.

'Maureen, I've got to talk to you.'

'Yeah?'

'What's going on?'

'Whattayamean what's going on?'

'What's going on with Julia Vernon?'

I looked blank, trying non-comprehension at base one. 'Julia?'

'Yes. Julia.'

'There's a couple of letters if that's what you mean ...'

'And what kind of letters would they be, eh? I notice you don't leave them lying around with your other letters.'

'Have you been sniffing through my letters now?' A nauseating thought. She ignored the query.

'Maureen, it's unnatural.'

'What's unnatural?' I knew what she was talking about. How she knew, though, puzzled me.

'All these letters. You carry on as if you're in love with the girl.'

Could I have said: well I am? Not likely. But I must have jumped.

'Yes,' she snarled. 'Caught you there!'

'What?' said I feebly.

'There's no bloody use denying it, Maureen. It's a shock to me and I don't know what it'll do to your father when I tell him and as for your old Granny ...'

'What the hell are you talking about, Mother?' False calm.

'You know bloody well what I'm talking about. I brought you up to be a decent clean-living girl; that's all I've ever wanted from you, and now—this.' She was starting to weep, a look of real anguish. To my halting assertions of innocence she replied, through sobs, 'There's no point in denying it Maureen. I'm not bloody well blind.'

'You're just a suspicious bitch.'

'And it's just as well, isn't it? At least I can put a stop to it now. To think my own daughter ...'

'For Christ's sake, what are you talking about?' It was clear that this tack was exhausted, but I could not think of another.

'Oh my God, anything but this. This ... this ... unnatural ... anything but this ...'

'Anything but what?'

Her face was mad with disgust, horror deeper than anger, a vast loathing. What it must have cost her to say that word.

'This ... this ... this lesbian business.'

The word. That word. Still shocking, even to me.

'I am not a lesbian. I am not.' A child of maybe five, redhot in the face, guilty in the eyes, half-tearful, trapped, denying its mother's accusation. 'I am not.' I looked down at the chessboard tiling of the big kitchen; our voices high-pitched, matched, vehement. For a moment I understood that her suspicion was certainty. I saw that she (somehow) knew. All my retreats were cut off.

'What's so unnatural about it anyway?' I'd defined my defensive. Tacitly admitted. She broke down. Hysterical, unbearable sobbing.

'My God ... my daughter ... unnatural ... you ask what's unnatural ... oh my God ...'

I knew I should walk out. Leave a shred of doubt. I knew that nothing either of us said could make the slightest difference. That I would not give Julia up nor she accept it. Despite myself, the truth was out and the truth admitted of no resolution between us. But

I stood still, tears starting in my eyes, stood still and waited. She kept muttering about her God and her daughter through the sobs. 'To think it'd come to this ... my God ... this business ...'. Finally she quieted and looked at me.

I stood, swimming in a maelstrom of black and white checks, drowning and unable to move. Although I knew she was gathering for the counterattack. She took a weighty breath and said, as if it pained her, 'This is going to have to stop, you know.'

'This is *not* going to have to stop.'

'I won't have my daughter indulging in this kind of filth.'

'This is *not* filth.'

'Oh, and what is it then? Eh?'

'I love Julia.' As if that'd be any defence.

She sneered. 'Love? You've never known what love is. You've always been too selfish. Look at you now.'

'What about me?'

'Standing there in your jeans with your thumbs in your belt like some sort of boy.'

'What's that got to do with it?'

'Do you think that's normal?'

'I don't give a stuff whether it's normal.'

'And your language.'

'Stuff my language.'

'Maureen, for God's sake ...'

'I don't believe in your bloody God.'

'Maureen, please, you've got to be reasonable.'

'You can talk.'

'Well you can't expect me to take this sort of thing lightly. Your whole life's at stake.'

'It's my life.'

'Oh my God, if only you were pregnant I'd at least be able to talk to my friends. But this ...' So much easier, pregnancy. A respectable scandal.

'You'd like to see me knocked up, would you?'

'You know I don't want to see you in *any* sort of trouble.'

'Bullshit. You've been making trouble for me ever since I can remember.'

'I've been making trouble, have I? I give you music lessons, speech lessons. I leave Cobb Swamp and all my friends so you can go to a good school ...'

'It was a lousy school.'

'We didn't know that then. I make sure you get a good education, get you to University ...'

'You wanted board when I was saving to study.'

'We were never well-off, Maureen, you know that as well as I do. We had to scrape and scratch year in, year out for you and Ken to have all the things we missed out on.'

'Oh shit yes, I appreciate all that.'

'You never showed it.'

'How did you expect me to when you hated me the whole bloody time?'

'Don't talk nonsense, Maureen.'

Suddenly the possibility of making her understand.

'I'll tell you something Mother. It's about time you knew. Sure you gave me speech lessons—and showed me off to those precious friends you had to leave behind. Sure you left, and every argument since you've rubbed in your great sacrifice and my ingratitude, when I hated that bloody school—full of snobs and half-wits. On top of that you blamed me for Ken turning into a juvenile delinquent. Little Kennyboy wouldn't've had that sort of thing in him, now, would he? And all the bloody time I was slaving my guts out doing your cooking, your housework, your shopping, at your beck and call, and always under your thumb. Shit, I wasn't even allowed to go out with other girls because you thought something might happen to me. Lose your little slave.'

'You always grumbled ...'

'Yeah. But I always did it—and you hardly ever said a word of thanks. You talk about ingratitude. Yours stinks to the high heaven. And all that time you favoured Ken as if he was the one helping you out.'

'He's a boy.'

'Yeah, and I wish I'd been one. You believed him when he lied, the little bastard, you belted the shit out of me for the things he did and made out I'd done. You were blind to everything he did because he was a boy and boys get away with everything. The way he came in the other night—and laughed at you—and you still make all the allowances for him. You never made any for me. You even belted me once for trying to get away to see Granny.'

'You're making it up.'

'No, Mother, I'm not bloody well making it up. You caught me at the back fence by the gums, dragged me inside, locked me up in the bathroom and took to me with that bloody great canvas belt you used to have. I suppose it's not the kind of thing you like to remember. I wouldn't like to have treated a kid like that.'

'But why would I have done a thing like that?'

'Search me. How should I know? You said Granny was spoiling me and wouldn't let me visit her for months.'

'Well she did spoil you.'

'Yeah. Look how spoiled I am now, eh?'

'It's no laughing matter.'

'If you loved me, you bitch ...'

'Maureen!'

'... if you loved me you kept it a bloody dark secret.'

'No, no, Maureen. NO. You've got it all wrong. Of course I loved you. No other girl would see it like this.'

'That's how I see it. That's how I feel it. That's how it was.'

'I wasn't to know you felt like that ...'

I sniggered through my tears.

'Maureen, please ... if you feel like this I'm sorry, really sorry ...'

'Thanks.'

My throat felt lacerated, my eyes hot as if I had suffered the attack myself. I would have liked to be able to put my arms around her and make peace. I couldn't do that any more than leave her. No peace and no exit.

She cornered me at the end of my tirade.

'I want to help you.'

'I do not need your help.'

'Come on now, Maureen. You must be worried yourself. It's no way to live.'

'It's my business.'

'You need help.'

'I do not.'

'A psychiatrist then, if you won't let me ...'

'There's nothing you or any headshrinker or anyone else can do. It's my business.'

'There's your family to think of. Do you want to be known as one of those all your life?'

'I don't give a shit.'

'I'll have to take drastic steps if you won't do something about this yourself.'

Fleetingly I wished I could humorously promise to be good, as Ken would have done, and leave jovially. I stood. Defiant.

'If this doesn't stop I'll contact Mrs Vernon—I'm sure she wouldn't be too pleased.'

'She's in Sydney.'

'She'll be back.'

'Anyway, she's enlightened I bet. Not everyone's living in the nineteenth century still.'

'It's got nothing to do with being old-fashioned, Maureen. It's a simple question of morals.'

'Bullshit.'

'What's more, I should think the College Principal would be anxious to put a stop to your carryings-on.'

'Jesus mother, you can't go telling the college.'

'We'll see.'

'You wouldn't.'

She raised her eyebrows with an air of despair.

'I might be forced to.'

Visions of Julia's mother clouting me with a lecture-board—yet surely a sociologist might have some tolerance ... And college ... Maureen Craig, expelled 1965, for lesbian practices. An awful warning. A public affair it'd be: there Emma stands smiling wanly, there Libby Stace and her fresher-cronies tittering. Dr Heath appears in full academic regalia—ermine and red velvet—wielding a mace, as the college music students strike up the Funeral March and the tutors file past in black, each signing the expulsion warrant with a flourish. Craig shivers in a bath-towel. 'Who put you in?' Emma inquires in a stage whisper. 'My mother.' The assembly gets their laugh out of it, great waves of swelling hilarity. A couple of hefty seniors step forward for the public flogging and Craig is finally carted out to the nature-strip, dumped in the big bad world, while students aim pebbles from upstairs windows.

Through the panic and desperation I couldn't follow my mother's torrent of propositions for my immediate relief from sin.

'You can't do this to me,' I screamed. 'You can't.'

'Just promise me you'll stop.'

'I can't. And I won't.'

'Well you're not staying under my roof then. We've always been respectable people. Your grandmother'd die of shame ...'

'I don't want to stay here. You begged me to come home. I never wanted it. I'll be gone by morning.'

'Maureen. Please. I only want to help you.'

'All you're worried about is the scandal—and your old-hat morals. I'm not interested in your morals—they never did you any good, that's for sure. And I don't give a stuff what you try. I hate your moral guts.'

As I clattered down the steps she yelled after me.

'These aren't idle threats, Maureen. I'll take action. I'll stop you. I'll have to help you if you won't help yourself.'

I emptied all my change out in the telephone box and shakily dialled trunks. Get through to Julia. Get help.

'That'll be eighteen shillings for three minutes.'

'I've only got twelve.'

'That won't be enough, I'm sorry.' Frenzy.

'Please, please give me two minutes—it's a matter of life and death.'

He connected me; must've enjoyed the situation that was life and death to me—he didn't cut us off. I babbled on for an hour. Julia agreed to sound out her mother and suggested I try the Vice-Principal, who knew and liked me.

'Come back soon,' I begged foolishly.

'Saturday.'

'I'll be back in college.'

'I love you, Maureen. Don't worry. We'll find a way through.'

I packed my suitcase and went to sleep in the armchair for an hour or so. Terrified of meeting my mother I got up at dawn, wandered the drizzling Bentleigh streets until nine, had my mail redirected and caught the train to Flinders Street. I'd lasted eight days with the family. This looked like the end.

If I'd stopped to think, it would've been clear that Mother's fear of scandal was her deepest-rooted, and that no thirst either for rectitude or revenge would balance it out. The choice between two risks. If the Principal didn't know already, it had to come from me, not my mother. My best chance, I calculated, lay in coming clean with the authorities. Dr Doyle, the Vice-Principal, was a bulwark of a woman, old and reputedly crazy: to me the epitome of civilised sanity. She ushered me into her study, sat me in a leather chair and asked the problem.

'Er ... Well ... The thing is. Well, first I would like to come back into college for the rest of the vacation.'

'Of course.'

'Er ... Well ... I won't be able to pay the extra fees for a while. I ...'

'We can postpone that, Maureen,' she said gently.

'I ... can't stay at home. My mother's thrown me out.' The embarrassing tears would start any minute.

'Goodness me, that's no good.'

'No. That's the other thing I have to say. My mother's threatening to contact Dr Heath to get me thrown out of here, too.'

'Well, I'm sure Dr Heath's not ... '

'It's because of my relationship with Julia Vernon. I want to ask you if maybe I should see Dr Heath. I don't know if my mother would go through with it. You see, well, it's sexual.'

'I see. These things do happen in a women's college.'

'Yes.'

'And college decisions are not within your mother's influence.'

'No.'

'So I'd just leave it. I don't know the Principal's exact attitude to the matter. But she'd hardly dismiss two of our best students, would she?'

'I suppose not.'

'Don't worry about it at all. I'll speak to her on your behalf if it should crop up.'

I was effusively grateful, but, with unaffected delicacy, she ignored the snivelling and nose-blowing, steered gently into academic waters and asked about my essays.

In my pigeon-hole was a telegram. All is well. Love Julia.

'What did your mother say?'

'She didn't seem at all perturbed. She just said it happened to quite a lot of people really—like Florence Nightingale.'

I grinned.

'Yes,' she continued, 'I was surprised—she took it as a matter of course. Said she thought your mother's tactics were utterly stupid.'

'And brutally one-eyed.'

'She did not say that, but she couldn't see how throwing you out and threatening to expose you would do anything but push you closer to me.'

'I guess that's true.' I hugged her.

'And she said to tell you you can stay at our place in vacations if it's still hard to go home. She's got nothing against you at all.'

'That's incredible.'

'It makes me feel better, you know—her reaction. She said it's the kind of thing you grow out of.'

'Could be.'

'So the best thing's to let it ride.'

'She sounds pretty bloody enlightened.'

'I suppose an education helps.'

'Maybe that's it.'

Mrs Vernon and Dr Doyle offered a glimmer of tolerance, a willingness to let us be. The desire: to exist in isolation from the pressure which provoked a defiance no more free than knuckling under would have been.

Libby Stace had adopted me as her intellectual mentor—guide, philosopher and friend, as she put it. She dropped in often with her problems and questions. She had none of Emma's discreet avoidance of things and I often got to the point of telling her what was happening to me. I was tempted to shock her, to dare her to reject me on the simple sexual basis although she'd enjoyed my company. Evidently she had not guessed that my association with Julia was anything other than the closeness of a couple of women with fine minds attuned. It was her own confession that finally triggered it off.

An evening of unusual confidences.

'You know, I'm not a virgin,' she told Julia and me. Julia covered up her faint shock. I said, 'Shit, eh?'

'I was only fourteen. Went up to my uncle's farm at Mooroopna one holiday. A kid of seventeen or so, Charlie I think his name was, took me off in his Chev and—well—seduced me.' She looked down, ashamed or feigning it. Julia's mouth hung open a fraction.

'Was it any good?' I asked.

'No. It hurt. And I felt bad. My mother would've been angry.'

'Did you do it again, after?'

'Not much. There were a lot of fellows at the Youth Club at home wanted me to, but all their parents knew mine. Anyway, there didn't seem much point.' I felt glad that Libby had gone beyond the sexual pale, though I recognised at the same time that if pregnancy itself was better than being lesbian, Lib was by no means the sinner I was.

'Didn't you feel guilty?' Julia asked, wide-eyed and wondering.

'Oh yes. Terribly. I knew I shouldn't have done it. I was terrified my Uncle Bob'd get wind of it and let Mum know.'

'I'd've been scared of that too—it's the sort of thing mothers belt you for.'

'Oh, not that.' Her tone slid into patronage. 'My mother never did anything of that kind. She'd just have been terribly disappointed.'

I let out the bitter Craig laugh, but provoked no reaction.

'It does something to your self-respect, you know,' she continued, almost proudly, adopting a tone of superiority. 'It's just as well I'm so resilient. It could've had an awful effect on me, but I just put it behind.'

'Don't you think it's better to get married first?' Julia asked her. It was quite a curiosity to see Julia in the guise of puzzled inquirer. Libby laughed outright.

'I can't very well afford to, can I? A boy asked me to marry him, you know, about two years ago. But I felt I was too young for it—and he was so earnest! Yuck! Anyway you don't want to commit yourself until you're old enough to know what you're doing.'

Libby's self-possession amazed us—she sounded outrageously mature.

'You're both virgins then, I suppose?'

I glanced at Julia briefly and we agreed to risk it.

'More or less,' I said.

'It's not the sort of thing you can be half and half, I wouldn't have thought.'

I smiled and felt nervous. Take the plunge. 'What's your attitude to homosexuality?' Hard to gauge her reaction—but whether her self-styled maturity was a pose or not, she wasn't going back on it.

'I don't have any tendency towards it myself,' she answered coolly, 'but I do regard it as a personal affair. There shouldn't be a law against it, for example.'

'Shit no.' I spoke a bit too explosively. 'You see Julia and I are in love with each other.'

She glanced from one to the other, coyly, half-smiling, and said, 'Really?'

There was a trace of panic in Julia's face, a sudden fear of blunder. She clammed up.

'Yes,' I continued, 'but you have to choose the people you confide in pretty carefully. Of course we're not ashamed of it ...'

'Of course not,' she cut in readily.

'If you love someone' (gazing shyly at Julia, who blenched) 'you've got a right to express it as you feel it.'

'I've always thought that. Had to in a way. I'm terribly honoured that you're trusting me in this way.'

'Well, you're one of the few freshers who seems to have a bit of imagination and maturity.'

She pursed her lips in pleasure.

'I don't need to ask you not to spread it about.'

'Of course not.' Then, as an afterthought, she added, 'So don't.'

'There are people here who think we're freaks.'

'Who?' she flashed in.

'Oh I dunno. Just the atmosphere sometimes.'

'Must be awful.'

'Is.'

'Well I think you're great. Hell of a lot of courage to go through with a thing like this. And you're so good together. Sympatico.'

Even Julia responded to the compliment.

Pleasure grows with time, meshed with distaste; rarely free of unease, but growing. I prefer the love-making motions fully-dressed, prefer contact filtered through blue jeans and shirts. Flesh on flesh horrifies. Until one night Julia comes to my room and, fear of intruders notwithstanding, I let her strip off my blue boy's pyjamas. Hair embarrasses me. I hate catching glimpses of myself in mirrors—moments of vertigo. We've been together for nearly a year, now, and I'm still in semi-horror. She's not going to kiss that bunch of hair? Or? Relief as she kisses my navel and bundles her long breast between my legs, feeds its nipple into the soft bit where the flesh yields and opens. She moves it gently, bulging it up over the mound, delicious rubbing. I'm going up, no striving, no strain, effortless powerful glide to the top. Every fraction of skin is curiously awake, backbone shivers. This is different. No turning back, calming down, cooling off—the vast arching wave is bound, somehow, to break—and me with it. Out of nowhere blue flame shimmers and shudders in the flesh of cunt, arse, back; spreads, without consuming, into the edges of my body. Whole flesh luminous leaps and leaps and leaps. 'Like blue flames,' I say. A total surprise, unexpected, unawaited.

We look at each other amazed. Mistily. She seems exultant. I discomfited by this, but floating free, detached.

'Orgasm?'

I shrug. 'Like blue flames.'

A fantastical world. Unconscious; free of every consideration but itself, limitless because untempered by past and future, undisturbed by guilt. My body floats, contained; for the first time it seems properly to be the thing I call myself; I bear it no grudge.

I think: if she can make it happen, so can I. Pull on the blue pants with their soft thick crutch. And rub. And discover it's there, always there. Can always be released. I do it daily and more. Learning to appreciate my own body. My unthinkably pleasant cunt.

Unfortunately Julia didn't see it as quite the stroke of luck I did. It convinced her that she'd made me a Confirmed Homosexual. 'If you get that much out of it, you'll never want a man.'

'So what?'

'So that's terrible.'

'Terrible? It's the best thing ever happened to me. I don't see anything bad about it at all.' And if I wanted her forever? she must have been thinking. She started expatiating with new intensity on the necessity of being just good friends, letting herself believe that she'd led me way downhill. No way out for either of us—except, just possibly, this desperate denial of our feeling for each other. I was distraught at the possibility of losing her, of living without her unfailing support, her kindliness, her love.

'Please, Maureen, go off to bed. It's for the best. We can't sleep together—and we have to make a start somewhere.'

She was lying in her bed, worried in her winceyette nightdress. I tried slipping in, was clouted on the shoulder; I tried arguing, but she was adamant. Grip on her slipping. Complaisant Julia had frozen up.

'All right then, I'll have to go and masturbate.'

Julia's mouth fell open; her eyes distended.

'Maureen, don't say that.'

'Why not?'

'You don't do it, do you?'

'No,' I lied, 'but I'll have to if you don't let me sleep with you.' Undisguised blackmail—but it worked. Once. She threw back the blankets and embraced me in her voluminous nightdress, held me tenderly and, skirting the word itself, lectured me on masturbation.

The ploy didn't work a second time. Fear, guilt and the pressure of place had finally driven Julia to take a firm and apparently unalterable stand. Understanding only a part of the extremities which forced it on her, I felt cheated and thrown out in the cold. Being alone was bleak after Julia's warmth and companionship.

There was no other woman—not even her Christopher, now; she simply couldn't go on. Scared out of her wits of being lesbian for life. When I suggested that I might in fact prefer women, that I might not be, as her mother put it, going through a stage, she reacted with fear and a distaste as real as my mother's. She set herself the insane task of helping me to be normal; refused to think about herself. Orgasm—jealously desired; but feared desperately as the seal on her pervertedness.

As the guilt shrank, I identified its origins—not in any fabled conscience, not in some hypothetical moral sense; it came entirely

70

from the outside, the parents, the encrustation of slime on a handful of simple words, the college women with an inlay of obscene notions so thick they'd never know them as distinct from themselves. Even in me, the mirror of malicious eyes hopelessly qualified the knowledge of innocence.

My activities had always been directed towards someone else—futile lavishings of effort on my mother. Latterly an absorption with Julia which usually excluded the rest of the world. Dependence a sour word nagging in my head. All very well, I'd thought, because Julia thrives on it. Let Julia withdraw a scrap of herself and putty-for-guts Craig is in limbo. General formless misery. Method of counter-attack: work. I dived doggedly into the literature course, spent hours attacking Jane Austen to Emma's unyielding defence.

'It's just because she's got your name, Emma.'

'Rubbish.'

Emma's forthright cheerfulness rubbed off occasionally—I never worked out how anyone could be so thoroughly in command of herself and her life. Her reticence kept me from bemoaning the broken heart. When I showed her the maudlin verse she was never harsh. 'You seem to be battling, Maureen. All very well—but not poetry.'

The last thing I needed was a sympathetic ear—knowing, however dimly, that any avid listener was bound to become Julia II. Libby was all too anxious to provide one.

'What's wrong with you and Julia? You don't seem to be together much these days.'

'Ah well. You know. All's fair in love and war.'

'You made such an interesting pair.'

Scornful laughter from me. 'That was the trouble I expect. Julia couldn't stand the guilt any more.'

'You felt guilty then?'

'Not me so much. I'd've gone on anyway.'

'It's a pity,' she said, 'to see it break up. It's like two people you like an awful lot got engaged ... and then split up.' Libby put her arm across my shoulder and told me to come down to her room whenever I felt like tea and sympathy.

When I began to tell her about my struggles at home I found Libby wry and slightly sceptical. Her family was orderly and harmonious, she told me, and she seemed not much interested in my staple tales of battle.

'What's your father do, Lib?'

'He's a kind of salesman, but that's misleading in a way—he preferred to stay with people instead of taking the executive job they've offered him for years—didn't want to work behind a desk.'

'Don't blame him.'

71

'He's a good sort of person—sticking to a job he likes, even when it's not very well paid.'

'Yeah. I approve of that.'

'All the more amazing really when he's always been embarrassed at earning so little—Mum has a private income, you see.'

'Oh.'

'He felt he ought to be supporting her. It's so hard for a man if he marries a woman with a bit of money.'

'Shouldn't be.'

'I suppose not.'

'Your mother went to University?'

'Oh yes, she was here in college—got a double first in History and English.'

'Why didn't she go on with it?'

'I don't think she fancied the academic world—women weren't terribly welcome. And dad wouldn't let her teach school.'

'He what?'

'Well she liked teaching and I think she must've been very good. She was teaching when they met. But ... well it was the forties and things were different. Dad thought he should give his wife her leisure.'

'But y'said she liked teaching.'

'She would've preferred to teach, yes. But he believed that women shouldn't work. And he's a bit of a kid about the things he thinks are important. It's much easier to give in. He gets sulky ...' She grinned.

'I think it's criminal.'

'They've been happy enough.'

'But doesn't your mother resent it? She must've been bright.'

'Very. Still is. But she got a good man, utterly devoted and loyal. I suppose you have to give up something.'

'I'm never giving things up—not those things.'

'You might have had to—in the forties.'

'Not me.'

The remorseless pursuit of sympathy, disguised as tea, took me stalking down to D-Wing with inveterate regularity. Libby was always interested—and my mask of gloom was bound to invite questions anyway.

'Did you or Julia ever have a lesbian relationship before?'

'No. Neither of us.'

'How did it happen then?'

'Accidentally, I'd say. We liked each other a lot.'

'Isn't it hard if you find yourself looking at girls with a sort of sexual interest?' Her blue eyes wide open with a studied innocence. I felt curiously unnerved and babbled, 'Well no, not so much. I mean.

72

I don't really.' That's not the point, I thought, but couldn't sound convincing. She said nothing.

'It's not like that, Libby. It's not sexual interest. Julia and me liked each other, got to know each other. I don't look at anybody that way. I don't size people up. It isn't like that.'

A patch of silence; she was still watching intently.

'I mean, I like women. They're easier to get on with; it's impossible to get to know men at all. That's all it is really.'

'Really?' She smiled.

'On the whole.'

'On the hole, eh?' Libby roared. 'I'm interested. When I get to really like a boy there's always some sort of physical attraction involved.'

'Mmm?'

'So I would have thought, once you've had a relationship with a girl, it'd remain a perpetual possibility ...'

'Only in a world of speculation,' I countered in her style. We laughed.

But she wasn't having any evasions; her face went suddenly solemn. 'But seriously, Maureen?'

'Shit, I've known Emma and Erif and half a dozen other friends for over a year. They're attractive—as people—but I don't want to dive into bed with any of them. What you're saying just doesn't follow.'

'But what if the friend were willing? What if she wanted it too?'

'There's a difference. Like Julia. I don't know.' But I was quite aware of what she might be driving at.

Opening the books was taking a tepid plunge. Concentration febrile and short-lived, always interrupted by the plausible borrowing of a book from Libby, the need to consult Emma over hastily-conceived intellectual problems or tragic poems hot from the pen, the ambiguous impulse to offer coffee to Julia. Always feelers going out to anyone who'd come close, support the shaky grip, or even simply talk. A clean break, I told myself. That's what I need. Stop pursuing Julia. Stop crawling. And watch yourself, Craig—however much you congratulate yourself on detaching from Julia, it's only because there's someone else to tackle. Libby was sometimes withdrawn, often attacked me for self-indulgence and amateur dramatics; there would be no percentage in a switch of personnel. What I need, I said to myself, is a complete change inside, a spine of my own. But I was baffled at how to find it. I could feel no strength in myself. Strength came from outside.

In the afternoon I met Libby and walked back from the University through the gardens, arms linked. Just acceptable. She sheered off up the corridor, waving.

'Must work. See you later.'

I forced a smile and retreated to my room; dumped my books and notes, sank down by the desk and flopped onto my arms. Coffee. Yes, I'll take Libby some coffee. Won't stay. Just a gesture. I made it rapidly, spilling the milk and breaking a cup. Then off round the corridors, thumping heart and slopping mugs. I stood at the door, listening for voices, heard none, and waited. I turned around and headed back up the corridor. But I've made the bloody stuff. I wheeled and went back to D-Wing. I stood and waited for the involuntary plunge. Suddenly I knocked very gently.

'Thought you might like some coffee if you're going to work.'

'Oh thanks.'

'I won't stay.'

'But you've brought your coffee.'

'Yeah. Well ... on the way ...'

'Stay for the coffee, Maureen.'

'Can't stay long ...' I muttered, sitting down and spilling more. It was with a sense of my superhuman strength that I got up ten minutes later—voluntarily.

'I'll be off then.' She came over to me as I stood stiffly, displaying massive control.

'Sorry it's so tough for you.' She put her arms warmly around me and, after a moment, kissed my lips. I hung on. She parted her lips against mine, pressed harder. Then she swung back and said, 'See you later.'

'Yeah, later, yeah, see you ... ' I jabbered. The corridor reeled, my throat ached. 'How long is later?' I wondered as usual.

Julia was getting jumpy.

'What's happening between you and Libby?'

I snorted. 'We've got plenty in common. I like talking to her. And *you* won't see me very often.'

'Well be careful, Maureen. You know I am only doing this for your own good. I don't want to see you muck yourself up all over again.'

'Ah don't give me that. It's my funeral, not yours. You'll get to be normal. You're safe.'

She burst into tears and rushed out. I didn't want to follow.

Libby and I drifted in and out of sympathy, every reversal a blow.

I like you Maureen, you're so wise and witty and helpful ...

Oh shut up Maureen; you're always going on about Julia—I'm sick of it ...

Sorry, Maureen, must work—see you later.

Hey Maureen, don't forget to come up tonight—straight after dinner, so we've got plenty of time to talk.

74

You dramatise everything, Maureen. Nothing's ever as bad as you make out. I'm sure your mother's all right really.

Marionette Maureen.

Must cut loose, I adjured myself every day as I made the interminable journeys down the D-Wing corridors.

MUST CUT LOOSE.

Might as well be talking to a brick wall.

'I'm going to bed, now,' she said, 'but why don't you stay for a while?' She took her hairbrush off the table, staring an instant into the mirror and tossing the thing nonchalantly onto her pillow. She made none of the usual coy concessions to modesty, stripped off in the middle of the room, rummaged for her pyjamas, and threw herself into bed. She patted the blanket beside her and beckoned me to sit down. Her lips pursed in a smile that was charming and inviting. I felt uncomfortable.

'I love to have my hair brushed. Will you?' Thrusting the brush into my hands.

'I'm sure I won't do it well.'

'I'm sure you will.'

She responded to my frankly non-sensual grip on her shoulder by throwing her arms around my waist, touching breast to breast. I dropped the brush, leaned back with her and kissed her. A moment of acquiescence, lips parting. Then the recoil and the thrust aside.

'Oh. No. Maureen. No.'

She seized my hands though, as I stood up, and pulled me back beside her. 'Don't go.'

'I don't want to go, but I think I should.'

She looked at me baffled as if she'd not known what she was doing. I've got to get out, I thought uneasily, not knowing why and not wanting to.

'I wish we could,' I said.

'Sometimes, you see, I want you,' she answered and finished off my guilty self-denying impulses for good. I felt culpable and buoyant.

'I don't think you should have told me that,' I announced dramatically, setting up another line of defence.

She touched my arm delicately. 'It's true—often now.'

'It's not an easy life to lead,' I went on, in automatic retreat.

'Oh it's obviously impossible.' A trace of flippancy. 'Yeah. Maybe you'd better go now. Switch off the light, will you?'

I got up angrily but as I flipped the switch she called.

'Maureen?'

'Yeah.'

'Kiss me goodnight.'

I felt my way back to the bed under the window and sat down. Both our bodies were as tense as tightrope.

'Yeah,' I said, 'I really like you.'

Her mouth brushed my face, lips parted. I bent a fraction to kiss her. She fell back, pulling me after her and I lay beside her kissing her tenderly, wrapping myself around her blanketed body and rubbing my warm wet cunt against her. 'I suppose I'll be sorry,' flashed gloomily through my mind, a half-thought in the midst of my pleasure.

'Good night,' I said suddenly.

'Don't leave me here, Maureen. I've never wanted anyone like this.'

'You just said it's impossible.'

'You will have to cope, then. I can't.'

I'll be held responsible for this, I thought, but it can't be helped. Cut loose. Hook up. The latter always seemed easier once it was offered. An endless succession of monkey-traps. And yet I liked Libby, liked her unilateral style, admired her self-possession, loved the way she'd accepted me even if she didn't quite approve of joining in. I wanted a relationship where everything could be said, everything could be confessed—all the time. In flight from being alone, I wanted to act inseparably, in concert. So bloody easy: When I'm with you, if I like you, I haven't the suggestion of an impulse of my own. I will bend to anyone who gives me affection, bend with amiable grace. In fact I am always prepared to do anything except leave, pretending at the same time that some obscure principle forces me to leave, and hoping Libby will oppose it.

'Libby, I think I'd better clear off.'

'All right,' she said unexpectedly.

'But we'll have to sort something out, you know.'

'Yeah. See y'later.'

'Shall I come down tomorrow?'

'Please yourself. Dunno when I'll be around.'

'OK,' I muttered, shaken, and went to my room.

It's a dog's life, a rat's life. I sleep fitfully. I feel sick. I shit all the time. And I travel the corridors like a yo-yo. I must've done a few miles the next morning before I finally caught Libby, leaving.

'You're elusive today.'

'Busy.'

'How'd you like some tea?'

'No time.'

'Later?'

'Maybe.' I shrugged and turned.

'Maureen.'

'Yes.'

'I'll be up in about ten minutes. Must give this book to Cleo.'

My displeasure at their arriving together, Cleo uninvited, must have been obvious. She looked at me hard from behind her horn-rimmed glasses. I smiled wanly and asked them to sit down. Cleo had red hair and a pudding-basin haircut that played up her round face and accentuated its chubbiness. She was a loner, as far as I could make out, seen relatively rarely in the company of the fresher coffee-cronies; not much given to idle chatter, a bit timid. Libby had talked about her before—one of the Pass students who should be doing Honours, intelligent, astute and keen. 'She could get a second I should think,' Libby had told me. 'Undervalues herself, but Cleo's not stupid you know, not by any means.'

Cleo was watching us with an altogether too astute gaze. I supposed Libby had told her and, deciding to put up with that, put on a show of conviviality—punctured at no decent interval by Libby's announcement that she'd just remembered a vital lunchtime meeting.

'You look rather gloomy, Maureen,' Cleo ventured after she'd left.

'Oh I feel good sometimes,' I countered, showing the nerves.

'Look Maureen, I don't know if you want to know this, but you don't have to be scared of me "finding out"—I've been through it all before.'

'What?' I said flatly.

'At school. I loved a girl—very much—and for years.'

'What happened?'

'It was strange. Not very physical, Just intense. She kissed me once in the back of a car.' She was speaking levelly, emotionless. 'It had to finish when I came to University.'

'Why?'

'She still lives in Upton. Anyway there was another girl—older, different from me.'

'Why the hell are you telling me all this, anyway?'

'I don't know. Except to say give up on Libby.'

'She told you?'

'I saw.'

'Maybe we would be better off if we gave up on each other. But I don't seem to have a lot of control over it.'

'It's a dead-end business.'

'Was for you.'

'And for you—with Julia.'

'You know about that too, eh?'

'I think everyone suspects it at least.'

'Ah shit. No bloody privacy.'

'I doubt if there ever would be.'

'Well it's their fault, isn't it? Not ours. We didn't ask for their surveillance or protection or spying or whatever you like to call it.'

'No. But you'll never change them. And they've got the weight of numbers.'

'I tell you what, Cleo. They won't change me either.'

'I'm not challenging you,' she said calmly. 'I just think you'll make yourself incredibly miserable. And Libby too.'

'Libby knows what she's doing.'

'Maybe. But that's beside the point. You'll both be sorry.'

'But it's the way we feel.'

'Why don't you try?'

'Try what?'

'Keep to yourself for a while.'

'Like you do?'

'Yes.'

'That's why, is it?'

'More or less. I don't like too many of these people anyway; but I'd rather be alone and free and uncriticised than in love with a girl and tied up in knots.'

'Yeah. So would I. But there's a principle involved. Nobody should be able to dictate my private behaviour.'

'There's hardly much point in establishing a principle—even if you could—when it's agony all the way.'

I shrugged and got up for lunch. 'I wish everything was different.' I opened the door for her and followed her down the corridor feeling doomed.

Days of coming and going. Sensual moments, extended and curtailed. Sometimes we kept distance for a day; sometimes we lay warm and tightly embraced. One night I slept in Libby's bed, feeling good to wake up beside her and bury my head in her long brown hair. Freewheeling—downhill. No brakes. The only expedient being for one of us to hurl herself out of the situation—to return an hour or a day later. I talked about the principle to be established, tried to believe that I ought to be free to do this thing ... Ought to be. I drew back whenever Libby wanted to strip off and get on with it. I love this girl, I told myself. You've got to be free to express it. But I couldn't convince myself. I'd better try to save her, I thought, and waited until this would emerge as impossible. 'My body,' she said, 'wants one thing and my mind another.' It didn't occur to me that such a state of affairs was itself unnatural; neither of us questioned that our minds, our feelings and our bodies were separate, that the mind was the higher being and ought to have been able to exact obedience from the flesh. Skull-love, mind-love, Christian love was supposed to overcome the sick wet cunt, the writhing, the disgusting proliferation of kissing, stroking and playing. As for our feelings—we hardly noticed their relevance.

'I'm sick of this,' she said one evening as we looked at each other after one more flash of shame.

'Sick of me?'

'No. Sick of this turning right on and then cold water.'

'You're not the only one.'

'Well I'm not going on with it. It's all worry, tears and strain. I'm getting out.'

I raised my eyebrows.

'Or ...' she said, distinctly, and stopped.

'Getting in?'

She smiled. 'In a manner of speaking.'

'It'll be difficult.' More Craig warnings.

'Love always is, anyway,' she answered easily.

I hadn't the slightest wish to deter her and simply nodded, taking her hand gently and stroking her palm.

'Why not?' she went on with an uncommon seriousness. 'We love each other, we turn each other on. If it's sin we've done it anyway in thought and almost in deed. And I don't see that it's wrong. You make me feel fantastically good.'

'And you me.'

I felt I ought to ask her if she'd given this due consideration, if she'd calmed her puritanical mind, if she really knew what she was suggesting. But such questions were finicky and irrelevant, and had been asked a hundred times before.

'Do you expect anyone?' I asked her.

'Veronica might come in. But I'll go and say good night first—she's only across the passage. Once the light's out, no-one'd come in I don't think. Won't be long ...' She came back almost immediately, stood a moment in the doorway, grinning, with her finger on the light-switch.

'Ready?' she asked softly.

I stood by the bed and took off my jacket. We undressed in silence; I was nervous still, despite myself, and glad of the dark. She straightened and faced me, slim body and long falling hair. 'You look very fine,' I said quietly, letting my hands rest on her hips, feeling the smoothness and liveness. She wrapped her arms around my bare back, drew me inwards. Touch of breasts, folding into each other. Hair friction. I sank on my heels, bent and kissed her flat breasts. Friendly, exuberant. And so easy, after all—to deny the guilt; as easy as opening a door to the air. 'Come to bed,' she said and pulled me in beside her, cunt dripping, gleaming, body charged to the fingertips. 'This is what it feels like,' I thought, 'to be invincible.' My hands traced the moulding of her body, fingers curled in hair and hair. 'Go on,' she said, squirming with pleasure. I was embarrassed again suddenly, without the courage to define what we might do. Masterful prim Craig engulfed in confusion, aware, too, that it was entirely up to me. 'Do whatever you like,' she whispered and redoubled the confusion. 'There's nothing to be shy about,' I assured myself and was unconvinced. 'Slowly, slowly,' I repeated. The sureness of my voice surprised me, reassured me. I lay facing her, my hand just beneath her shoulder, stroking hair and arse and spine-base, moving closer to her cunt. Palm on hair, I parted the smooth lips, moving into muscle-throat and velvet inside. 'Feels beautiful,' I said. Her body rippled, sinuous and alive, with a snake-like unity. She pulled my head towards hers, thrust her tongue into my mouth, licking the insides of my checks. Cunt, arms, body smouldered as I rubbed my bright cunt against her thigh. I disappeared into the unqualified darkness. Release from self, from shyness, from guilt, from strangeness.

'Did you ever have an orgasm?' I asked her, after a while. She shook her head. 'No wonder the Elizabethans called it dying—I feel as if I'm shining, giving off bright stuff.'

'You are.'

'We'll make it for you sometime. It'll come.'

'I can't imagine anything better than I feel,' she said. 'I feel amazing.' I grinned in the dark. 'Imagine—that everything happens all at once and you're in it. Not a nice feeling that you identify and enjoy; something bigger than you altogether—like a bloody great blue fire. Not burning, but the way flame moves. Can't explain. But it's more. It's something else.'

'I'm happy,' she said, and fell asleep on my lucky shoulder.

Weeks of unbounded merriment. Even reticent Emma said she thought we were doing each other a lot of good. Julia didn't say much to me; she looked sad and regretful whenever I passed her in the corridor and though she obviously wanted to speak, to stop me perhaps, she could only raise her eyebrows occasionally in mute question. Cleo often looked me in the eye meaningfully, but rarely spoke. Libby threw caution to the winds, reminding me that we had a principle to establish. I flinched, but followed. The demonic glee, anyway, was an internal insurance. The slimy gaze and the hushed voice only sent us into contemptuous laughter. 'Immature twits,' Libby declared. 'They don't know a thing about love—let alone sex.' She told her irrepressible love to Veronica, the girl across the corridor; and took Veronica's strained tolerance and disguised jealousy for approval. I figured that I would, in the end, suffer for all this—and hoped the end would be far-off. Whatever the undercurrent of unease, the spirit of daring and the strength of our magical bond kept me euphorically gay. I even faced the August vacation without anguish, sure that things would continue fair when we came back. For a time I forgot all about the ancient imperative of cutting loose.

Secretly I admired Ken. The confident will, the unilateral action. His relations with Mother were bitterer than ever that August. Always a sneaking relief to see them at war; it loaded the balance of power in my favour. Or, rather, her vigilance was, for a while, divided. Robby Hitchin was mother's last straw. Hitchin the dumb brute. Ken ought to have picked up with a nicer class of boy. Not a sneak-thief runt who didn't so much as deign to play at politeness for her benefit. He was as short as Ken, but slight; wiry and invincible. And he hadn't even the dubious status of being an old mate from Brighton High. Permanent truant turned bad, he hadn't seen the inside of a classroom for years. Ken led astray by older boys ... Hitchin worked a petrol pump, fixed engines and drove a beat-up, souped-up car. Ken was bound to get out of his depth ... He looked as though he thought so, too, the day he got rolled.

He must have staggered in some time in the afternoon and lain down out in the bungalow where he slept. Mother didn't expect him home on a Saturday at all, found him by accident when she went out to straighten his things. Lying half-conscious with blood still oozing out of a gash in his forehead and dry blood caked around his nose and down his shirt. His newish suit was shredded at the armpits and slashed down one thigh. She screamed for me. As I came in he lay there squinting and murmuring, 'Shut up, shut up, shut up, shut up ...'

'Get water and rags and Dettol. Quickly.'

'Don't worry,' Ken muttered. 'Leave me alone. Go away.' I got her the first-aid gear.

She was sitting on the bed hunched over him, nearly keening.

'You must tell me what happened, Kenny. You must at least tell me how it happened.' She spoke softly, almost coaxing him.

'Nothing.'

'Oh, Kenny.'

'Got rolled.'

'Rolled?'

'Yeah. You know. Rolled.' His eyes rolled and the whites showed, riddled with bloodshot tracks.

She dipped the cloth in Dettol-whitened water, gingerly hovering over his forehead.

'NO,' Ken roared. 'Christ, NO, it hurts. Leave it. Leave it.'

She was weeping, pleading. 'We'll have to know how deep it is, darling. You might need stitches. I'll be gentle. Don't worry.'

He groaned through grinding teeth as she squeezed the cloth, bathed, uncovered a swollen triangular wound with flesh-edges widened apart and blood seeping through faster than she could clear it.

'Kenny darling, how did they do it?'

'Some ... bastard ... hit me ... Ma.' His eyes rolled again. 'It hurts.'

'I know. I know. But a fist couldn't have cut this deep ... it must've been a weapon.'

'Jus' knuckle dusters. That's all.'

She drew her breath fast and sudden. 'This is Hitchin's crowd for you.'

'It wasn't me mates, y'silly bitch.'

'Where were your mates, then?'

'Ah shut up.'

'They left you, didn't they?'

'Leave me alone, woman. Can't you see I'm feeling crook.'

'Maureen,' she said, 'I think he needs a doctor. Will you find your father and tell him to get the car out.'

'I'm not going to any bloody doctor. For Chrissake just leave me alone. I'll clean meself up later.'

'But Ken ...'

'I'm staying here. Now piss off.'

'Try to sleep then dear,' she said lamely and, gathering up the bowl of tepid brownish water, she went out.

'Is there anything you want Ken?'

'It's OK Maureen. I jus' don't want any fuss.'

'OK.'

'What were you saying to him?' she shot out as I came in.

'Nothing. Just asked him if he wanted anything. I think he'll go to sleep.'

'What are we going to do?'

'What do you mean? He'll be all right.'

'You don't care a damn about him. Never did.'

'That's not the point, Mother. That cut won't kill him you know.'

'He could bleed to death and you wouldn't care.'

'There's no arteries in your forehead. It'll stop when the blood cakes.'

'It should be bathed properly.'

'Let him do it later. He doesn't want to be interrogated right now.'

'That cut could be infected.'

'He wants to be left alone.'

'He doesn't know what's good for him.'

'Probably not.'

'He'll have to answer for this.'

'Looks like he's answered for it already.'

Later he defied all Mother's attempts to supervise his wounds and dressings, locked himself in the bathroom for an hour and came out patched.

'You must eat some tea, Ken.'

'Mum, I've been bashed up, I feel sick and I don't want any food, thanks.'

'But you need it.'

'Gimme some coffee then.' When she disappeared, he asked me to lend him ten bob.

'Yeah, sure, but didn't you get paid yesterday?'

'Keep your voice down. The bastards got my wallet—pay packet and all.'

'Shit. Yeah, I'll give you a quid if you like.'

Mother came back with steaming coffee and a hunk of bread and sausage, moved the table near his chair and placed the tray. Then:

'What were you two whispering about?'

'Since when was it a crime to talk to your sister on a Saturday night?'

'What were you talking about?'

'Talking about how bloody cold it is for August. Don't you agree?'

'I heard you mentioning money.'

'Oh, did you now,' he said, curling his lip, wrinkling the plaster. 'Got a good ear, haven't you Ma?'

'Well?' she continued, not to be gainsaid.

'Well what?' Ken blew innocently on his coffee.

'You'll have to tell us what happened Ken.'

'Now why would I have to do that, Ma?'

'Otherwise I'll have to call the police.' Ken spluttered, then laughed. 'Jesus, do you really think the cops'd be interested in one of the Bentleigh kids getting rolled?'

'I'm sure they'd like to talk to you and try to clean up those youths wandering around in gangs. It's dreadful.'

Ken clammed up, gazed at the idiot box with rapt attention. It wasn't even on.

'So they got your wallet, did they?' she continued. 'And ruined your suit. Don't think we'll be paying.'

'Nobody asked you to pay, did they?'

'What'll you wear to work now?'

'I got jeans.'

'I'm sure Mr Ferguson'll be pleased.'

'I'm his best salesman. He'll like it all right.'

'And what about your board this week?'

'Looks like you'll have to wait, doesn't it ... you mean old bitch.' But he was sweet. No rancour. No recrimination. No asking her to waive it.

'Were you with Hitchin today?'

'For a while.'

'Where?'

'Brighton.'

'Where in Brighton?'

'Look, just to shut you up. I was coming down the alleyway out the back of where that friend of Maureen's lives—the fat one—Julia. I was with Willy and Rob and Pete and Joey Murphy. It was two-fifty-eight and a half. And about twenty sharpies come burning down from the Golf Links end. We turned around and ran. But it's about half a mile down that alley and you know how I lose my breath. So I was just leaning against the fence trying to get meself moving, with a bit of a pain in me chest holding me up, when the first of those creeps caught up.'

'And hit you?' Mother was distressed.

'Of course he hit me. And got so mad when I ducked that he got his mates to hang onto me while he got a punch in. It took all twenty of 'em.'

'And Hitchin ran away?'

'What bloody good would there be in two getting rolled instead of one?'

'Fine sort of friend I must say—he could've helped you get away.'

'Bullshit. I couldn't even breathe, let alone run.'

'Who were these boys then?'

'I dunno. Just sharpies. We'll get even.'

'You'll do no such thing. You'll stay home for a while and keep clear of that type of person.'

'We'll see,' he said in good-natured disagreement.

'Want to get yourself killed, do you? Scarred for life?'

'Don't worry, Ma. I'll be taking care next time. We'll get 'em.' She pursed her lips indicating disciplinary intent ... and went out.

'How'd you get home then?' I asked him.

'Walked. Somehow.'

'Didn't Robby come back for you?'

'No. But I'm not telling the old woman that.'

'What happened to him?'

'Dunno. I'll see him tomorrow down the Bowl. Might've run into trouble himself. He's a good guy though. Something must've come up.'

'You don't reckon he just cleared off?'

'Nah. Not Robby.'

When I went to stay with Libby, Mrs Stace threw me out. I heard the whirlwind in the corridor and fell out of Libby's bed, my pants off, disguising the palpable nakedness with a blanket; I jerked back onto the stretcher-bed they'd set up for me and aimed at the semblance of quiet separate chatter. 'Oh you really think so ...'. But Mrs Stace was well past bluffing. She came through the door at a charge, an entrance so singular, so dramatic, that there was no door opening, no handle turning, only the *fait accompli*. A woman with a fine theatrical sense. She stalked to the window and threw up the blind. 'It is late.' Ice in her voice. She stood there glowering. I felt sick. She didn't say much.

'I don't like lesbians and I will not have one in my house. Get out.' I must have done a (fake) double-take. She wheeled on Libby.

'You, before you left this home to go to college, were a perfectly normal girl.' Pause for impact. 'And you—although I don't like the word—are a lesbian. Now will you go.'

I wondered with appropriate brevity what was wrong with the word. Maybe she heard the bed creaking—always a problem for illicit lovers; or maybe she could sense the way we felt about each other. Her instant sweeping exit left no margin for sweet reasonings, even had my assaulted mind been capable. Judgement had been passed and sentence handed out. I was the predator, the lesbian hunter, dangerous, destructive, intolerable. I got out.

Mrs Stace had been cool ever since I arrived. Being a quick-enough thinker and a currier of favour in such situations (after all, I was in love with her daughter), it took me only seconds to locate Charles Morgan on her bookshelves—he had been a favourite of Mrs Grantly's.

'Oh, you've got Charles Morgan's *Sparkenbroke*.' A study of surprised glee in my energetic young voice. But the gay little sky-rocket backfired.

'Morgan! Intellect functioning in a vacuum. None of the smell of good honest sweat about him.' Cool scorn. I resented her implying that I knew nothing about good honest sweat, but could hardly start explaining how hard I'd always worked. I went red and said nothing while the three of us stalked pointlessly around the living-room, examining in silence the intellectual resources of the Stace clan.

Libby's father, a stubby man, was quiet and well-behaved. He never raised his voice to my knowledge, never seemed to exert his will. I wondered how he could have prevented his wife from doing anything she chose, though the fact was that he had, and Libby claimed proudly that he made all the important decisions. Mrs Stace had made a career of serving him; she treated him like a pampered son, cooked his favourite vegetables and puddings, and saved him the bother of demanding anything by making sure he had it.

It worried her that her own father had finished himself with his head in a gas oven and, regarding this as insanity and insanity as hereditary, she had set about insulating the children from stress. The mainspring of her method was laughter; both the young Staces could recite a variety of comedy-discs at length, both knew countless jokes, both loved anecdotes and collected cute speech habits. It must have been a shock to her when Geoff tried to fuck his sister at fourteen—

or worse, the day he took the carving-knife to Libby and chased her around the kitchen. Incest and homicidal mania. Her face whitening, she dashes to the gramophone to dose them up with a humorous titbit ... which magically transforms the festering insanity into chuckling harmony. The funlust she instilled was, after all, an impulse seeking outward, craving amusement. Would Libby, at the point of poisoning her old man and drowning the babies in the bath, suddenly remember the wicker whatnot and refrain? Could Geoff quell the impulse to leap naked from the Ming Wing?

That I came to the Stace household, that August, in woe, escaping the throes of another campaign in the endless struggle with my mother, was the first signal for Mrs Stace's disapproval. No decent girl with a smile in the heart could find it necessary to flee the maternal breast. She of all people, with her text of lightsome laughter and tolerance where tolerance is due, must have had scant idea of the blitzkrieg conditions prevailing in the Craig household. Had she confronted my mother on this question of the dangerous daughter she might have ended pitying me after the hail of loudspeaker yells, outlandish accusations, pots, china and finally light furniture which she would inevitably have received. Ironic that both were under the illusion that it was all the other girl's fault, spinning ghastly imaginings of the vile snotty-nosed seductress and their own straying innocent.

Libby was sorry, sympathetic, hugged me, offered comfort; she walked with me to the railway station, promising a new start when we were safely back in college. She was glibly certain of her love; probably scared stiff of her mother, anything to get rid of me as quickly as possible. My premonitions, as I caught the train, were more realistic. The railway network at Flinders Street Station was inveterately grey; in fine misting rain the wires, the countless wires and uprights, endlessly divided up the grey grey space. That monstrous station oozed mud at the pores and the asphalt ramps and platforms gleamed with the cockroach sheen of bootmud under pale electric glimmer. The next morning I fled the city.

Hitching out of Melbourne for the first time. On the train out to Dandenong, I read Eliot. I wanted quite literally to be not the same person *who left the station or who will arrive at any terminus*; and how could I *consider the future and the past with an equal mind?* Mrs Stace's accusing face was everywhere; even much later, in equanimity, I sometimes saw it in trains and crowds—and recoiled.

I got as far as Lakes Entrance that afternoon. There was only a glimpse of sea, a blue patch between the hills, before the road burst out of the bush and commanded the sudden water everywhere. To the west the Gippsland Lakes stretched away, intricate pattern of water and island, with a long sandy spit separating them from the sea. I topped the rise at sunset. The lakes were long pools of glittering light; the islands, dark and distinct, looked like a scattering of cut-outs. Beyond them and far to the east lay the straight white coastline, its breakers miniature from the cliff-top. Dead ahead, a fishing boat the size of a toy ploughed up through the walled entrance; and another slid round the signal tower and made for the smoky town. The car wound down the hillside and across the small bridge that spanned the north arm of the inlet. A truckie had told me that Jamieson, the Presbyterian preacher, had a youth camp just out of town, deserted now in the winter months; that he was an original saint and turned no-one down. I decided to stay the night—visions of pressing on to Sydney next day and stowing away on a tramp-steamer or other suitable vessel of deliverance.

I got out in the middle of the town, a strip of houses and shops fronting on the wharves. Across the road the Co-op fish shop fried flake and flathead under the tatty pines along the quay. I bought a bundle and walked out on one of the jetties to eat, swung my legs over the edge and looked down at the purple-shot oily water. Ropes as thick as my arm strained around the stout wooden bollards, the kind that rounded out in a smooth ball and looked the perfect seat for a Hornblower or Hawkins. The boats were spewing out sludge from the holds and smelled of diesel and fish. I crunched my chips, swung my feet indolently and watched the men as they fastened ropes, swilled decks or squatted smoking.

After a while I inquired for Jamieson's house and made my request over the tea and cakes which his wife brought instantly to his study. He had a craggy, beaten-up face, looked more like a gangster than a pastor, no unction or greasy well-being; he had, in fact, been a sailor, welder, fighter and no doubt sinner. One leg, shot half-away in the war, gave him constant pain which he embraced as his appointed cross. The youth camp, it turned out, was miles away in the scrub— he asked me to stay the night with his family. Over tea we hit on the Reformation, history which I knew and he loved. When he suggested that I stay as long as I cared to, a bit alarmed at my grandiose open-ended travelling program, I accepted with a sneaking relief. Certainly he thought I was someone other than myself—but he did offer his home to a dusty scruffy student, which is hardly the rule with dedicated Christians. In return for a few sessions with him discussing Luther and Calvin, I had a place to sleep and the freedom of the long beaches.

In Lakes Entrance that August it seemed as if there had been no winter nor ever could be. I spent days wandering the town and the seashore. Still numb at first with shock; later on growing warmer and calmer under the benign late-August sun. One afternoon I crossed the footbridge which led over the silty eastern end of the harbour to the ocean beach. The day was turbulent; black clouds stacked up and turned the sea metal-grey, tossing fiercely up the beach. Amazingly, the black bolts tattered apart at intervals and shafted white light hit the sea which immediately glowed green, and the surf which dazzled as if flashing its own blinding brilliance. I turned east along the beach and ran as the light failed and flashed, and the sea growled and played. Lake Bunga was silted up and I rolled down the sandbank near the dark stagnant water and rested from the wind. The sun, when it came out, was hot there out of the breeze; I hauled my jumper off and felt my winter-pale arms soak up the blaze of heat. Under sooty sky I crawled back up the sandbank and jumped over the top onto the sand-whipped beach, running further with the wind behind. Like a feather or a leaf, I was bowled up the beach, almost flying. Ahead was Shelly Point, a blunt rocky headland with a short spit of grey rock strung straight out to sea. I had never been there. As kids we were confined to the footbridge beach near the town. But this reddish cliff jutting out from the scrubby dunes felt like my destination.

As I came near, the wind blew viciously, scattering the piled cloud and driving it all towards the horizon. Within minutes the sky shone unbroken blue and the wind followed the clouds over the edge. The orange rock shivered in heat-haze. Languid blue waves lapped the still, burning beach. I dived onto the sand, churning it with my fists, rubbing my face and body against its warmth, spitting grains through my teeth with a wild pleasure. Not a human being for miles, the village way down the coast, no farmers, no fishermen. A world with no dangers either within or without. Tranquil blueness, the unhurried topple of waves, the smallest of them breaking with a faint splash into the lazy swish of the undertow. I stripped off slowly, shy even here, and ashamed of a shyness which seemed to have no real source. I stood straight and slapped my thigh-fat, looked around cautiously and grinned at myself. The dry caked sand under the cliff squeaked as I drove my bare toes into it, sliding one sole after the other across its slippery feel. A sound as bright as sunlight. With a yell I ran down the sand and into the sea, splashing the shallow foam into the air until, waist-deep in the surge, I could dive through the crests of the breakers, catapult out into space and drop back into the trough beyond. Coalescence of wave and body for this unaccountable instant tossed up in air. I swam out, pivoted and wallowed like a seal, watched for a big swell to build up behind me. Then I hurled myself, windmill arms, driving every grain of energy into a sprinting all-out stroke; swimming fast and perilously in the tottering wall of water. It followed, overtook me, caved in and shot me in through the surge with a roar and a cushion of exploding bubbles. Near the red cliff I found a hot flat rock, shook myself and lay down on it. I felt strong—as if this magical afternoon had been given to me.

As soon as I turned to walk back to Lakes Entrance, cloud began banking above the sea, big white clumps at first—returning to the coast. The sun shone on, getting low, and the sea went sea-green. All along the miles of beach, out beyond the sandbar, gulls and gannets hovered and plunged. Each bird hit the sea at dizzy speed, sheer stone-like fall, disappeared a few seconds, then erupted, fish threshing in beak. Hundreds of them. I scurried down the coast with the rising wind and sand in my teeth. Over the sea the cloud darkened and thickened, blotting out the sun and sweeping away the blue. The birds disappeared. Rain drove in from the south, stippling the ocean and drenching the sand. I crossed the footbridge in the misty grey aftermath and admired the day's symmetry, its astonishing island of summer. In bed that night, I listened to rain on tin and the occasional crack of the surf—undertow slapping back against the off-shore reef like a rifle-report.

Most of the nights were clear; the moon nearing the full. After tea I took the kid's bike and rode out of town a few miles before cutting through the scrub to the sea. The night-sea was small, and I sat watching the peculiar sheen of moonshine on moving water. The waves caught the gleam at the instant before breaking; looked as smooth and slippery as a fish's belly while they curled; then broke up into the gentle boiling of a phosphorescent foam. The moment was brief and I watched for hours, to catch each subtle variation of the light-play. I came back night after night.

Jamieson's house fronted on the north arm of the lake where dozens of small boats were moored to rickety jetties. The ex-cop who hired out boats gave me a rowing-boat for nothing. Three miles across the broad ruffled lake the channel closed into a reed-bound snake of water known as the Narrows. The sun poured down in the windless air; the gum trees grew thick on the hillsides above; gnarled tea-tree straggled down to the reedy edges. Cattle crashed through the scrub occasionally on the patches of firm land along the deep edge. The Narrows curved ahead in stillness—only the bursts of magpie-warble and the squark of crow, the rhythmic creak of oars and the faint slap of placid water against the bow. The brown water itself lay so slick and smooth that reflections ran down into it, solid upside-down hillsides, and the small wake splayed out behind with perfect geometry. Miles up I came to a square jetty, just as the Narrows phased off into muddy waterholes and rivulets blocked by a rotting tree-trunk. I steered in, tied up and climbed the dirt pathway to the tea-house.

Two old people lived there. He was shrivelled, gnome-like, waving his knotty bush-stick and speaking with the piercing clarity of the deaf; she was ample and dignified, wreathed in thick grey curls. In the winter their customers were few, the tourist riverboats operated rarely and single rowers must have been unknown. The old woman brought me into the kitchen for tea—huge smoking woodstove, worn wooden rolling-pins, scarred marble chopping-block. She baked fresh scones, produced thick cream and jam full of whole sweet plums. Her craggy little man told stories of mighty exploits on the jetty hauling in the garfish—and watched for the response he couldn't hear. She was deft and easy, perhaps pretending that I was her own granddaughter from the University whom she hadn't seen for a year. I stayed on through the afternoon and, at twilight, I rowed back to the town.

During the week I wrote to Mrs Stace, begging forgiveness along lines Macbeth might have used addressing Duncan. Horrified at myself and seeking a pointless reconciliation, I half-accepted the guilt she laid on me. What self-distrust, I wonder, prompted me to say that I had difficulty sorting out the nature of my responsibility honestly? Why treat it as a matter of wrong-doing again, anyway, when Libby and I had broken through that? Why try to settle between criminal or psychopath when neither fitted?

Inwardly, I still doubted whether it was a question of guilt; even if it was, the seduction had been mutual. Julia and I had expected mild tolerance, not charmed envy bordering on the jealous. There Libby was: a girl brought up with a proper dread of homosexual activities (much more explicit than mine), already fucking at fourteen, recipient of a proposal of marriage in between; a fun-loving seventeen-year-old with no real peculiarities, no Home Front, enjoying a solid and blamelessly natural connection with the girlfriend of her youth. There she was: enchanted by Julia and me. There she was: loving me and proud of it. An unlikely story, Mrs Stace would have felt.

I arrived back after my break in the sunshine to find her prompt reply in my letterbox. It took full advantage of the Craig bafflement.

Dear Maureen,

I am so glad that you realise the enormity of your conduct. Of course it must be hard for you to be honest and, indeed, I congratulate you on the clarity you have achieved. Being clear-sighted, you will naturally understand that, should the college authorities be informed of your behaviour, their attitude could not but be adverse. With my guidance, Elizabeth has recognised the weakness and stupidity of her acquiescence, and has decided to sever the unfortunate relationship. It is best that you are aware that I am a member of the College Council, which can overrule even decisions of the Principal. Consequently it will be pleasanter and easier for you if you make no attempt to approach Elizabeth and undermine her resolve. I shall have no compunction about informing the Council if you do. Despite your difficulties with honesty, you ought to be mature enough to recognise without my assistance that allowing your ambivalent tendencies play is jeopardising your own career as much as Elizabeth's. Bear this in mind; and realise that I do you a great favour in giving you the opportunity to improve your attitude. No college is happy about your kind of disruption.

Maud Stace

A cool woman, Maud Stace. I had no equipment to deal with such a letter, even less than to accept Libby's companion-piece, the expected, edged with endearments, larded with apologies, a neat brush-off. Mrs Stace had a vast pull even on me; I dreaded public ignominy, hadn't a shadow of the courage to face expulsion. Libby was petrified before her, incapable of decision outside her mother's explicit approval. The idyll was bound to collapse.

By Sunday everyone was back in college. I was on wire. I saw Libby at tea, froze a smile and nodded; she looked away. She was deep in animated discussion with Veronica and a half-dozen others. I swallowed a bowl of soup at one of the far tables with the feel of eyes on me and beat it through the kitchen up the narrow corkscrew stairs of D-Wing. At the top of the stairwell I met Cleo coming down. She must have noticed my panic; she stopped and said, gently, 'They all know.'

'What?'

'Everything.'

'Everything?'

'That Libby's mother threw you out and that Libby's decided to drop you.'

'Oh.' Tears of rage welling in my throat.

'They're very self-righteous,' she said.

'Libby told them?'

'Just Veronica and Sheila Grounds first, but they told Priscilla—and now everyone seems to know.'

'Jesus.'

'I tried to defend you but they don't really listen. They just talk about protecting Libby.'

'This is going to be awful.'

'Yes. They're holding meetings and working themselves into a fever. They're even talking about getting the Student Exec. to inform Dr Heath and have you disciplined—or that's how they put it.'

I groaned.

'But I don't think the Seniors'll pay much attention. The freshers just feel Libby's been led astray and needs their help to save her. They don't think about you at all really, as a real person. But they'll calm down after a while—there are other things to be interested in.'

'But it's not true, Jesus, Cleo ...' I stammered, too angry to speak. She grasped my hand warmly and said she'd do her best to talk them out of public action. I turned up the corridor, vision tear-stained, mind appalled.

I was emerging as the villain, the deftly publicised ring-leader, as if there was some sort of gang whose recruits, before contact with me, had been normal and natural people. The Craig Scare. The entire fresher-population devoted itself to Libby's virtue—all except Cleo. They got together to discuss the problem and decide on a line of action—a regular Society for the Prevention. From Cleo I learned now and again of their plans. They were preparing to approach the Principal and ask her to deal with me officially, whatever that might mean. Day after day I lived with the tension of waiting for a summons from her.

To walk out of my room and down the corridors was a continual ordeal. They looked away when I passed or hurried by with a look of contempt and disgust. A known lesbian. I was treated as someone utterly different from anyone else, who was setting out to drag others after her. Sheila Grounds cornered me in the College Library one afternoon and explained that the anti-Craig measures were entirely for my own good; too bad that I had made this shocking blunder of finding women attractive since I denied myself the overwhelming richness (and cleanliness to boot) of the Platonic friendship. I felt driven into a corner and couldn't argue.

I decided to go and ask Libby what had happened. There was light under the door but no sound. I went in. Libby was reading at the desk, Sheila sat in the armchair smoking and Veronica was sprawled out on the bed.

'Oh,' I said.

Libby smirked. 'What can we do for you?'

'Just came to say hello.'

'Hello', she said.

Veronica smiled slightly and Sheila looked stern.

'I'd like to talk to you, Libby,' I managed to stammer.

'Fire away,' she said pleasantly.

I knew they knew I could say nothing in front of them all, but they leaned back, relaxing ostentatiously. I could do nothing but beat a retreat, blushing and confused.

Whenever I went down to D-Wing there were doors open onto the corridor, and people glancing casually up from their work to note my arrival. Stealthily as I might approach, one or more of the self-appointed guards would appear within seconds to keep the encounter respectable, no doubt to protect Libby from herself as well as me. Whatever the motive, I was effectively isolated from her. Libby had capitulated to the freshers and they drank in her penitence.

When we had first acknowledged the affair and decided to enjoy it, she was unabashed, unafraid, ready for any amount of hostile chatter. I was as shit-scared as ever of the probing eyes and the darting tongues between greased lips, fear which she had tossed aside as my persecution-complex. She made a parade of it, tenderly grasping my hand in the caf or playing footsies in the college dining-room. Cold sweat. At least Julia had understood the proprieties. Libby simply refused to hide what she felt delighted about, refused to be intimidated by the possibility of judgement. If I was still in bed with her at ten in the morning she'd invite the casual caller in and discuss the last lecture on the Spanish Inquisition, smiling the while a consciously naughty smile. To my wan requests for a bit more secrecy she asked, with a faultless emotional logic, how I could possibly want to hide such a great love. She was unashamed, I said I was unashamed, so what was there to hide? What could they do to us? Free country or not, what they could do to us was never doubtful in my mind, and Mrs Stace's letter did tend to prove my point. It was not without fury that I realised Libby had slipped out the back way and left me alone to take the rap. Her bodyguard constantly insured her against confrontation with my end of what had happened. Knowing her to be strong and normally self-determining, I was forced to admit that their protective function was exercised with her total approval—perhaps instigation.

At meals she sat away from me, with Sheila and Priscilla Slinn or Veronica. I was aware of her timetable, her usual movements, and came down each day hoping to catch her alone. She always filled her table fast while I collected my grub from the kitchen. I was angry as they heaved the sausages out of the stainless steel vats. I sat alone. She would watch me out of the corner of her face and pretend to her companions that this coy observation was a joke. She laughed too much, too hard, jabbing it into me. I felt weak and contemptible; could think of no action which would affirm my dubious dignity. I was glad when Julia or Emma turned up, since they saved me the shame of eating my meal in silence, either alone or surrounded by senior med-students for whom I was an inferior whether they knew the scandal or not, and who bored me thoroughly with their conversational compound of corpse-dissection and males.

I couldn't grasp the change; I imagined love to be capable of survival, to be something bigger than Mrs Stace. I expected Libby to obey her enraged mother and break with me, but I failed to understand how she could square this with herself—unless the whole affair had been shallow deceptions. I floundered in the morass of alternative explanations. I remembered, or thought I did, that there had been a total commitment—Libby had even used those words. 'Let's have a total relationship,' she'd said blithely. I remembered that we had been amazingly happy in the last weeks. I remembered myself as a bombshell of energy, running sure-footed on the stairs, walking with such vigour that I felt tall. I seemed to remember nakedness with pleasure rather than shame, seemed to recall the most extraordinary

93

feeling of strength and tenderness combined. Most puzzling, I remembered it all as incontestably mutual. It had been as final, I believed, as such things could be. She had planned to take me to her summer paradise, surfing and lazing with her brother Geoff; she had wanted to share her delights with me and, naïvely, regretted that one of us was not a man so we could marry. Marriages, I was certain, were often built on less. Evidently, then, Libby had changed her mind, 'woken up to herself' in the freshers' scheme of thinking. Which made delusory nonsense of the idyllic memories. Thoroughly implausible; but staring me in the face.

Or had Libby gone down fighting? Accepted her mother's authority because she had to, and sealed herself off from me because any alternative would be agonising? Better grow away than wade back into the guilt-swamp. This was, to me, much more probable—and certainly it made less of a fool of me. But why, then, did she have to draw support from the freshers, why did she turn to them for approval? Interpretation, deductions, counter-arguments revolved for hours at a time in my fuzzed brain and refused to submit to syllogistic analysis. I dedicated myself to the dubious pursuit of finding out exactly what had happened in Libby's mind, and why. Libby was less than co-operative, even on those rare occasions when I managed to corner her alone.

'It's all over then?'

She nodded, tight-lipped.

'You want to have nothing to do with me?'

'Easier.'

'Then what happened with us meant nothing to you?'

'There's no point in talking about it. It's just easier if we don't see each other at all.'

'And you don't miss me, eh?'

'No,' she said with the trace of a smirk.

'I miss you,' I blurted out.

'Don't tell me your troubles.' A catch-phrase which she used often, always as a conversation-stopper.

'Look Libby, I have to know. This indifference—it's not just a defence?'

'No.'

But I found it hard to believe her.

Sin seeped back into my thought-streams. Mrs Stace held me responsible, the college held me responsible. The offence was clearly and generally recognised and reckoned to be serious. I was the common denominator of the scandals, the obvious candidate for blame. Briefly, in the halcyon days, I had broken with that terminology, buttressed by Libby's reciprocal assurance and apparently greater willingness to be honest about herself. The carpet whipped out,

I spreadeagled amongst my regrets. If it hadn't been for me, Libby would still be able to regard herself as normal and untainted. Now, even her affection for Veronica was being spread about with fierce innuendo. Libby had been discovered by Sheila in Veronica's bed; they had stressed the extreme chill of the evening but evidently not allayed Sheila's distressing suspicions—which were communicated through Priscilla Slinn to the rest of the college. I was the source of the disease.

'The way I talk,' Cleo told me, 'they're wondering if you've been at me, too.'

'I hope you put them right.'

'I don't say too much,' she said. 'This place is like Salem.'

I half-woke from a dream I could not remember, to find myself paralysed from head to foot. I could scarcely breathe and knew I had to rouse myself. Panic and darkness. I was disappearing back into sleep, into terrible danger. I tried to move my arm. Nothing. I must sit up. But my body did not respond. I wanted to scream. No sound came. Sleep came washing up to my stiff body in threatening waves. This'll go on forever. The end, maybe. I fought to clench my fist, but the fingers stayed immobile, rigid. I tried to mouth the word help; not even a squeak. The panic redoubled, my throat constricting and refusing to breathe. One finger. With a superhuman effort I bent one little finger into my palm, then another. The sleep kept coming at me. Help, I whispered. I jerked my hand off the sheet with the kind of effort it takes to lift a sack of flour, and kicked the blankets back with my feet. Alive, I struggled up on one elbow and reached out for the light, my eyes and head heavy as if I'd been doped. The light dazzled me, which seemed to help. I shuddered and shook my head. I gazed at the clock on the desk. Must've been asleep for an hour or so. The college was deathly quiet. I gazed and gazed, and finally got up to make some coffee. The heavy drowsiness was slowly retreating.

There were lines of light under a few doors, but absolutely no-one I could go to and sit with for a while. I sat alone, afraid to lie down in case I fell asleep again. I picked up book after book and flipped the pages without attention. I thought of writing something—a letter, a poem, but didn't even begin. A truck roared in the distance, stopped, then wound up through its gears again, growling. I thought of going for a walk but felt no energy. The clock ticked relentlessly.

I could neither sleep nor do anything else. My mind meandered on, thinking about Libby and the sleeping women who despised me. I tried to remember what dream I'd been having and found only a blank. There was no memory before the moment when I had become aware of my rigid body. I must be utterly petrified of something, I thought. Paralysis, powerlessness. And that was probably the way I felt all the time, though I didn't feel it so badly when I was awake.

Have I, perhaps, done evil? Even Julia thought that way, and she'd been involved. Cleo was noncommittal, but was herself taking a path which would avoid any recurrence of her childhood experience. Mrs Stace had warned Libby that I belonged to the 'ambivalent sex', shady customers who might not be able to help themselves, and, for this reason alone, should be more strenuously avoided. Maureen the moral leper. There wasn't much to choose between disease and depravity, though it was easier to live with the vagrant hope of reform than with the ignominy of being a helpless defective. Sometimes I cherished a residual defiance, believing angrily that neither of these images was my own; more often they existed in my mind with a life of their own.

In Yeats I found a poem which gave me a little sense of solidarity.

How in the name of heaven can I escape
That defiling and disfigured shape
The mirror of malicious eyes
Casts upon my eyes until at last
I think that shape must be my shape?
And what's the good of an escape
If honour find me in the wintry blast? ...

I am content to follow to its source
Every event in action or in thought;
Measure the lot; forgive myself the lot!
When such as I cast out remorse
So great a sweetness flows into the breast
We must laugh and we must sing,
We are blest by everything,
Everything we look upon is blest.

I read the poem again and again. That shape is not my shape, even though they have nearly persuaded me that it is. Forgive myself the lot. Cast out remorse. Was it going to take me until I was sixty-seven or so? Still, my right to measure and judge for myself suddenly seemed reasonable, even if I couldn't do it. It might be a long time before I'd have the guts to define myself in contradiction to the hateful Craig image, weight of numbers as Cleo once put it; but I saw the way out, realised that it lay in a forgiving attitude to myself. I won't go under, I thought, if I can fight their disfigurement from my own embryonic sense of my innocence. A tangible distant hope. The everyday reality of hostility and judgement couldn't fail to come between me and an acceptance of myself. For while I kept silent, I was accepting the fresher view of myself. If I rejected it outright I'd be on my own.

Hard to stand alone. But no one to stand with. I try for Emma's support. Emma the complete humanist, the intelligent flexible thinker. And yet I wonder what she thinks of me in between the times I talk to her. There's something neutral, detached and, so, unconvincing about her. I desperately want acceptance entirely on my terms—it isn't to be had; if I can't generate it myself I won't get it at all. This is a burden I cannot, easily, carry. My friends are in books. Using the poets for my maps. Shakespeare's sonnets, Yeats's forgiving impulse and Blake's marriage of heaven and hell: *Chains are the cunning of weak and tame minds which have the power to resist energy. Energy is eternal Delight ... Those who restrain desire, do so because theirs is weak enough to be restrained ... Good is the passive that obeys reason. Evil is the active springing from energy.* I am grateful to these three men. They make it possible to dream of the daring premise that my natural impulses are inviolable, unimpeachable.

Whatever halting confidence I could gather transformed itself into fury against the rigid righteous women of the college and contempt for safe-play Libby Stace. I considered leaving, seeking out Erif in Carlton and finding myself a private whole place to live in. But I struck flint. I would not allow any of these women the triumph of having made it too hot for Maureen Craig. I stayed on, stewing between anger and fear.

Finally I found Libby alone one afternoon, and inexplicably vulnerable. Nothing to lose anyway.

'What's the matter?' I asked, feigning a formal curiosity.

'Oh nothing much ...' I noticed her voice was dry and rasping as if she were on the point of tears. 'Oh you know,' she went on dryly, 'a lot of work, didn't do so well in my last essay.'

'Suffering must be good for the work,' I said. 'I got a really good first for my Wordsworth job.'

She visibly repressed her anger at my unfair tack and managed to say, 'Oh good.'

'You haven't got much to be sorry about, though, have you Lib? Stacks of friends, a whole army of supporters; people looking after you. Real concern ... No-one's talking about you every time you turn around.'

'No.'

'Well count your blessings, kid. Essays don't make anybody happy, do they? You've got it all over somebody like me, you know. You've got an unerring knack for survival. Never get too far in, do you?'

'Stop. Please.'

'Stop what? I'm only congratulating you on your quite fantastic—in the true sense of the word—your fantastic ability to avoid anything that's a bit nasty.'

'Stop it.'

'Why should I, for Christ's sake? I've been trying to talk to you for weeks. All the time you've been hiding behind these clap-witted friends of yours. I'm surprised you haven't called one or two in this afternoon.'

'That's crap.'

'Crap is it? I needed you Libby, and you sealed yourself off to save your skin.'

'So would you have if you'd been in my position.'

'Maybe—don't think I'm blaming you for going along with your mother. Most people do. And anyway, she had the whip-hand. She could've made it too hot for me.'

'What do you mean?'

'Oh she wrote to me. Told me to lay off or else.'

'Or else what?'

'Council action. Expulsion I imagine.'

'She didn't tell me this.'

'Really?' I said with a mock-rise of the eyebrows. 'Didn't she now? She's been playing quite a game, hasn't she?'

Libby looked angry but said nothing more.

'That's beside the point—we did have to give in to your good old Mum, I think. What we didn't have to do was to broadcast the news through the college and sponsor a tiny club for the isolation and ostracism of M. Craig.'

'I only told Veronica.'

'Such a discreet young lady, too. How decorous of you both.'

'Maureen I didn't think ...'

'Exactly,' I cut in—her style—'You didn't bloody well think. That, I would say, is the crux of the matter. All your bullshit about love and concern—even marriage you used to talk about ... Concerned people do think.'

'Not that many people know.'

'Who the hell are you trying to kid? You can tell by their lean and hungry looks even when you don't know for sure. But your oafish mate Grounds has been lecturing me, you see, so I'm not labouring under any false sense of security.'

'Is it that bad?' she asked, showing signs of relenting.

'Worse,' said I, showing none. 'It's purgatorial. You can give yourself top marks for getting out of it—it's something no-one should have to live through.'

'Maureen, I'm very sorry about this.'

'Too bloody late to be sorry. Being sorry doesn't change anything. I should never have got mixed up with you—anyone who trusted you would have to be a half-wit ...'

'Go away,' she whined, sobbing into her pillow. I made for the door, teeth clenched.

'Maureen,' she muttered, barely audible, 'please don't go like this. Please sit down for a minute. I am sorry.'

And despite the bravado I am still soft Craig. I sat down in the armchair.

'Sit here, beside me.'

I went to her. She threw her arms around me weeping bitterly into my shoulder. I found myself stroking her hair, gently, slowly, compassionately—with all the old deep-frozen tenderness.

Cripple Craig

Summer came with thunder and sticky rain. Coming out of the bungalow at my parents' house again, I disturbed the hydrangeas and covered my white shirt with their load of raindrops. Oppressive mornings—I slept through them and stood outside when the storm broke, cooling through as the shower fell, one sheet humming across the back lawn.

Ken, still the current scapegoat, provided a basis for truce-like solidarity between the rest of us—even Mother and Father went into fits of co-operation. And Mother, desperately aware that Ken's car-pinching mates were riding for the fall, was too bothered about the forthcoming criminal record to stir with me. She welcomed me, threw a birthday party, set me up in the bungalow and never said a word about rent.

Ken had got himself a sheath-knife, evil-looking blade in slick black leather.

'Watch out, sharpies,' he murmured and grinned at me.

'I just hope you don't make yourself into bad news this Christmas,' I said to him.

Ken slid it out and, flicking it handle first, pegged it into the wall across the room. 'No worries, sis. I'll be all right now.'

'Shit, boy. Take care.'

But I didn't tell the parents who might've managed to get it off him. He would've bought another.

That cavalier parting of Libby's. 'We'll start again some time if we feel like it—can't see you anyway because of Mother. Have a good summer ...'. Fuck her, I say to myself, but can't see how. One could at least be grateful that the strain's off—I'm sure she is. Indeed, how much more could either of us have taken of reckless passion and superguilt in lock-progression? One day: dammit I want you. The next: what about Mother? What about the Principal? What if it's... sin? A destructive vacillation, eating away all the warmth between us. Pasternak gave me a myth, Zhivago the loser thrown in and out of a blighted passion. *You fling your dress from you As the coppice flings away its leaves. In a dressing gown with a silk tassel You fall into my arms. You are the good gift of the road to destruction When life is more sickening than disease And boldness the root of beauty. This is what draws us together.*

The Zhivago poems danced in my head, lending me an adaptable tragedy, making heroic sense of that hectic springtime and this empty summer. Zhivago went with me to Junee, an ambiguous solace through the hot dusty days.

The trains again: those crowded Christmas runs without an instant to think twice, and Junee baking under the sun at the other end. Full of sharp bird cries and the seagull sound of children at the pool. Still evenings with the sunset colours lingering and the low hills delicately, elegantly outlined in the slow-fade dusk.

'Students, you see, can work with the best of them,' I pointed out to Edith who, as tart as ever, pursed her lips and informed me that I was the exception that proves the rule. I refrained from mentioning the flaw in that conception of the proverb and bathed gently in the false glory. Edith was surprised that Erif, too, proved the rule when she showed up on our crew. We must have established it solid by the end of the summer.

The Bentleigh house was as quiet as a tomb after the parents left for their summer holiday. Granny's slippers shuffled briefly and rarely from room to room, or out to the rocking-chair where she'd watch the traffic and crowds pass and pass on the road. She'd had that chair maybe fifty years; one of its rockers had split off at the back but the cane webbing was still solid, worn and shiny the way it had always been while I was around. I cooked her meals, shifted her chair to sun or shade, changed her sheets when she wet them through, fixed up the TV when the frames rolled or the snow came on. She seemed scarcely to notice if it gave out—or, more likely, it was her old determination not to give anybody any trouble, to bear in silence what she couldn't change herself. During my thirty-hour absences on each Junee trip I left her food and hoped she would manage. And always, when I got to Bentleigh station, I'd start to run the half-mile back, always suddenly scared that she'd pitched down the back steps or tripped over a cat, scared that I'd find her cut and helpless, or—just a half-thought—dead.

New Year's Eve in Junee. The crew were all expectant at the prospect of RSL festivities—with poker thrown in. At tea they came down in dressing-gowns, hair in rollers, faces sparkling.

'Well,' I said to Erif. 'We might as well go along.'

She smirked. 'Could be fun. Have a dance with a few local hoods.'

'Yeah.'

Short of glamorous, but neat withal, we arrived in the wake of the gorgeous Buffet Car crew. Even old Edith had got herself up in a tastefully quiet floral and applied a solid coat of paint to her bitter wrinkles.

'Of course we're twenty-one.' Erif stood haughtily on her dignity as she addressed the RSL bouncer in bow-tie and tails, sweating visibly around the collar. We waited beside the aspidistra while he retired within to verify with Gertrude who, I never fathomed why, admitted that we weren't.

Junee seemed practically deserted, hot nightstreets between the unlit terraces, their wrought-iron balconies dim and lacy under old-style one-bulb streetlamps. 'Let's celebrate anyway.' But it sounded downright absurd in these dead streets.

'I think,' said Erif, 'a bottle of Passiona.'

We sat down on the stationyard fountain, more disillusioned than ever with the Returned Soldiers.

'Pass the bottle.'

The paint on the concrete frog was flaking and mouldering; the plaster nymph pirouetted with broken toes on the brink; a thin layer of green slime rotted in the pond. *However many rings of pain The night welds round me, The opposing pull is stronger, The passion to break away.*

'Going to make any resolutions?' Erif asked.

'Dunno. Could do with a few.'

'Yeah?'

'Well—only if the resolution guaranteed its own success.'

'Pass the bottle.'

'I'd like to do something big enough to wipe out all this fruitless strife I seem to get mixed up in.'

'I know,' she said gently. 'You have to just make up your mind not to let the small minds bugger you up.'

She knows, I thought.

At midnight the trains set up a howling of sirens from Junee's vast shunting-yard. Long steam blasts and whistle salutes—as if, in the faceless hot blackness, it was the trains themselves offering greeting.

Mind is constantly taxed with the puzzle of acquiring independence. Getting nowhere. The notion of going back to it next March is just as intolerable as the notion of doing anything else. 'I'm not sure I want to go on with the course,' I tell Erif.

'No?'

'This kind of life's easier on me—less strain.'

'Yes, but you got great results.'

'Well. Means I don't have to feel a failure if I give up. It's easier knowing I could get the degree if I wanted.'

'You'd get sick of waitressing on the railways.'

'Must be something else ...'

'Nothing as easy or free as being a student.'

'I suppose not.'

The opposing pull, anyway, is not stronger.

The parents returned, tanned and testy. The handbrake jerked on with the familiar tired screech; they got out of the car chattering towards the back steps; the phone rang.

Libby.

'Well hullo, how've you been?' Sounding cheery.

'Oh fine thanks, just got back from Torquay ...'

'Hang on.'

'Great surf. And lovely brother down there too ...'

'Hullo, Ma.' Grinning broadly at Mother.

'Who's that, Maureen?'

'Lib.'

'... had fantastic weather and ...'

'Just a sec, Mother, I'll get her to ring back.'

'... and anyway Maureen how's the railways?'

'Oh really good. Got the same crew as last year and Erif's joined our crew. Always get a swim in the pool. And the trips aren't so bad—getting easier now Christmas is over.'

'... yeah. Christmas was really great—spent the day on the beach and Mother did a barbecue—even got a bit boozed, Geoff and me, and went ...'

'Hang on.'

'You could have made the beds some time this last three weeks, Maureen.'

'Sorry, Mum. Didn't think you'd be back till tomorrow.'

'... whatever's going on Maureen?'

'Oh the family's just this minute arrived from Queensland.'

'... sounds like bedlam ...'

'Is. Could you ring back in a couple of hours? When they've settled down?'

'... no—I've got to get back home. Some other time.'

'I'm sure I said today in that card,' Mother grumbled.

'What card?'

'Oh, Maureen!'

'OK, Libby, you know when I'll be here.'

'... sure. I got your trip table ...'

'OK. Hope you're feeling good.'

'Never better. I'll ring again. Bye.'

Click. *Take your hand off my breast We are high tension cables. Look out, or unawares We will again be thrown together.* Some hope.

Mother wasn't looking pleased.

I replaced the receiver and headed for the kettle. Must make amends for this terrible beginning.

'Everyone for tea?'

'Too right,' said Dad, passing by with a suitcase or two.

'Here Mother, let me just throw these beds together while the kettle's boiling. I really thought it was tomorrow.'

'I'm sure I said today in that card. I might've even said yesterday.'

'What card?'

'From Kiama.'
'Haven't got it yet.'
'Oh.'

'I'm going to meet Steve.' Erif looked exuberant.
'Yeah?'
'In Rockhampton.'
'Jesus. When?'
'Next week.'
'No kidding?'
'Yes. We're going to hitch back through Mount Isa and Alice Springs.'
'Sounds great.'
Erif grinned.
'Tell you what though—have you got anyone to take your room?'
'Would you like to?'
'Not sure, but things look a little torrid at home. We're spoiling for another battle.'
'Well you're welcome.'

We get up at two and start work when the train pulls into Junee and the New South Wales girls get off. It's quiet the first hours, before Wagga, a few dazed passengers hunched over coffee. The conductors sit around yarning and swapping stories with the Buffet crew. You get your meal in the dark—too hectic, after five, for anyone to have a break. One morning, reeling back after breakfast, I stop dead at the window and watch the dawn growing in the landscape as it rushes by.

Black sky still starry up top, but the east already streaked with pink and violet, intense red just where the sun will come. A round hill rises out of the plain, a crescent-shaped waterhole lying in perfect symmetry at the base of its northern slope. Three gum trees stand black across the water, and throw their impassive reflections into the billabong, where the red runs like dye into pools of darkness and the water's own dawn-green. The hill rises up black. For an instant, this waterhole freezes in its perfection; the train thunders close behind the hill; night returns.

Until, as January passes by, the nights grow longer. One morning it is gone.

Mother had been scowling at me on and off since I had arrived back from Junee that morning. When Father was settled in to watch *Homicide*, she came out to the kitchen and stood over me.

'It's this Stace girl now, is it?' she asked icily.
'That's over,' I replied wearily. 'Everything's over.'

'Why did you hide it, Maureen?'

'What would have been the point in telling you? You were better off not knowing.'

'You've always hidden things from me.'

'Yeah.'

'Why?'

'Mother, I'm sick of it. I'm sick of your worries. I've got my own.'

'Obviously. I imagine they're all involved. That Erif girl and Emma what's-her-name? Brightfort.'

'Bullshit.'

'Well, what am I supposed to think?'

'I don't give a shit what you think. Mind your own business.'

She frowned with an air of doing her disagreeable duty. 'I'm going to have to do something about it this time—it's getting serious.'

'There's nothing you can do. The college knows and so do all the mothers.'

'Maureen,' she gasped. 'And what about Mrs Stace?'

'Mrs Stace threw me out last August. If you want to know. She'd hang up on you.'

'She WHAT!'

'You'd've done the same.'

'Oh Maureen, I don't know how you can bear the shame.'

'Neither do I. So skip it.'

When I got out to the bungalow, pleased at this one having passed off in such a tired low key, I found letters on the floor and the cupboard in a shambles. She's been through this ... Only a few of Libby's letters were there at all—the rest ... *I'm ready to smash everything to splinters. And bring them to their knees.*

She was still in the kitchen, fiddling with the dishes. I strode hard across the checked floor, grabbed her shoulder and turned her towards me, brutally shaking her small unhappy body. Through clenched teeth:

'You've read my letters.'

'I had to know.' Lamely, breaking free.

'And you've still got some.'

'Don't come near me, Maureen. You're going mad. Keep back.' She spoke quickly, in panic.

'Get me those letters. Now.'

'I will not.'

'Get them.'

'I may need the evidence.'

I lunged, she dodged, screaming, 'Joe. Joe. Help. Help.' Father made no response as she fled down the back steps. Right. She's in the garden. I'll find the bloody things. I went through her papers, her drawers, all her things. Nowhere. And suddenly remembered the rice tin where she used to hide money back in Cobb Swamp—there were the letters, stuffed in amongst the sago.

The Gunning Street place. Iron picket fence, black wrought-iron balcony above; rough-cast walls painted with light purple wash. Under the downstairs window stood a long iron earth-bed on legs, which Erif had planted with red geraniums and which Sonny Stoop, the landlord, always called the Garden. Out the back, the stony strip of earth was stacked with beer bottles. Except for a crab-apple struggling out of the ash-heap and a few stalks of rank grass, the backyard was bare.

Sonny welcomed me with an enthusiasm I didn't understand, a friendliness which was nevertheless a relief. He dashed down the corridor to put the kettle on; I looked around. A stiff pink mattress lay on the low iron bed-frame. Erif had painted the whole place white except for the high puce ceiling and the firegrate. The window opened onto the street with its fine trees. I sat on the edge of the mattress and waited, not bold enough to follow Sonny out to the kitchen, though a part of my mind was telling me that the natural course of action would be to wander nonchalantly into the living-room and look about. I just sat.

Sonny was short and slight, close on forty; his small frame and scored face gave him the look of a gnome. He squinted sideways behind his glasses and he spoke from only part of his mouth, usually the corner, emphasising his oddity. He sat down close beside me and began explaining the mechanics of this community in his reedy measured voice.

'I hope you'll like being with us, even if it *is* only for three weeks. We all put in a pound for food—you'll eat with us. We share all the work—Erif's been on my team so I hope you'll join up with me. Max and Martin, the incredible brothers O'Hearn, are the other team. Glad we've got a girl. We were going to miss Mother when she went.'

I laughed politely.

'One team cooks for the week and the other cleans up—then we swap. The object of the cooking team is to produce a cordon bleu meal.'

'Oh.'

'This means using everything in the kitchen, giving the other team plenty of scope for cleaning.'

'Is there much to use?'

'Heaps of stuff. Come and look.'

He paused in the living-room and pointed to the long trestle-table right down one wall. 'That's the banqueting table.'

The kitchen was pretty greasy and was in fact equipped with pots, pans and dishes of every conceivable shape, size and origin. Sonny remarked that they really needed a mother to keep them in line and rinsed a couple of mugs under the tap.

'We bring the hot water in from the bathroom heater. I ripped a sink-heater out of one of those houses they're wrecking down in Rathdowne Street but no-one knows how to put it in.'

I feared Sonny might think my attitude critical, so smiled as much as I could and asked if there was anything I could do.

'Not a thing—our team's cooking this week, so we'll have to get Max into this mess.'

Sonny poured out the tea. 'I live in the front room upstairs,' he went on. 'It's the biggest—I've been here longest. We all share the rent equally. Martin has the suite in the East Wing and Max's got the Hardboard Cell at the top of the stairs. Everyone's happy with quarters at the moment.' Sonny beamed. 'I'll call you later if you'd like to help with dinner.'

I made up the bed, threw my clothes into the sawn-off bottom drawer of an old wardrobe, painted bright white. The sun disappeared behind the bottle-yard across Gunning Street.

Max came in swinging a crash-helmet by the strap, threw it and his goggles on the sofa and collapsed.

'Do you have a motor-bike?' I asked him.

'Scooter. Shit heap. Had a blow-out up in Ringwood. Tyres are rotting, the engine'll blow up any day. And there's something wrong with the clutch.'

'Sounds bad.'

'Yeah.'

He lapsed into silence. A tall thin man with a soft boyish face and a discordant hook-nose. He ran a hand through his fair hair, his eyes fixed on the wall somewhere. I could think of nothing to say and, being the mother they wanted, went out to make him some tea.

'What do you do, Max?'

'Oh nothing mostly. I'm supposed to be studying architecture but I usually fail. It's part-time teaching this year. Bugger it.

'Teaching?'

'They'll probably give me maths or something. I haven't got a clue. They take anyone, though—and the money's not too bad.'

Dinner was set out on the banqueting trestle along with several bottles of Fosters. Martin—Max described him as the brains of the family—wandered in after a Greek lecture and congratulated Sonny on his remarkable use of kitchen resources.

'You're studying Greek?' I asked tentatively.

'That's only a side-line,' Max said.

'Oh?'

'Yes. I'm an engineer, really—lecturing at Monash. Y'need something more to broaden the old mind, so I'm doing a bit of Greek and

Ancient History.' Martin spoke casually, as if any engineer might do as much, and Max raised his eyebrows as if to say: you see what I mean.

'I suppose you like a beer, eh?' said Sonny, winking.

'Oh, love it,' I replied, wondering how I'd choke it down, but deciding it was a taste badly in need of acquisition. Could hardly admit to expensive feminine tastes. I tossed down a few glasses, drinking with a mouth full of food to minimise the taste. Bitter bloody stuff.

'Oh no more.' Feeble as Sonny offered to fill it again. 'Don't drink much, you know.'

'You'll get the hang of it,' he said, pouring a half-glass and winking again. 'Maureen's got a guitar you know, Max.'

'Mmm.' His eyes came alive. 'What sort?'

'Wouldn't know. Looks like somebody knocked it together in a back shed. Sounds all right though.'

'Mine's a bloody ripper. Spanish. Sounds terrific. Only trouble is you can't tune the bastard. Got pegs like a violin. Wooden. Always slipping out to buggery.' Max closed back into total silence.

I got a letter from Libby. Darling, it said, I'll be in town Tue. and Fri. Can you sort out that crazy roster of yours and ring me if you'll be accessible.

Look out.

So Libby paid a visit; the first since we parted for the holidays. Desired and dreaded. We were slow, restrained, talked of her summer, my trains, Menzies out at last, Max's beautiful guitar—desultory and disconnected.

Years will pass, you will marry. You will forget these unsettled ways.

But she turns, slim in blue, and says: 'I like you very much, you know.'

'Yeah. Me too. Still.'

'May I come again?'

'If you like—yes, do.'

'I want to look after you, Maureen. See you through. I'll come if you need me.'

'I'd like to see more of you.'

And I cannot draw the frontier.

The dining-room was always dim; its one window looked down the back yard between the walls of the East Wing and the next house in the terrace. The flies droned there at night when the light came on, having clung, sleepy, to the walls all day. As I came in Max was curled up on the sofa, a black gun pointed at some specific spot on the ceiling, steadied murderously across his left wrist. Absorbed by the dead-eye process of taking aim. He let out an imitation gun-shot roar and sent a volley of water at the wall. A big fly started off, stunned, and spiralled to the floor, buzzing dully.

'Got him!'

'Some shot.'

'Oh hullo, Maureen. Just getting me eye in.'

'Where'd you get it?'

'Confiscated.'

'You look done.'

'Brains beaten to a pulp.'

I made tea.

We both sat in silence for a half-hour until Max suggested, as one of us always did, 'What about a drink?'

'Lemon Tree?'

'Yeah. 's hot.'

A fringe pub, never the student scene, old guys down-and-out and shaky women. We laboured at openings.

'How's school?'

'Shithouse.'

Silence.

'What's the trouble?'

'Fuckin' kids.'

Silence.

''nother drink?'

'Yeah. Get some chips, eh?'

'OK.'

Silence. Two pairs of grey eyes staring out, or across tin tables, or into the beer.

'Better get back and see about some tea, eh?'

'Guess so. Sonny and you are cooking. I'll get a bottle.'

'Great.'

Libby showed up again, right on time.

'Glad to see you,' I said, embracing her, surprised to find her stiff and unresponsive. 'What's the matter?'

'Oh nothing.'

'Tea?'

'Yeah.'

High tension cables.

'Are you going back to college, then?' I asked her.

'Me? Yes. I am.'

'I thought I might too.'

'Mmm.'

'Aren't you pleased?'

'Doesn't matter to me.' It's changed again.

'No?'

'Maureen, I can't. I can't help it. I can't help you. So don't come back because of me.'

'But ... last week ...'

'I'm sorry. Must've been lonely I guess ... I didn't mean that.'

'You didn't.' Flat as a tack, not even a question.

'I was talking to Emma yesterday. She said she agrees—that everyone has to stand on their own feet.'

'You suggesting I don't?'

'I don't know. And I don't care either.'

'Shit, Libby, why these visits then? I didn't ask you to come.'

'Had to come today. Had to tell you.'

'I don't understand how come you change your mind all the time.'

'That's too bad.' Then, distinctly. 'I hate cripples, Maureen. And that's what you are. A cripple.'

Way below the belt. I doubled up inside. Groaned. Beat it, I wanted to say. BEAT IT. GET THE HELL OUT OF HERE. But I sat, silent until she got up and started out. Be brave, Craig. Sit here and just say gentle goodbyes. I got up, opened the door, mock-gallant, ushered her out. Don't spit, Craig, don't show a thing. Don't even speak.

'Bye Lib,' I said suddenly, 'See you back at the University—if I'm still here.'

Max was gloomy as usual and I gloomier than ever. Our afternoon drink deteriorated into rare monosyllabic exchange, until Harold Holt gave us something to talk about. Max, who'd been to a small Catholic college in the eastern suburbs, seemed indifferent to the increase in the Vietnam contingent.

'Somebody's got to fight them,' he said.

'You reckon?'

'Well I don't know much about it, Maureen. But it's them or us, isn't it?'

'You think so?'

'Well they're moving. Taking over Asia.'

'Who, for Christsake?'

'Oh. The Chinese, I suppose.'

'But there aren't any Chinese in Vietnam.'

'There must be.'

'No. The Viet Cong are Vietnamese—southerners at that.'

'You must be joking.'

'No fear. And they haven't even got Chinese guns. They capture most of their stuff off the Americans—and shoot it back.'

'Fuck me. I never read any of that.'

'It's not the kind of thing they put on the front page.'

'Doesn't sound right, though, does it? Spending all that money if there isn't a real threat.'

Our drinking-sessions became more frequent and, at last, we had something to talk about, to fill our shy inept silences.

In which Maureen begins to see

Libby remains just around the bend in any thought-stream, comes dancing in boxer-like, singing Cripple Craig and grinning. I dodge and swing back into the French Revolution. But I cannot keep her from skipping across the barricaded streets, intruding a presence in whatever heroic world I've slipped into. I'm fighting with shoddy equipment, an alarm clock chiefly with which I get myself off the college scene each morning before she comes on it; a reckless and boring cultivation of innumerable companions—anyone, in fact, who has no truck with the Stace Connection; and (this might work) the campaign to join the University. About time. I can be grateful that someone has forced me into this—since, once I am sitting in the caf amongst people who are unobsessed, some of them, with either passing or getting a man, I begin to feel sorry for those cribbed women back in college, with all the old secure familiar faces and conversations.

At Easter Cleo invited me to the Evangelical Assembly in the mountains. College was empty except for the librarian and sundry trapped unwilling helpers. Jesus Creek could hardly be less entertaining.

'Please don't swear, though', Cleo whispered as we drove up from the station. One of the preachers had been good enough to collect me.

'Blood oath,' I breathed back.

Up at the Creek we drew into the Methodist Camp, neat bunk-houses built under the pines and a big meeting-house and cook-room.

'Bloody nice,' I told Cleo in an undertone. 'This is just the Metho camp, then?'

'Sssh. Yes. All the camps meet down the hill in the big tent.' She paused. 'Those two,' Cleo remarked, 'are lesbians.'

'In a Methodist prayer-camp.'

'Sssh. Yes, they've lived together for years, sort of married.'

'But Jesus, what do the religious cohorts think of it?'

'If they know, they pretend not to. Sheila and Marj don't give them anything obvious—so they can refrain from noticing.'

'I shoulda been a Metho.'

'You'd never be able to be that discreet.'

I liked Cleo's ease with the subject, her casual neutrality.

We walked down the hill for the evening meeting; the mountains folded away in the quiet April light.

'Do we have to go?' I asked her, loath to leave the evening for a prayer-meeting.

'Yes. We should.'

'We wouldn't be missed.'

'Our own people would notice.'

'OK.'

We circled the mighty tabernacle and stood at the back leaning against the outer boom. Thousands of heads bowed in prayer as the nasal preacher-in-black thanked the Lord for bringing us together and blessing our meeting with clear skies and sunny hearts. I looked sideways at Cleo, sunburnt and childlike, her head bent with the rest.

> *He owns the cattle on a thousand hills*
> *He owns the mountains and the stars and the rills*
> *He owns etc.*
>
> *And so I know he loves me ...*

Cleo was singing with gusto. I fingered the songsheets and wondered where all these maniacs, some of them stoutly middle-aged, got their simplicity. Voices beefing out chorus after chorus of stirring mindless nonsense. I saw Sheila and Marj standing together at the back, rapt along with the others, and wondered how they coped with sin.

Back in the Methodist meeting-hall, after coffee, the Camp Warden got up on the platform and asked if we wouldn't like to hear a few of our number give testimonials. All around me the faithful murmured yes, yes, and began to clap decorously.

'Well, if you'll all take a seat.'

'Too late to escape, I'm afraid,' Cleo whispered.

'Now who'll begin?'

Everyone was deathly quiet, heads lowered. For a minute a silence so profound that I could hear the pines outside, soughing in the lightest of winds.

The first came forward and launched his story—rampant fleshly sin, the Lord's messenger who awakened his sleeping conscience, the days and nights of stubborn resistance until the Lord in His Mercy just took over and flooded his sinful soul with His Light. 'We are all instruments of the Lord, if only we will open our sinful hearts to His Love and Guidance.'

'Amen,' said the warden.

'Amen,' chorused the eager crowd.

Others followed, flocking to the platform itching to spin their personal variations on this mesmerising theme of sin forgiven and weakness overcome. Finally, just on midnight, while my backside ached from its confinement on the wooden bench, the warden raised his white palm to stem the flood, and called on us to join him in prayer; thanking the Lord for the strengthening tales we had heard and for His Divine Guidance to our brethren in their sin and affliction.

The star-turn was Sunday's mass drive for converts; for this we had ringside seats. The evangelist rose, a dapper, grey-suited, open-collar figure, tall and lean, with a prominent Adam's apple. The tent hushed and the harangue began. An hour he went on, merciless with the unrepentant sinner, secure in the Lord. The tension mounted as he approached his master-stroke. 'YOU CAN BE SAVED NOW!' he bellowed. He had, he told us, gathered for the Lord numberless men and women at just such meetings. NOW IS THE HOUR, THE SPIRIT IS AMONGST US. FEEL HIM. FEEL HIM. BE LIT UP BY HIS COUNTENANCE. FEEL HIM. LET HIM RAISE YOU TO YOUR FEET. FEEL HIM. LET HIS OVERWHELMING POWER GUIDE YOU TO THIS PLATFORM. MAKE YOUR CONFESSION NOW. BE SAVED TODAY.

And they started moving; slowly at first, then streaming down the aisles. Recruited for the Lord as the preacher carried on ranting, demanding, cajoling, tidying the bait. A long line raising their arms in unison, the lucky, lucky Saved. Rejoice and Hallelujah.

'Cleo, it's madness.'

'Yes. I suppose it is.'

Libby came and Libby went. At first I was haughty and distant, though never hardliner enough to tell her: No. Don't come to my room. Not so much out of hope as out of kindness. I, at any rate, forgave. My impulse was one of yielding and loving (to her, always, helplessness); I was open, friendly. She came for advice, comfort, coffee. I gave it. When I was in the college, sitting at my desk between the white walls, my mind still wandered towards her; I still wondered if and when she might seek me out. Gradually, I had to put more and more effort, it seemed, into staying out of college whenever I could and staying in my own room while I was there.

The project to join the University had led me to get a part in student theatre. The performance was only a few weeks off when the cast and crew went up to a cheap old boarding-house in the mountains for a weekend rehearsal. I shared a room with Erif.

'Jesus, Erif, I don't know how I'll ever get my life in order.' We'd been drinking.

'Yes, it's hard. Hard even without the scandals and stuff you've been through.'

'Yeah. I feel so hopeless sometimes.'

'But you know if you don't like it, if it's no good for you—you can make it different if you give yourself a chance.'

'You reckon?'

'Steve used to be attracted to men. Right up to when we first got together. It got easier—but only slowly. And there's other people, too. A lot more than you'd think. A lot more than most people think because they're all hiding it from each other. You just have to give yourself a go. It's not that you can't stand men.'

'No. Just shy. Hopelessly. Steve's good—and Max. I like Max.'

'Just try to keep clear of it for a while—say a year or so. Things change. If you can let them.'

'Yeah,' I agreed, though I couldn't see how I could avoid the way I felt inside, or even why I should try to do this. I stared into space for a moment and decided to say it.

'You see I ... I really loved Libby—you know, at first, before her mother stopped her, we were really close, and happy, too. It wasn't the sort of thing that there was any need to steer clear of—in itself.'

'But there'll always be something to fuck it up, don't you think?'

'I guess so. It's hard to know. If I felt stronger, felt I could ... put up with the people who judge me ...'

'You know,' she said, 'there's a place I know where you can see a psychiatrist for free. It's a church clinic but they don't push Christian morals or anything. Steve went once—they were kind and friendly ... Maybe just to talk to someone—help you sort it all out a bit.'

'That's not a bad idea,' I said. 'It might do me some good.'

I was wary of Dr Sam Hudson, the small neat collar-and-tie psychiatrist.

'I haven't come here to get normal,' I told him the first time, a grain of truth in that. 'More to get independent of approval.'

'That's the main problem,' he agreed.

'I wouldn't mind if other people didn't mind.'

'Perhaps not. But they will mind. We must try to sort out why the other people make all the difference.'

'The disapproval isn't inside me. It's out there. Most of it.'

'You're sure?'

'Just about. It's hard to tell where it is when they get half-inside your own skull.'

'What do you mean?'

'Well. Guilt. I felt that for a long time.'

'Not now?'

'Yes. But less. Like with Libby I started to feel fine, just before her mother came into it. For a while I knew I was right. I felt good about it.'

'And now?'

'Well. I'm on my own. It's not as bad as last year. There's new people who don't know.'

'Would it upset you if they did?'

'It'd upset them, more like it. And then me, of course. Yeah. And it does feel bad wondering if they've found out and what they think and if they judge and whether they want to know me. Knowing people are like that—makes it a bit hard when you know you're hiding something. It feels like cheating when people like me, and even worse when they don't. And last year's freshers, they think I should be ashamed and they look at me a funny way.'

'Why do you think you're cheating when people like you?'

'I always think they wouldn't if they knew. People are all so narrow.'

'And you care what they think?'

'It's always there. I never forget how they see me; never forget for a minute about their labels and their interpretations. It's not as if I dwell on it morbidly. It just happens like that. Thoughts go through my head, and I'm imagining what Priscilla has told someone, and how she says it, or how my tutor would react. And the word, lesbian, I hate it.'

'Why?'

'It sounds horrible. And it's so ... total. As if it's my distinguishing feature, my definition. Maureen Craig ... oh, she's a lesbian. And it's always pushing in on me. One word and they think they know everything about me that they need to know.'

Hudson was a patient listener. He asked quiet, detached questions, never condemning, always allowing me the space to believe in myself.

I was in bed early one night reading, when Cleo came in.

'How are you, little Maureen?' she asked, perching on the bed and looking glum.

'Oh, bearing up. And you?'

'I don't know. All right, I suppose.' She looked questioning.

'Libby's hard,' I said. 'She keeps coming to see me, keeps being friendly and throwing her arms around me and then clears off laughing.'

'Tell her not to come then.'

'Some chance.'

'I saw you,' she said suddenly, 'from the roof, yesterday.'

'Yeah?'

'You were sitting at your desk, working, completely unaware.'

'Why didn't you yell out and say hello.'

'No. It was nice, seeing you like that. I didn't want to disturb you.'
I felt vaguely disappointed, vaguely pleased.

'And I had a dream about you, too.'

I smiled.

'You were in a play with Syd Anger, my English tutor, and you whirled in the middle of a stage, in a red dress, with your hair flying everywhere, saying sex, sex, sex.'

'I was *what!*'

She looked slightly apologetic.

'What a weird idea you must have of me.'

'I don't know,' she said, reflecting.

'Were you in the dream?'

115

'I was watching, outside of it.' She crouched on the side of the bed, knees bent, arms around them. 'I'm always watching.'

'Poor Cleo.'

'Oh nonsense,' she said, brusquely, but her face remained dark.

I held out my hand to touch hers, wanting her to be sure that the feeling behind it was simply warmth, but having no way to express this, anyway. She uncurled, lay down, and hugged me tight.

'I'm vulnerable, now,' she said abruptly. She jumped off the bed and was gone.

Vacation came. A wrestle with the unwritten essays at the end of a term criss-crossed by unresolved tensions. Desperately I'd been thinking that isolation was the only possible solution. A thought born of my helpless drive to go on seeking Libby through the successive rebuffs. Always hoping for the occasional friendliness and the even rarer sense of love restored. Only if she were dead or a thousand miles away could I conceive of locking her out. 'Detachment,' I'd mutter. 'It would be better not to get involved at all.'

I went to look after a friend's flat near the northern gate of the vast old cemetery. Relishing the calm, I began to work. The Committee of Public Safety came alive in my head; with Robespierre I suffered and fought the paranoid nightmare. In the afternoons, I walked through the unkempt cemetery with its rampant weeds and the wild plenty of coloured leaves.

The parents came to pay a Sunday visit to the flat, an afternoon tea-party, passing off well with Mother delighted by this clean shiny kitchen in quiet North Carlton. No signs of irregularity, books strewn about indicating study and calm. Genuinely, she was pleased to see me 'looking contented' in a context she could approve. Her face was weary and noticeably older since Ken's disappearance. He had shot through one night after a family brawl. 'I was only trying to protect the silly boy from that Hitchin. He was going on about a Jag that night and of course I knew Hitchin would never have the money for that sort of car. Kenny tried to get out of it but he had to admit Hitchin pinched it—for a joyride, he said. Really, Maureen, he'll end up in jail if he doesn't pull himself together. Your father never takes any action,' (my father was sitting across the table listening passively), 'so it was all up to me as usual. And Kenny won't take any notice of me any more. He just packed his little bag and cleared out. He's done that before, though, and I thought he'd be back.' She sighed, long and exhausted, took a gulp of tea, and hurried on. 'I rang the shop a day later and Mr Ferguson was terribly upset when he realised what had really happened. Ken'd been in all right on the Monday and told some cock-and-bull story about a good job with executive prospects. Collected his wages and left in a blaze of glory. The crafty little bugger's made sure we can't trace him. All a pack of lies—I rang BHP but they've never heard of him. Unless he's using a false name, but the manager seemed to think that none of the new lads answered the description. We just don't know anything.'

Father had taken the No News Good News line, to Mother's horror, and insisted that if Ken were dead or in jail we'd find out all too soon. 'He might need us,' Mother said, often, but Dad relaxed in the assumption that Ken was canny enough to get what he wanted and self-interested enough to show up back home if he couldn't get it anywhere else. Even if disaster had not yet struck, Mother countered, there was no reason to suppose that it wasn't about to, and every reason to find Ken and help him avert it. She had 'put the matter in the hands of the police' who had interviewed her, taken the names of likely confederates and drawn a blank. 'Honestly,' Mother told me, 'I don't think they tried. I don't think they care.'

Away from college, I no longer had to live with that boiled pumpkin self which had spent yesterday combing the corridors for Libby and would probably take over and do the same today. I toyed with the idea of leaving the place for good. Outside, in this other air, perhaps I could lay Libby's ghost; perhaps, finally, be free. The notion might have frothed away if Cleo hadn't treated it with exasperating scepticism. Having spent days belabouring the pros and cons, I had decided to stick to the known and stay on. It was the last week of the vacation and Cleo was already back from Upton.

'Oh ho,' she chortled, when I came in for tea, 'I bet you haven't got round to leaving yet.'

'No.'

'Thought you wouldn't.'

'Why wouldn't I?'

'It's too big for you. You're a conservative.'

'You might be right ... but then again. Erif's gone to live with Steve. Her room's free at Gunning Street.'

'But you haven't taken it.'

'Er ... No. I'd have to see Dr Heath first, wouldn't I?'

'She's around. I saw her at lunch.'

'I'll go down then.'

'Come and see me again soon.' A quizzical open-ended expression on her face.

Everything was, quite instantly, easy. A bout of amazing assurance. I wandered down, asked if the Principal was free. I was shown straight in and ushered into a big leather chair.

'What can I do for you, Maureen?'

'Dr Heath, I'm sorry I've left it so late and all but I ... want to leave college.'

'I believe we can fill the room easily enough—but we would, of course, rather not lose you.'

'I'll be able to live much cheaper Carlton. I'm terribly short of money.'

'We'd be happy to cut down the fees, you know, to whatever you can pay.'

'Oh that's very kind,' I shot out, 'but, er ... no. I've really got to leave.'

'Tell me, Maureen, has Elizabeth Stace got something to do with your decision?'

I must have always known she would know. And it was an almighty relief to lay it on the line. 'Yes. Yes. That's why. That's the real reason.'

'I think we could arrange for Elizabeth to ... perhaps ... live somewhere else. At home for example. That alternative is at least open to her.'

Can she be serious? I thought, leaping through the possibilities. If I happened to like the idea of revenge, now, what a ripper. But I didn't. Nor did I care to get involved in the infinite nastiness of a Mrs Stace-College Council Retaliation. Nor could I imagine, since I left Cleo's room, staying in college at all.

'I appreciate that, very much. But I think it's better for me if I go—there's a room free in a house where I lived last vac. I get on with the guys there. And, really. I don't want any trouble. Not for Libby either.'

'Well then, Maureen, I hope you will remain a non-resident on our roll. We'll waive the fees.'

'Thank you. I'm glad to accept.'

She shook my hand, wished me luck and hoped to see me about.

I got on the bike and made it through Tin Alley at speed.

'Well we've had a bikie along to see it,' Sonny told me, 'but nothing beats having Mother back. Wait till I tell Max.'

'Wait till I tell Cleo,' I thought.

I rode over to college in the first week of term and knocked on Libby's door.

'Come in. Oh, it's you.'

'Yeah. The latest Carlton scrag.'

She averted her head to look out the window. And wouldn't say a word.

'Have a good vac?' Silence.

'Want to come over and have a Stoop-Craig cordon bleu dinner?' Silence.

'Sorry then, Lib. I had to do it. See you.'

She never turned an inch.

I brooded on Libby's churlishness at times, but living at Gunning Street made all the difference. Meals to cook, company whenever I wanted it (and male at that), Max always willing to crack a few bottles or play chess. One Sunday evening, when Martin had dragged Max off to St Mary's and Sonny was upstairs with his woman, I decided to go and see Libby again. She's at Evensong, Cleo told me. I parked my bike at the gate, and walked up to the archway. It was cold, a light icy breeze scuttling around the corners of the chapel. I found a sheltering buttress and waited.

People filed out, talking and smiling. College men swept by in their academic gowns, wrapping themselves against the chill. I wondered if Libby had left early or left by the side—and noticed I wasn't anguished at the thought of having missed her. Near the end, she appeared in the doorway, blue skirt, blue shirt, blue jumper and a tentative smile on her face.

'Maureen!' She stopped on the path beside me.

'Hullo.'

'Haven't seen you for ages.' She was nervous and pleased.

'No, I didn't see much point in bothering you.'

'Well, yes. You know, Maureen, we're so stuck with ourselves. I was so angry that you'd left, that you didn't tell me first ... and I didn't think it was necessary.'

'It was. For me.'

'I know that. I suppose I wasn't thinking of you ...' She smiled bleakly. 'That's always the snag.'

'Yeah.'

'And I miss you.'

'Oh, Libby, me too. But I try not to, and I succeed better over in Carlton.'

'Sure,' she said gruffly, and paused. 'Sometimes I get so pissed off with everything. We had a good thing going in the beginning.'

I smiled quietly. 'Yeah. I thought so too.'

'I couldn't do anything else. I had to do those things.'

'I understand. Friend.' I looked up as I said it and took her hand gently.

'Sure. And I don't want to be at loggerheads with you. You're one of the most important people for me, really.'

I wondered if I could ask her over to Gunning Street, but said nothing.

'And I'd like to come and see you, really I would.'

'Any time you like.'

'I will. This week. Or soon. Do you want to come back and have coffee in college?'

'No. I'll go on home tonight.'

'OK Maureen.' She slipped her arm around my shoulders and we walked slowly, companionably, down to my bike at the gate.

I came out of the lecture into frosty air. Blue sky and brittle sunshine. I considered some history reading for a split second and turned away towards Carlton. Up Swanston Street the trees were bare, standing out against the pale crisp sky. I banged my feet down to keep warm and wondered where I'd walk to.

I hardly knew Andy, an engineering student of Martin's who had come to dinner once, but he greeted me like an old friend.

'The very person ... Hullo!'

I shuffled to a stop as he came up, and put my lecture-board under the other arm. I couldn't remember his name. I smiled.

'Marianne, isn't it?'

'Maureen,' I said accommodatingly.

'That's right. I've just moved into a room up there.' He spun around and pointed up towards the cemetery, slapped his sides and breathed deeply. 'Beautiful morning.'

'Oh yes,' I said, having forgotten all about it. I shifted and looked about brightly.

'Where are you off to?'

I shrugged. 'Going for a walk,' I muttered.

'Been to the cemetery lately?'

'Oh yes, I...'

I noticed that we had begun to drift on together. I felt unhappy, my exuberance clean gone. It wasn't anything about Andy so much as my feeling of having no alternative but to go with him and give up my quiet walk. I was literally unable to affect what was happening to me—flattered and entrapped. I found Andy noisy but felt sure I liked him. And anyway, what could be more irresistible than being whisked away by a comparative stranger, whoever he was. I kept hoping, however, that he would somehow let his name drop. I was too ashamed of forgetting to bring myself to ask him.

He spoke cheerfully and almost excitedly of his new room, his reasons for living in Carlton now, how easy it was to drive to Monash if you picked the right time of day, the price of BHP and Mr Whippy shares, the Vietnam War, Lowell's poetry, Bordeaux wines and count-less other matters. I listened in a silence which he appeared not to notice. We swept around the Crescent and in by the cemetery clock, with me deftly following his lead. I did it as if by second nature. No-one had taught me; yet I knew the rules. I tried to imagine myself waltzing up to him (or any bloke) and wafting him off for the morn-ing, on an undisclosed mission, raving the while without noticing whether he said anything. Where did they get their confidence?

'... don't you think?' he ended up.

120

'Oh yes,' I said quickly, ashamed that I hadn't heard.

'Well, let's go back to my room and have some coffee.' He touched me lightly on the arm to steer me, and we strolled back the way we had come. I nerved myself to turn away across the cemetery as we came to the gate. I would remark on the sunshine and escape. Here we were.

'The sunshine's so lovely,' I said.

'Yes, the nicest for weeks.'

And we were already out the gate and heading for his place.

The room was dark and very cold. While he went to get the coffee I could, at least, look inside a couple of his books and find out his name, which set one problem to rest. We drank the coffee, he talked some more, I wondered how to leave and he finally said how sorry he was but he had to go out to Monash that afternoon.

'Oh well,' I said, 'I have to work anyway.' Avoiding a tone of relief, I probably sounded disappointed.

A note from Ken. Dear Sis, I've got a great job in advertising and everything's fine. I'll come to Carlton and see you if you promise not to tell *her* anything. I'm trusting you, so do the right thing.

He came a few days later; stood at the door with his thumbs in his strides, looking tough.

'Hullo, Ken.'

'Do you promise?'

'Sure.'

'OK. How are you?'

'Pretty good.'

'Got yourself a fella yet?'

'Not yet, you bastard.'

'About time. You can't go on reading books forever.'

He was affable, friendlier towards me than he'd ever been, full of his job. He was learning design, setting-up, PR, the lot. And, on his account, was already the pride of the firm.

'Let's have a few drinks, Maureen.'

'OK. There's a pub just around the corner.'

'Nah—full of students I bet.'

'No, in fact—Max and me seem to be the only students that ever go there much.'

'Deros, eh?'

'I guess so.'

'All right. Dero came up to me in the city the other day, wanted twenty cents—and I knew why. Dunno. Tried to think what I'd feel like if I was a sixty-odd alkie. Guess I'd rather have the grog. Anyway I took him into a little caf and gave him a big lunch instead. Reckon I'd rather have the booze if I was him, but maybe I'd be better off anyway if some young smart-alec gave me a feed instead.'

'Getting good money, Ken?'

'Beats old man Fergo's pittance. And I've already had one rise. They're bloody keen to keep me. What are you drinking?'

'Beer, thanks.'

'Jesus—gone off the Black Tulip shit have ya?'

'Yeah—we all drink beer at the house.'

'One of the boys still, aren't ya?'

He got two pots and came back to the tin table, walking loose with long assertive strides and a studied indolence, striking the floor with the soles of his feet to draw attention to his command of the situation.

'Hole of a place. No wonder there's only deros—and Max.' Ken hadn't met Max, but assumed from my account that O'Hearn was a slack-arse.

'Mum's worried, you know.'

'Let her worry.'

'Why don't you let her know you're alive—and got a good job—she'd be pleased.'

'She'd be after me with the bloody feds, that's what. She can get me sent home until I'm eighteen—and I'm buggered if I'm going to give her the chance.'

'Please yourself, but I'm sure she'd be happy just knowing you're OK.'

'I'm not taking any risks. I'm not telling her and you're not telling her. Right?'

'Well, all right, then. Where are you living?'

'Spying are you?'

'Just wondered.'

'Bentleigh. With Robby. Old lady'd be shat off if she knew I was just around the corner.'

'You never run into her?'

'Saw her shopping one night. And headed off.'

'And how's things? You bastards still pinching cars?'

'Who told y'that?'

'Mother.'

'She would. Never knocked one off myself, ever. Robby's going into Nasho soon; he's going to get a GT of his own.'

'He got called up?'

'Lucky bastard. Pity I had the rheumatic fever—they'd never take me. It's bloody good brass if you go to Vietnam. He'll have a few thou before he's twenty-one.'

'If he's still alive.'

'He's too fuckin' smart to get killed. Excuse the language.'

'No worries—I use the word myself.'

'Jesus, Maureen,' he said, suddenly serious, 'you shouldn't you know. It wouldn't suit you.'

'Fuck that.'

He goggled a bit. 'Well, if you want to sound like a fella that's your own business. But it sounds bloody awful from a woman, if you want my honest opinion.'

'We've all got our opinions.'

'I bet you wouldn't say it to a fella if you had one.'

'Don't see why not.'

'Jesus, you're off your head.'

'Listen, Ken, we're having a party soon for Martin—he's moving. Would you like to come?'

'Students.'

'Most of 'em are all right, you know.'

'Commies.'

'Oh come on.'

He agreed to drop in and made me renew my promise. We parted friends, oddly enough, for the first time.

'Student Housing have said me to come.' A tall blonde olive-skinned girl in a black coat, collar up, stood at the door.

'Right. The room'll be free next week. Come in.'

'My English is from school and a little time in England. So please to speak slow.'

'OK. I'm Maureen. And you?'

'What is that?'

'What's your name?'

'Oh. Inga Schmidt.'

'You're from Germany?'

'Berlin.' She pronounced it the German way.

'That's great. Have you been in Australia long?'

'Only a little time.'

I turned the wireless down.

'I know this music very well,' she volunteered.

'You like Brahms?'

'Much. I have some concertos from Brahms in my trunk. You also play guitar?'

'A bit. That one belongs to Max. He lives here.'

'I have also a guitar. I did play cello at home, but it was big to carry.'

'I bet. Did you ever play the cello suites?'

'I tried but I was not so good. We played together my sister and brother and me, trios and so. Things not so compliz ...'

'Complicated?'

'Yes.'

'We're having a party on Saturday for Martin, the guy who's moving out. Will you come?'

'Oh, it is my cousin from Manangatang that I am going this week-end to stay.'

I wondered what she thought of the general chaos, but she smiled and said she'd move in on Monday.

'It'll be nice to have another woman. The other two tenants are guys.'

'I look forward,' she said and, unexpectedly, shook my hand.

I had tea with Libby before Martin's party, a friendly meal with a few beers. Libby bought a bottle of vodka for the occasion and we walked back through the University and Carlton, huddled against the wind and gusty rain. 'It'll be good to get in out of this,' she said as we turned down Gunning Street.

'Sure will,' I answered, turning my head and grinning.

She caught my look and laughed. 'That's an amazing thing about us,' she said. 'I never had a guy that could be friends after an affair. When the sex stops, that's it. As if the sex was the only thing that counted.'

'I only thought of cutting off because it seemed hard to see you and not think about it all. But it is so crazy—that we could be friends before, and really get on well, but not be able to be friends after. I could never quite see why making love has to destroy everything else.'

'Well, it didn't.'

We laughed and collided with Max in the gateway. Steve and Erif were staggering along in his wake.

'Poynton threw us out.' Max blinked. 'Threw Steve out, really.'

'Doesn't like me drinking b-b-b-bottles inside to s-s-s-ave a b-bit of brass.' Max sniffed and sighted Libby's bottle. 'Vodka, eh? That'll really finish us off.' Steve burst into affable hysteria.

'Later,' Libby answered.

Martin sauntered down the corridor. 'Pissed already, you bastards, eh?'

'And why not brother?' Max answered airily, sliding past him. I saw Ken standing near the stairs by himself. A reflex way in the back of my mind noted that I looked as if I was arriving with Steve and Max, not just with another woman.

'Ken. You came.'

'Sure did. Lotta weirdos here but.'

'Oh nonsense. This is Libby.'

'Hullo, Ken,' she said.

He nodded and waved her past him, spinning back to say, 'Looks like a bloody flagpole with nobs on.'

'Ken!'

'And that sissy bastard in the corner over there. Powder-blue T-shirt. What a horrible little creep.'

'Come off it brother. No need to pick the shit out of the people.'

'I'll pick what I like.'

'Sure. Let's have a beer.'

'Yeah. I'll get you a glass,' he responded, instantly chivalrous.

'Hey, Max,' I yelled from the kitchen door, 'don't put the bloody Kingston Trio on. Let's have some music.'

'The Kingston Trio? Not music?' Max looked mystified.

Libby wandered over to the sofa and told Max she didn't object to the Kingston Trio. 'Everyone else does', he said and hummed the *Ballad of the Thresher* as he got Dylan out.

'Here's a bottle, sis. Can't find the glasses. Don't just stand there. One of these bastards should give you a seat.' Ken glared at Martin.

'Plenty of floor,' I said, and leant against the wall.

'Who is he?' Ken pursued. 'The curly-headed baby-face?'

'Somebody's boyfriend. I don't know.'

'Looks like a poofter to me.' Ken spoke loud, so that the man in pale blue could not fail to hear. He started and half-turned.

'Yeah. You.'

'Shut up, Ken.'

He tossed his beer down his upturned throat and stumbled across to stand, legs apart, over the fellow. 'What's your name?'

'Rick,' said the young man quietly.

'Gotta dick, Rick? Y'look like a baby girl to me.'

'Oh really?' he said coolly, and turned calmly away towards the girl beside him. 'You were just saying you'd like to see a few of my paintings?'

Ken rattled out a laugh. 'Fancy yourself, don't you?'

Rick looked steadfastly away.

'All you poofs are scared shitless, that's your trouble,' Ken sneered, his smooth good-looking face suddenly contorted by some kind of disfiguring hatred. I looked at Libby who was leaning back, smoking.

'What a family!' she shouted.

Someone collided with me and we collapsed on the floor.

'Hullo.'

'Hi.' I looked at him and discovered it was Andy.

'Who's that awful youngster?' he asked.

'My brother, I'm afraid. Poor Rick.'

'Oh, Rick can manage. He's tougher than he looks.'

'Friend of yours?'

'Martin's. He's an engineering student, too. We're not typical. I don't like engineers much.'

'I don't meet many.' I grinned up at him, feeling somewhat silly.

'You're lucky.'

The fridge door slammed, flew open of itself and was coaxed shut by another hand.

'What a dead-shit party y'got here, O'Hearn.'

'Now whatever gives you that idea?' Max asked him with quizzical innocence. Ken swept a few dozen empties off the kitchen table— sturdy glass tubes bounced and broke on the lino-covered concrete.

'That's a party-trick is it, Ken?' Good-humoured puzzlement.

'Ah shit, O'Hearn, don't y'see? There's not a drop left to drink.'

'Jesus!' Max exclaimed as the truth hit him. 'Here, give us a hand to cart these out the back and we'll investigate. Have a feeling I saw a bottle of vodka out there on somebody's lap.' Max winked and Ken, miraculously won by his mateyness, began to pick up the bottles and sweep together the glass, giggling the while. 'Not that bony cunt that came with Maureen?' Max gave a secretive smile. 'The very same,' he replied.

'Max is bloody amazing,' Andy said to me. 'He's already won the kid's confidence.'

They emerged smiling and, with a show of earnest honesty, Max approached Libby.

'Libby,' he said, 'the regrettable truth of the matter is this: that the beer is finished and there's terrible thirsts unslaked. I wonder is there any chance at all of a nip of the old vodka?'

Libby smirked. 'Have as much as you like, mate.'

'Well thank you kindly,' as he bowed to her and took the vodka. Max nonchalantly flicked off the cap and took a timid swallow; he managed to pass it on to Ken before bringing his hand to his lips and breaking into a wrenching cough. 'Jesus. Dunno how those Russians manage.'

'It's a matter of experience, Max,' Ken told him airily and poured the vodka down like beer. Max recovered and grabbed, but Ken dodged and leapt gracefully, to poise on the two-inch wooden arm of the sofa with the bottle extended high in the air. Not a splutter—the kid had swallowed a quarter of it without flinching. His cheeks puffed a fraction, but he would obviously have preferred to die than to cough.

'You're carrying on like an idiot—dangerous at that,' Andy told him.

'Danger's a man's game. Trouble with you sissy bastards is you don't like being shown up. I could swallow the whole fuckin' bottle without batting an eyelid.'

'Bullshit,' Rick said softly.

'You want a bet, Dickie?'

'You'll make yourself sick, you half-wit.'

Ken curled his lip, his face instantly mean and brutal again. 'It'd make you sick, pansy, not me.' Then he grinned. 'All right, I'll lay you good odds, three to one. What about a dollar, Max?'

'Can't risk it, Ken me lad. I'm sure you'd win.'

'And there's a discerning man.' Ken socked back another huge dose and handed the remainder triumphantly to Max before passing out neatly, full-length on the sofa.

They threw a glass of water over his face and smacked him. His eyes rolled open. 'Drink this, Ken.' He spluttered over the water until they'd poured a pint of it down his throat. 'Dilution. He'll sleep for a day or so I suppose.' They heaved him down the corridor and dumped him on my bed.

Rick stopped in the kitchen. 'What's wrong with the poor bugger?'

'I don't know. He's got a lot to prove. He left home. Wants to be a man. Maybe he's scared of the er ... homosexual er ... possibility.'

'We all got something to prove. Pitiful, isn't it?'

'Yeah. Pitiful.' A drove of indistinguishable thoughts flooded my brain. I wanted to say something but could not make out what. I bent over the can of orange juice, abdicating. Rick went on in.

'Ever been out to the Notting Hill?' Andy asked me on the doorstep.

'No.'

'Well how about coming out for end-of-term? Good cheap food, open fires, it's a good scene.'

'It's miles, though.'

'I'll pick you up. No worries. How about it?'

Out of the blue a bloke had asked me out. Incredible. 'Yes,' I said, 'I'd love to.' He squeezed my hand and sauntered off to his car.

Part Three

Ladies don't move

Cleo. She was amazing. Sure to be as tight and guilty as the rest of us, I thought, particularly after I'd met the parents. Cleo and I were collected from the Upton station in the Atkins' gun-metal Valiant, their sole visible luxury. I was by that time extremely wary of anybody's parents, and prone to blundering badly whilst attempting to keep on unexceptionable ground. This pair struck terror, breathed morality at every turn. Mr Atkin was distant, said nothing and looked grave as he ushered me to the car. She smiled unsmilingly, the tight lips parting for a split second and closing primly. Neither of them laughed at any time that day and his smiles, if not as entirely humourless as hers, had an inbuilt sternness which indicated that a slight relaxation of his lips did not indicate any relaxation of his authority. They had all the earnestness and seriousness of the pastor from Lakes Entrance without a trace of his warmth. Cleo had evidently let out that I lived in Carlton (with men) even though my parents were in the suburbs at Bentleigh; for the Atkins, this must have been my measure and they made little attempt at friendliness. I began to wonder how Cleo had persuaded them to let me come.

Her mother had that chilling habit of referring to her father as Mr Atkin even in his presence. The house was spotless; the meal was prepared with meticulous orderliness, Mrs Atkin's small hands working with an impersonal efficiency. It was the kind of kitchen where you hesitated to offer assistance—and yet her aura demanded a show of feminine willingness; the kind of atmosphere where your terror of making a mistake was bound to provoke one, and where the penalty would be an icy invitation not to worry. Throughout the preparation of the meal and the cleaning up afterwards, Mr Atkin sat back on the settee under the window, sucked on his pipe and glanced up approvingly from time to time over the top of his newspaper. His whole demeanour was of benevolent surveillance. I was disproportionately relieved to get through the drying-up without breaking so much as a saucer; but I saw Mrs Atkin deftly inspect every item as she stacked the dishes away in the cupboard. They gave me the creeps.

Cleo said grace and was quiet through the meal, Sunday roast and baked custard. No Cleo-glee showed up here, no acid wit, no puns, no jokes and not a hint of her boisterous irreverence. We were to have the car for the afternoon. This must be why she brought me, I thought. No-one could've imagined me hitting it off with Mr and Mrs Atkin.

'Cleo,' her father said sharply, 'I don't want you to go as far as Lorne—' (Cleo had been talking about going to Lorne for weeks before) 'the roads are busy of a Sunday.' Cleo gulped and said 'All right,' just a hint of pique which her mother identified with unerring accuracy. 'Really, dear, it's dangerous on Sundays.'

'Yes,' Cleo answered sweetly. 'We'll go to Torquay.'

'Christ,' I said as I closed the car door—carefully so as to avoid Mr Atkin's probable reproof. 'They're pretty serious.'

She backed out carefully, drove the first block sedately, took the corner out of view, then gunned exuberantly down the main road.

'Isn't this nice?' she said.

'There's one thing I can't make out whatever way I look at it. Those people can't have decided to call you Cleo.'

'What should they have called me?'

'Them? Oh—Betty, Barbara, Jill, even Josephine. But not Cleo.'

'It was Daddy's mother's name. Or the one she adopted. Nobody ever talks about her. She was Irish and Grandpa met her in the First War and brought her back. Apparently he never talked about how he came to meet her, but she was low-class and the Atkins didn't like her. Besides, she used to drink whisky and everyone was afraid she'd lead Grandpa astray.'

'Did she?'

'Oh, he's pretty good, Grandpa. I don't think she did him any harm.'

'She's dead?'

'Yes. Ages ago. There are dark rumours that she died of something terrible.'

'Syphilis?'

'Maureen! Cirrhosis I think. Still, that's just as bad for an Atkin.'

'Well how come ...'

'The name? I don't really know. It must've been Daddy wanted it. I've never even heard Mummy mention Grandma.'

'So you're named after an evil woman.'

'Yes. Just as well, isn't it?'

The Torquay turn-off slid past.

'Hey, aren't we going to Torquay?'

'No.' She lifted her hands off the wheel in rare ecstasy and said we were going to Lorne anyway.

'But what about your parents?'

'They won't know till afterwards. This is now.'

Down through the scrub and pine plantations to the coast at

Anglesea, where the Great Ocean Road began winding along cliffs that dropped sheer to the Southern Ocean. Giant headlands with the road carved into them, S-bend detours where it threaded back inland to cross the steep valleys of dozens of small fierce streams, occasional straight stretches where it ran on a ledge close to the sea's edge, with the dense bush rising up beside. A blue day, sky and sea in reciprocal splendour, thunderheads rising bright white and thick at the horizon's edge. And Cleo Atkin the Second, poised over the wheel, looking flushed, intensely young and so buoyant she might zap out like a cork.

'By Jesus, Cleo, you're looking beautiful.'

She laughed and glanced sideways; modest, sceptical, pleased.

'Sit beside me,' she said. 'If you like,' and shot out her left hand to grasp mine.

'You turn me on.'

'Oh dear me,' she replied, swiftly—pretending prim outrage; but she held on to my hand and smiled when I slid over beside her. 'Perhaps not,' as I put my arm around her shoulder, 'you never know which of Daddy's friends mightn't be out on a Sunday cruise.' But she kept hold of my hand, gently, firmly.

I was totally aware of her, totally involved by her unexpected physical being. Her body smelt strong, smelt good. The old lusts, I thought to myself, and felt vaguely ashamed.

'Hey, Cleo. Stop somewhere. Stop awhile. Let me kiss you.'

'No.' And I felt her thinking *Not you; I'm not going to be a casual stop along your way.*

'You're really something,' I said, and must've sounded as if it surprised me. *It's Andy you're going out with. I'm a woman. It's lust. Nothing else.* Her thoughts hung, almost as tangible as if she'd spoken. Yet not puncturing her effervescent mood, not reducing the odd, fascinated flow between us.

'Won't you?' I tried again.

'No.'

'You don't want to?'

'No.'

But this liveness in my body, this sudden overwhelming desire was a response to her. She held my hand; her palm sweated a fraction; she smiled.

We took a narrow dirt road near Lorne and began to climb, winding slowly up amongst the huge gum trees wading in bracken. We stopped in a grassy space amongst the trees.

'We walk from here,' she said, leaning over to lock the back door. 'Better lock your door as you get out.'

I made to put my arm around her but she laughed and jumped out. 'Come on. Don't you want to see the falls?'

We walked. I hooked my arm around hers and looked up at her. She had disappeared now, behind a solemn and equally unexpected face. Sunk in her thoughts or under the spell of the soaring trees that cut out the sky and left us deep in shadow. She caught my glance and smiled, a grave smile, almost like her father's. Down the track came children's voices. A well-dressed Sunday couple strolled by, circled by two small boys dressed identically in red shorts and striped shirts. They played and dodged amongst the trunks and tree-ferns, aware of no-one but themselves. Cleo dropped her arm when the people came in sight and we went on in silence.

The water fell in shadow, curtains of mist coming together in a turbulent pool well below us. The dim opulence of rain forest. Big tree-ferns held out still fronds, their trunks damp-brown, nearly black. On the rocks the moss grew lush and dark. Logs lay rotting. Around the tree-trunks fungi clung, flower-like, ledge-like, bulbous; most of them pale, but some brilliant orange. *Woods decaying never to be decayed*. I was about to offer the Wordsworthian insight to Cleo, but stopped. She stood quite still, staring across the water into the shades, scarcely blinking, mysteriously absorbed into the forest. 'I'll start back,' I muttered, though I sensed that explanations were alien to Cleo. I turned down the path, an intruder in the moment.

I ran like hell, jumping the jutting roots, dodging the logs and another Sunday couple who frowned and obviously thought I was mad. A rock ledged out on the left where the track fell away sheer to the fern-thick gully; I sank onto it, out of breath, and waited. A long quiet time. Hidden in the valley the stream bubbled down its rocky course; from above the boom of Erskine Falls spread its blanket bass note. For a time I ceased observation, the shadow and the water music flooded space, and me with it.

Cleo came slowly down the path, in her eyes that shyness and uncertainty accentuated in people behind glasses. I rose to meet her and we exchanged grave smiles.

'Anything wrong?' I asked.

'Something happened.' I questioned with my eyes. 'Don't know. Something strange.'

'It's a strange place. Total.'

'Yes. Like God.'

At Aireys we stopped and went down to the sea. The sun was hot for October, but the water too cold for either of us. We rolled up our jeans, paddled in the edges of the waves, following the undertow down across the hard wet sand and retreating as the next wave slapped down and swept up the shore. Stretched out on the beach I pillowed my arms and turned my head to look at Cleo, gazing off up the inlet towards the town and the mountains beyond. She woke me up I don't know how much later and told me we must go. I wondered if she was annoyed that I'd fallen so instantly asleep, and suspected that she was.

'I'm sorry,' I said. 'Didn't sleep much last night.'

'I know,' she answered without a sign of hurt.

The night before, Andy had been at Gunning Street, along with the usual small party of dedicated drinkers. Andy, the first guy who'd ever taken me out, who got me feeling—and how necessary this seemed—like a regular woman. Initially, his opening the car door produced an ambiguous pleasure, but one which became so rapidly uneasy that I began to defy the pattern, to leap out (without mishap) and surprise him by divining how a Holden may be locked from the outside provided one closed the door with the catch pressed in. He always checked anyway. As for walking on the gutter side of the pavement, this was a foreign and evidently middle-class habit, which at first only mystified me. What kind of nervous energy, I wondered, compelled Andy to dodge around me whenever we crossed a road? Finally I asked him, and he explained in his unfailingly jolly tenor that a gentleman owed it to his lady to keep the sword hand free in case of ruckus.

'Oh yeah?' I replied, amazed. 'What if he's left-handed?'

'Whoever heard of a left-handed hero?' he parried, elegantly evasive.

'OK Andy. But what if we were walking down the other side of the road. Your sword hand would be hampered, especially if it was round me.'

'Well, a modern gentleman has to think of mud, and the constant splashing of fast cars. Walter Raleigh in mufti.'

'In high summer?'

'Summer storms.'

'My gear's always scungier than yours anyway. Why bother?'

But Andy only smiled as if the point were incontestable. He thrived on the rituals of the gentleman mystique. And continued to move gutterward despite my own counter-manoeuvres and amused ingratitude. If I walked on the kerb, he walked *in* the gutter.

Nevertheless, when he took me to his Monash parties out in the south-eastern suburbs, he paid me the compliment of handing over the street-map and allowing me to navigate—even though I occasionally suspected that he knew his way anyway. Whatever else—Andy was willing to admit me as His Girl and, to my own astonishment, was proud of it. He was overjoyed at having a bird to drink with, a bird who drank beer (paying off); he seemed never to have contracted the notion that women ought not to drink. An unlikely coalescence of stuffy convention and radical eccentricity.

His friends were of two distinct kinds, between which he hung somewhere. The Brighton and district students: amiable well-boozed men; pretty, nicely-dressed women, their evident intelligences half in abeyance. The others were perhaps the first wave of dropouts and probably came from Brighton too. Dave, the unmatched giant amongst Monash physicists (a genius, Andy intimated), assured of every break and success and achievement, had got bored with physics as taught, found his own life more interesting than his course and hit on the idea of having himself certified—at a hospital which allowed him to move freely during the day, return at night and draw a small pension. Dave was tough, caustic, unhappy. On weekend leave he made expeditions to the Hunter River and brought back grass; but, if he shared it with Andy, he certainly didn't offer it at large.

Andy staggered me with his continuing invitations to his turns and his occasional unannounced arrivals with a bottle of wine and a carnation. Obscurely, I was aware that I was using him, standing him up between myself and my reputation, especially to deflect Max and Sonny from the scent. Sonny, who was old enough to feel fatherly although he called me mother, had taken me to the pictures. Ostensibly to see *The Knack*, but the support—*The Man With the Green Carnation*—was the subject of his chatter as we walked back to Carlton. His off-hand condemnation of Wilde, his unqualified approval of the Family Intervention (a game played the world over)— these revealed his attitude and left me in doubt as to his intention, and what he knew. Again, Andy gave me a wider status, self-reducing but imperative—just as drinking with Max had done. To sit in a pub or a park, even to walk on the street, without a man was a shame for any nice girl and a scandal once you hit twenty.

When I got drunk enough to blank out the past I even felt a sex-tremor from Andy's touch, though it never ceased to puzzle me that he could kiss without noticing unresponse, something I thought inconceivable. He wanted too much sex-play, just limited play at that, too often. His rapid gross initiations left me no space to open towards him, even if that had been possible—which I couldn't find out. Certainly I couldn't suggest that we sit apart, say, and wait awhile; or kiss gently and explore. Andy could desist, thinking 'Girls!' and leave me be; but he couldn't understand why, and neither could he see that it was something about the pace, not the fact, which blocked me. We went out; we drank a lot; we bought hamburgers and ate them in the moonlight—the right set for 1966 Romance. Andy usually remained fully-dressed, as if his body were of no interest or concern. He must often have had an erection, but he never hinted about that, never wanted to show me. My body was for the play. I could've done with a break. Always my shirt was unbuttoned, my breasts kneaded, my cunt stroked. I wondered if one ought to touch a man, apart from his

133

spine, in the embrace. Men probably didn't care to be touched. I'd have to be invited—hadn't the courage to risk whatever it was that I thought I was risking. I was terrified of blunder, almost convinced that there existed a body of precise rules governing the minutest details, something which couldn't possibly be in print, yet something which everyone but myself appeared to be in command of ... I wondered if Andy's world of activity might split apart if I made any move. Shit-scared of giving offence. Crazy.

We had spent the latter part of that Saturday night engaged in these futile pursuits, until Andy went home about five. Cleo had knocked on the window at eight— she'd had to get me out of bed for our day at the falls.

We arrived back at the Atkins' to the chilly barrage of inevitable questions.

'Did you have a good time, girls?' he asked.

'Super day,' said Cleo readily. I nodded, enthusiastic.

'Were there many at Torquay?'

'Er,' said Cleo who, I discovered to my horror, could not tell a lie. Not even an important one.

'Mmmm?' asked her mother.

'We didn't go to Torquay.'

'Oh Cleo,' was all her mother said, voice mild, even, unmistakably hurt.

'There wasn't much traffic, Mummy, and such a lovely day. So we went on to Lorne. The road's so beautiful.'

Her father looked up under contracted brows and said nothing. Her mother put the kettle on and suggested we have tea.

'Really, Mummy. And here we are safe and sound.' Cleo spoke brightly, trying to pass it off.

'Fortunately,' came the brief cool reply. Mrs Atkin busied herself with the cups, laid out the teaspoons at identical angles on the saucers.

'Torquay's just a beach Mummy—I wanted to show Maureen the falls. She's never been before.'

'Oh yes. And did you like Erskine, Maureen?'

'Oh very much,' I launched, wishing to Christ I could vanish through the floor. 'Such dense forest, and the falls are marvellous.'

Mrs Atkin declined to comment further and I felt positive that she suspected me of importuning the divided Cleo to go on, go on, not bother about her silly parents. Odd that she was wrong. Cleo must have caught the thought. 'It was me, Mummy. Maureen said we oughtn't to go on. But I so wanted to show her.'

More silence, broken by the dribble of tea into cups. What a purgatorial climate to have grown up in, I thought, and felt fortunate for the first time in my life to have had a family that lost its temper and screamed. Worse to come, as we gingerly took our places at the kitchen table and Mrs Atkin offered around dainty slices of delicious fruitcake. 'I'm sure you must be hungry, Maureen, after your long drive. Do have another slice.' Mr Atkin swallowed his cake sparrow-like, lips clamping shut after every nibble.

He broke the portentous silence.

'I dare say I don't need to tell you how disappointed we are, Cleo. We will have to think twice about letting you have the car again, since your attitude is so casual.'

'We would like to think we could trust you, dear,' her mother added. Cleo literally hung her head.

To compound the sport we missed the last train back to Melbourne and the Atkins had to drive us the fifty-odd miles—all with an air of unreproaching reproach. I held Cleo's hand in the back while Mr Atkin slammed the grey Valiant steadily down the freeway. An additional hour of that diabolically stilted atmosphere. Did I want a lift over to Gunning Street? *Not on your life.* 'Oh thanks awfully, but I'll just drop in on Libby and walk back later.'

'Very well.'

'Thanks for having me,' I said dutifully and retired across the nature-strip while Cleo kissed them goodbye and no doubt went through some more deathly, kindly, all-for-the-best reproof.

'Come on Cleo. I'll put you to bed and then piss off. The Falls part of the day was matchless.' She got into bed and I sat beside her for a moment. 'I do like you,' I said. 'A lot.' I bent over to kiss her cheek but she turned her mouth and we touched lips. 'And don't let those parents of yours terrorise you.' The imperative desire of the afternoon was gone. She didn't want that kind of relationship with me. Perhaps with nobody ever. I accepted, kissed her and went out, switching off the light. Anyway, must I not somehow try harder with Andy? Try to make it? Erif had thought that normality might be acquired by habit—like beer-drinking perhaps, bitter at first, but excellent once habituated.

I might have given her up, if she hadn't said to me the next day: 'I wish you'd stayed last night. I was tired, but you went away.'

'I shan't go away next time.'

'You won't want to stay.'

Max and I introduced Inga to the local haunts—Watson's the wine shop, Poynton's the trendy dim-lit pub, the Clyde with its plastic replicas of old masters alternating with fake lanterns along polythene imitation brick-work, the modest tin-table Lemon Tree, the Alfred's steaks and juke-boxes. Inga was wide-eyed most of the time. A

European taste for schnapps, a total indifference to Fosters and what it meant, wonderment that a race of such dedicated drinkers should be cribbed by such inexplicably short licensing hours and a quite incredulous response to public bars for men only.

As third term went on, Max punctuated his drinking with frenetic bursts of work on long-overdue design projects. 'Hardly worth trying when they'll say it's shit anyway.' Inga began to sit up with him at night as, taciturn and concentrated, he hacked out bar after bar of his Eiffel Tower in black cardboard; a precise replica done to scale with slide-rule and razor. Near dawn one morning I came out to the kitchen and found them sitting, in a silence so tangible that it must have been long, on separate sides of the fire-grate, wide awake and staring into space.

'You're up early, Craig.' Max looked up and smiled ruefully with his lips closed and drawn tight.

'I'm not staying up, that's for sure. Just after a piss and a glass of water.'

'Want to make some tea?'

'Oh yeah.' I never refused company.

'Will you have a cup of tea, Inga?' he said, solicitous.

'It is late,' she said and stood up. 'Good night.'

'I'm hopeless, Maureen,' Max said when she'd gone. 'I can never think of anything to say and then she always goes to bed like a shot when I'm warming up to it.'

'She's shy, I guess. And she still doesn't always understand what we're saying. She thought you and me were married until a few weeks ago.'

'Shit, did she?' He paused to reflect. 'She's told me about Berlin and her family. I keep forgetting what it was I wanted to ask her. I think of things every day. And when she's actually there I haven't got a clue. I just don't know how to talk to women.'

'She likes you Max. She stays up with you.'

He squinted. 'Yeah. S'pose you're right. It's hard though.'

There's no way of getting any nearer to Andy, I thought, unless we do the whole thing; everything else was a pale and inferior version of things I knew well already. A stunted formridden game. Prickless prim Andy—whose harsh blundering touch and authoritarian attitude had me thoroughly disillusioned with 'normal' sex. So, tanked up as usual for the night, I finally proposed that we 'do it'.

'No,' he said.

'Why not?'

'You're a virgin.'

'So what?'

'So when a guy wants to marry you, he'll want ...'

136

'No guy is going to marry me.'

'I bet dozens'd want to.'

'I'm sure they wouldn't. But that's not the point anyway. Guys do what they like before they get married. I don't see why I shouldn't do the same.'

'Guys like to marry virgins.'

'That's too bloody bad. Let 'em practice what they preach. Come on Andy—I want to do it all.'

I was half-naked as usual and, taking the world in my hands, I began to unbuckle his belt.

'It's no good, Maureen. I've never done it before.'

'We're in the same boat. It's OK.'

'And I can't. Not until I get married.'

'You what?'

'Because ... I had a girl when I was about fourteen. We were going to get married when we got older. We were in love, completely. She died.'

'She died?'

'Yeah.' It still made him ache, his eyes looked misty though he didn't cry. I could think only of consolation clichés, and said nothing.

'We were just kids, I guess—but we would have got married, we would've stayed together.'

'And that's why you won't.'

'She was dying. Nearly the last time I saw her. Hospital. Leukaemia. She asked me to marry someone else some day. Not to get stuck on her. She knew she was done for. I said yeah, all right; numb as hell. And then she said, But promise me one thing. Anything, I said. She asked me to promise never to sleep with anyone until I loved a girl enough to marry her. I promised her that.'

'And she died?'

'Yeah. And I won't break that promise.'

'But shit, Andy, people are starting to realise that getting married is just formal. You're not religious.'

'No.'

'So marriage is nothing but paper.'

'Perhaps if I'm going to live with one girl all my life, it's all right. But it has to be that. I can't break a promise, not when she's dead.'

'But she'd see by now that it's crazy.'

'I can't do it.'

'How old was she?'

'Thirteen.'

'Jesus. A girl of thirteen—and that must've been ages ago. It's like Thomas Hardy.'

'I can't do it.'

'And you didn't—with her?'

'We were going to. Then she got sick, quite suddenly. She was in hospital mostly—after that.'

'Don't,' I said sharply. 'Don't touch me now. It's pointless.'

'It's not pointless. You're beautiful.'

'I am not beautiful.' I felt sorry for him, sorry his bride had died; but, more immediately, cheated. This was a dead-end. One day I'd try to tell him why. Just then I wanted none of him. Gentleman Andy with his promises to the dead. I reflected that a woman who had recited a similar tale to some ardent male lover would have been charged with neurosis and laughed out of court.

Jake, a suave egotistical woman-hater who taught at the High School where Max suffered three days a week, arrived late in the afternoon and found Max and Inga at the banqueting-table playing a game of the impoverished chess which served all of us as an alternative to conversation.

'Fucking hot mate. Let's go down the Alfred Bar and have a game of billiards. They've got the fans on full.'

Max knocked over his king, smiling his conceded defeat and jumped up with enthusiasm. He mumbled something to Inga about a few quickies and threw his jacket over his shoulder by the tag.

'But Max. We will also come with.' She rose, faintly puzzled. Jake threw a look at Max which he caught deftly and passed on to me.

'They're going to have a drink in the bar,' I explained. 'Without us.'

Her anger was vastly amusing to Jake. Max looked embarrassed. His awkward placations brought stony silence as she set up the pieces for a game with me and ignored him. A puzzled cigarette fell out of his mouth. He picked it up and followed Jake down the passage. 'Bloody women,' Jake muttered through his beard.

'It is incredible,' she said angrily. 'You move first.'

'Come on. Let's go and have a beer ourselves.'

'I do not feel like it.'

'OK.'

'I do not understand Max. It is not like this at home. That bloke (bloke is the word?), that bloke in Berlin, he will sometimes go off with that other girl I have told you, but he is never leaving me to drink with such idiots.' She stressed the word at the end as if it rhymed with pots and gave it a silliness which put Jake admirably in his place.

'All guys do. They like to get together and talk without the women.'

'But what is so different that they can say?'

'Search me. They seem to talk about twin carbies and who they fucked.'

'Wink arbis?'

'Motor-cars, motor-bikes, engines, all that.'

'It makes me mad ... Because he is so nice when there is not Jake and these other twits. He is never talking about wink arbis to me.'

'I don't think Max really cares much about all that. He just goes along with them. They always back each other up.'

'Idiots.'

I had begun to tell Dr Hudson about Cleo, the girl who (probably) loved me but was afraid I would simply use her.

'Would you? Only use her?'

'No,' I said, 'I don't think so. But I'm not in love with her, not that really strong feeling ...'

'And Cleo?'

'She's more involved than I am—even though it's me that's been making the moves. I feel safe because of that. If there's trouble, if she backs out—I can shrug it off.'

Hudson smiled.

Cleo arrived one night, quite late. We sat around the banqueting-table with Steve and Erif; Max was slumped on the sofa designing mousetraps; Inga, still perplexed by our conversations, was reading Kierkegaard in German. At midnight Steve offered Cleo a lift back to college on his scooter, a heap nearly as decrepit as Max's.

'It's OK, thanks,' she said, 'I like walking back at night, it's warm and quiet.'

We left Max and Inga to their nightly talking and went upstairs. I switched on the radio—the first movement of Beethoven's Seventh, energy and strength. I sat up on the table, looking down at her. I saw her hesitancy and waited. Cleo, with no sexual past beyond a back-seat kiss back in childhood, seemed to have a physical core which came naturally. Odd in a woman, I thought, having been rescued from a world without physical pleasure by fortuitous paths myself. Perhaps Erif was without division, but most women were victims of their minds; minds niggling fear and circumspection at straight-jacket bodies. Cleo was at home in her own skin. I asked, almost flippantly, if she wasn't going to stay the night with me then? Yes, came the staggering answer.

'You intended to stay tonight?'

'I chose.'

I slid off the desk beside her, put my arm gently across her shoulder, brushed her neck with my lips. She looked ahead, at the sawn-off wardrobe and white wall, traces of fear—yet I knew with certainty that it had nothing to do with the sable sin-bound fear which I'd seen too much of. Her eyes darted sideways, her head still, and she smiled at an angle.

'What do you want of me?' she asked, her levelness covering everything else.

I couldn't answer.

'I love you.' More a statement of fact than the usual declaration.

I couldn't return the words. 'Perhaps I will love you, Cleo,' I said lamely.

A smile flickered as she saw clean through me. 'No undertakings. Let it happen—if it happens.'

She turned and I leant across her, plunging into her lips. A minute perhaps, she responding vividly. I opened my eyes, expecting to observe an absorbed blind face. I met watchful bright eyes.

'You keep your eyes open,' I said later.

'That's a question of trust, not desire.'

It had been months since I'd fucked with a woman, months of Andy's hard forward mouth, his meaningless end-stopped approaches. A relief to meet gentleness, and knowledge. I lay on Cleo, kissed her, tangled with her, satisfying myself without noticing whether she did or not—hardly expecting it of a virgin. Delusions of the male. Without glasses she looked defenceless, myopic gaze into the shadows. And it was good—to make it again with a woman, a woman who, in some restrained way, already loved me.

'I may never want to do this again.' My warning.

'Nor I,' came the answer. She left at dawn.

But the next afternoon I went to see her. Wanting to hold her; be good to her. She was sleeping. I let her be.

'I could love Cleo,' I told Hudson. 'I trust her.' I wondered if he would interpose some discreet warning, try to dissuade me. Instead he asked if I felt any surer than I had done.

'I think, yes. She loves me. But she's not sentimental. And she doesn't judge, even me.'

'Why should she judge you?'

'I used to trudge around after Libby. Cleo knows that. I've been weak and breaking down. She accepted that. Most people judge.'

'You see Maureen,' he said evenly, 'it's all up to you. These other relationships have broken up because of your guilt and the guilt of the others, and because you have needed too much, leaned too heavily. You must decide if the situation is different, if you can meet your friend Cleo equally.'

'You don't think another relationship with a woman will be bad for me?'

'It seems to me that the sex of anyone's lover is irrelevant. Love if you're able. It's for you to decide if you are able to love Cleo. I can tell you very little. And I certainly can't answer that question.'

140

'Cleo might be the person.'
'It's up to you.'

Looking back, it strikes me as scarcely credible that I'd have gone home again at the beginning of that summer. But I'd had appendicitis and Mother had been happy to help despite months of tenuous communication; she had visited the hospital and prepared the bungalow for a comfortable convalescence. I must be looked after, something of which she believed Sonny and Max incapable. Suburban backyard all over again. Cut grass. Lemon tree. The back fence a blaze of early red roses, perfect petals closing around each other, dropping dew gently from their secret centres. At night, the clang of the level crossing bells came up from the railway, and the whistle changed pitch nearing and retreating, an eerie parabola of sound.

Mother's attitude to Andy was a tense compound of potential relief and fear of sin. His hair, long, was loathsome, and she was sure that his beard only served as a disguise for a weak chin, notoriously unacceptable to any woman. Indeed, his only claim to forbearance was this: Andy (oh Christ, can she be reforming?) was a male.

'Now, Maureen, I don't want to fight with you again, but it's not done.' Referring to Andy's extended presence in the bungalow the night before.

'Er, what? Not done?' I always knew exactly what she was talking about, guessed her suspicions before she hatched them.

'I heard Andy drive off this morning. It was already getting light.'

'Goodness, Mother, didn't you sleep well?'

'How can I be expected to sleep well while my daughter is entertaining a boy in her room until all hours of the night?'

Here we were again. With this hide-bound, stiff mother of mine there was just no hope. No placation. Tempted to tell her that I-thought-she-thought pregnancy was a lesser evil. Or that I was really keener on Cleo. But I refrained from baiting. Bound to end badly. I took a marginally safer line.

'Andy doesn't believe in premarital sex, Mother, so ...'

'I SHOULD BLOODYWELL HOPE NOT.'

'... so don't worry about him. He's a nice boy. A regular next-door lad.'

'And don't sound so scathing about that.'

'I'm not scathing,' I lied. 'It's true.'

'Well, I don't know of course what you two were doing out there all night, but I won't stand for it. Think what it looks like. It's a respectable area here; and I simply won't have you spending the night with a boy under my very nose.'

'Did y'come out for a sniff?'

'I'm serious Maureen.'

'And so am I. If you're going to start the interference bit all over again, I'll go back to Carlton.'

'You would.'

'Yes. I would.'

'You can't take care of yourself after you've been so sick.'

'You'd be surprised.' She dropped the subject.

Just as well she didn't have a sniff the night before.

I was invincibly shy with Andy, however kind and solicitous he appeared. His adolescent oath hung in my own mind, redoubling the fear of forbidden territories and acts. Must not offend him. For me there existed no line of initiation anyway. He wouldn't fuck, whatever that was like—and he knew nothing about easing me to the orgasm any other way. He made it in his underpants no doubt, but I was not permitted to remain in mine, where I might have been able to make the masturbation mutual. I was stripped off or (more unsettling) I found myself with a T-shirt strangling me, rope-like, and pants hobbling the ankles—only the torso-cunt centre of attention laid bare. I couldn't find the courage to criticise nor even to whisper the request for a moment's truce to remove the offensive remnants. 'The male ego is very fragile, Maureen,' Andy had proudly warned. Most fragile, I imagined, in this sort of situation.

I grew angry with him, and anger inevitably dried up the sources of desire. There was no trace of intuition; disenchantment with any move had to be spoken. Of the bruised silences or the grunts of pain Andy was totally unaware. To say something like: 'I'd rather you didn't bite my nipple so viciously' was, naturally, unthinkable. The vocabulary for what my mother described as 'down there' even more severely limited. Please don't rub that bit. Move left two centimetres and touch lightly. I should, perhaps, have compiled a guide-book for private study.

He brushed my backside; accidental shiver-touch, renewing the frayed pleasure. Yes, I said, low. I reached for his hand, with rare daring drew it around to the spot where I'd got the unexpected charge. 'No,' said Andy, sharply and suddenly. *Too near the arsehole.* 'No,' he repeated, 'not that sort of thing.' His thoughts rang out. 'Sorry,' I murmured, angrier still and not in the least sorry.

Andy appeared to have forgotten his long manicured fingernails. I yelped. 'Oooh, Maureen, sorry,' he said tenderly, and continued scraping. *He wants to put those fingers in.* My body went rigid as a fence post, tense from hair-roots to toenails. Andy didn't notice. How, I wondered, could he miss it? What incredible quality in him enabled him to slam on while the contact between us dissolved and my sexual engagement decreased in inverse ratio to his own? I could scarcely credit his blindness to non-participation, his pushing on into that

142

bleak no man's land of alienated crutch-play. Even if Andy was at sea with women, new to sex and inexperienced, there was a more frustrating inadequacy: he was dead to every non-verbal nuance. At the same time accurate words were few, and to tell Andy he was blowing it was tantamount to attacking the shaky ego. Impasse.

Andy dived in, muscular stirring, faintly reminiscent of a pudding-basin action, with those nails ripping around somewhere inside me. Panic and disgust. I reached for his wrist and pulled at him. 'Hey, you no like?' he asked with a Chinese accent of sorts, intensely surprised. 'Come out,' I replied, still trapped in the masquerade of giving no offence. Phrases formed inside my brain. You're scraping the inside outa me. Ever think what fingernails do to passion? Wake up, you stupid prick, and take a look at my face for a start. Why the fuck do y'think I'm lying here like a corpse? Phrases forming, rehearsed a second, abandoned as too much for him. 'You silly bitch,' one guy says to me years later, when I must have gripped his prick too tightly. 'That's flesh, not a garden rake.' Could've fooled me, but I envied him his ability to object loudly and spontaneously to a rough touch, however inadvertent. Nevertheless he, along with countless others, was mysteriously insensible to the obvious analogy, that cunt is flesh too, not gutter-pipe.

Libby's visit finally finished my stay at home. In the preliminary skirmish it was acridly accepted that, grateful as I was for the care, I would prefer discomfort and peace to the old smothering curtailments. When Libby arrived, they exchanged frigid greetings and we retired to the bungalow. Mother, helpless victim of her own suspicion and drive to know the worst, left us alone for scarcely twenty minutes, and might have been disappointed to discover us on opposite sides of the room painting bookshelves. She stood in the doorway, brow furrowed, eyes nervous and angry.

'I would prefer you two girls to spend the afternoon indoors. I'll make you tea.'

'We've got things to do here. Painting.'

'I think you had better go into the house.'

I cocked my head, dipped the paintbrush and said, lazily, 'Want to keep an eye on us, Ma?'

She erupted. 'You can either work inside or Libby can go. I will not have you both out here. In my home. I won't have it.'

I looked straight into her light agitated eyes. 'If Libby goes, I go. You treat me right. You treat my friends right. And you don't order me anywhere any more. See?'

'This is your last chance.'

'This is *your* last chance, Mother. To wake up to the fact that I know my own mind and I don't like your ideas one scrap.'

143

'Go then,' she screamed. 'GO. Go on. GO.'

'I will,' I answered softly.

'You only asked this double-faced bitch here so you'd have an excuse to clear out again.'

'Watch it, Mother. I don't need excuses.'

Libby stood behind, near the bed, absolutely silent and quite obviously amazed that family conflict could take such a torrid form. My mother glared at us both, hate for Libby, disgust and heartbreak that, in the crunch, I should have taken the water-over-blood alternative. She went out quivering. We heard the door wrench on its hinges and bang so ferociously it vibrated on like a drum-roll.

'Your mother's dynamite,' she said after a moment.

'Got to get back to Carlton; help me pack.'

I was almost inured to the inevitable. I packed, storm-faced, and hardly cried a tear. Finally I collected one of the black kittens from the shed—for company—and lit out for home.

'Darling, you're back,' Max offered cheerfully.

'Yes. I brought it with me.' A favourite Milliganism.

'Not another cat!'

'Why not?'

'Janus'll rape him.'

'I'll keep him inside.'

'Jesus. Must you?'

'He's clean.'

'An illusion. Cats are just cunning. Do you feel like a drink?'

'Sure. Just left home for the fiftieth time—the usual. Where's Inga?'

'In her room. Sulking.'

'But I thought things were really going well.'

'I asked her to come home with me for Christmas. She wasn't keen.'

'Well you're not usually keen yourself.'

'They'd be better if she came.'

'What about her saying fuck so innocently? Your mother'd have fits.'

'And she'd know who taught her, too,' he agreed glumly.

'Shall we ask her to come for a drink?'

'We're not speaking this afternoon.'

'Shit Max, why?'

'I always say the wrong thing.'

We walked around to the Lemon Tree in silence; Max gazed off across the neighbouring park, hopelessly puzzled. 'I couldn't see anything wrong with it—I just said I thought if she was sleeping with me it'd be natural to come home when she hasn't got a family here. She just snorted and asked me if my mother knew. Good God. Of course not. And I bet she wouldn't tell hers either. She got high and mighty and told me she wasn't pretending anything for my family's peace of mind. She's not even a Catholic. The old man'd blow a fuse.'

'But you wanted her to go?'

'I thought it'd make things smoother. Mother's a different woman when there's visitors around. Inga reckoned she couldn't think of anything worse than an Australian Christmas. Having to stay with my mother, she said, while I went off to the RSL Club with the fellas.'

'Do you?'

'Not for the whole fucking week.'

'Y'can't blame her.'

'I suppose not. But she was so scornful. And she's going off to some fat German cousin's place instead. At Manangatang!'

'Shit. Not much of an improvement on Wodonga, is it?'

'We could've got away together a bit,' he said, and finished his beer without another word.

The geometry of innocence

The old railway viaduct at Rosewood was thick with blackberries, a steep thorny climb; but it commanded the road in from the Dandenongs, bluish humps in the distance. I squatted to wait, a long stick slanted over the shoulder, self-styled solitary sentry. Saturday-arvo trippers tore round the bend and roared under my position, never a sign of Cleo—but then I didn't even know what make of car I was watching for. From the town-side of the viaduct I could see the small weatherboard house where she had stayed this last month. The Worthgolds of Rosewood had been just Baptist and moral enough for the Atkins to swallow their misgivings about Cleo's likely decline and allow her to stay away from home for the December cherry-picking. In fact, the orchard where Cleo was taken each morning with the Worthgold kids was owned by a god-fearing, drink-detesting stalwart of a farmer who would have no bad language in the orchard, least of all the taking of the Lord's name in vain. Even Cleo had to steel herself sometimes; upon falling from a ten-foot ladder, for example, the strongest permissible profanity was 'bother'. Cleo hated lies and must have been relieved to write home to Upton about the nicely-behaved cherry-harvesters, and the lovely Christian orchardist, who didn't employ the itinerants—rough and ready customers with no respect for decency.

For weeks after term ended Cleo was not much on my mind. Her letters came, at first, from Upton when she returned to her morbid, moral parents. Letters which showed her constricted and well under the thumb, almost conned into a dutiful dreary summer proselytising with the Beach Mission. Just as well not to go any deeper when Mrs Atkin was (icily I had no doubt) disapproving of such peccadilloes as port. Cleo had accepted some wayward uncle's invitation after a respectable family dinner; her mother had choked, frozen and later insinuated that Maureen Craig's rough working-class ways and undesirable male co-habitants were leading Cleo to a drunken fate. I had not the slightest doubt that the real situation, though relatively sober, would afford her no consolation. Sometimes Cleo indicated that she missed me and my opposed world; that she'd been again to Aireys and felt cheated to be with anyone but me; that she envied Andy his ready access and continuous contact.

She remained at Upton, unwilling to face the confrontation which visits to Carlton would have involved. I did without her. Andy was there. Andy was preferable for social reasons, no secrecy, no public restraint or pretence. And Andy was a tenuous link with the possibility of normality. All this contrasted with the sharp memory of Cleo's animal-shy eyes, my acute physical response to her, her extraordinary tenderness. The comparison did Andy no good; I resolved not to make it, deciding that men must be clumsy and unsensual by nature.

At Rosewood, Cleo chafed under the burden of ubiquitous people, all cast in the mould which assumed mild-mannered sobriety of every sort, never supposing it might be an effort. I wondered how she kept up the charade; how she had acquired her matchless talent for the double life, something I singularly lacked. If Cleo suffered under her disguises, she revealed nothing; while her parents, confident enough of her basic virtue, were too civilised to probe anyway. Evidently her disobedience with the Valiant and her flirtation with port had frayed only slightly the veil that she kept taut between her increasingly disparate lives. Perhaps it was this precise facility which allowed her to move in both worlds without guilt, which enabled her to love me.

I stood on the viaduct and mused on the futility of my grandiose project—to bring Cleo back after her last day of cherries, to rescue her instantly from the Worthgold prison, take her back to Gunning Street and tell her the abrupt new truth, that I loved her. It was after six, the Worthgold house deserted in the evening sun. A chill breeze blew off the mountains and I shivered. Damn, I said to myself gently, no doubt affected by the Baptist ambience. Not a particularly romantic day at all. Hitching out from Carlton, I'd spent an hour with a Baptist-looking, middle-aged gent who turned off just short of Rosewood.

'Ah hum,' he said as the motor idled, 'if I may call you Maureen ...'

'Sure.'

'I'm sure a student like yourself, Maureen, could do with five dollars.' *Sure could but no dice buster.*

'Oh you've given me a lift sir,' I said sweetly. 'That's saved me a lot. Many thanks.'

'I don't want you to do anything.' *No?* 'And there's a spot up the road where no-one'll be able to see. I could then take you on to Rosewood.'

'Er ... see what?'

'Now don't get the wrong idea. I don't want to touch you at all, in any way. I simply want you to watch.' He moved in his grey business pants, his prick hard and buckled up inside. He flicked it straight with his thumb and turned back to me.

'No thanks,' I shot out without thinking, both curious and curiously unwilling to let him have his kicks. Even if it only took watching, even if I half-wanted to watch. 'No thanks. Thanks for the ride.'

'Well, I thought ten dollars might've helped you out, you know,' said he, bargaining consummately.

'No thanks. I'm getting a loan from the University. No worries. Thanks a lot.'

I was shaking when I got out of the car. Neither panic nor fear nor disgust. I was incapable of prim reactions, found them more hateful

147

than sexual predation itself. It was anger, rather, that a man could provoke and control such situations. It certainly struck me as unlikely that I'd pay a guy to watch me fuck myself. It was inconceivable that I'd have the gall to ask. Women must not admit these notions, even to themselves. He acted, I reacted. The wild oats story every time. Grey-suit wasn't repulsive—men simply acted on their impulses. While women were cracked up to be so different that their behaviour required a separate moral system, an alternative code for action. Why? The trees gave no answer. I thumbed on down the road.

Cleo had come to Gunning Street once during the cherry season, agreed to stay the night and taken the early train the next morning. She had given me weeks to reflect before returning to my room in any but social guise—but, then, I had repeated in talk and letters that I had no intention of getting involved with her or anyone. 'I just want a lover. And you're a great lover.' Another myth—or an old one: Free-Ranging Craig, Liberated Craig, or, beat this, Detached Craig.

We drank wine with Max and Inga, sitting on the floor, *Blonde on Blonde* in the background. Cleo apart and quiet. She answered the inquiries about her results, listened intently to the talk and, when I caught her glance, she smiled fractionally, like a child musing. Brown from the orchard and lean from the work, her orange hair longer now and curling around her face, despite Mrs Atkin's approaches with the pudding-basin. Cleo was pretty, a young summer face.

She seemed shy, but she wasn't. Sometimes the shyness of Wyatt's deer: *They flee from me that somtime did me seke, With naked fote stalkyng within my chamber.* Cleo had animal ambiguity, even in Gunning Street's prosaic dirt and clutter—as likely wild as scared, powerful as frail. And wholly at ease. I doubted if I had ever known Cleo's kind of physical innocence.

'You're not sensual,' she said, after we had made love and lay sleepy.

'No?' I felt disappointment though I'd been thinking the identical thought. 'I've never much liked my body. I can understand Swift.'

'I can't.'

'You've no idea how bad it once was. Before the first orgasm.'

'When?'

'With Julia. I never got undressed with her. And only sometimes since, with other people. I need clothes over it.'

Cleo giggled. 'Aren't you funny?'

'Am I?'

'I wouldn't wear clothes ever, if I could help it.'

'I guess you're lucky.'

'I guess I am,' she said definitely and moved her warm body against me. 'You're good to look at, those neat full breasts, all of it. Strange that you don't like it.'

'Oh now, I don't know ...' I stammered, confused. 'It's easier, really is. With you. You show me. The others didn't.'

'Not Julia?'

'I suspect Julia hates her body.'

'Libby then?'

'Libby ... she's ... in bed she's absorbed in herself—she's after her pleasure, bored once she's happy. And she's a seeker. Always looking for kicks. You don't seem to strive, anywhere. You're with me and we're together in all of it ... you're weird, Cleo—you teach me.'

There was a flicker of solemn pleasure, breaking into laughter. 'It's you that's experienced,' she said.

'It's you that knows, darling.' She kissed me instantly, fire and love, thrusting her tongue into my mouth, daring to act without thought, without waiting. *This woman is amazing.* I accepted, passive but alive in every lambent muscle. She leaned over me, setting my skin alive at every touch, gently drawing my body into her simmering excitement. Her palm swept swiftly down my backbone, feathered my backside, parted cunt open from behind. 'I want to go in you ...' 'Yes.' Voices small and passing. She sank her fingers into that jumping-jack-flash warm wet cunt; I felt her sense me, concentrate, drive, relax, measure rhythm, court me, mouth on mine again, on my face, my eyelids, my neck until the split waves resolve in the last slow rollers up that weird cliff, smooth slow dance into nowhere everywhere firework super-come fuck complete. I yelled—enough to make you want to scream. *Cleo.* Running my limp fingers over her skin in mute grateful amaze-ment. 'I must call you darling more often.' 'Ah, I like it,' she said, simply, nestling into my shoulder and closing her eyes. I lay a while and gazed through her hair at the opaque window, glanced a moment down at her quiet head, and went to sleep, a deep shared sleep.

The morning was cool, still dark; I woke with her, got out to make breakfast and went up the dark street to call a taxi. We said goodbye on the chilly, shadowy pavement. I promised to ring her at Worth-golds and wanted to drop the façade of sex-and-sex-only-don't-expect-more. I could only look at her and think that something had really changed, that I would break it off with Andy, that it was Cleo I loved.

A car swung into the Worthgold driveway and disappeared behind the house. I sprinted along the old railroad to keep the vehicle in sight but saw only a tubby man in cricket whites. He went inside. Must be Worthgold Senior, just back from a match with the Rosewood Baptist Fourths. I decided to ask him where Cleo was, though I baulked at the possibility of a prolonged conversation.

149

He came to the front door, carrying a bath-towel.

'Excuse me, but you must be Mr Worthgold.'

'Yes.' He was surprised that the strange girl knew him.

'I'm a friend of Cleo Atkin, you see and er ... I was out this way er ... visiting my family and thought I might drop in and say hullo to her.' I smiled engagingly. Worthgold looked guardedly annoyed, en route to the bath, I guessed, and unwilling to be interrupted.

'Well, Cleo's not here. Mrs Worthgold's been giving the youngsters a trip around the district since it's their last day. It is Cleo's last day here, you see.' I let the pause go until he was obliged to comment that they would all be back fairly soon if I had the time to wait, hoping I wouldn't.

'Oh I'm in no hurry, Mr Worthgold. I'll wait if I may.'

'Come in, then. Come in. Adrian!'

He seated me on the sofa in a small sitting-room, TV, immaculate antimacassars, china ducks pulsing in technicolor across one wall, bookshelf lined with old volumes—titles like *Sin and Predestination*, *The Layman's Approach to Calvin*. On the table was a stack of magazines, the *Baptist Chronicle*.

'Adrian, perhaps you'll entertain this er ... young lady, what did you say your name was?'

'I didn't, but it's Maureen. Maureen Craig.'

'Scots is it?'

'Possibly. Most of the family is Irish.'

'Oh,' he said, faintly disappointed.

'Protestants, though.'

'Well, this is my second son, Adrian. Excuse me. I must bathe before the cherry-pickers—they're always filthy.' He turned and marched out.

Adrian was a lank youth, his face disfigured by thick pimples, and a mawkish pair of horn-rimmed spectacles tilted forward on his nose in parody, it seemed, of some aged statesman. He wore a tie, even on a Saturday. I shook a sweaty limp palm and sat down again quickly.

'Maureen, is it?'

'Yes, a friend of Cleo's,' I answered, helping him out of his puzzlement.

'University?'

'Yes. Just finished third year. And you?'

'I'm studying for the ministry.'

'I see. Is it interesting?'

'Oh yes. And more. It's a vocation.'

'Yes.'

He broke the silence by offering me a cup of tea, and went out. The sitting-room was dark, heavy drapes half across its single window, full of old awkward furniture, dominated by Worthgold's theological collection. The only colour was the ducks'. Unexception-able hands Cleo had been placed in, if only her parents could have seen.

The young man and I recognised mutually that we had nothing in common and little to say to each other; both of us covertly listening for the car which would deliver us from each other's company, meanwhile falling back on the perennials.

'It's been a good year for the cherries,' he said. 'At least since the rain.'

'Were you picking?'

'Oh no. Sarah, that's my sister, she tells me.'

'Oh.'

'Chilly evening, though.'

'But clear. It'll be fine tomorrow.'

'Most likely,' he replied and shot out of his chair with unexpected speed as we heard the crunch of wheel on gravel and the low note of a quiet engine. 'That's them. Do go out to meet Cleo if you like, through here.'

Nervous and suddenly afraid that Cleo would hate seeing me here, in the other world, I stood outside the kitchen door as a crowd of Worthgolds exploded out of the car, bearing bags of cherries. She got out on the far side and straightened up, brown face, nose red and peeled off, a small white sun-hat moulded on her head, her shirt stained with cherry juice, her hands, face, clothes, all covered in red earth.

'Whatever are you doing here, Maureen?' she called out, to my embarrassment. I walked over, trying to be slow and relaxed. *How fucking lovely you are.* 'Oh I was out this way, thought I'd say hullo to the cherry hero.' *She's not pleased to see me. Thinks I'll show her up.*

We walked towards each other and she said, quietly, 'What would you be doing out this way?' A mixture of irritation and a potential giggle at my transparency.

'Lookin' for you,' I answered in an undertone.

'Thought so. Come on, silly. Meet Mrs Worthgold.'

I met Mrs Worthgold, who exuded an unexpected flair and warmth, and all the little Worthgolds. Cleo was utterly surrounded and the chances of exchanging even a private sentence looked slim. I caught her getting her washing off the line. 'I'll go soon. But please walk with me to the station.'

She frowned. 'Dinner's ready, cold because Mrs W's been giving us a tour of the sights. I can't leave before the meal.'

'And I can't stay.'

'You haven't been asked. Oh Maureen, how crazy you are—I'm coming down tomorrow anyway. Why this?'

'Yeah. I'm off my head. I ... wanted to take you back with me.'

151

'Tonight?'

'Yeah.'

'But Libby and that bloke of hers are coming up to collect me—tomorrow.'

'I didn't know.'

'You never hinted you'd come—on the phone.'

'I only decided this morning. I got your letter. I wanted to see you.'

'Take a look then.'

'Look, I'll just say goodbye to all that lot then.'

'You don't belong in this,' she persisted.

'I know. But neither do you.' She tacitly dissented.

Mrs Worthgold, however, wouldn't hear of me going off so soon, an unlooked-for reprieve.

'I didn't realise it'd be so late when you got back,' I offered by way of apology.

'Of course not,' she answered kindly. 'Sit anywhere. We'll have tea soon.'

After the grace (for what we were about to receive), the meal, the grace (for what we had received) and the dishes, I suggested a walk to Cleo, an idea welcomed on all sides by the clamouring Worthgolds. A platoon to accompany the unsuspected lovers. Jesus. Up on the old railway we let the others forge ahead with the torch and stumbled in the darkness over the sleepers, blackberries whipping at our legs. Starlight only, and the rest ahead shouting. Only her round white hat showed up in the darkness. I took her hand and she held mine willingly.

'I came to tell you something, Cleo. I love you. Suppose it wasn't true in the beginning. I was playing all my chances, escaping, but I've chosen. I really do love you.'

She was silent, squeezed my hand just perceptibly; and we walked on as if nothing had happened.

At the station, with another squad of Worthgolds buzzing about to wave me off and take Cleo back to the house, I found a moment to follow her into the empty drab waiting-room while the others broke into a lightning game of tag up the platform. I kissed her.

'I'll stay with you tomorrow,' she said. 'I'll get Libby and Fred to bring me to Gunning Street.'

'That's great. Till tomorrow.'

Inga was waiting for the Manangatang cousin when I got home. I collapsed while she made tea. 'When's he coming?'

'He is at a concert from Mahler. Perhaps ten. You have been in the sun.'

'Yeah, I hitched out to Rosewood—it's at the foot of the mountains.'

'Max has gone tonight on the Spirit,' she said, preoccupied. 'I was at the station.'

'I thought he was going tomorrow.'

'Oh, he still wanted that I should go with him. He said he did not want to put eyes on my Kraut cousin.'

'Poor Max.'

'It is this hypocrisy that makes me leave my family. My father he ruled always like Hitler. Breakfast is at seven and we must all be there. And he is saying nothing the whole meal unless I am late or someone is not dressed proper. It is just all forms like this. Always I am shit-scared too, climbing in the basement window if it is late. And I do not even sleep with Gustave. I am escaping families. And Max, he does not understand why I do not like to go with him.'

'He just thought you might stop his parents being so hard on him. And he wanted to be with you.'

'Yes. It is silly that we quarrel about this.'

'Yeah. I bet Max wouldn't mind being on the other side of the world so he didn't have to face his parents and try to convince them he's doing what they want.'

'I am harsh because now it is more easy for me. We are not so different.'

She looked at me, shy and inquiring. 'You know. We are each the first for the other. It was so funny, so sad, this first night. We try and try. And it will not go in.' She brought her fist up to nuzzle her palm. 'We think will it fit at all? So we try again and again. And it is not working. Max cried. We both cried. For hours and hours, nearly all night. Now we think that is funny. But it was so sad. Max is a man of gentleness. Not like Jake. It is a pity he is still pretending so much.'

'You made it though?'

'The next night. Shall we try again? Max said. Just like that. He was a bit grim and also a bit laughing. We start to giggle. And it was not so hard.'

I wanted to ask her what it was like but felt the question intolerably naïve. 'I've never done it,' I said simply.

'Andy is not wanting?'

'No, he thinks he shouldn't until he gets married.' I laughed. 'Anyway I broke it off last week. It wasn't any good with him. Really,' I went on suddenly, 'the thing is I love Cleo. I went to see her today at Rosewood.'

Inga was evidently at ease. 'It is all right, no worries?' she asked.

'Just beginning. Yeah. It's fine. It's different from before. Yeah. It's good.' I grinned, a bit red in the face.

'You are not ashamed?'

'No. A bit embarrassed, I suppose. I'm always scared of what people might think. I mean you might've stopped talking to me or moved out.'

'Shit,' she said succinctly.

'I don't even know if Max knows. I'd never tell him.'

'No?'

'He'd disapprove.'

'I do not know, but I do not think so. But perhaps it is more bad in Australia.'

'Perhaps it is,' I repeated, 'more bad.' It had, on the other hand, never seemed better.

Trouble, the kitten, sat on my chest purring. Nine o'clock. I'd have liked to sleep until she came. Sunday in Carlton, hot summer streets with no-one in them, the city in the grip of its Sunday sleep, everyone departed for the string of coastal beaches. Even the fish and chip shop closed. The Kraut cousin had duly called for Inga and Max was already in Wodonga beginning the nightmare Christmas holiday, a week ridden with obligatory Masses, naggings and other memorials to his Catholic youth. Probably right now he was providing his annual explanation for his failure to measure up to Martin.

Sonny was downstairs singing in his inimitable low-key whine, making tea. I opened the window, warm sun, still air, and leaned out over the back yard. 'Hey Sonny!' He shuffled out from the kitchen, looked up at me and saluted military-style. 'Mother! You're awake early. Tea coming up.' I lay back watching Trouble arrange his neat black body along the window-sill in the sun.

Max had shifted his rifle-rack, pith-helmets, spare muffler and guitar into the East Wing when Martin left, leaving me the option on his tiny upstairs room, where I could escape the eternal bottle-yard with its resonant outdoor telephone bell. Facing east across the jumbled pattern of terrace roofs, it was a simple room with an unobtrusive ceiling and a hardboard wall decorated with Max's graphics—plans, blue-pencil views of house-designs, etchings of every conceivable kind of architecture, interspersed with comic-strip mice and designs for the traps that might catch them.

Sonny brought tea and announced that he was going to Rosebud with his new girl. 'Come along,' he suggested. 'Got any food?'

'I'll find some.'

She'll be there already, I thought, as we arrived back having killed the day, numb from the windy ride up the Bay Road in Sonny's open car. On the back of my note to her Cleo had written: Gone to Libby's. It's for the best; for us both. Cryptic, but unmistakably a backdown. Never show anyone you mean it. This is the blunder. I hate it—all the games, all that fencing, all that not letting on so as to gain the desired one by circuitous appearances of non-interest.

I went out on Monday very early, walked two or three times around the city, block for block, all over, buying a Christmas present here and there. I came back along Royal Parade, had a drink at Naughton's and returned in the evening through the deserted University, savouring the warmth of sun-drenched asphalt on the soles of my feet, the peculiar miracle of warm wind on shirt sleeves, that faint flutter of cloth in mild air.

'Hi, Erif.'

'Hello, Maureen. Cleo's upstairs.'

'Cleo?'

'Yes. She came at lunchtime. I thought you'd've been back.'

She was standing in the corner of the room.

'You've come,' I said quietly.

She looked straight at me, expecting rage perhaps, anxious and supplicatory.

'I thought you'd decided against it.'

'Forgive me, Maureen. Libby wanted me to stay with her. You weren't here. I didn't know what to do.'

'And if I had been here?'

'You weren't.'

'But you have come ... to stay with me awhile ... have you?'

She looked down, then up again, almost defiant. 'Please,' she said. I closed the door behind me and walked to her, wanting simply to kiss her shy brown cherry-orchard face and love her.

'You've been here all day?'

'I looked for you everywhere, college, the library, the caf. I thought you'd never come home.'

'I never imagined you'd be here.'

'I'm sorry.'

'Doesn't matter.'

'It was mean and weak. I let you down. I'm afraid a bit—but it is still the best thing that's ever happened to me. I'm glad you came to Rosewood—you were so silly, but so nice.'

'Ah shit, was I?' I took her hand and pulled her to the window. 'What a day!'

'What did you do?'

'Walked. Decided you could have it your way without a struggle. I wasn't sure what your note meant, except it stank of the old moral bind.'

'I've been uncertain. And you weren't here to balance that. To make me remember we're pure, and that none of that moral stuff applies or ever could.'

We stood together, arms around each other, looking out over the roofs. Free gift Cleo. I stroked her neck. 'D'y'want to make love?'

That look, that wild tameless shameless burn of a look.

'Jesus, Cleo. I love you. I want you. Everything.' There's sun slanting on the roofs, sheer blue sky. And this great stroke of luck: she's come. She's come to me.

Undressing, silently, with relief. Facing her. Holding her body to mine; held. Kissing her soft lips; kissed. Taking her to my bed; taken. The limp needless words unspoken. Body whole and invincible, giving myself up to the long lazy ride, the towering set.

'Stay still,' she said.

'And you?'

'I came with you—all the way.'

'Yeah?'

'Yes. And the other times too.'

'Hey, I didn't know that. I didn't notice. I didn't expect it.'

'Why not?'

'Well. You'd never made love before me, had you?'

'No.'

'I thought probably you wouldn't at first. I didn't for a long time.'

'It's always been there.' Staggering matter-of-fact statement.

'Always?' I asked.

'Shall I tell you?'

'Please.'

'I can remember it as far back as when I was five. I used to wake up in the middle of the night all alone. And the cock would crow. It frightened me, the empty screeching in the darkness and silence. And then I ... would do it. It made me feel nice, and safe, and warm. I'd go back to sleep soon if I did that. I liked it. Always.'

'That's amazing. I don't know anyone like you. Anyone who never had to find it, anyone at all who had it all along. In fact, I suppose I thought it couldn't happen before ... er ... puberty anyway.'

'It did.'

'So strange. And your parents. They're the coldest, most anti-sex parents I've ever met. They didn't know?'

'Perhaps they thought it was impossible.'

'Yeah. I would've.'

'And as far back as I can remember I was making sure they wouldn't see. Only in the middle of the night when I needed it. They never came in. They went to bed early and stayed there. I knew they wouldn't like it somehow. But I knew that that must be their silliness; because it was good, and it took away the fear and made the rooster quiet.'

'Must be your grandmother's blood.'

'Didn't you ever do anything like that when you were a kid?'

'Not that I remember. Could easily have been belted out of me at an early age. But I don't have the vaguest recollection of ever finding my body pleasant or fun. I was very careful not to touch it. I never ... er ... masturbated until after I discovered you could have an orgasm.'

We grinned at each other, almost blushing at our own frankness; we lay a long time in companionable silence, my arm under her neck, legs linked, exchanging looks only occasionally, not asleep but at mutual peace. I could talk to Cleo. Or I could be quiet. There seemed never to be any strain.

The masters make the rules

I felt uneasy when Cleo went back Upton. Staying in Melbourne was wholly out of the question for her—vacation time was parent time, and Carlton was as much a sink of iniquity for Mrs Atkin as for my own mother. I shivered at the possibility of Mrs Atkin divining Cleo's thoughts, suspecting Cleo's sinister affair with me. Nervous but determined, I accepted the long-sought invitation to spend a weekend at the Atkin holiday house. A weird weekend split between courting the parents with good manners, household help and charming humour, and devising ways to be alone with Cleo. At night we gave them half an hour to go to sleep after the lights went out.

'All quiet, Cleo?'

'All quiet. Come over.'

Breathing shallow, listening, listening. 'I bet your mother could move as quietly as a mouse.'

'She doesn't suspect. As long as we make no noise ...'

Fortunately, the ancient holiday beds consisted of mountains of kapok loaded onto bare boards. Safe silent bunks, sinking without a creak. Conscious of danger, scarcely speaking, moving together slow and almost silent, we fucked for hours—through Cleo's third orgasm into the dead of the Anglesea night. In pitch darkness, I kissed her forehead and went back to my own bunk to sleep.

The next evening, after tea, we walked over to Roadknight and climbed up onto the high ridge of sand which shelters its quiet bay from the south. We stood arm in arm on the edge of a hollow amongst the dunes and looked down to the ocean below, the rocks laid bare by the tide, the flat still pools reflecting the fading colours of the sky. I felt quiet and untroubled.

'It's too risky back there,' she said.

'It was good though.'

'Yeah. But I think we'd better not. Imagine if they heard.'

'We'd tell them we love each other and ask them to discuss the matter in the clearer light of day.'

'Oh yeah? My mother would give you an even icier time than Mrs Stace did, you can bet your boots.'

'Wouldn't like to risk my boots.'

'It's not worth it. The trouble would ruin everything.'

A faint misgiving, the knowledge that Cleo would never stand up to her parents, whatever the loss. 'I see,' I said quietly. 'You are right, of course. It'd be bloody nasty.'

Night was coming down on the sea; light wind ruffled the tussocks around our hollow. Sand rose steep on three sides but swelled only slightly towards the ocean, where the dune dropped down fifty feet, sloping sharply to the rocks. Tussock and hummock blocked off the mainland and the world, everything out of sight except the sea where it met the sapphire sky. The evening star began to flicker; the moon, already risen in the east, grew bright. Cleo slipped her hand into mine, face earnest and childlike, eyes defiant and inviting.

'It's better here, anyway,' I said simply, and took off my jacket and jeans, laying them out in the most sheltered angle of the hollow.

'This is our sort of place,' she said.

'Yeah. No-one for miles. Just the beach down there.'

In the morning we went swimming near the town, waves blunted by warm vertical rain, spattered oily swells.

'Will you come to Lakes Entrance?'

'My parents would never agree.'

'Can't you tell them you're just going to Cobb Swamp?'

'Maybe.'

'They seem to have taken a liking to me.'

'Your achievement. I would never have believed you could stop yourself saying shit.'

'Shit. Only if there's something at stake. Like you. I'd do anything to keep us smooth.'

'I bet you would.'

'Come to Lakes.'

'Perhaps.'

New Years Eve. Gunning Street was deserted—Sonny was off courting his teenage girlfriend; Erif was down with Steve's family at their holiday house on the Bay. My family, whose New Year's Eves I had suffered for most of my natural life, were back at Cobb Swamp now, celebrating with Mother's old friends at last. And Cleo was undoubtedly sipping lemonade and picking at morsels of fruitcake.

Andy's car stopped out front.

'You're not all alone?'

'Yeah.'

'Want to come to a party? There's about six I know of. We could check 'em all and have a ball.'

'Ah shit, Andy, you know how it is.'

'Come on. I haven't got a bird to take along. You haven't got a party to crash. Let's just go together.'

I looked at his merry face, and saw that it was impossible to gauge whether we were in fact doing each other a good turn or plunging back in where I had already drawn out. 'Is there someone else?' he had asked dramatically, since he thought not. 'No,' I had replied, since any explanation must involve her identity—at least the fact of her being a woman. I had told him about loving Libby, long before. But a straight statement that Andy was a lousy insensitive lover who didn't

159

measure up to childish-Cleo-running-home-to-Mummy? I doubted if any credible truth could be told about my decision to break. And doubted that my version of the truth was in any way important to Andy.

We bought a few bottles and drove out to Malvern. Music, laughter, a bath full of beer, and most of Andy's friends. 'Bull's-eye!' he shouted over the Beatles. 'This is the scene.' We sat in a corner by the record-player, near enough to let the music fill our silence. How was Anglesea? Fine. How was his own holiday at Torquay? Great. Eleanor Rigby pulsed out. I sang along. Andy hummed flat. People danced.

'Wanna dance?'

'OK.'

We danced, enthusiasm muted. What were we going to do with each other?

'Another beer?'

'I'll get it Andy.'

'You will not. Sit down again—it's up to me to struggle through all those guys in the kitchen.'

'I don't mind.' But he was gone, manoeuvring through the crowd and exchanging greetings and guffaws.

This was impossible. I was not Andy's girl. Perhaps I never had been. And no other role appeared to be open. Except to sit and listen and pass the time. However much Andy had given me status, his friends didn't approach. Because I was his girl—or possibly they found me as inadequately feminine as I had always feared. I recalled parties in first year where I had sat alone, studied indifference to my situation and gone home feeling worthless. Cleo? A hope, a happiness. But our love remained a passion in isolation, a brightness with no conceivable context. To be Cleo's girl was no solution to this uneasiness—rather a complication. I would have wanted to dance with Cleo but, if she had been there, I would have remained paralysed.

Andy dumped a beer. 'Back soon. Must talk to Pete.'

'Right.'

'You don't mind?'

'Of course not. We're both free.'

He looked doubtful, pouted a little and turned away. Along the wall a small blond boy took nervous gulps from his glass, put it down and began twisting his hands together, knotting his fingers and painfully unravelling them to pick up his glass and begin again. He looked sideways and caught me looking sideways at him. I smiled slightly. *He's a real Nowhere Man, sitting in his Nowhere Land, making all his Nowhere Plans for nobody.* 'That's me,' he said, looking towards me again. 'Yeah?' I felt impelled to answer. 'Yeah,' he said. He picked up his glass and sidled a few inches closer along the wall. What's your name, what do you do, who do you know here—limp exchange. Andy was laughing his head off with Pete.

'He your boyfriend?'

'No. Just a friend. Why do you think you're the Nowhere Man?'

'I am.'

'I'm going,' I told Andy after Auld Lang Syne and the kissing.

'I'll drive you.'

'We'll hitch.'

'Who?'

'That blond guy over there can't get back to Hastings. He can crash in the East Wing. Max is still away.'

'Oh.' Andy looked hurt.

'Come on, Andy. I don't really know anyone here. You're in your element. Don't worry. And please don't get upset.'

'No,' he said, frowning. 'OK. Maureen. See you.'

'Thanks for coming around tonight and bringing me out.'

He waved a not-at-all.

'You notice,' Julien remarked, 'that I've got bow-legs.' I looked at them and agreed provisionally.

'You know why?'

'People do have them, sometimes.'

'But I didn't used to. Once. My father told me why, too, when he caught me. And it's obvious. I've twisted them out of shape.' His pale parboiled eyes registered the horror of his having inflicted irreparable damage on himself.

'How do you mean?'

'From er ...' He hesitated, took a deep breath and launched in. 'I'm so bloody lonely down there on the farm. There's nobody for miles. And I lied. I'm not at Monash. Not even at school. I work on the farm. I crashed that party. I do sometimes—come up to Melbourne at the weekend and look for a place where there's a party and the door's open and that. And where there's students, usually, because they don't get so snooty if they find out you're a crasher. I have to get away. It's paddocks and paddocks and dirt roads and just my father and sister and he hates me. You must think I'm weird.'

'Everyone's weird if they stop pretending.'

'And that's why. That's why my bloody legs are like bloody boomerangs. He used to even stop me going into Hastings. And what's there? The worst thing, he caught me trying to get onto my sister. I s'pose you think that's terrible.'

'No.'

'And he beat the living daylights out of me. I couldn't walk for a week, couldn't even drive the tractor. They had to tell the doctor I'd got beaten up by a gang in Melbourne. Purple all over and big welts. He used his horsewhip.'

'Jesus, what a brutal bastard.'

161

'S'pose he was making sure I wouldn't try it again. And that's why my bloody legs got so bloody crooked. From ... masturbating. Might as well say it. I s'pose you think that's terrible.'

'No. I do it.'

'*You* do it???'

'Most people do, at least sometimes. I bet your father does.'

He looked incredulous.

'Why don't you leave?'

'Leave? Dad and Bessie?'

'Yeah.'

'I don't know. Where would I go? What would I do?' He gazed hopelessly into space.

'Really, Julien, I'm certain you couldn't have bent your bones. You must have been born like that. Tough luck, but not your fault.'

'My father said I used to have straight legs and he ought to know.' Julien was beyond the reach of reasonable argument and looked as if he would remain so, convinced of the damage he had done himself.

'Come on, then,' I said gently. 'Come upstairs.'

I pointed into Max's room and said, 'You can sleep there if you like, or with me if you'd prefer.'

He glanced sharply at me. 'All right, I'll come in with you. Nice to have company.'

Julien had the usual reservations about actually fucking a virgin—much as he believed that only normal sex might mitigate the problem of his ever-bowing legs. I was thankful for his moral restraint by the time we'd been in bed for five minutes. 'You shouldn't put your tongue in my mouth,' he gasped. 'That's not right.'

'Why not?'

'Not normal. Jeez. Aren't you funny or something. You keep moving around and that. I picked up girls before at parties—for a bit of a cuddle—but none of 'em ever moved. They stay still and let you do it to 'em. Like a bloke's s'posed to.'

What hope does this poor bastard have? I thought. What hope in the world? He's so bloody shackled, a whole lifetime won't be long enough to free him, even if he knew how to start—or even wanted to start.

I kissed his smooth hairless cheek, avoided his watery eyes and turned my back to him, murmuring good night.

'Never been able to talk to a girl before, like that,' he told me next morning at the front door.

'Hope it helps,' I said.

'I'd like to see a lot of you.'

'But Hastings is a hell of a way out,' I parried, certain that I could not take him on.

'I come up weekends.'

He's lonely, I was thinking, knotted to buggery in his own mind—beyond help probably. And I'm no paragon of sexual normality or simplicity. Not to mention Cleo. I should tell him this, that I have a lover, a woman; that I won't be any good to him. Yet I identified with his trap and his loneliness.

'I don't think I can help you, Julien,' I said tenuously.

'Just to talk.'

'Call in then, if you're here. But don't come specially. It won't be worth it.' I spoke detachedly, but blunted it with a helpless smile. He pecked me on the cheek and turned down Gunning Street, ambling on his wide legs like a cartoon Popeye, looking back again and again to wave.

Father drove us out of Cobb to the highway. Six bundles—tent, camping gear, sleeping-bags—stacked up on the gravel. The morning sun was hot, the Gippsland paddocks hazy and yellowish. Cleo was overcome by her own daring, not only at agreeing to hitch to Lakes Entrance with me, but at spinning the tacit lie to her parents who thought she was spending a safe week at Cobb Swamp with the newly-returned Craig family. My mother, long unhappy with the isolation of suburban life and increasingly certain that the city was the source of all human shame and infamy, had decided at last to return to the place where she belonged—leaving both her wayward salvationless children to ruin their lives as they wished, she having done everything that could have been expected of her.

The hitch from Cobb was easy, though Lakes was full of people. Finally, at the far end of town, a woman whose camping ground was full agreed to let us pitch our tent in her garden under the apple tree. Free at last. No-one knew us; no-one bothered. We could tie up the flap and lie together with impunity.

In the afternoon we shot waves and stretched out on the beach, so amazed at finding ourselves alone together that we could say little and do nothing but exchange grins and laughter, walk arm in arm with a sense of daring. 'That's where I nearly drowned Ken.' 'There's bream under this bridge.' Schoolboys leaned on the railings, dangling lines wound around cork. I threw five cents in the Wishing-Well. 'What did you wish?' she asked. 'Nothing. I don't want anything else.'

Naked in our impregnable tent, listening to the familiar rifle-report of the undertow on the reef. Time stops and the rules are as meaningless as the absent masters.

'You are beautiful, Cleo.'

'Beauty's in the eye of the beholder.'

'It's in mine, all right.'

'It sure is.'

Earth solid under us; apples hitting the ground now and then or sagging the canvas and rolling down the tent.

'So good to be alone, now,' I say.

'No-one knows.'

'No enemies.'

My fascinated hands trace the lines of her body, her breasts, her spine, arms, feet, thighs. Contact so complementary that to touch and to be touched are the same, are merged. Her breast touches my hand, my feet stroke her legs. *I am whole. Shared undifferentiated desire. That's what is strange with men—they are unilateral.*

Beneath her hair her cunt is closed, but swelled-soft and moist.

'I want to go in.' Echoing her.

'It's closed. There's no way.'

'I'll make way.'

'Might hurt.'

'I'm gentle.'

'Slowly.'

'Always.'

Tenderly, exploring cunt. Find the place. And stroke the tight muscle, moving into her. Privileged. I do not know for sure if something must be broken. Hope not. No pain. Sinew and tension. 'Must push.' Gathering her flow on my fingertips moving and retreating slowly until she is immersed in the rhythm; yielding; away, back. The tight neck opens, she cries out, I slide into her narrow cunt, hold an instant, come out, return.

'Do I hurt you?'

'Not now. Just at first.'

'Will you come?'

'No,' she says simply. 'It's too new, too strange. I will, another time.'

'Shall I stay?'

'A little.'

'Feels nice in there.'

'For me too. Like nothing else. To discover a new bit to my body.'

I took her to see Jamieson, the preacher; I took her fishing for bream under the bridge. We rowed up the north arm taking turns at rowing and at sitting back in the stern under the scorching sun. She met the people of the Tea House who treated us both to scones with jam and cream and were delighted by our visit, remembering me better than I had imagined they would. We went to the red cliff past Lake Bunga, to the entrance and to the lookout where the road winds down above the lakes and sea. All over the town and to all the places I'd found there or known as a child. And between our explorations we returned to the tent and shut the world out.

Dr Hudson wanted me to do group therapy—a repulsive notion, yet I trusted a man whose priorities put love before normality. 'It's a social model, in a way,' he said. 'All kinds of people, all kinds of problems. The difference is that you can and must say exactly what you please; you can bring the conflicts out in the open. It's a group with a lot of men—this might disturb you but you can probably see why I advise such a group. The situation is closed. Everyone can afford to be himself or herself. It might be a way to learn to say what you think and, in the long run, how to deal effectively with the fact that people disapprove of you. Because, of course, the others will be free to criticise you, just as you are free to do that too.'

A challenge, I thought, and agreed to go along with it. Might turn out useful, after all, the way he described it. I had said very little through the summer sessions, listening to the handsome young man who discussed his impotency; to Bruce, the stout-faced man of fifty who puzzled and complained about his breaking marriage; to Nigel, the urbane Englishman who liked young boys and drew on himself the condemnation of the entire group. I remained quiet. Until the day that Cleo's letter arrived. 'Don't write or ring me at home, C.' She had scrawled this across a torn scrap of foolscap. I stood utterly still in the hallway, head bent over the bombshell fragment. Can't mean that. Must mean that. Flash to Mrs Atkin pursing tight lips, perpetrating awful silences, manic earnest woman faced with, only explanation, Cleo's affair with me. How? When? Too delayed to be the result of any indiscretion of ours. Cleo had come to Cobb Swamp with as much of her parents' blessing as she ever got. Burning need to know. Yet that knowledge was trivial if the truth was out.

'I would like to speak tonight,' I said awkwardly, as if to announce myself. They looked at me. 'Something bad happened today. I got a letter from my girl calling it off because her parents found out.'

'So you're a lesbian are you?' George drawled lazily. A big-muscled, oblong-faced man who had rarely talked, except to hint that he did not much like people, especially women, and that his difficulties were with aggression. Don't get defensive Craig. Calmly.

'Well,' I said, 'most of my sexual relationships have been with women.'

'Why?' George asked, a mixture of taunt and curiosity.

'I loved them; it happened naturally—it grew out of friendship. I doubt if there is any other reason. And now this has happened.' I sounded calmer than I was.

'Didn't you ever fancy boys?' he pursued sarcastically.

'I don't want to talk about what's wrong with me in your eyes ...' I hesitated. Stomach sinking, I was already beginning to regret my boldness.

'Maureen is in some ... distress, George, I should think. You might at least remain silent if you've nothing constructive to offer.' Nigel uncrossed his legs and crossed them again, neatly, leaning forward intently.

'I don't see why. We say what we want to say. I don't like you, anyway. I don't like poofters.' Nigel raised his eyebrows and stared a moment at George, then withdrew under his hooded eyes.

'You sound as if you've accepted your affairs with women. You don't seem to fight it. Now don't you think that's dangerous for you?' Bruce's reedy voice coaxed.

'Dangerous?'

'If you don't in fact struggle to get out of it, you might spend your whole life ... like that.'

'So what?'

'Personally, I don't hold with it,' he explained with a faint show of tolerance. 'And besides, every woman needs a man. That's nature.'

'Look Bruce, I'm not going to have the argument about what's natural and what's not. It would appear to me to be solely a matter of opinion. But I do want to ask you something. If you reckon a man and a woman are the perfect answer to each other, how come you're here? Because you're always telling us that your wife treats you horribly.'

'She does,' he squeaked. 'Never cleans a floor except if I tell her to and ...'

'You've told us before. What I never asked you before is why she should clean the floors? Personally, I hate cleaning floors. Why is it such a disgrace that she doesn't keep the house spotless for you?'

'It's a woman's business. And she has nothing else to do.'

'Nothing except to be your servant. I'd jack up too if I'd been your servant for thirty bloody years. If I was her, I'd not only leave the place filthy on purpose, I'd put sleeping-pills in your coffee whenever you complained—and shut you up. You spend all your time whining—even here.'

'I wouldn't expect a girl like you to see eye-to-eye with me.' Bruce pouted and shut up.

I sat there, the dreadful implications of Cleo's letter whirling in my brain, surrounded by fourteen hostile faces, only Nigel neutral, withdrawn from George and silently playing with his cane. I looked towards the handsome young man with erective difficulties; his gaze was averted towards a frieze of children's chalk drawings at the end of the room. I glanced covertly at the women: a warm intelligent housewife who had never mentioned her own reason for attending but had offered unfailingly sympathetic advice to almost everyone; a quiet student who had spoken of conflicts with her family; and a stern

166

advertising executive who was obsessed with her career. They all sat silent, eyes on Hudson. If he thought he was working with a model of Aussie society, he was obviously absolutely right.

The men stared at me. I said nothing. The air was vibrating with their hostility. Bloody queers. She won't get anywhere with me.

'Maureen.' Hudson addressed me with a kindness which relieved some of the strain. 'Tell us what happened with the girl you mentioned. I think that is what you set out to attempt.' He glanced around the group for confirmation of his suggestion, got none, but looked back at me, questioning.

'Yes,' I said. 'Cleo and I love each other. We've been together a few times through the summer. It was only the beginning, but we were coming close, trusting, teaching each other.'

'What?' George cut in.

'She was ... she was showing me that there is nothing to be ashamed of. That sex is not sick, not evil. That it's bloody marvellous to make love with someone you really care about.' They were embarrassed by this. 'But you can all be at peace in your minds. Because it's over. Because her parents have found out somehow. And she won't oppose her mother.'

'I should think not.' Bruce again.

'You got children, Bruce?'

'Yes. Three, all married I'm happy to say.'

'And if one of them had been homosexual, what would you have done?'

'None of my children could have been like that.'

I gave a false sarcastic snigger and saw Nigel smile covertly in his corner. 'The way you describe your wreck of a marriage, it surprises me that any of your kids was normal.'

'You blame it all on your parents, I suppose?'

'I don't blame it on anyone now. There is no blame.'

'Pretty cocky, aren't you, Maureen?' George sneered.

Nightmare. Black light. Fuck them.

'Jesus!' I said, very loud. 'I'm not bloody cocky now. They've smashed it up again. I'm just trying to hang on to what I believe is true.'

'And what if it's not?' George spoke slowly, needling, mocking. 'What makes you think you know the truth? Going to University?'

'I have only the subjective evidence of my love for Cleo and hers for me. That was real. That was beyond doubt.'

'Her parents doubt it, obviously. I doubt it.'

'You've admitted you don't even like people, so what do you know about it? And her parents—they don't find it relevant. They're not interested in love; they're interested in morality.'

167

'We all need morality,' Bruce added.

'I'm not suggesting we drop all our ethics and start killing each other. Sex is my business, and yours, and George's and Cleo's.'

'How old is she?'

'Twenty.'

'Well she's under age, isn't she?'

'The age of consent is eighteen.'

'Legally perhaps. But parents are right to feel responsible until their children are twenty-one. That's what I've always believed.'

'Cleo's parents'll try to shape her until she's eighty-one if they're still around.'

'Well—you'd only understand if you were a parent. Of course I'm concerned about my kids. Always was. Always will be. And the oldest is over thirty now.'

'Don't you realise that a child just might happen to be the kind of person its parents detest?'

'They've failed then, haven't they?'

'So they go on interfering, trying to force the child back into the mould of their expectations.'

'If they take their responsibility seriously, of course.'

I was getting close to screaming point. 'I just can't talk to you. You are so bloody blind, so bloody complacent, so bloody conservative— we're wasting each other's time.'

'You opened the subject,' he replied, nettled. 'And I'm supposed to say what I think.'

'I've never liked Bruce's moaning,' George said, just to keep the record straight, 'but I'm pleased to see he's got a bit of spirit about something. First time I've ever seen him stand up like a man instead of whining.'

Bruce blushed, then smiled a qualified small smile. I realised suddenly that no-one else was going to speak. Tacit accord, or embarrassment, or both.

'Anyway,' George continued, 'I don't like aggressive women.'

'You're not aggressive yourself, I suppose?'

'I'm not a woman.' He smiled thinly.

'You all believe everything you've been told. That's what's wrong with you all. You think you know what a woman should be like. You know nothing.'

George raised his eyebrows, smiled and said, 'Really? Surprising that you're here yourself when you know so much.'

'I have to live with ignorance. That's my hang-up.'

'That's your story.'

Hudson always summed up, gave us his account of what had happened. 'I'm disappointed,' he said flatly and swept his eyes around the circle. 'We are here, after all, to help each other. Each of us is in

168

some kind of trouble, which most of you appear to have forgotten this evening. Maureen has been asking you for help, for support, for some kind of human understanding. At the very least, she has asked you not to judge. Most of you have said nothing, by which we must assume that you do pass judgement along with Bruce and George. There is no rule that the group is obliged to attempt to understand its members—but I would have imagined that that was an unwritten imperative. I won't say you've failed. Perhaps you've all learned something. I will only ask you to be aware of what you have refused and to ask yourselves why. Goodnight.'

I waited until they'd gone, not daring to look at any of them. Only Nigel stopped as he passed my chair and said, 'Good night now, and cheer up if you can.' He extended his hand and I shook it. He smiled and went out.

'I doubt if I will come again,' I told Hudson.

'That would be a pity. They need to sort it out now, too.'

'If I saw a glimmer of any kind of ... contact ... with any of them, I might. But they're cold as stone and they know they're right, whatever you say to them.'

'Perhaps.'

'Thank you anyway.'

'Do you want a private appointment again, Maureen?'

'Yes. I'd like a chance to talk to someone.'

'OK.'

I stepped out into the night, alone and terrified, and walked down Dandenong Road towards Emma's flat. Sorrow at losing Cleo, rage and frustration with those fiendish group bigots; intense and confused all of it. Emma's light was on and I trod softly up the concrete stairs wondering why I had come.

'Maureen. What a splendid surprise.'

'My psychiatrist is out here, you know.' Condemn that for a start if you like.

'Of course. Come in.'

'Thanks. I think I want to talk to you. Do you mind?' I'd always been equivocal with Emma, pretended detachment on her lines, avoided admitting confusion.

'Not at all. You look done. Have a cup of tea?'

'Might save my life.'

'What's wrong then?' she said gently. Emma didn't like scenes.

'Just about everything. I'm really stuffed.'

She waited, attentive.

'I'm in love with Cleo. You remember Cleo?'

'Of course.'

'It only happened this summer. She was great. She's not caught up

169

in shame like most people. About sex, about being with a woman. We went to Lakes Entrance together, explored all the places. Had our tent to ourselves, some privacy. We were good together.'

'Yes. I've always liked Cleo.' Warmer than I was expecting.

'Well, I got a letter this morning. Her mother's found out—Jesus, the same story all over again. I'll go off my head.' Be cool and noncommittal, Emma. Slip off to make tea and come back talking about Benjamin Britten.

But Emma frowned, ran her hand back through her hair and looked me in the face. 'Maureen, that's dreadful. How did she find out?'

'Looks to me as if someone from college told her mother, who passed it on to Mrs Atkin in true public spirit. One of last year's freshers who made it so hot over Libby, I guess.'

'Narrow-minded bunch, aren't they?'

'Cleo'll do exactly as her bloody parents prescribe. She wouldn't hurt Mummy and Daddy.'

'She probably can't.'

'I know. I know. I sound meaner than I am.'

'Fair enough, too.'

I looked at her and realised that Emma was not going to knock me. She sat with her head thrown back, helpless in the situation, but unquestionably friendly. I talked for a while—about Cleo, about the therapy group, about the new bleak future. She listened squarely and without dutifulness. However wary I had been of Emma's probable opinions, it suddenly hit me, like a counterblast to Bruce and George, that Emma was not among the enemy, not one of the pseudo-tolerant covert judges. I had never dared to find out.

'Thank you,' I said as I left. 'You've no idea ... '

'That's all right. I just hope things look up. Drop in if you're at therapy—and if you need a break, come to Sydney next month and stay. I'll be settling in for the new job before term starts.'

'That'd be great. Thank you.'

She put her arm lightly across my shoulder, a rare gesture. 'Good night and good luck.'

'What I must tell you because it is the most important thing—to me—is that I love you more than anything in the world—but—because you are a woman and because I must "Think of my future" and because my parents are afraid I will degrade myself and never recover my "standards", I shall no longer be your lover, your associate or anything more than a casual friend. I cannot bear to tell you this—I cannot seem to do anything else—now my parents know. I refuse to deceive them and I have not the courage or rather the unfeelingness—for them—nor the trust in you to desert them—even though I know they would still love me.

'I hate my parents. I don't feel that I, nor anything the future may offer will be worth it. Darling, darling, my dearest.'

At times I hoped for Cleo's sake that she hadn't been as hopeful and elated about us as I. Yet I knew she had. Cleo was in the family trap, no doubt about that. *'They couldn't understand that our love might be valid and worthy. Comparisons with my former evangelical self were made. They saw I was changed—to my detriment. They say I am too fine a person. Eventually I would not talk of our love—they could see it only as hideous, unnatural and dishonourable. (I insisted I did not feel any loss of self-respect—they were ashamed of my lack of standards.) They could see my feeling is deep and genuine but it is "dirty". They think of you as a seducing bitch—they cannot see, I despair. I love you but I shall no longer tell you. I hate this.'*

I tried to imagine what it would have been like if I had not been able to oppose my mother the first time, and leave; if the horror of hurting her had been stronger than the necessity to continue what had been begun. I couldn't quite conceive of parents with ultimate control over me. Cleo lived with it. My history of conflict turned out, after all, to be an unlikely asset. Cleo's subtler oppression, disguised more plausibly as love, was a cage without loopholes—unhealthy, unspoken, unbreakable.

'You should've lied,' I said to her the day she escaped to Melbourne to pick up her teacher-training pay.

'I can't lie well,' she told me helplessly. 'No practice. And anyway, they had information; they definitely had an informer—there was a confusion about you and Libby, which it was or maybe both. Horrors. So someone from college let my mother know. There's no doubt of that.' Spies and informants. Paradigm Calvinist methods. In Geneva they prowled about ferreting for sabbath-breakers, gamblers, dancers, adulterers. A lot of those poor college women would have been at home in Calvin's Geneva.

The Atkins had acted with despatch and placed Cleo under maximum security immediately. It had taken her days to post the first letter since her parents played warder by turns and kept her under constant surveillance in and out of the house.

'Why didn't you just tell them you were posting the bloody thing?'

'I don't know. It wasn't that it would confirm their suspicions. They already had it sewn up. Just that they had me. I had to obey.' Cleo accepted being in custody—indeed it was surprising that they refrained from chaperoning her that day. But she came alone and filled in the picture for me.

Not only did they exercise moral suasion, their forte, they were also prepared to play dirty. As her guarantors with the Education Department they were in the neat position of being able to withdraw the signature and stop Cleo's allowance. 'I'll find someone else to sign it,'

I told her, willing to approach the Student Counsellors, the College, even Mrs Vernon. But there was an answer to that, too. A diabolical strategy. If Cleo got an alternative guarantor, Mr Atkin would inform the Secondary Teachers' College and the Education Department of Cleo's tendencies, putting paid at one fell swoop to any possibility of Cleo's ever being accepted as a teacher. There was little chance of her encountering maverick enlightenment in a government department. Cleo would risk her studentship and her career. Even I had to admit that I probably wasn't worth the sacrifice.

'He wouldn't do it,' I said wistfully.

'I'm not taking the risk,' she replied.

'What is important to them is my social image, my reputation, my future career. I am too fine a person—they say—to ruin my future with you. I would prefer to call this fineness well-brought-up ignorance. When I said that I felt no shame, they felt only sorrow that I should have fallen so low. "This is going to take effort, Cleo, and self-discipline—it's going to hurt and only you can do anything about it." You can understand the line and objectively, materialistically, you know they are right. But they have no conception of the depth and purity and reality of our love. I insisted that nothing so genuine, so honest, could be wrong. But the answer came pat. Lust is honestly felt, and wrong; hate is honestly felt and bad; and therefore ...'

They've fucked it up, anyway. They've set us at loggerheads. They've got me close to accusing Cleo of cowardice and they've got her, in consequence, on the run, begging me not to be emotional and hating me for loving her. They've forced us to meet in the shadow of our own most dangerous weaknesses. They've already changed us. Real spanner in the works syndrome.

'I, in my confusion, do not know what to ask of you—all I know is that I love you and I don't want to lose you—though I think I could bear it, back to "I am a Rock" pose. I hate this hurting you and me and my parents. I want you to hold me; hold me together; but the resolution you would bring me might be false and degrading. And yet I refuse to let my parents badger me their way—I have kept aloof and unapproachable. I feel at the mercy of two winds—yours warm and sandy and small perhaps—theirs biting, cold and empty ...' She had broken off and scrawled, in different ink, this conclusion—

'I shall never again come to see you and you must leave me to myself—I mean this, Maureen. I must cease from loving you and in time I shall. In return you must remember only now. Your love for me was *in the past only. 1, I do not think our love was wrong; but 2, I do think it was inadvisable socially—that in the eyes of people it was wrong. And people don't change.*

My parents do love me, which excuses much. Goodbye, Cleo.'

The final word. Cleo had chosen them—she was willing to live by the rules and to set her own feelings aside. Their cast-iron morality admitted neither tolerance nor understanding and they held all the cards. Held prisoner until she would recant, and held prisoner so easily because the Atkins had prepared Cleo, from a time she couldn't even remember, for obedience to their will and submission to their bleak decent world of sins and reputations.

She would not step out of line now and she would never smash them as they deserved. I spent my time stunned and sorrowful, with no apparent motive for doing anything, or even living. Somehow or other I would have to gather myself and live without her, wishing that it had not fallen out this way. Finally I answered her letter.

My dear Cleo,
It seems to me now that, loving you, I can only accept your decisions as you've made them, and say goodbye, keep away as you've asked me. It's going to be hard, as you must know, especially hard because loving you has been the most real and honest-to-the-core relationship I've had. The only one that made me grow and understand more all the time, free of those awful games of guilt, free even of the possibility of blame. You've given me a lot anyway, so no regrets, no hard feelings. I'll try to forget you, I guess. I love you though—and I'll always hate them for destroying us. I hope you will be all right, with my love. Maureen.

Trying to force myself to act right. To love so true that I refrain from pushing her. Unlike her parents' love. I'm trying.

I will go to Upton. Here's a possibility. I will put it to them. Get on my pushbike and cycle down the fifty-mile freeway to lovely Upton-on-Slush. It's a fine summer morning and I'm up at dawn to beat the heat, pedalling along the fortunate flatlands south of Melbourne. Crash-helmeted, sun-visored Craig, pushing a twelve-inch toy bike into Mission Impossible.

Clatter the knocker. 'GOOD morning, Mrs Atkin.' The pinched little woman levitates as if she's seen a mouse, screams faintly and slams the door. Baffled for only an instant, I speed to my bike parked amongst the roses, get out the billy and the white flag. I knot the banner to the birch tree and, gathering loose sticks from the wood-shed, I build a campfire amongst the rhododendrons and hoe into morning tea. It's the powder-blue Falcon with flashing blue light and siren that ruins this strategy, as I slew down the kerb and the chase through Upton's quiet streets begins. So how am I to prevent Mrs Atkin from calling the law? 'There's a mad lesbian eating breakfast in my rose-patch.'

OR. Wearing solid mountaineering boots, I stand with my nose to the knocker. As she opens the door I sweep my crash-helmet from my head in an elegant and gallant bow, and intrude my left boot into the doorway.

'What are you doing here?' she asks venomously.

I'm courteous and straightforward. 'Mrs Atkin, I have come to discuss our future. If I may step inside for a moment ...' Stepping in and ushering her into her own spic-span kitchen. 'I'll have tea, thank you.'

'Get out, you vile, degraded creature.'

'Come, Mrs Atkin,' I say, coaxing, 'I think you should know that I have treated Cleo impeccably. She will probably never have a more faithful and devoted lover.' The Emily Atkin nerves of steel are bending. She's ruffled as she's never been before. For never has anyone challenged her rules and guideposts for the evasion of everything she considers unpleasant. 'Get out.' And her tone is more than menacing.

'Mrs Atkin, please take a seat. We have a lot to discuss and I have to ride all the way back to Melbourne before nightfall, as I have no reflector on my back mudguard.'

'Get out,' she says, voice rising.

'Mrs Atkin the time has come to face the world. You'd be fifty now, wouldn't you?' Muffled umbrage. 'And you've had a good few years to discover that you're incapable of any sort of enjoyment.' She makes to speak, but I raise my gloved hand for silence. 'Now don't imagine for a moment that I'm blaming you for this—you are just a victim of this society and, I shouldn't be surprised, of your own family.'

'I'll ring the police if you aren't out of here in five seconds,' she says, setting a convenient stopwatch.

'You will do no such thing,' I say authoritatively, seating her firmly at the table. 'A terrible warning, Mrs Atkin. You and your husband are attempting to turn Cleo into someone exactly like yourselves—mean, tight-lipped and moral; shrivelled, earnest and frigid. The most disturbing thing about this, of course, is that you may succeed as thoroughly as your own parents once succeeded.'

Mrs Atkin goes white as a sheet and groans. The truth is out.

'You will not remember the words of Mr Dylan's song, but let me refresh you. I regret that I have not brought my guitar, but it goes like this.'

I belt out the fourth verse of *The Times They Are A-Changin'*, a tuneful, persuasive performance: *Come mothers* ... I sing, *your daughters are beyond your command* and I rip out the order to get out of the way if she can't lend a hand, staring her straight in the eye, cool and confident, a half smile playing on my lips.

She sits, somewhat stunned. 'Mrs Atkin, the regrettable truth is that people like your good self may resist change to the bitter end—but the bitter end will nevertheless come. You are asking Cleo to share your grave with you. Mrs Atkin, please don't try to strangle yourself. Mrs Atkin. It's not too late ...'

But, by the time I get to her side, her head has begun to blow apart, fragments of skull plastering themselves about the ceiling and walls of her spotless kitchen. It is too late. I can only flee the wild scene, sink a few ice-cold beers in Lower Upton and pedal off across the Slush and up the freeway, my crash-helmet strapped gratefully to my solid sane skull.

Part Four

---

*In which Inga returns for a week
and Maureen thinks of going for good*

It was three years later that I drove Max to the airport to meet Inga's plane. She had gone back to Germany a year before, bored with Australia and dissatisfied with Max. He was nervous and absorbed, hardly bothering to watch the road and traffic as he usually did. In the terminal we waited for Inga to come in from the tarmac. We sat, shuffled over to the glass and sat again. Half a dozen flights came in from Sydney. Max straightened his jacket, tore at his beard and said nothing.

'Want a whisky, Max?'

'Ah shit I don't think so. Bit bloody early. What's happened to her?'

'She might've forgotten about the dateline—in which case she'll be here tomorrow, same time, just a day late?'

'She couldn't be that stupid.'

But we waited in vain.

'Think I'll go to work this afternoon,' he said, wrinkling his nose.

'Nothing else to do.'

'OK. Let's go.'

'Got any cat food?'

'Yeah.'

'Must feed the goannas.'

'All right.'

The goannas, trophy of one of Max's shotless shooting-trips, lived in the cockatoo cage and had received his undivided attention since Inga left. On cold nights he brought them in for a warm-up by the radiator and had tried, unsuccessfully, to induce them to smooge. They spat and bit.

In the afternoon I went down to the University to mark a few more exam papers. Nearly two years as a tutor and I still felt like a student. Too much strain to be somebody in the staff-room, too much dazzling cut-and-thrust wit. No-one appeared to relax for an instant. I came in from the quadrangle and up the back stairs to my hole-in-the-wall office hollowed out of the bowels of Old Arts. The University, having superseded most of its lawns, could grow only upwards or underground. A small muffled room, thick carpet, stout desk, telephone. It was never an environment I could take for granted; a stage-set where Craig the brilliant impostor avoided the inevitable denouement, fleeing to her first-year tutorials as if to a haven. The unguarded friendly table where sophistication was mercifully unknown and jokes owed nothing to scintillating malice.

How much do they know? I had asked myself for two years. Cleo drifted further and further back—we only made love once up on the thick blue carpet in the Office, and few of my colleagues had ever known her. But the insecurity was more general. Dithering, the self-possessed jester, asked with monotonous regularity if my boots betokened a steed a-waiting, or had I joined the secret police? I gave up initial feeble attempts to answer in kind and tried to ignore him. Dithering disapproved of tutors using their first names in class, he disapproved of improper dress and he detested everything which undermined the structures of respect for the academic. It required a considerable effort to resist the attempt to tidy me up and accommodate me to the system.

'You can't wear jeans, Maureen,' Mrs Abernathy told me, an emissary from above.

'But I'm allergic to stockings,' I replied.

'But surely your students will not respect you if you don't dress decently.'

'I have no decent clothes,' I lied. 'Besides, we get on fine. We like each other. That's the thing.'

'But the older ones?' she insisted. 'The part-timers?'

I laughed. 'They feel maternal. Scruffy little Miss Craig. I'm sure they don't feel they've been placed in unworthy hands—in fact it makes them more willing to have a go. Too much respect and they're too scared to think.' I felt relieved to have stumbled on a convenient ideology. The jeans controversy subsided without further pressure, but the staff-room remained a gauntlet to be run twice daily. The kindly left-wing lecturers and the odd youthful radical provided little antidote to the needlings of Dithering and his kind. I was stuck with an endless unease, as if I were always waiting to be found out. A civilised casual climate which nevertheless left their hostility ungauged and uncharted, and my partial self always in a state of mild fright amongst them.

'Righto Max, what would you like to eat?' I asked him that evening.

'Dunno,' he answered, gloomy.

'Oysters at the Railway?'

'Ugh.'

'Steak at the Alfred?'

'OK.'

'You two going off boozing?' It was Ken. We'd ignored our

misgivings and let him move in to Inga's vacant room when he'd been thrown out of his flat after a wild party. Sometimes we wished we'd left him on the streets.

'Yeah,' I said, 'and for a feed.'

'I'll come along for the feed, eh?'

'OK,' I said.

'Want to race down?'

'You can race, Ken. I can't be fucked.'

'Want to come down with me, O'Hearn? You'll be safer.'

'Oh it's all right thanks, Ken,' Max answered, pretending to hide a craven fear.

'I'll have a few while I'm waiting,' Ken said, and strode out to the beat-up brown Fiat which he'd improved with a set of wide wire racing-wheels ingeniously fitted from an Alfa wreck. Ken and Robby Hitchin left the Alfa on blocks. He swung behind the wheel, started the car, revved up hard and, one of Ken's flawless stunts, shot off at instant speed dropping a pair of wheelies. The intersection wasn't above thirty yards from our gate, so he was obliged to brake viciously to avoid the trams. An excellent opportunity to drop a second pair of wheelies. Ken had been known to stop and measure them.

'He'll kill himself one day,' said Max, wistfully.

'Not a chance.'

'By Jesus,' Ken said when we got to the pub, 'it's good now. Those Pirellis—best thing I ever got on the shit. She'll take those corners over the back of the house at fifty-odd. Used to nearly flip on forty.'

Max was thinking about Inga and didn't bother to listen while Ken rambled on about his wheels and sank beers so fast that Max and I kept up only with conscious effort.

'Outa practice, O'Hearn? You're drinking like a baby.'

'Not feeling extra good, Ken,' he replied, offering Ken a meekness and docility which was his strategy for avoiding the eternal challenges. Ken slapped his hands on the table-top and levered himself up. 'Well. Must be off. Got a lot of solid drinking to get through tonight.'

'Righto, Ken, don't drown yourself.'

'Don't be funny, smart-arse. Bye sis.'

'Y'feeling nervous, Max?'

'Ah shit yeah. I'd say from the letters that she's not looking forward to seeing me at all. Bet she's got some other fella back in Berlin.'

'She never mentioned anyone?'

'No. But she writes less and less often. And always kicking the shit out of me—and Australia—but mostly me. She's doing this Marxist course and seems to think we're all fucking Fascists out here.'

'A lot of us are.'

'Yeah. But I'm not. I don't give a damn. And anyway, I'm not in favour of Gorton or conscription or Vietnam or F1-11s or any of that Liberal shit.'

'Maybe being neutral isn't enough for her.'

'Used to be. She never bothered while she was here.'

'I'm beginning to think there's no point in bothering anyway. The more people bother, the tighter it gets.'

'She reckons I'm lax, though, to use one of Ken's priceless expressions. We had a terrible fight when I brought Hank home.'

'Hank. Shit.'

'He's a decent guy, Maureen. And you just can't expect a fella who's been three years fighting the bloody war to agree that it's a foul bit of pointless imperialism.'

'I guess he's been through the brainwashing.'

'Yeah. And he's been through the war. He's got to believe some of it.'

'Oh, I can see why he would—if you've been through it, you have to believe it. That's what's behind the RSL. But I can also see why Inga didn't like having the bastard around.'

'It was bloody embarrassing. The guy's probably completely fucked up and all Inga can do is argue politics and tell him he's been suffering for nuts.'

'But it's true.'

'No need to tell him that.'

Basil was sitting on the front fence when we got home, picking his nose and looking disconsolate. 'Thought you two might be back about now, so I waited.'

'Good thing you did,' Max said. 'We've got a half-dozen to get through if you'd like to lend a hand.'

'No worries.'

Basil Ponsonby was a small, sugar-blond maths-student. Never really at home except when spinning the web of his superiority, he regarded mathematics as poetry and the mathematician as the Universal Man—qualified to pronounce on all branches of learning. He had lived with us for a few terms before Inga left, and antagonised no-one more than Ken, for whom he epitomised all that is worst in the smart-alec intellectual. One of Ken's delights was to beat Basil blind at pontoon, knowing that, secretly, Basil believed that the Universal Man is a superb gambler as well. 'Fuck,' he would say as Ken turned up a pontoon, grinning broadly and saying, 'Only two bob this time, you lucky bugger.' Yet Basil moved on to the next deal with a show of cocky confidence and rarely took Ken's baits. Indeed, Basil kept everything in check, even his bitter unhappiness.

Ken burst in after his regular booze with the mates; he was drunker than usual and cackling about the tape-recorder they'd haggled from a pawnbroker. 'Serves the bugger right—too much brass.' He laughed hysterically, slapping his sides and letting out whoops and howls of pleasure. Finally he noticed Basil at the table wearing his inimitable smirk.

'Oh ho! So it's you Ponce, Ponsonby, Poncie-Ponce.'

'Had a few too many, eh, Ken?' Basil tried jollying, but Ken cut in.

'It'd be too many for you little pansy-ponce. Takes a man to hold his liquor.' Loud fart. Basil looked up over his glasses, his staple show of amused self-confidence. 'Yeah, you're not really a man at all, are you Ponce?'

'Oh I wouldn't say that, Ken.' Still jolly.

Ken danced in, clumsy boxer-style, windmill fists, darting them out close to Basil's face. He put his hand up and Ken stood off laughing.

'Afraid of me, aren't you?' He flattened his right palm and flipped Basil across the top of the head.

'No, Ken, not at all.'

'Put up your fists then.'

Basil smiled toleration. 'No, Ken. I don't want to fight.'

Ken curled his lip and wagged his finger. 'And we all know why, don't we? Because I'd make a heap of shit out of you.'

'That's beside the point, Ken. I don't fight.'

'Of course not. Poofters don't know how to fight.'

'For Christ's sake go to bed, Ken,' I said to him.

'I'm not going to bed till I beat this little queer to pulp.'

'What the hell makes you think he's queer?'

Basil muttered shut up, there's no point arguing with him.

'What makes me think he's queer? It's written all over him. Got the poofter cringe, haven't you, Ponce? You're sitting there shitting yourself and hoping I won't thump you.'

'Thump me if you like, Ken. I'm not hitting back.'

'You don't bloodywell know how to hit back.'

Basil raised his eyebrows, cocked his head to one side, said nothing.

'That's the trouble with pansies, haven't got the guts to stand up for 'emselves. Sickly little pervs like Ponce here.'

'I'm not staying to hear any more of your shit, Ken.' Basil rose calmly to his feet, steady and level.

'I don't want to talk, Ponce; put up your fists.'

Basil put on his jacket and walked around Ken towards the door. Ken jumped back and braced himself at the doorway. 'Put up your fists.'

Basil cocked his head and smiled with effort. 'Let me pass, Ken. It's assault, you know, if you try it. And I'll get you into court for it.'

Ken spat out the pellets of paper he was chewing. 'I'm standing at me own door, Bazza. Nothing illegal in that, is there?'

'Do you want a lift, Basil?' I asked him.

'No, I want nothing. But I *am* leaving.' He spun around, and walked quietly out the back door and down the alleyway. Ken laughed and laughed until the tears rolled down his cheeks. 'Poor little Ponce, crawling out the back way.' Max went silently to bed.

'Jesus, Ken, I wish to Christ I'd never let you move in here. No-one's super-Aussies here. Why don't you go and live with Hitchin or one of your brutal bloody mates. You'd get on better, boy.'

'Robby's still in Nasho, smart-arse.'

'I told you you'd have to fit in if you lived with us. No poofter-baitings and no slacking. I warned you that we needed to co-operate and that no-one'd play mother and do your share of the work. Even if I can take the way you clear off whenever anybody mentions the washing-up—this other bit is too fucking much. Do you understand?'

'Shit, Maureen,' he said, insolently coaxing, 'you can't like that little creep very much. He probably is a poofter.'

'So?'

'So that's no decent sort of fella t'be around my sister.'

'You bloody half-wit. There's plenty of people who are homo-sexual. I know a few.'

'Like who?'

'I wouldn't tell you, would I? They're no different from anybody else—no nastier, no meaner—*some* are a bloody sight pleasanter than you, for example.'

'Oh fuck off.'

'And I'm one of them.' He raised his eyebrows. 'I've had several relationships with women.'

'I don't believe you.'

'It's nevertheless true.'

Ken was speechless. 'Any beer left?' he managed to ask.

'In the fridge. Get it yourself.'

He was rotten drunk already. He lurched through the doorway saving a fall by clapping a hand on the doorhandle.

'You gotta glass, sis?'

'Yeah.'

'You want a smoke?'

'Yeah. Thanks.'

We smoked and drank in silence, eyeing each other. If Ken had often seemed a bad bet to live with, a parasite-male who arrived to be fed and disappeared speedily to get drunk, this evening pointed to total disaster. I glared at him.

'I don't understand you, Maureen. I'm your own brother and you look at me like poison.'

'Sometimes I can't stand you.'

'Sometimes I can't stand you either.'

'Go then. Find someone else to work for you; find some other people to take it out on. I'm sick of it.'

'O'Hearn never cooks either.'

'Max does a bit. And he doesn't expect to be waited on as if it's his right.'

'I don't either.'

'Bullshit.'

'I don't. You do things off your own bat. I never ask you to make my food for me.'

'Skip it, Ken. It's the other thing that gets on my nerves. What the fuck do you get out of stirring someone like Basil—he's not strong, he's not good at getting on with people, he's unhappy as hell, he's ...'

'He's a fucking arrogant know-all.'

'Y'could try to see why.'

'I detest the bastard.'

'So that gives you the right to blow in here and break it up when Max and me are just sitting and talking to him?'

'Jesus, Maureen,' he said, quite suddenly, eyes dull and perplexed. 'I don't know what happens. Sure I don't like the idea of poofters, but picking on Ponce is like picking on a fly. It's like ... once you get started you just have to go on, have to fight if they fight, have to push and push till they break or try to shoot through. Then you can let 'em go if you're bored or—you can belt 'em to pulp.'

'You? Belt people to pulp?'

'No, but I sometimes feel like trying to. Not that it'd be much fun. But you just get that kind of a feeling.'

Ken's head thudded on the table; a teaspoon flew up and tinkled against his glass; a bottle keeled over and hit the floor.

'You OK?'

'Leave me alone,' he growled. 'Leave me alone.' His throat rasped and he held his shoulders taut to disguise the sobs.

'Ken. I'll help you to get to bed.' I spoke gently and he looked up, faced steeled and quivering to stop the tears. 'I don't like it. I don't like anything. I'd rather be fucking dead.' He cried, his whole body shaking, his lips twisted with pain.

'Jesus, brother,' I said, putting my arm across his shoulder. 'If it makes you this miserable, isn't it worth trying to change?'

'Change?' he groaned scornfully. 'Change. How am I supposed to change? You gotta live with it, don't you? I couldn't do University—too bloody dumb ...'

'Bullshit.'

'Too bloody dumb for that lot ...'

'I couldn't have passed maths, either.'

'Couldn't do Nasho. Too bloody weak ...'

'Nasho wouldn't've helped.'

'You make some brass out of it.'

'Brass doesn't help.'

'Brass is something.' He gazed at me. 'Do you remember Pauline, that bird from Sunshine. You drove her home one night last year?'

'Yeah.'

'She was a silly bitch, but bloody good-hearted. She's never got in touch with me for months.'

'Well you've got Margie now, haven't you?'

'That's different. I wouldn't screw Margie—I'm going to marry her. Pauline knew that, though. She told me once, you know, how she had to have an abortion and she told the fella and asked him to help her out with a bit of dough, she's only a shopgirl and doesn't make much. He promised her half, to her face, said he'd have it in a week— and just shot through. She never saw him again. Had to find about a hundred dollars or get it done cheap, and that's risky. So she went down to the docks around the pubs, picking up sailors—and made the brass that way. She's never done it since, either. Fuckin' brave sort of broad, going out there and doing it all alone. Couldn't even tell her mother—she just thought Pauline was off-colour the day she had it done. And she said to me if it ever happened again she'd never tell the fella, never ask a guy for anything. That's the point y'see. Last time I went with her it was risky and I ... er ... wasn't careful, told her it'd be all right, and now ... she never rang me up since.'

'And you think ...'

'Probably. And I would've helped her. I would've. She should've known. She was good to me that time I left home. Used to do my washing and mend things. She never hurt anyone.'

'Can't you ring her?'

'No phone.'

'Go and see her. She probably just got sick of you.'

'It wouldn't work. She'd hate me and she'd probably throw me out. She's tough when she's angry.' He looked at me with his eyes red and swollen. 'I'm no fucking good at anything. So how do you expect me to be nice to all you geniuses?'

'None of us is that bloody clever.'

'You're a tutor—that's big. That's getting somewhere.'

'But you don't have to get anywhere.'

'Of course I do. It's all right for you. You've made it.'

'Things aren't that rosy for me, Ken. Because the real problem isn't making it—it's getting your own mind straight, finding out what you're like and doing it right.'

'I don't like it,' he said again. 'I hate myself. I can't do anything right.'

'Why don't y'try?'

'Fuck. I try. It's hopeless.'

'What is it you don't like then?'

'Everything. Jesus. Everything ...'

'She'll be right, sis,' he said as I got him to his room. 'Jus' don't tell anybody I been crying.'

I smiled. 'Sure. It's no disgrace though.'

'Jus' don't tell anybody.'

'Sure. Good night. Get a good sleep. And call me, will you, before y'go to work. Max and I have got to get out to Essendon and see if Inga shows up.'

'OK. Good night.'

Max put his arm around her and escorted her gently across the tarmac, gazing down tenderly at her bright blonde hair. She looked ahead at the glass corridor, amazed that a whole day had dissolved somewhere in mid-Pacific, amazed to be back in the familiar city.

Max had worked with meticulous determination to make Inga's welcome smooth. This was a brief holiday and he had only two weeks to win her back. He'd finally attacked the musty trunk where he stored his washing—a sacrificial bonfire fed with rotting socks from the Gunning Street era and dozens of intermediate shirts and underpants. The Eiffel Tower was repaired and mounted on the wardrobe; the sheets were clean; his room was purged of dust and debris, and he had gone so far as to get up early to clear the bottles and ashtrays out of the dining-room.

He brought her home almost with pride, failed in his attempt to put her suitcase in the room they had shared, and went on into the kitchen to make breakfast. 'Don't bother, Maureen, I'll do it.' I sat down with Inga while he did it with tightrope efficiency, hoping to counter her old accusations of his laziness, his passive willingness to be served, fed and looked after.

'Tell me though, Inga,' he said after we'd eaten and begun the duty-free whisky. 'Why didn't you answer the letters when I said I'd come to Germany?'

She looked at him sharply. *It's started already*. 'Shit, Max, I have already said in other letters that it is impossible. You do not know German and there is not much work for architect assistant in Berlin anyway—it does not grow, now, that city.'

'I said I'd do anything until I got the hang of the German and I've got a lot saved for the first few months.'

'So you want to go to Berlin. I will study and you will do shit-work and that will be beautiful for you?'

'I wanted to be with you,' he said, just audible. 'Something would've turned up.'

184

'Here, you get at last a job with drafting where you can do some interesting things; you get away from this rotten teaching and start to work with architecture. And you think it is good to leave all that for nothing?'

'There's you,' he said, puzzled that the premises of their arguments seemed not to meet.

'But it is your life, Max.'

'I could've gone to England to study.' She laughed. 'Well, at least to work.'

'Yes, Max. But I know what you are like. You could, but you would not. You would sit around in Berlin getting unhappy and unsatisfied and you would wait for me to find you some answer. That is not good for you or for me.'

'You underestimate me,' he said, nettled. 'And you forget that I love you. Isn't that a reason?'

'It is not enough, though.'

'It would be enough if you still loved me.'

'Bullshit.' His face contracted; her answer dismissed him without admitting the feared truth. 'I'm tired. It is twenty hours in that plane, or two days, I do not know which.'

He rose quickly. 'Sorry, Inga. My bed's fresh made-up, if you'd like to sleep.'

'The couch here is good, thanks.' And she closed her eyes.

'Fuck,' he said under his breath. 'I think I'll go to work this afternoon.'

'Want a lift?'

'Sure.' He hovered by Inga to kiss her goodbye, but her eyes remained shut.

I followed him down the hallway. 'It's a fucking foregone conclusion,' he said, bitter and angry.

'She doesn't want to talk now. Maybe later.' Offering him flimsy hope.

'No, Maureen. I've got the eyes to see it. She hates seeing me. She wants me to pretend we never were together. I don't know what fucked it up but it's well and truly fucked now. Plain as day. Don't bother. I'll walk. See you.'

Inga stretched. 'It is not much fun travelling all this way and Max so unhappy. I am sure it will get worse.'

'You're finished with him, are you?'

She shrugged. 'It is hard. But yes. It is true.'

'You should tell him that, straight off.'

'I can't. He doesn't seem able to believe it.'

'Jesus, Inga, he used to winnow your letters for the bits that gave him some kind of hope.'

'He should have been able to tell.'

'He couldn't bear to. He loves you.'

'It is not love. He does not even know me. I was just a woman to look after him. That is what he misses.'

'Surely more than that. And it is love, to him.'

'He is so fucking limited, Maureen. And he will be always so, staying in Australia where it is the right thing to be limited.'

'But you wouldn't let him come to Berlin.'

'He must do it on his own. If it is just for me he goes, it will be exactly the same old story.'

'You're hard on him.'

'I cannot live with him. I could not live in Australia. He could not survive in Germany. I am only sensible.'

'I guess so.'

'He is the kind of bloke that must get married. One woman for the whole lifetime trap. That is what he wants. That is what I do not agree to. Never. But he will not be able to understand what I am talking about.'

'Maybe not.'

'All his letters come. It is always what went wrong that you suddenly do not want to be with me forever? I just woke up Maureen. I went home and woke up. Max is an Aussie. He wants a cosy flat, all private, all for him and me. It's a bullshit. Max is not my whole life and I am not Max's. Whatever he thinks, I am not everything. No-one is that much, really, for anyone.'

'Maybe you could've helped Max.'

'I decide that it is not possible. The only way he will want it is the way which he sees. He wants marriage.'

'That's the way he's been brought up.'

'Me too. But I am wanting to be free.'

'Yeah, I understand. I'm with you.'

'You should leave here, Maureen.'

'I've been meaning to for ages. I'd like to get away from the whole bloody narrow-minded fuck-up. But if I start another year tutoring, I'll have to stay.'

'Don't.'

'No. Perhaps I'll go.'

'When?'

'I could, any time after Christmas. Need to go back to Mallacoota for a while—say goodbye to the boats. Early next year, if I wanted.'

'Then do it.'

'I suppose I still don't really want to leave Cleo.'

'Shit, Maureen, you are bad as Max.'

'Worse. She would never even have lived with me. And its been three years. Three fucking years! And now she's teaching down in

Maffra—will be next year, too, probably. It's the only way they can staff the country schools, sending out the new teachers. I'm an embarrassment to her down there, when I go to see her. I don't fit into her model-teacher pose at all. Our lives seem to point in totally different directions.'

'It is better to finish this, then.'

'I'm a hopeless finisher. I'd rather patch.'

'Then, in the end, you just have got the patches and this is nothing to do with love.'

'Sure. Yeah. All I need to do y'know is leave Australia, shoot off somewhere where I can't get in the car and go to her. Get out of range. I'm always going back to check if she's changed her mind—she does sometimes. Jesus it'd be good to be on the other side of the world. No temptations. No trying.'

'Oh, the other side is always going to have some temptations, too.'

'Of course,' I agreed. But I did not really believe her.

In which Maureen reflects on Cleo's limitations, and her own

Three years of the same pattern. In the immediate aftermath of her mother's intervention I stopped writing to Cleo and spent the rest of that vacation getting by. Luck, I thought, what foul luck that her mother should have been informed. Without losing sight of the loaded dice; the sapping likelihood that you simply couldn't win. It amazed me to find Timid Craig turning out to be the sole resister, the only tentative advocate of living at odds with the parents and their rules. Cleo saw it all and was paralysed. Strange double Cleo with her infectious sexuality, her refusal of shame. And her bondage. I couldn't help believing that Cleo ought to have noticed and confronted the manifest contradiction in herself, but how could I accuse? 'You said ... you gave ... you wanted ...' Mummy's and Daddy's love was their excuse, their justification. And their power gave their love a right to mould and fiddle which mine was denied. I suspected that their love was the very urge to imprison that I wanted to avoid; Cleo did not appear to entertain the suspicion. Heady thought, that I might, however isolated, consult my good faith and find myself guilty of nothing greater than having desired too much in a hostile world. For, when Cleo's mother had me cast as 'the personification of evil', I could scarcely agree.

At the same time, I felt obliged to treat Cleo's loyalty to those unspeakable parents with an alien and primordial respect. I understood Cleo's dilemma and I accepted her decision to break off and bury the regrettable intensity of the past. All of us infected with the creeping Atkin ethos, more powerful in its insidious assumptions than in any of its direct discipline. 'I'm not a child now, Cleo-baby. Back to Mummy if you must—I'm off on the ocean wave, goodbye.' But I said nothing of the sort. I decided to take Emma up on her offer of a stay in her new flat in Sydney and hitched up the coast road alone and without Cleo's knowledge. Dwelt a bleak midday at Lakes Entrance, withered hopes, and continued north. I preferred to be hidden from her, taking my own action almost in secret. She wanted none of me. She'd get none. And yet my mind was often flooded with her, and always I reeled back to the point of disbelief that she could about-face on the finger-snap of her parents.

Back from Sydney a few days before term started, I wondered if she might not have changed her mind and couldn't resist a visit to find out. I knocked at her door.

'Maureen!'

'Hullo', I said coolly, stepping inside the door and taking up an attitude of relaxed aloofness. 'How was the rest of your vacation?'

'Terrible. I got a job though and wasn't so much at home.' I smiled the smile of knowledge. Suddenly, without thought, she ran across the room and hugged me. 'Darling. My Maureen. You shouldn't have come today.' I was conscious enough to ask why.

'Because I gave myself a break, like tossing a coin. If you came before term started I wouldn't be cold. I'd act as I felt.'

'You knew I would come.'

'Perhaps. You never wrote to me from Sydney.'

'No.'

'I only found out by accident. Libby got a card of the Harbour Bridge. "Whoever's up there?" I asked gaily. "Maureen," she said, "didn't you know?" I felt mortified.'

'You didn't want me to write.'

'I told you not to.'

All my defences to keep Cleo at a distance are crumbling as I hold her, touch her neck and feel her cunt pressed against me. What the hell's she think she's doing? 'I've missed you,' I say. This'll compound the cool for sure. 'I love you.' Never admit it. Panic. 'Christ I love you.' I'll be sorry. About fifteen seconds and I've kissed her, loved her, altered the balance of power.

'Come to Gunning Street,' I entreated. 'Have a meal. Come on.'

She looked up as if noticing what she was doing for the first time. 'No. No. I can't do that.'

'Of course you can.'

'I mustn't go there at all, especially so soon. I promised.'

'What?'

'Not to see you.'

'So you don't want to break your promise so blatantly so soon?'

'I'd rather not at all.'

'But you decided you would if I showed up before term.'

'I don't know,' she said, bemused and breaking away.

'OK,' I said bitterly, swallowing the stray hope. 'OK. I'll leave you to it. Nice room you've got this term anyway. Have a good year.'

'Have coffee,' she offered, returning.

'All right.' I should go away, of course.

We sat and talked of the things we'd done. She touched me occasionally, smoothed my hair, patted my knee, as if to verify my physical presence. After a time I gathered myself and went.

While I kept my distance she fretted for me, longed for me, feared that I really was through with her. If I could stay cold she would, eventually, invite me to betray my guarded feeling. What was rarely a game became solely that.

A few weeks later. It was hot, late March. I met her sweating in after a lecture.

'Whew! Hullo! There's orange juice in the fridge. Cold. Want some?'

'Sure. But I won't stay. I'm going off this afternoon, down the beach.'

'Where?'

'Dunno.'

'What about Portsea?'

'It's a hell of a way. I thought a bit closer.'

'I'd like to go to Portsea,' she announced.

'You want to come?'

'It'll take ages, but we could sleep on the beach.' These sudden half-serious flashes of daring.

'Why not?' I said, smiling.

'Maybe,' she answered, retreating.

Walking some kind of tightrope. At the restaurant in Frankston I courted her, attended to her, opened. She grew quiet. In the bus I buried myself in a book, ignoring her silence, and she came back, interrupted me to point out hawks and hills and road plants. I shut the book and took her extended hand, secretly in the back seat. We walked across the grass in the blazing afternoon, arms linked; climbed down to the long, yellow surf-beach; lay out in the sun. She gazed off, face closing. OK, I thought, and slung my towel over my shoulder, headed off down the beach to the rocks. Tide-pools, green and limpid, sunned warm since morning. Just now, the rising tide was spilling in at the edges, foam and cold disturbing the silence. I stripped, swam fast across a deep emerald pool to its ruffled edge, came slowly back, head down, eyes open on the rippled greenish sand at the bottom. I went back.

She lay still on the sand as I ran up declaring that I'd just caught a huge wave, and ridden it all the way in.

'Oh,' she offered, distant and detached. 'Shall we go?'

'Don't you want to stay?' I asked, disappointed.

'No. Not at all.'

I did not want to spend another three hours on buses and trains with this unfathomable capricious woman; neither did I want to stay alone on the deserted beach. I thought vaguely of going to the town for food and returning, but I knew I would not. Still hot. We trudged up the path.

'It is over then?' I asked.

'Yes. Completely.'

I passed the purgatorial hours in the bus cracking bitter jokes; angry and sad.

Always the revelation, always accepting her overture, even when the sequel had become a well-worn foregone conclusion. Cleo, re-assured of me, would stay sometimes a day, sometimes a week; always, sooner or later, slip away. When she wanted me she sought me. I was there. Without fail. Habits die hard, especially this one. And what a paradigm woman I was, after all, if only some fellow had the sense to see it. Self-effacing and loyal, responsive to the least dim indication of renewal. The impulse to find a separate way—always caught and strangled by considerations for the interminable others. When Cleo came back I welcomed her, perpetuated the bind, powerless to break in my own clear interests. I had been shown a forkless path of submission and had trodden it too long to be conscious of alternatives. A hard road, but familiar. At the very least I must appear to submit and keep the goodwill, at all costs the goodwill. If there were conflicts, I must capitulate and apologise, must afterlard with favours and comings-across. Cleo might wake up one morning and find she still wanted me. How then could I leave my monumental perseverance to this end and turn my back?

And yet, if I cannot turn my back, I am lost.

A beginner's approach to normality

Not long after the excruciating trip to Portsea, I bought my first car. A total shit-heap, a jungle-green 1952 FX, the nearest thing to the tank in Holden motoring history. Man's inalienable right—to drive a motor-car. I didn't bother for months with the mere licence and learnt from experience—experience curtailed at frequent intervals by the limit-ations of the vehicle itself. A three-point turn? Why not? Zoom into the sidetrack, slide the sticky gears ever so expertly into reverse. Stall. The tank starts only under gross physical pressure, weighs some tons, is pointing downhill into a fence, cannot be rolled back, must not roll further forward. Indeed, ace-driver Craig must admit that wedging the wheels and keeping FX stationary is the sole influence to be exerted. On the road, we hail a Main Roads Board tray-truck full of shovels and chivalrous shovellers, splitting their belted and ample sides. I'm prickly. 'Always stalls, the bastard.' Leading Alf and Jacko with rope to the stranded tank. Craig knows the axle's the place to knot it; scrambles under. Jacko climbs in and pushes the starter. 'No starter-motor,' I yell. 'Won't work.' But Jacko makes sure, goes through the choke-routine, gazes awhile at the ignition wiring, yawns as he gets the familiar dead click out of the button. 'I think you're right there.' 'That'll hold,' I tell Alf, but he's on his knees investigating. Rises like a coiled wire unbending. Yawns. 'Might do, lady.' 'Oh we often tow it out of here and there—it always held before.' *I'm not a fucking idiot, mate.*

Inga was the ideal passenger; she never suffered from the imperative of controlling the inanimate object which offered stubborn resistance. In fact, the stallings, towings, pushings and shovings were her eternal delight. While I swore and fumed at the shameful nature of my situation—driver without power over this hulking tank of mine—Inga laughed and laughed, tears spilling down her merry brown face. 'It's not funny,' I roared, causing irresistible gales of hilarity. She had a taste for adventure, however prosaic, and was never more comfortable than with the 'unexpected' disaster. 'The unexpected happens!' she would announce as if a curtain were going up out front on Craig and Francis Xavier locked in mortal combat again. FX having stolen another march on never-vigilant-enough Craig who has not, until this instant, deduced that Frank's tank can refuse to disgorge its last gallon of fuel, the fuel-gauge showing half-full the while. 'We are not out of petrol,' says Craig, quietly and with menace. The tank rolls coughing, feigning exhaustion, motor in doubt. Inga mutters maddeningly about the unexpected and the super car. 'Shut up, Kraut. I always expect it.' 'You pessimistic twit,' she counters. 'Grrrr,' I growl. 'Brrrmmm. Brrrmmm-brrrmmm.' FX responds with a splutter and the silence of the Australian bush is all as we roll on another half-mile closer to Cann River. Until the tank lumbers to a final self-satisfied halt. 'We can't be out of petrol,' Practical Craig repeats, thinking what a laugh and raising an internal giggle. There is, however, too much at stake to be openly frivolous in the inalienable motor-car.

The government had finally decided to pay my living allowance without reference to the family income; a sudden bonus lifting me well above the bread-line. Without hesitation I decided on wheels. No man complete without them.

'Well,' said Cliff, ex-Loyola school-mate of Max's, fled to Carlton, 'a woman needs a small reliable car.'

'Axiomatic,' I muttered.

'Axe who?'

'Sure, Cliff. But—well—I need a bit of speed and power as well.' Cliff drove his deep purple Austin Healey Sprite at maximum speeds on all occasions.

'Yeah. You can't drag 'em off without acceleration. Saves you the embarrassment, though, of dragging off some peanut, only to discover the bastard's a cop as you hit seventy up the main street.'

'It happened?'

'It happened all right. Cost me thirty bucks.'

'Bastard.'

'Yeah, he revved up real cocky, just to stir me. I was driving along peaceful and quiet, thinking about Joanne when the smart bugger just hacked in beside me and threw down the glove. Is it?'

'Yeah. Gauntlet.'

'So. Power, yeah. Can be a liability.'

'I can handle it.' I had driven Cliff's car, once, on the open flat road. But ignorance could not be allowed to interfere with the premise of motoring skill and confidence.

(Craig steals out after dark, sinks the keys in the ignition; flick. Out on the bitumen, running on the spot, hands braced onto the FX. Collect momentum and hurl self forward down the slow Gunning Street hill. Tank shudders and catches. Mind vibrates with the impact of the realisation—handbrake or gear. Check. 'Hopeless, Craig,' I mutter, releasing both, and resume the onslaught. Frank gives up, wheels roll, over the hump. Craig sprinting alongside the rapidly accelerating juggernaut; moment of action; hurl the body onto its cushioned driver's seat, hit the clutch and get in gear; magic moment as clutch foot retracts. Cough, lurch, cough, consumptive and wrenching; every instant in the balance as Frank builds doubtfully to a full-throated roar. So, the nocturnal driving-lessons with Francis Xavier the only teacher and task-master. Learning early to sight the flashing blue lights and counter with impeccable steersmanship and sobriety. At the Johnston Street lights I'm revving ever so happily when the speed-cop strolls over and leans. *They've got me—without a licence.* Heart thunders and heroic Craig's solitary zoom crumples in a niche of the nervous brain. 'Good evening, Officer,' I blurt, trying to infect my voice with cultured academic calm. The cop unaccountably sweeps off his peak-hat and smiles. 'Good heavens, madam' (he's blushing), 'I ... I ... thought you were a young fellow up to no good ... er ... the cloth cap I think. So sorry to bother you. Good night.' And he melts into the traffic leaving Invincible Cloth-cap Craig to wrestle the gears, avoid stalling, and slip on out Studley Park Road to the quiet practice circuits of outer suburban streets.)

'On the other hand, the parts are tuppence a bunch. You'd never have any trouble with FX parts. There's literally thousands of the old Holdens rusting to buggery all over the place. Parts are cheap—and plenty of 'em.

'How about it, then?'

'Well they're hefty, Maureen, to handle, and you'll have a lot of trouble seeing out the front windscreen. But they've got the old chassis base, they're safe enough. Like they'd go right through a car made ten years later. It'd take a reinforced concrete wall to crumple up an FX.'

'Sounds all right.'

Visions of impregnable masterful driver controlling tons of jungle-green metal. It was no disadvantage in the nature of things that women rarely attempted beat-up motor-cars, let alone the original GMH tank. I was on the brink of the Great Motor Car Romance.

Max and I, with Inga gradually getting used to our mystifying Australian habits, ended up drinking our way through that winter, against the background of an unimaginable '67 San Francisco summer. Nightly we repaired to Poynton's, lined up the jugs, fed the juke-box and settled down to our gallons of ice-cold beer. The heater burned; sometimes we heard the Melbourne wind whining above the invitation to wear some flowers in our hair, the possibility that 'All You Need Is Love', and the information that although our eyes were o-o-o-open they might just as well be closed. The hangover lent the morning to sleep, the afternoons allowed for an occasional lecture and brief bursts of manic research for the imminent Finals. By evening Max arrived from school, Cliff returned from his job in the city, Inga or I offered food and the four of us finally put on our jackets and pushed off.

There appeared to be no feasible alternative to becoming a formidable drinker, a drinker to be reckoned with. Indeed, practice applies to all skills, and Cliff, seeing its value, was delighted to engage in competition, regarding me as a serious and dedicated opponent. A jug each, with Max to pour, we skolled glass for glass—a challenging game, this, to be played near closing time, when Cliff had the taste. Without the taste, we agreed, the game became a meaningless exercise. Cliff won, at first, though he conceded a bigger mouth and gut as advantageous and devised a handicap system. 'Come on, Maureen—it's not a matter of pride—they do it with horses and sprinters and all kinds of contests.' After a few weeks of the system Cliff had to admit that his handicaps had been too generous to allow for my own stunning increase in power, and we skolled together from scratch again. 'You're amazing, though, Craig. I've never met a bird could drink me under the table before—and I have to admit you come bloody close.'

'Shit, Cliff, I'd win if you didn't always leave it till closing time so we never push on to the killer stages.'

He grinned. 'Wanna try one day?'

'Neither of us'd ever get home ...'

'Yeah. Let's agree at that. A couple of drinkers like us should be taking on the weak—not exhausting ourselves on each other.'

'Count me out,' said Max, quickly.

'Wouldn't even bother with you, O'Hearn. You're a piker from way back.' Cliff laughed.

'Can't ... just can't face 2B at nine in the morning after a session with you lot, even the usual.'

'I face the customers, Max.'

'Yeah. That's all right selling shirts, Cliff. The customers don't throw parties in the shop, scream at the tops of their voices, fire off their water-pistols and leave cryptic messages like Cliff Malloy is a shit all over the counter.'

'I see your point, Max.'

Poynton hovered, changeless smirk and pink carnation. 'Ten fifteen,' he smiled. 'And be so good as to leave your glasses behind this evening, gentlemen.'

'Glasses?' I said, indignant.

'Yes,' he smiled, 'you might care to return the half-dozen you carried off last night?'

'Couldn't've been us,' I replied.

He raised his slick eyebrows, smiled a knowing smile and turned to the next table.

'Slimy brute,' Max remarked.

'At least he's not calling the cops,' I said.

'We're small fry. And anyway, we're his best customers ever.'

'Right again Cliff m'boy. Let's go.'

Cliff turned to me. 'I got a few tubes back at the house. Shall we finish 'em off, Maureen?'

'No worries.'

'By Jesus you're amazing.'

I took Cliff's compliments at face value and glowed with manly pride.

The Melbourne winter as usual. The Mayfair was crowded when I got there, mud underfoot, coats dripping; I bought a beer and sought a seat, considered the bleak concrete of the beer-garden, tin tables puddled on top, decided to stand near the bar and wait for Tony. Sometime since the party where I'd met him I'd made up my mind about tonight—a simple affair, and I knew exactly what was going to happen. We would buy an armful of grog, take it back to Gunning Street, drink the lot and go to bed. Tony would fuck me. Having led a full and fulfilled sexual life, it is perhaps surprising that my first fuck with a male should have had any special significance in my mind. Virginity was something, however, that every woman had to reckon with and its common definition was purely mechanical. Woman is virgin until the prick enters. Julia used to say she didn't see herself as a virgin, but I accepted their terms and couldn't quite understand her—I knew instinctively that women didn't count. Having swallowed at some early age the bizarre assumption, force-fed to all women, that we are incomplete without men, I knew that Tony would count. Hardly consciously, I wanted a smokescreen, not only from the eyes of the world but from myself; I understood and attached myself to the groovy, easy, free-as-a-man image, a perfect if intolerable alternative to being seen as one of those. Since my move to Carlton I had surrounded myself with men, looked out for their company and tried to belong to and with them. The involuntary search for validity in their eyes.

When Tony arrived, he suggested that it might be pleasanter to take some beer back to my place on such a foul evening. I wondered if I'd be normal afterwards.

We sat for hours in the dining-room drinking methodically through the beer. I outlined the image of Craig as Great Poet; he marvelled, and explained his own miserable fate—National Service.

'But people get out of it without too much bother—students that is. You can postpone through several degrees and get so old they won't take you.'

'Don't feel like being that old and still at Melbourne University. I'd rather do it now than lose the chance to start a good job after I get through.'

'But the war might end. They'll have to realise they can't win—soon.'

'They'll keep conscription, though.'

'Better without Vietnam in the picture.'

'I don't think so. I'd like to see for myself.'

'And you don't mind fighting, then, in that war?'

'It's not for me to say. I'm prepared to do my duty by the rest of the fellas my age. Someone's always going to have to go, aren't they?'

'They'll brainwash you.'

'Not me. I'm a clear thinker with a First in Logic last year.'

'That's no armour.'

'I've got to go some time. I might as well get it over with.'

In a drunken haze we threw caution to the winds and held hands. I asked if he would care to continue upstairs and led the way, locked the door behind us, directed him to my narrow bed. A tight fit all round. Abrasive surfaces, that thing of his too bloody big, desire entirely in the head, cunt bone-dry.

'I did it once before,' he said. 'It seems so difficult—the girl didn't like it, it wasn't much fun. But they say it gets better.'

At least this'll stretch it a bit, I thought, ream it out for later. I can't be heterosexual, I thought, if I don't learn to like it. I have faith in habituation.

'Do you use ... er ... contraceptives?' he asked afterwards.

'No.'

'Oh.'

'Y'never get pregnant the first time.'

'I read about a girl who did.'

'No worries,' I continued, concentrating principally on the sore patch. 'I could always get rid of it.'

'Maureen, that's frivolous.'

'Frivolous?'

'Michelangelo was a bastard.'

'And Michelangelo wouldn't've wanted to be bothered with a kid if he'd had the misfortune to be female.'

'I don't follow.'

'Doesn't matter. It's my problem.'

Tony lay there half the night, lean and dank, sweating into the sheets, half-sickly traces of semen disappearing in the heavy smell of his damp body. I was delighted when he made his fond farewells and apologies for going. 'Call in when you're in Carlton and don't let the army make an animal out of you—or a fool.'

'No fear. Goodbye.' He kissed me chastely and was gone.

Five in the morning. I crawled out of the stinking sheets and stripped the bed. So that's fucking a man is it? A dull sore affair. But Tony, who touched me with a token gentleness, who thought it might be better, who wanted to stay on after the action—Tony, for all the fumbling and sweating, turned out to have been exceptional.

I dumped the sheets in hot water, disliking the smell of man, took a long shower and drank tea until the light showed. That's over. That burden's gone. And even if I do not feel substantially more normal, I am relieved that no repulsion has been revealed to me. The prick must fit, logically speaking, and though it remains unseen and untouchable, it is, surprisingly, less than threatening.

I unchained my bike, jumped on, pedalled a few yards and decided to walk. Winter Carlton showed a cool blue that dawn; the frosty orange sun lifted over the streets and splayed cold rays across Royal Park. Free at last, thought Maureen, as she strolled back through the terraces. And sunny into the bargain.

An alloy of fascination and pretension, this dive into the enigmatic engine. Ken always spoke with confidence of cracked heads, cams, crankshafts, diffs, plugs and the like; a vocabulary as glibly accessible as the language of literary criticism. The jargon itself was diagnosis and cure, only inadequate in practice. The FX, however, plunged me into intimate and continuous conflict with the motor itself. On the extreme fringes of a wildly-coveted competence, each breakdown expanded the diagnostic flair. On the level of the simplest solution Craig pushes ahead, cleaning plugs, ramming the coil back together when it falls apart, adjusting the clutch, which slips, at every second traffic light. A new frontier under the bonnet where the Lone Craig challenges male territory and thinks about a big victory.

The new used petrol pump looked elegantly easy, needed only to be fastened to the fuel lines. Spanner in hand, I had driven off into the back alley the better to make my blunders in peace. I screwed off the joints and lifted the old pump out. Child's play, I reflected, flipping the spanner about in a manner appropriate to the old hand. By Jesus. Looks neat. I jumped in, started it and rushed back under the bonnet to observe petrol spouting freely from the connections. A moment of thought. Always wanting to try it out too soon.

'You'll never get that back together.' A man stood behind me, grinning and leaning on the mudguard.

'Just needs tightening.' *You bastard.*

'Jesus, are you simple? Needs a man to tighten that kinda joint.'

'I disagree,' I replied curtly as he burst into derisive laughter.

'We'll see.'

How liberating it would be, I thought, to break this bastard's nose. Deciding rapidly that fighting was another frontier and not yet accessible. Besides, his nose was feet above me. 'Piss off,' I growled from between clenched teeth.

'Some lady, aren't ya?'

I tossed the spanner into my left hand, caught it with menacing deftness and flipped the coil apart to stop the engine.

'Very smart,' he said, sarcastically.

Feeling increasingly frayed; must appear cool. I wiped my hand professionally on my backside to recover dignity and swung back into the job. With relief I heard his feet crunch the gravel, his giggles retreat. Wrench, puff and feel the cheeks red-hot. Tighter, you bastard. Oouff. A sensation of ultimate outrage took the edge off my success. I revved the motor. Through the pump's transparent dome the amber petrol swirled and bubbled; vapour came off the joints—not a sign of leakage. 'Fuck his arrogance,' I said aloud.

I was surprised that Steve should visit me without Erif, and puzzled when he took my hand on the way back from the pub. How friendly he is, I thought. This man with his wild black hair and explosive laughter, who charmed women without trying, could scarcely be expected to take an interest in shy, awkward Maureen Craig, denim-clad and armoured with a comfortable virile manner.

'Let's drink in your room, eh, Maureen? I'm s-s-sick of S-S-Sonny's s-s-safari record. Whew.'

'OK.'

He sat beside me on the bed, his arm resting across my shoulders. 'You're a little ripper, Craig, aren't you?'

I blushed, lost for words. He laughed. 'Yeah. You really are. I s-s-see you s-s-sitting there in those s-s-seminars never saying a word. And you're there all the time, thinking away.'

'Yeah. I listen.'

'P-p-pity some of the other p-p-preten ... tious idiots don't follow the Craig example.'

'It's only that I can never think of anything intelligent enough.'

Steve exploded again, and left me mystified that he should be so charmed. He let his glass fall to the floor, turned to hold me by the shoulders and looked at me.

'You're wasted on women,' he said. 'No. I shouldn't s-s-say that.'

'Erif told you?'

'You don't mind?'

'No. No. I don't mind.'

'Erif and me are fucked up,' he said quietly.

'I'm sorry.'

'No. Don't be. It's my fault. I suppose I wanted to get away. Maureen. Let me stay with you. Just to sleep with you, to lie near you. Let me stay.' He let his head fall against mine and flashed a shy smile.

'Er. I've always liked you,' I said, awkwardness somehow vitiating the sincerity. 'Please stay if you like.'

He undressed, tossing his clothes at his feet; and stood in the middle of the room. His smooth firm body swayed a little, brown and solid even in winter. He threw his arms in the air and yawned, stretching. I began to undress, fighting off the unbidden embarrassment, my eyes drawn to his cock. Astounding, this column of hard flesh standing straight out from his black hair. And amazing his unself-conscious stretch, his accord with himself. An erection, I deduced, and wondered what that would mean.

'It's narrow, but big enough,' I said for something to say, pointing to the bed. I stood, removed from my ungainly body, discomfited and longing to be easy.

He moves and embraces me, his prick strange and alive against my skin. Cunt grows warm, comes full awake; I touch his back and arse with fingertips, feel him tremble and draw closer. In bed we lie arms encircling, faces meeting, bodies closed together, effortless rhythms of flow. 'Oh, Maureen,' he groans. We relate. We connect. Incredible.

'Lie still, lie quiet with me,' he whispers. 'I just want the peace of you. I didn't come here to make you.'

'I know. But I want to. I never felt this good with a guy.'

'No.' He frowns, black hair sweeping my face as he shakes his head. 'It's not right, not fair when you're a virgin.'

'Er ... I'm not,' I say, embarrassed. 'I did it once already.' He looks disappointed. 'I don't suppose I liked the guy that much. I didn't know him at all. And I didn't feel much. I calculated. But I wanted to know what it was like and to see if I could ...' I have taken the defensive despite myself.

'But it's not the way. It's downhill. It's nowhere. I've known girls go on and on as it all got more meaningless. Like men, predatory and meaningless. And me. Look at me. I can't even be faithful to Erif— I despise myself.'

'For being here?'

'No. No. Not for being here. You're different. You mean a lot of things. You've got guts and you live it out. Things I can respect and love. It's not that. It's just that everyone is responsible, every bit of the self-defeating chain, every prick who takes his advantage. I don't want to be that for you.'

'But that's the old double standard, Steve. Am I really any different for you?'

'Women don't make things any better by behaving like men. I need women. I need Erif. I need her purity.'

'Jesus, Steve. Are you telling me I'm impure?'

'Ah shit, Maureen, I don't mean you are. I'm lost, lost, trying to fathom it out.' He trailed off, then asked, 'You want me?'

'Yes.'

Suddenly man-woman equality begins to slide off into the darkness. Mounted. The word flickers through my mind and disappears. Steve kisses my breasts, towering in the dimness. I am below, flat, forked, receptacle. His cock snuffs wet open cunt and presses inward. 'Be gentle,' I say wanly, afraid of failure. Walls stretching near to taut snap. Rest, I want to say, aware that I need time to feel him sunk in me, to arrange myself around him. I cannot speak. Dare not say anything which might seem to accuse him of insensitivity. Throat paralysed, as he moves, inwards like a cannonball, jarring guts, away and back with rapid thrusting strokes. While the lighted ready cunt squeals and dries; and my voice is silent. Slow. Slow. Easy. Don't drive. I can't say it, not even to arrest this equivocal confused suffering. Not pain so much as impotence before the growing failure. Don't you know, baby? That your fucking excludes me from the experience? And why, at this closeness, can I not tell you? My tongue tied in indecipherable knots; my body reduced, disintegrating; my mind mystified and horrified by its own inability to change what is so patently unbearable. And afterwards the anger carefully disguised, because it's anger beamed back on my powerless self, and out beyond Steve or any single man. Anger at the seamless web of our fuck-up.

'You're marvellous, Maureen.'

Glad you liked it. 'Yeah?'

'Yeah. Do you like it then? Fucking with a man?'

'Mmmm,' A noncommittal agreement, a self-betrayal, a Steve-betrayal. *Being fucked you mean.*

I noticed with faint shock that I intended to steal his wallet. The foray was quickly over as usual and Walt had put his jacket on and gone in search of booze. I dressed, sore drilled cunt and affronted soul, and combed out the hair-knots with my fingers. As I bent for my shoes, I saw it lying half-under the bed. With ginger determination I immediately flicked it open and whistled. Fifty bucks. A bloody good price you'd have to admit. He fucks with his pants on—he'd have to lose a wallet now and again. I stuffed it down my jeans. For what, after all, do I ever seem to get out of these brief assaults? Fair compensation, surely.

Walt was holding a glass and a fag and looked worried.

'Can't seem to find my wallet,' he said. 'Would you run up and have a look around, Maureen?' *You must be joking.*

'Shit, Walt, go yourself. I want a drink.'

He scowled and made for the stairs. I realised, blushing, that I hadn't counted on his noticing the disappearance before I left. Shit. I went through the crowd and out the back to the rank weedy garden, bottle stack and decrepit shithouse. Someone was pissing noisily amongst the daisies. I fled into the bog and sat down to decide, fingering the leather and wondering by what process I had become convinced it was mine for the taking. He will after all be certain that I took it.

'Ha ha,' I laughed weakly, 'that had you worried. Here it is, you bastard.' Walt's face was distorted with rage and suspicion.

'Why didn't you tell me before I went up?'

'You expected me to go. I thought I'd give you a bit of suspense.' Bitch, he was thinking, devious smart-arse bitch, and she wouldn't've let on if I hadn't noticed. We eyed each other. Then he said, abruptly, 'I'm going home. Give me your phone number and I'll come by sometime.' Curt and hostile. The request made no sense.

'Oh you can get me during the day at the University. Extension 666 and ask for Miss Craig. I've got an office.'

'Thanks,' he said. 'Good night.' He hung a moment, decided not to kiss me and turned on his heel.

Shit, I thought. I nearly did that.

The little blond bloke pounds it out in thirty seconds flat. 'Shit, Maureen, you can't expect a fella to hang onto it—he can't control it, you know. Don't get so peevish. You get sore?' (Laughs) 'Shit that's all right me dear, I've got a gallon of Nivea over there. Of course it makes a difference.' He begins to ramble. 'Sharlene, now, you remember Sharlene. You know, the bird out at the farm, she wanted to marry me just when I was leaving dear old Mallacoota last year, abs just about finished, not much dough in it any more. Yeah, I liked Sharlene, pretty little thing. Funny I never got onto you down there—you musta been getting it from Bony Tony were you?' (Laughs) 'Sharlene wanted to get married. Mug's game that. A man doesn't want to tie himself down. Pity I knocked her up though. She thought that'd do the trick, but I'm no fool. We got the brass out of her old man in the end, got rid of it. Yeah, I liked Sharlene, lovely little bird, but shit, Maureen, think of it! I'm only twenty-eight. Got a lot of slap and tickle left in me yet' (demonstrates) 'couldn't get meself tied down.'

Sharlene appears in my mind, little and pretty and quiet, hanging on Joey's imbecile words across the table in the pub. Sharlene, Maggie and Jen on the lookout amongst the divers and shellers in the pub. No local lads in this part of the world—only Georgie from the General Store, thin face, thin colourless eyes, thin hips, only Georgie and the abalone boys. Sharlene after Joey (Maggie after Slam the Clam, Jen moving her big cheerful body from table to table), trading cunt for promises, hoping to spin the myth that she is his girl right into his mind. No wonder Joey didn't 'get onto Maureen' down in Malla-coota—he liked them docile, he liked them feminine and well-dressed, he liked them well away from the boats.

Joey's voice intrudes ... mate of his used to make his women struggle, they used to end up calling him a brute and worse. He loved it, used to end up raping them more or less, bloody funny sort of bugger he was, this mate of Joey's, used to have Joey in stitches over his exploits, but making the birds fight, now, that was genius. A bloody genius all right. Joey works his prick back to par, grabs the jar of Nivea, wants to jam it in again. 'Come on, Maureen, you wanted another round.'

I don't care one way or the other now. Desire thumped right out of me; I can't find his mate as salacious as Joey does. His double-quick performance is a repeat anyway. Machine-gun rat-a-tat injuring cunt subtly, bony white arse joggling at speed in the darkness. Why am I here? This hard unfleshy flesh ramming, cramming, feeding itself. Why don't I clear out? Piledriver Joey rams it home again, snoring five minutes later.

Mallacoota was paradise to those who knew it. The same campers returned year after year to pitch their tents amongst the tea-tree and mosquitoes. The Genoa lakes ran into the wide quiet inlet, flanked by dense bush folding up to the Howe Ranges and scrubby dunes towards the sea. Birds flourished out on the Goodwin Sands; pelicans cruised, herons and white egrets tiptoed in the shallows, gulls cut the air. People fished for flathead all along the lake-edges and out in boats.

The town itself was built where the channel curved inshore past jetty and moorings and met the sea in ever-changing patterns of sandbar and water. South of the bar Bastian Point rose, the end of the seven mile beach which curved from Gabo Island, broken only by the estuary. Beyond Bastian the coast alternated rugged cliffs, short encircled beaches, rock and more rock. From the shore right out to sea lay the reefs where abalone had once abounded, where the ab-boats swung at anchor on a good day and the divers went on fishing for diminishing loads.

Up at dawn, I roll out of the sleeping-bag and hunt for jeans and shirt, step out the front flap into still magnetic morning. The boiler-smoke rises in a column from the shower-block along the foreshore. The pale sky is clear, the thin drift of cloud from the north barely perceptible. Yawning, stretching, coming full awake, I start the car and burn past the sleeping campers to the cliff that scans the bar. Sea stretches flat blue to the horizon; two-foot toy breakers flop lazily along the beach; nowhere a broken surface; even on Bastian Point and the bombie beyond, the quiet swells slap and suck without white water. We'll be going out then. And I grin with pleasure, go back to wake Inga and arrive at the moorings feeling overwhelmingly good.

Stan the Man prances down in his wet-suit; battered scarred face, unshakable faith in his own charm. One of those bodies with muscles rippling, he usually jogs eight miles out to the airport and back before breakfast and stands around on the jetty flexing his biceps, playing with his prick inside his swimming-trunks. Stan makes the usual jokes about fishing with a pair of sexy chicks (Inga and I sexlessly con-tained in huge men's shirts and stinking jeans, zinc-cream noses, green rubber gloves in hand), revs up the motor and slams into reverse. I fling the painter inboard, leap onto the deck, run down the gunwale as he slides the boat back into mid-stream in an elegant arc. Past the jetty, campers are making breakfast and idling around their tents, looking up as the boat gathers pace and throws its wake at the shore. We curve around Captain's Point for the last sweep up to the bar; Stan throttles down to make sure of the channel, then points out through the sunrise breakers. Up the wave. The boat takes off into air and skims slap into the trough; two, three times, until we're clear of the sandbar and cruising on the oil-shiny calm swells of a blue world. Sun spins off bow-rail and water; the shore rises—rock, surf and tea-tree; the town recedes; the flawless sea encompasses us.

At first I lived in dread of the accident, the mistake which would put a stop to this sporting and comic gesture of Stan's—to take women on as shellers. Some afternoons the wind drove big seas in from the south and we clung, wet exhausted bodies, with a limpet hand to the windscreen frame. 'Took a bird of mine out once for the ride; poor little thing couldn't keep a hold on the boat in the rough, sprained a wrist and split her face open on the bins, went sliding to buggery down the back in the ab-slime. Lucky I had Joey out with me that time—I couldn't've left the wheel to fish her out of the bilge—the swells were breaking all over the place.' Stan chuckled at his meaningful anecdote and waited patiently for the sea to prove too much for us.

We found Stan's tent on the foreshore the night we arrived in town and sauntered down hopefully at dusk.

'Jesus now, light the lamp, Jack, and we'll have a look at these two tough chicks.' Gales of laughter from the men in the tent. Jack got up from his stretcher and struck a match over the gas-lamp. Light blazed up and threw his shadow on the back of the tent. Rampant red hair surrounded his face, beard gleaming gold in the gas light. Behind him two men were sprawled out, laughing. Stan chucked Inga under the chin. 'You're a pretty one. It's hard work, girls. Not a holiday at sea.'

'I like hard work,' I said firmly.

Stan shuddered with laughter. 'You must be off your head,' he managed to stammer.

'We can do it, anyway.' Inga spoke curtly and drew out of range of Stan's neck-caressing fingers.

'Never knew a woman could spend a day at sea without chucking her guts out, specially with the ab-slime and the stink and that.'

'We won't get sick,' I told him with a false confidence.

'Well, what man can refuse a beautiful woman?' Stan bowed and giggled again. 'You're in luck, ladies. Joey's gone to Sydney and your humble servant lacks a sheller. Tomorrow at dawn. No buggerising around, you know. We'll be working if it's fine.'

'No kidding?'

'Fair dinkum, baby. Now what kind of a hand would you be at frying fish?'

'Medium-good,' I replied.

'There's the stove, then. I'll get 'em cleaned. Have a beer if you like. I never touch it myself. Here, Jack, open a couple of cans for these luscious women.' Stan swept out. We stood at the flap and waited.

'Come and sit down, then. There's an airmattress in the corner if you can shift Bony there.'

'That's all right,' Bony said, sitting up to make space. 'Hullo there.' And he laughed again.

'Do you all live here in the tent?' I asked, anxious to keep talking.

'I'm in the next tent down,' Bony answered. 'We lie about here. It belongs to Jack and Stan.'

The fourth man got up, about six and a half feet of him, and ambled out. 'Oh Jack,' he called back over his shoulder, 'Could you tell Stan I collected the petrol for tomorrow—got his drum while I was at it. 'S down by the boats.'

'Good skill,' Jack told him and ripped the cans open.

'You fry a mean fish, Maureen. How come you didn't get married?' An abysmal unanswerable question. 'You must be joking.'

'No.' Bland and agreeable.

'I don't care to tie myself down, Stan. You wouldn't want to either.'

'Oh, women are different—only too happy to get chained to a bloke, in my experience. Seems to be how they're made.'

'Bullshit.'

He raised his eyebrows and continued. 'Well, what about the lovely Inga?' Inga scowled. 'Couldn't imagine you without a boyfriend.' He rolled his eyes over her, an appraisal which was insult disguised as appreciation.

'What a bullshit,' she answered levelly; saying nothing about Max who was doing his annual Christmas penance at Wodonga.

The mythical man's world. And we measured up. That satisfying uncomplicated pride in shelling with the best of them, wasting no meat, getting the floor clean before Stan arrived with the next haul and, between the two of us, hauling the dripping bags of abalone from the sea. Getting the anchor hooked and tied off, pulling it up in heavy seas, never falling overboard, never giving in to exhaustion, ignoring the shell-cuts on our fingers, and showing up at the pub after the day out, to drink and sing with the men. Proof positive of something obscurely necessary. Women were ace shellers, even if the men in their innocence could never see why we chose to be. After all, I reflected, why all the comedy? The money was good; the bar-crossing, the blue, the sea itself cancelled out any sensation of working for it. I was unable to imagine any more appropriate way of making a living—indeed I wondered often that summer why I accepted as inevitable that I must go back to Melbourne to teach. Here was work that demanded strength, indifference to comfort, indifference to appearance, toughness—qualities just as much anathema in the academic woman as in the wife-and-mother; qualities unacceptable in any woman; qualities which I found in myself and liked. Work without pretence or pretension; mind engaged with body and sea.

'Joey's back,' Stan said. A little blond bloke stood at the door of the bar, twisting his white moustache and running a systematic eye over the women. He noticed Stan with us and came over.

'This is Maureen and Inga—Joey. They've been out shelling with me for a week.'

'Good girls,' Joey said. 'That'll show a fella—going off to the Big Smoke and losing his job to a pair of wenches.'

'The ladies've been filling in, Joey-boy. But they've done wonders. You'll have to be on your toes with competition like this around.'

Inga curled her lip; I smiled feebly, unable to distinguish bullshit from bullshit. Joey laughed. 'I've got some news you girls'll be interested in, then. I saw Johnno running his boat in and I guess Anton'll go back with him.'

Stan beamed. 'So you're not out of a job, Jack!' he bellowed across the bar. 'You'll be needing our mermaids here.'

'Will I now?' Jack leaned on the table and looked from Stan to me. 'How's that?'

'Johnno's back.'

'Delighted,' he said and held out his hand. 'Welcome aboard, crew. I was getting sick of Anton—singing his French love-songs off-key for days at a time.' He smiled down, his pleasure undisguised.

'Watch out, Jack,' I said. 'I sing all the time out there.'

'Ah, but you sing beautifully.' I staved off a blush by draining my glass into my face. Mere flattery. 'Tomorrow then, if the weather holds.'

Bony sauntered over to the table with a dozen cans dangling from the little finger of each hand. 'What about a few tinnies down in the tent?'

'Have to be your tent, Bones,' Jack said. 'I'm figuring on the big kill tomorrow.'

Bony laughed. 'Come along for a while then—Stan? Joey? girls?'

'I'll get some lemonade,' Stan remarked with gravity and, non-chalantly rearranging his prick, he got up to get it.

Bony looked at me. 'Wanna drive down with me, Maureen?'

Bony swung out from the pub and wound up through the gears. At the corner he swerved left at the last minute and we were tearing out of town along the Betka Road.

'Where the fuck are we supposed to be going?' I asked him, shamming a cool curiosity.

'Have a look at Bastian, eh?' he answered, rocketing left again towards the Point. We shot to a hair's-breadth halt on the cliff and looked down over the dark sea, the black rocks, the Gabo Light flashing away in the distance.

'Have a can while we're here, eh?' He ripped it open and passed it over.

I must be as casual as he is, I calculated. Matter-of-fact. No wile-and-titillation stalling. If I agreed to be driven to the tent, I agreed to this, too. Didn't I? Or did I? But what overwhelming programming, superbly integrated into the female mind, takes charge of the ambiguous situation and elects to fight? Why is it always a question of giving in? To succumb at once is to fork the legs in passive annihilation; to succumb later is to have suffered the insanity of a losing battle. To refuse is to lie, anyway; to refuse is to see my live self sheer off into the night; leaving a hateful foreign prude sitting stock-still and rigid in Bony's embrace. It is easier to risk annihilation than to shuffle desperately through this nightmarish nonsense. As for initiatives, I know none. I have never understood the method allowed women—the ambiguous, retreating, stalking approach. And whatever is straightforward and willing and playful in me stiffens and atrophies under the undisguised male demand for the only part of me he has any interest in. Have another can, Craig, and blur those insoluble misgivings.

'What's wrong?' he asked me, as I glared up at him.

'You really don't know?'

'Can't imagine. It was great.'

'For you.'

'Yeah. Bloody marvellous.'

'For you,' I repeated.

'Birds've never complained before.'

'They wouldn't,' I said.

'Oh come on. I been screwing a long time. You can't tell me they all felt badly done by. I'm no brute.'

Nothing to lose, I thought, and decided to continue. 'You feel pretty good, now, don't you?'

'Of course. You're a nice lay.'

'And what about me?' Feeling perilously close to the indignity of the whinge.

'Well, what about you?'

'Oh yeah. It was fine. But then you finish in two minutes and I'm left in the air. Have to ease off without coming and pretend I like it anyway.

'But women don't come,' he said.

'What?' I yelled, shocked into raising my voice.

'Well they don't. Not really. Not like men.'

'How fucking ignorant can you be?'

'Of course,' he said sarcastically, 'I haven't been to University, have I?'

'That's got nothing to do with anything.'

'They never did with me—you're the first girl ever mentioned it.'

'It just goes to show, doesn't it?'

'Show what?'

'How bloody scared we all are of hurting your fucking feelings.'

'Look, I'm not going to have an argument. But it's obvious that a bloke has to get it out if he's any good at all. It's biology. Birds've got nothing like that. It's all the same right through, I'd reckon.'

'But it's not.'

'Anyway,' he continued, 'I read it—whatever it's like for birds, there's only a few ever get it. And most of 'em never make it at all—any time.'

'Ever wondered why?'

'We ... ll.' Bony drew the word out, investing it with a wealth of wisdom. 'I guess it's just how things are. If it was meant to happen all the time—like men—it would, wouldn't it?'

'You don't think it might be the way women are brought up?'

'Shit, I s'pose it could be—but that's still how it is, no matter why.'

'Or it could be the way men go about fucking.'

'Bullshit,' he said angrily. 'If you reckon you get climaxes you're an exception.'

'The way most men fuck I'm not surprised.'

'Jesus,' Bony groaned, starting the motor and revving it hard till it screamed. 'You're off your head, Maureen. You just can't expect to get the same out of it as blokes do. Blokes're different.' He drove back to town at maximum speed, raising curtains of dust behind us on the dirt road.

'Drop me at the tent, will you?' I asked curtly.

'Sure. Good night.'

There was no point, obviously, in dialogue. Words did not convince. Indeed, I was beginning to wonder whether my expectations were unrealistic in their nature, whether sex was, as the moral tradition had darkly rumoured, an activity which women could only endure. Unlikely, if you thought of Cleo. Fucking men, I thought, is for when you feel really altruistic and want to hand it all out to someone else. Fucking men is for saints. You might have expected the entire female population to be lesbian at that rate, or did women believe, along with the men, that their own pleasure was of minor importance? Did they believe that men liked it and they didn't? That men took their piece of tail and women gave it? Out of love perhaps or the will to please, but always with an exterior purpose?

Inga and I watched for Jack to surface with his load and, arm over arm, towed him in, whipping the air line back across the boat to float out straight on the other side. He was fanatical about keeping the hose straight, told us the cautionary tale of how one diver lost a boat when his line jammed in the propellor. Jack came floating in across the swells, khaki air-parachute and black, goggled head pitching from trough to crest. We grabbed the parachute and pressed thighs against it to steady the dripping bag of abalone; leaning out, we fastened our hands on the ring as Jack dived underneath and shot the bag up to us.

Grappled with the netting, hand over hand, and rolled the bastard in. Jack handed up the weightbelt, vaulted over the side, sat, flippers splayed everywhere amongst the abs, as he reached for the sardine sandwiches.

'Bloody nice,' said Jack, 'the way you've always got plenty of food, girls. Anton never brought a crumb.' Inga swung up on the deck, bun in hand, and faced away in the sun towards the miles of towering sand-dunes rising out of the sea in front of the Howe Ranges.

I squatted in the boat with him, at home amongst the abs. 'They really hang on, these poor buggers.'

'Yeah,' he said. 'They miss the rock. We told a new fella once the best way to get 'em off is to swim round first and give 'em all a sharp tap on the shell. He reckoned he needed a crowbar when he'd finished warning 'em.'

I grinned and squinted up at him.

'You're beautiful,' he remarked.

'Me?' I answered automatically, incredulous and entirely unable to muster the appropriate feminine grace.

'Yeah. Just like you are. Sitting there in the abs with that rat-shit T-shirt hanging off your tits.' Sounded like a compliment; felt like an invasion. I blushed.

'Ah y'look bloody good yourself,' I managed, somewhat at a loss. We smiled, sound of sea lapping the sides, roaring onto the beach a mile away.

'We got a flying fish in the boat while you were down,' I told him. 'Came off a wave and hit Inga slap in the gut as she's standing there gazing out to sea. She turned round to hammer me and found the amazing fish lying at her feet.'

'Yeah?'

'Wings like ... I dunno ... sheets of thin ice shot through with mother-of-pearl.'

'You threw it back?'

'Yeah. Too fuckin' beautiful to die.'

'Don't tell Stan. He reckons they're the best fish in the sea. Y'never catch 'em with a line.'

'Didn't look as if she ought to be eaten.'

'No. Still, the old leather jacket's a fine-looking fish—and we eat them.' He paused. 'And we're making a living ripping ab, here, off the bottom and leaving the reefs to the sea-urchins. You should see some of these reefs they fished hard the last five years. Bare rock and the urchins really in charge. Wasteland under water.'

'Sounds bad.'

'They don't leave the little ones, the bastards. I saw Mel dump two bins in the inlet last week—co-op wouldn't take 'em. That's maybe ten thousand little abs.'

'Bastards.'

'In it for the money. Guess we all are. Too windy up here; the surge is dragging me round like a kid with a puppy. Want to go down behind Gabo?'

'Sure. Might hit a good spot.'

'Might try. Get the anchor, eh?'

Balancing as the deck pitched, I flung the coils of rope back over the windscreen until we pivoted just above the anchor. Jack eased around to drag it free; I jerked at the line till the iron lifted and hauled it in.

'I'm staying up here for the ride.'

'Watch it, Craig,' he yelled above the motor. 'It's rough.'

I took a grip on the bowrail and planted my bare feet apart on the deck. More than a mile steaming through the sea; spotting flying-fish catapult out of the crests and glide in winds across the water; watching bow point up into sky, slam down into sea; feeling body swing, suspended momentarily by hand only, almost flying in air, wind plastering T-shirt back against naked body.

This is the life.

We hit a good spot under the lighthouse and got two extra bins before we had to head for home. Little Rame, the first big headland south, showed black in a pool of fire as the sun spun red behind it. The spray flew up from the bow in spouts of pink water. Above and just behind us three gulls kept pace with the boat, flying home beside us; and the calm evening sea spread before us in sheets of pale violet. Jack sighed and smiled at me.

For Stan, Max's arrival in town was a wholly unexpected, wholly unwelcome development. 'Who's that bearded bloke showed up at your tent this morning?' he asked me, curious to know the worst.

'Oh, that's Max,' I said. 'Just arrived. Inga's been living with him for a year now.'

Stan made no effort to cover his displeasure. 'I thought you two didn't have guys,' he said briskly.

'That why you took us on, Stan?' I asked, with unusual cool.

'Women!' he said with scorn and prowled on up the hill flexing his muscles.

'We'll have to get you a job, Max.'

'Ah shit, Maureen. I don't know about that. Must be bloody cold and wet out there.'

'No. Sun nearly always shines when we work.'

'Sunburn,' he countered briefly.

We lay on the Secret Beach sipping our cans and warding off the sandflies. Down the beach's slope Inga was swimming in the breakers, a naked bronze fragment tossed in and out of view. Max lay carefully on two towels, his motor-cycle boots splayed in the sand, his shirtsleeves rolled down and his head shaded by Inga's straw hat.

'Wish she wouldn't swim without her bathers. Anyone might turn up.'

'People don't come here much—the cliffs are too steep.'

'There was a guy here the other day.'

'Anyway Max, it's Inga doing it—nothing to do with you.'

'Makes me nervous, that's all.'

'And you don't fancy the sheller's life?'

'Don't think so, Maureen. I don't like being uncomfortable.' He smiled ruefully. 'I don't even like the beach that much—sand in the sandwiches.'

'Jesus Max, you're a softie.'

'No good pretending, is it?'

Inga came sprinting up the beach and whipped out one of Max's sand-defying towels; she rubbed herself randomly, making no attempt at decency. Max blushed faintly and faced away from her, dusting the sand off his jeans and gazing intently down to the rocks which cut the Secret Beach off from the coastline to the south. His grey eyes concentrated; he seemed absorbed in the middle distance. She pulled a face at me and prodded him with her bare foot. 'What's down there?' she asked him.

'Rocks,' he replied, without turning.

'Look here, crew,' Jack announced one afternoon, 'we've been up here on the Prince for about three bloody hours and no abs to speak of. Besides which, the current's zapping through like a hurricane. Feel like calling it a day? Exploring Gabo?'

Inside the Gabo harbour we slid beside the jetty and tied up. The sheltered water was still and deep green. I jumped up on the side, balanced an instant and made a knife-dive into the green, surfacing rat-like, sleek hair flattened across my skull and down the back of my neck. I shook the water from my eyes and looked up. Inga was climbing up the jetty; Jack stood watching, musing, smiling.

'To the lighthouse? Or the rocks?'

'Rocks,' I spluttered; he reached down a hand as I swam to the boat.

'Let's get this wet-suit off me,' he said, bending in front of me for assistance. The rubber peeled reluctantly off. 'Beats me how I ever get a suntan with that thing on my back every second day.'

Inga had disappeared in the scrub up the path.

Jack had this over the other men—that the sea was his first principle and the money a fringe benefit. Stan, the super-efficient strong-man, got his kicks back in town. Jack was the thinking bit of his boat, which allowed him to move across the sea, to challenge it, to respect it. With Jack the dawn meetings at the boat were the exuberant prelude to this adventure. Most of the divers ambled about for hours, or sat studying the bar, waiting for the big wind to arrive and blow the day's work. Jack preferred to ride back in the rough, rather than waste a day on shore. Catch Jack's eye as the boat whacks out over the breakers and you catch life triumphant.

We bore right from the path and came to the rocks; hot flat stretches, limpid pools, jagged sheer rock-falls, big smooth boulders.

'You want to sit a while and watch the sea?' he asked, taking my hand and leading me to a flat corner in full still sunlight.

'Yeah.' I rested my arm around his waist, uncertain of his intention, and loath to disturb the simplicity of our mateship. He bent to kiss me.

Impossible to relax into his arms and accept simply that I liked and wanted this. My mind hesitating, straining at meanings; my body, sunwarm and vigorous, responding. Insurmountable divisions. Jack's got a wife in Sydney, anyway, and kids, I thought, though that was not itself the reason. I was unable to believe that a man gave himself to the isolated fuck without standing half-away and congratulating himself on the conquest. Conquest itself an alien and repugnant idea. Fear of it jamming my brains even though I remained certain that Jack and I shared the sea uniquely. I snatched at the straw, the mode of retreat. Wanting to postpone; at the back of my mind, wanting more control.

'Shit, Jack,' I said. 'You've got a wife.'

'She's hundreds of miles away. And I love you.'

Bullshit. Yet true in some indefinable way.

'I've never enjoyed it so much,' he said. 'The days out, the fishing, the good loads, the bad loads, the wind, every fucking thing. I never thought I'd share it with anyone, let alone a woman.'

'Yeah. I feel like that too. It's like getting electric current off you— in the mornings. Knowing that we're really in the same boat.'

He grinned, mouth open, moving quickly to kiss me.

Why the fuck can't I meet him? What is it has this grip on my limbs, stiff-resistant, unyielding. What tells me, with certainty, that fucking a bloke is somehow the end of everything? There is a kind of love between Jack and me—but nothing could have less to do with it than what is happening now. His hands on my back persuading, per-suasion another kind of force. The false deep notions of virtue knot in with fear of failure, hatred of being taken; close tight around the recalcitrant fortress. I am confused. My heart tells me sweetly, clearly, that I am at this moment a cunt with a passable body and head on, that the isolation of the genital comes to Jack as if it were natural.

'I hate saying no,' I blurted out. 'I hate it. I can't explain.'

He looked hard at me, as if women would be always beyond him. 'It's not that complicated,' he said. 'I'd like to make love right here on these baking-hot rocks.' And I'd be on my back with the pebbles crushed into my backside.

'No,' I answered, disappearing into the fake moral world which would cover my tracks. 'You think about it, Jack—I won't say no again. You just think about it; if you don't mind fucking behind your wife's back, OK.' Ingrained conservative excuses. We women say such things, finding it harder to believe our own feelings than to excuse them.

Inga was waiting on the boat when we rounded the rocks in front of the harbour.

'She'll think we did it anyway,' Jack said, and laughed ...

'We're late,' Jack yells over the motor. 'Channel must be bloody shallow by now.' In front, the line of breakers pounds on the bar; after a dry spring the entrance is so narrow and shallow that most of the boats have to cross within three hours of high tide. Jack circles behind the breakers, scans the water, begins to ride in on the back of a big one. The boat holds pace behind it as it breaks, running in on its boiling surf. Sand. The prop jars and whines. Jack throttles up, gets a scream out of the engine and cuts back. 'Missed the bastard.'

Out in the breakers Jack takes the deep side. 'Over there,' he shouts to me. I'm shoulder-deep, grappling for a footing on the sand, going under the big waves, shoving the cork-buoyant boat back towards the channel. Up along the side, Inga's straining. 'There is not fucking leverage,' she screams as a wave lifts us all off bottom and throws her back against the boat. 'Get the fuck in,' Jack yells. He's in the boat like a shot, gives Inga a hand and leaves her to take care of me slithering over the gunwale, while he starts the motor and rockets away from the next set. Flat inlet water beneath. Wet jeans and shirt clinging to my body, grateful for the afternoon sun. Wind dies as we slow into the wharf lined with kids fishing, divers weighing loads, tourists asking for shells. 'They must be envious,' I reflect, as usual.

'By the way,' Jack said to us, after we'd moored and gone ashore. 'I've got an old mate down from Sydney'd like to go out fishing tomorrow. Would one of you mind taking a holiday? Four's too heavy with the bar as it is.'

'I will stay tomorrow,' Inga said immediately.

'OK.' Jack smiled and threw his gear into his van. 'Be down by five, Maureen, and we'll beat the tide out. See you.'

'You don't mind?' I asked as we walked up to the bakery.

'No sweat,' she said.

'I'll split the brass anyway.'

'Bullshit, Maureen. I am not straining to go out. It is five days in a row already and Max will be glad if I am at home with him. He is getting miserable sometimes, playing billiards in Parker's and boozing with the divers that do not ever work. He needs to be amused more.'

Jack's mate was a big, broad-nosed, blue-eyed affable fellow, who greeted me with the inevitable male amusement. 'Not much of you, is there?'

'Just enough,' I said.

'You'd be surprised, Alfie. Maureen's my right hand out there. She even gets us back to good spots—and that's some navigation out on the Prince.'

'Yeah?'

'No landmarks. Y'line up the seagulls with the clouds, don't you, Craig?' I nodded and waved Alf aboard, casting off with special nonchalance. Alf smiled continuously as he stowed his deep-sea rods along the side-pockets. 'Which way?' he asked me as we cleared the bar. 'North. So we ride home with the wind behind us. Always freshens in the afternoon.' Alf looked suitably impressed.

In the shallow gut between Gabo and the mainland, we hit the light north wind and the big northerly swell which was sweeping across the Iron Prince, building up over the shallow reef. A huge smooth sea—without a sign of chop or whitecap. When we dropped anchor the boat swung slowly into the wind; the air line coiled lazily behind across the rollers.

'Dunno about your fish, Alf, but the abs'll be easy for a change, if we meet any—that rip-tide's fuckin' disappeared.'

'Rip-tide?'

'Yeah, that's the only trouble up here,' I explained. 'It's a big reef and most of it's shallow enough to fish easy—forty, fifty feet. But there's usually a current through it—so fast it's enough for the boat to hang back the way the current's running—instead of with the wind.' I pointed out across the swells. 'We'd be side-on to these monsters if it was running hard. Had to give up yesterday.' Alf nodded respectfully and sat down the back, out of the way.

'Will it be OK,' he asked me when Jack was in the water, 'if I sit up on the deck and do a bit of fishing?'

'Sure,' I said. 'Better cast away from Jack.'

'Oh yes, of course.'

The rip had kept patches on the Prince unlooted for years despite the boom and the hundreds of boats that had worked out of Malla-coota. Jack had well over three hundred pounds of meat on board before he took a break. I shut off the compressor, enjoyed the sudden quiet of the sea. We sat awhile without speaking, listening to the quiet slap of water. Jack gazed out over the unbroken succession of swells rolling in from the north-east; the boat rose, pivoted on top and plunged back into the trough.

'It's a foot or so bigger than when we arrived,' I remarked.

'All the better for getting us home. And all our juicy abs, here. There's another boat coming. White. Might be Johnno.'

The boat flew and disappeared, came closer each time it shot into view on a crest. Johnno bore alongside and gaped when Jack told him we had four hundred. 'Pig's arse,' he called amiably.

'Blood oath, Johnno—they're shelled up under the deck. And big, mate! You've never seen abs like 'em.'

Johnno flicked his thumb down with a smirk, turned in a tight circle on the side of a wave and gunned on up it in search of a patch of his own. Anton stood at the bowrail, stripped to the waist, one hand flung into the air, and his eyes on the water spying out reef.

Alf took a lesson on shelling the abs, praising me the while. 'It's just a knack, Alf. Get it right and it's right forever.' But Alf must've thought my ab-shelling ease extraordinary; he scarcely spoke any words but congratulations. I got a kick out of them—the 'remarkable woman' compliments; and at the same time I felt uneasy, half-aware that it was not me but the range of territories alien to women which was remarkable. For Inga was as much master of the shelling situation, and the truth was obvious: any woman could be.

Around four o'clock the cloud started to build behind Gabo, big black swarms released from the clear southern horizon. The swell, now over fifteen feet, was still rolling quietly from the north. When Jack surfaced I told him Johnno had headed back. He took a swift look at the thick grey which had covered most of the sky and shut off the sun.

'The wind's gone,' he pointed out.

'Sure,' I said, pointing south, 'but there's more coming.'

'One more bag. Get the boat together and you can shell the last as we travel.' I chucked the bag down to him, finished up the shelling with a little help from Alfie, stacked the full bins up front under the deck, and waited.

The air was ominously calm; the mammoth swells toppled by, unbelievably smooth as if the sea were made of oil. Every minute or so, a bigger one would tower over a shallow part of the reef, curling and half-breaking miles from the shore, its long tatters of spray falling slow-motion in the stillness.

'Storm, eh?' Alfie asked me.

'Looks like it.'

Alf had packed away his reels and sat across from me, scanning sea and sky, waiting. Suddenly I felt the chill southerly breeze whip my cheek. Within minutes the white water was everywhere and the surface of the sea transformed from oil into chaotic white cross-swells. We swung round on the rope to face the new wind so that the fifteen-footers came in side-on, curling and threatening to break into the boat. As I hurtled over the windscreen to warn Jack I saw him surface amongst the surf.

'Here, Alf. Tow him in.' Alf hauled, I got the air line coiled, the compressor covered. We lifted the anchor and ran for home.

'We've only got three-quarters of an hour before the tide's too low,' Jack muttered. 'It's going to be a wild trip.' He swung the boat round and headed into the wind as I inched my way down the side and dropped back in. 'Get 'em shelled if y'can, Craig. We need to be light.' The upturned bin I sat on kept sliding down the decking as we reeled through the steep waves; the abs slopped over on the floor and had to be chased as they slid round in their slime. Throw the meat towards a bin, and the bin's on the other side of the boat before the meat lands. Flick the empty shells off the end of the knife and cop the ab-gut blown back by the wind. I worked without looking up, until I heard his voice again. 'Stand up, Craig. Quick.' I staggered up and grabbed the windscreen. Ahead of us was the gut between Gabo and the mainland. The fragmented northern swells were colliding head-on with monstrous gale-driven waves from the south in a mass of boiling surf. We met the full fury of the southerly as we came into the narrow passage. The bar was going to be dynamite. I gripped the windscreen with both hands and looked across at the men. Alf's forehead was split by an intense frown as he glued his eyes on the sea and looked at neither of us. Jack's face was running with salt and sweat. He held the windscreen with one hand and the wheel with the other, his knuckles blue with the effort. Spray came over in floods. I hung on while we thrashed through the white water, then slid back and finished shelling.

We were a half-hour later than yesterday, but with the tide itself later, we might just make it over the bar. Jack lifted his hand from the windscreen and pointed ahead. 'Johnno's still out!' he yelled. The white boat was standing outside pitching around like a cork. Screaming over wind, water and engine we found out Johnno's motor had broken down. I looked across at the shore. Twelve-footers were piling in and thundering murderously, throwing up huge clouds of spray which scattered and ran along the dunes. Impossible without an engine. 'We can't tow you through that,' Jack shouted. Johnno nodded and pointed over towards Bastian where the point protected a small cove which had been used for beaching during the war. 'We'll have to beach,' he screamed. 'Can you tow us over?' Jack looked at his watch, looked at me and shouted back, 'Yeah.' We circled round Johnno's boat, climbing up and down the waves, and finally got a line across. Jack was muttering 'fast' between his clenched teeth.

As we swept in towards the cove with Johnno in tow, Jack suddenly saw the wave toppling behind us. He pulled round in the trough and climbed back as the huge thing began to spill down. Our eyes connected, tacitly admitting we were scared. Jack headed back out and swung in near Johnno again while I fought to keep the tow-line clear of the prop. I heard Jack's voice, a feeble hoarse cry in the teeth of the gale. 'We can't go inside those breakers,' he yelled. 'We'll drive in along the rocks and cast off at the last moment. Good luck.' Johnno screamed back his thanks. We waited for a smaller set and made the second run, sheering off again up the breaking wave. I cast off. As we headed out to make our run through the bar, I saw Johnno engulfed in the wave. Then he shot back into sight on the crest of the next which seemed to hurl him past the rocks into quieter water.

Jack scanned the breakers. I heard him faintly. 'If we miss the channel we've had it.' I recalled us all playing about in the surf yesterday—there was no margin for error. If we struck bottom we'd be there for good.

'Here,' Jack shouted, thrusting the anchor-line at Alfie. 'Hang onto this. If we go aground try to get ashore with it. Maybe we can save the boat.'

'Where's the fucking life-jackets, Jack?' Alf screamed back.

'Life-jackets be buggered. No bloody use in this. Better be free to swim for it.'

'Jesus, Jack, I can't ... er ... swim much.' Alf sounded desperate.

'Good luck then, mate, and say your prayers. Here Maureen. Take the rope.' Getting ashore looked unlikely and hauling in a sinking ship one of Jack's nautical fantasies. I knotted the line around my waist and acted confident.

We climbed up a wave and rode in just behind the crest, way up in the air, level with the huge crests following. The wave in front curved and hurled itself down with a terrific roar, drowning out the continuous thunder of the surf up and down the beaches. We held in behind our crest as it broke beneath us, and surfed its violent surge. Jack's eyes were riveted on the water in front, the wide ruffled estuary with its channel indecipherable. I looked over and saw bottom through the white water, yellowish-brown of churned sand. The wave behind started to break, looking as if all twelve feet of it would crumble into the stern, like a wall in an earthquake. I felt the sickening lurch and heard the prop whine against sand. The wall of water behind filled half the sky—green and menacing. Jack throttled up. The prop jarred again, once, then drew water. Behind, the wave collapsed in deafening explosion; its spray enveloped us and chased on up the inlet. We were through.

Jack looked over at me and we burst into crazy laughter. Alf said, 'Jesus, Jack,' and collapsed in the stern with his head in his hands.

I leaped onto the deck and rode up the inlet at the bow-rail, yelling incoherent cheers.

At the wharf we lifted out our load—the best that summer—success tempered by exhaustion. Inga jumped down and swabbed the decks and floor for me while I sat, suddenly dazed, on the jetty. Max squatted beside me. 'We were up watching the bar. Saw you come through. Jesus, it looked dicey.'

'Yeah. I think it was. Never seen anything like it.' I babbled on with an account of all the risks and exigencies. 'It was good, though, getting through, especially afterwards.'

'You're off your head, Craig,' he said.

'Could well be.'

Away across the inlet I could hear the ocean thrashing on the beach. The sky was darkening with evening and rain, the clouds rolling overhead in one vast swift dark dance. It's going to piss down, I thought, but couldn't move. 'You look really done,' Max said and reached down a hand. 'I'll give you a shoulder to lean on.' I got to my feet and staggered up to the tent just as the sky opened. There'll be no fishing for days, I thought. Max disappeared discreetly into the rain as I stripped off the slimy shelling gear, flicked a towel over my damp body and passed out on the stretcher.

I woke and stretched. Wind was grabbing the tent-flaps and slapping the canvas around with the flutter of sailcloth; but inside, the sun had already turned the place into an oven. Max and Inga must be up already. I rose unsteadily, shoulders aching, and rubbed off the sweat. A shower, a loaf of fresh bread and a day of rest. Outside, the shelling gear lay muddy from the night's rain. I'll throw that lot away, I decided radically and drove the hundred yards to the shower-block.

'I saw your car,' Jack said. 'So I waited.' He leaned on the bonnet, his red hair blowing out in the wind. 'How're you feeling this morning?'

'Bloody good now I'm clean. Bit of an ache in the shoulders, but pretty fit. Passed out last night like a shot.'

'Yeah. I saw Inga in the pub. She said you were dead to the world.'

'How's Alf?'

Jack grinned. 'Oh, Alf's never going to pass condescending remarks to you again, Craigie—I think he's still suffering from shock.'

'Did you know the poor bugger couldn't swim?'

'He never thought he'd have to. Shit, he's been coming out with me every summer to do a bit of fishing. He always got pretty days before.' We stood in the sun and watched each other for a moment.

'I'm going for a drive out Betka way,' he said. 'Like to come?'

'I need a feed.'

'Well, I'll shout you breakfast up at the cafe?'

'OK.'

'Want to try this road?' Jack slowed and turned into a dirt-track, puddled and muddy after the rain.

'Can we get through that?'

'Sure.'

We lurched down a few hundred yards into a grassy space surrounded by tea-tree and gum, the leaves bright with the exceptional shine of a morning after storm. Jack switched off the engine. Wind roared in the treetops; broken shadow danced across the clearing.

'Let's not get out,' he said. 'The mosquitoes are sudden death here. Sit near me.' I slid along the seat under his outstretched arm and stared at the glistening bush, determined to ignore my misgivings, Jack's wife and all the irrelevant data that crowds the strait-jacketed mind. 'You're not saying no, are you?' he asked in an undertone.

'No fear,' I answered, and kissed him.

'Let's get in the back. We can stretch out.'

I nodded and climbed over. He stripped in the front, rapidly and gracefully; I did the same with less finesse, cursing the uneasiness which arose suddenly in the crystal morning as if from nowhere. We lay a short time facing each other, his hands rolling over my shoulders, body rippling along mine. Slowly the mind's structures began to dissolve, leaving me alone with him, all there. I'd wanted to fuck this guy for weeks. The rest was an inevitable recoil from the experience as Jack thought of it.

Jack slides in, moves slow, supple fit, smooth frictionless pierce of keel on morning water—this is something else. One or two unbelievable cinched-in strokes, cunt alive, exultance rising, expansive climb to ... Until Jack hits the accelerator, prick pounds and explodes, me following lamely as it slips out flaccid and Jack throws his head back. I must look surly. I scarcely want to disguise it.

'That's the trouble—when a girl's so bloody desirable. That's what it's like—I mean I'd like it to last a bit longer, too. But a fella can't do a thing about it.' Poor sort of system then, if that's the score.

'You're just too fucking exciting, Maureen.' His face apologetic and smiling. Cold comfort. Trick bind. Jack performs at usual lightning speed, sits back with an air of amused self-criticism, and pleads smilingly for resignation to our fates. He might as well be telling me I'll have to make it faster in future—to have a chance in the big event. But I cannot make it faster, I don't know how to do so and I remain mystified by the rule of speed, the race with only one winner. Enough to confirm the most hesitant lesbian—if the fucking's always fraught with the tension of a speed-rally and loaded against the woman.

'Ah, Maureen,' he continues, 'I am sorry. But you never expect much the first time, do you? All that's built up for weeks. That's how it is. That's how we're built, baby.' At least there's a doubt, of which I can give Jack the benefit—bound to be better next time.

The clearing is quiet, the windy sun still supernaturally bright outside the van. Jack sits up, leans forward for his clothes, gives his shrunken prick a dust with his underpants and puts them on. I shiver and start to dress. We might as well be on different planets, the contact is so negligible. Post-coital indifference. So that by the time we have dressed, not looking at each other, not speaking, not touching, we are more totally out of tune than ever before. No messing about, even for Jack. Get it in, get it out, and wipe it.

In the evening, we went up to the pub as usual. Stan caught my eye as I gazed around vaguely, as if I were not seeking Jack. I strolled over obediently.

'Jack's left for Sydney,' he said. 'He asked me to tell you—couldn't find either of you this arvo.'

I gave him an impassive stare. 'Oh yeah,' I said, 'we were out at Betka.'

'No-one'll get over the bar for a week after yesterday. Jack thought he'd take the chance to see his wife and kids. He misses 'em sometimes.'

'Yeah,' I said. Who fucked who was usually common knowledge among the men; yet it was possible that Stan's bland information implied ignorance.

I was sprawled out on the sand by the Betka river watching the breakers crash up the beach's incline and musing, as I had for a week, on Jack's return. There were boats out working today, skimming across the sea like big white birds. Sound of feet scuffing the dry, squeaky sand. A shadow fell, cool, across my back.

'Speak of the devil.'

'Were you speaking of me?' Jack asked, smiling.

'Thinking.'

He dropped soundlessly into the sand at my side and wrapped his arms around me, friendly and warm.

'Inga said you were out here. I'm glad I found you.'

'Me too,' I said, surprised at the pleasure of seeing him. 'I've been wondering when you'd be back.'

'And I've been longing to be back. With you and the sea.'

'I've only got a week left.'

Jack nodded.

'We working tomorrow?'

'Better be.'

'I cleaned the boat yesterday,' I said, unable to moderate the pride in my voice. 'Side-pockets, bilge, the lot.'

'Fantastic. I think you love the boat better than me.'

'About the same,' I said and grinned.

'Wish you weren't going back to Melbourne. I'm going to miss you forever.'

'So am I.'

'Why don't y'stay?'

'I've got a job. Have to go.'

'Tell 'em you've changed your mind.'

'I might've, you know, if you'd been single.'

'I am down here.'

'Can't help it, Jack. I'd think of myself as your cheap sea-side mistress.'

'You wouldn't be that,' he said gravely.

'I'd find it hard to believe anything else.'

'Anyway. I guess you want to be Dr Craig with a string of letters after your name.'

'No fear. Not at all. It's not that.'

'Bet you do. That's what a career's about. You'll be a Professor at thirty.'

'Jesus, I hope not. It's just that I never thought of doing anything else until I came here. I was good at the aca stuff, and I thought that sealed my fate.'

'Let me know if you change your mind.'

'Sure.'

We lay in the afternoon sun, at one with its warmth and brightness. Jack touched my back lightly. 'Would you be angry if I said I wanted to make love to you?'

'I was wondering something similar.'

We got up, flesh warm through to the bone. And my mind a grateful blank.

'Stay please,' I mutter as he starts to withdraw. 'It won't stay, Craigie. I've spent my penny.'

I groan. 'So soon, you bastard.'

He shrugs slightly. 'It's done. I'm sorry.'

I feel violent, want to smash his smug face to pulp. He speaks so calmly, so glibly, just as before. He's had his fuck and looks onwards, outwards. I am the sexual adjunct, used and set aside with a show of apology. Fill me full and roll me over—might as well be a plastic bag. Disposable.

'She bangs like a shithouse door,' Ken said to Robby Hitchin, *and burst into uncontrollable laughter.*

'Twat like a concrete mixer, that's for sure.'

'Have another beer, mate.'

'Wouldn't mind another piece of tail.'
'Beer first. Brush later.'
'Cheers.'

I look up, half-expecting Robby Hitchin's tough pointed face. Jack lies propped on his elbow. 'Really. Believe me. I ache for you. I can't help myself. I'm sorry.'

'And if I ache for you?'

'I'm sorry,' he says again. His face is worried and soft; his spent vulnerable prick flops sideways against his thigh. Just lie against me, I want to say. It's not all over for me. Let me come. Don't leave this anger to breed. I am silent instead. If he only saw that I have needs like his own. But I cannot say it, and he does not move; lies a little apart, looking hopelessly apologetic.

'It's hopeless,' I say in an undertone.

'What is?' he asks gently.

'Everything. Sometimes I wonder if men and women are compatible as they. are. At all. I should've been just your mate. That's love. This isn't.'

'What do you mean?'

'Sex is exploitation. Always.'

'Not always. Really, Maureen. I've never been so bloody awful with anyone. And that's the irony. Because I don't think I ever wanted to fuck anyone so much.'

'Sounds like bullshit.'

'It's true.'

Sudden mitigating thought. Maybe he'll suggest we lie on the beach for a while and make it again when he's ready. I wait for him to suggest it as a few minutes grind by. And why don't you say it yourself, eh, Craig?

'Fuck these sandflies,' he says. 'Let's get back to town and have a beer.' Failure and alienation. No way out of the quick-fire pointless fuck. Warmth receding at lightning speed and pleasure, the male preserve, never to be shared. Maybe I should learn to like what I get. Or should I accept the lesbian alternative, where participation is not perversity and contact doesn't have to be demanded? Which would seem a sounder notion if I hadn't already known it as a world of secrecy and fear, vulnerable to everything around it.

There must be some way out of here

Alvin had stayed a week in Mallacoota one summer, camping with his friend Alex. They stuck together everywhere, quarrelled as lovers do, and they had all the classic camp gestures. But if anyone else in town had noticed that Alex and Alvin were homosexual, they had pretended as continuously as I that it had never crossed their minds. When they invited me to Alvin's twenty-first, I was curious to go to the party and see if they had a place where they could act openly and comfortably.

Alvin seemed delighted. 'Didn't think you'd come, darling. Have a martini.'

'Oh beer, thanks,' I said gruffly, discountenanced, for once, to be drinking the man's drink when men and women alike drifted around sipping various exotic mixtures. I went slinking through the crowd to a dark corner where the music was loud and my being alone might pass unnoticed. I watched people dance, men together, women together; Alvin and Alex waltzed by and waved. I felt as if I looked as if I was gaping. I felt envious and a long, long way away. I wished something would compel me to join in, catapult me into the action.

Two women were dancing together. One was freckled and wore a demin jacket open over a checked shirt. Her face was resolute, her back straight, her body strong and graceful. As they came near she noticed me crouched in the shadow, looked straight at me and smiled. I dropped my eyes, picked up my glass and drank from it. When I looked up again she was gone. I glanced around. A moment later she was sitting beside me offering me a cigarette.

'Thanks,' I said gratefully.

'You're by yourself, are you?' she asked, her voice deep and American.

'Yeah. Shouldn't've come I suppose—I don't know anyone.'

'I'm Jody,' she said.

'You're American?'

'From New York.'

'I'm Maureen. From Cobb Swamp.'

'Where?'

'It's in the country, a hundred miles or so. But I don't live there now—got a room in Carlton.'

'Nice people?'

'Oh yeah. Don't get on with Ken too well—he never does much.'

'Your boyfriend?'

'Oh shit no, he's my brother. We took pity on him and let him move in. He just lives there.'

'Oh,' she said, laughing a little. 'Men are hard to live with on any terms.'

'Max is different.'

She looked sceptical. 'Who's Max?'

'He's an old friend, we've been sharing the same house for years. His girlfriend's just gone back to Germany,' I added to make the situation clear.

'I'm staying over in Fitzroy,' she said. 'It's a big house. All women.'

'Yeah?' It sounded unlikely. 'Doesn't that get you down?'

'Get me down? How?'

'Oh, I don't know. I've always thought mixed houses were best. I was in college for a while and I got sick of girls. They're so narrow-minded.'

'In what way?'

I didn't want to say. 'Girls hate you if you're different,' I hinted darkly. 'Guys are more rational about it.'

She threw back her head and laughed heartily. I couldn't see what the joke was and asked her to explain.

'Oh—men and their rationality. It's only the exterior, only their image. We never hear their empty chatter until we strip it off.'

'Don't you like men, or something?'

'I haven't much reason to.'

'But ...' I stopped.

'I bet you haven't, either.'

'I suppose not,' I muttered cautiously. 'They don't know how to fuck, that's for sure. But, really, some of my best friends ...'

'A couple of mine are too.' She laughed again, without malice.

'But Jody,' I said, 'isn't that just you?'

'That is what they'd like to have us think. But no. Definitely not. *Definitely not.*'

I drank some more beer and looked hard at her.

'You don't agree, eh, Maureen?'

'Er, well, no ... I mean, I don't know.'

'Let me run it down for you.' I nodded. 'Right. First man I knew was my father. Now he was a nice man, quiet, sensitive, a beautiful sense of humour, enthusiastic, you know he really loved doing things. He built things, played baseball, he even left a great pile of manuscripts when he died, novels, poems, stories. Oh, and he suffered, too. He didn't want to hold a job down. He liked variety; he wanted to travel—but five kids and a wife ... So there he was—stuck. I can understand him. But it doesn't excuse how he came home and fucked his daughters at night.

'Shit no!' I said.

She nodded, looking at me levelly. 'Shit yes,' she said. 'And it's not like growing up helped that much. There were always men on streets, whistling, jeering, ogling, the usual. And always plenty of them. And I sure knew what *they* were on about. I took it, too, of course, the way women always have. I went to work in an office, fell in love once or twice, got married, left work and started sitting around in a nice apartment cooking cordon bleu, washing shirts and staring out the window. It was OK for a while, even if Raymond wasn't quite the adventure I'd expected. He was another nice guy, a decent guy. I think he did love me within his appalling limitations. But the more I tried to get through to him the less he noticed. He couldn't see what was bothering me. Isolation, boredom, panic, tranquillisers. I wondered what was wrong with me—he was a good man, we had a nice apartment. I felt guilty for feeling bad! Ray tried to help. Take up weaving, he used to say, take up pottery, take up something. Help yourself ... Well you might as well throw a two-year-old in at the deep end and tell her to swim. Later it was go to a shrink and find out what's wrong with you. Wrong with me! Ray didn't have a clue.'

'Bad luck,' I said.

Jody laughed. 'Oh I don't know about that—my second husband beat me up. There's a limit to what you can explain by bad luck. Unless you think women are born to it. It all adds up, Maureen. And it doesn't mean bad luck.'

I was not at all sure what she meant, but she spoke with a serene conviction which could not be gainsaid.

'The trouble is,' she went on, 'that we always believe it is ourselves, our filthy luck, our inferiority, our own failings which make us so vulnerable, such victims.'

'But if you want to lead a normal happy life, don't you just have to accept all that.'

Jody exploded in laughter. 'They sure got you bluffed, sister.' I blushed. 'Like I was leading one of those normal happy lives. Wow! Normal maybe, but I never did figure out where the motherfuckers got the happy bit from.' She laughed again. 'It certainly isn't for most women.'

'It never was for me,' I said with an odd formality, and hung my head.

'Once you quit putting up with things,' she said, 'you can start to choose.'

'Oh, I'm going to leave Australia after Christmas, that's one thing,' I told her without raising my head.

'Well, right on. The only snare with that is that you won't be leaving yourself.' I looked up. 'But I guess you know that.'

I stared at her. 'How come you're here?' I asked inadvertently.

'I came with one of the women from the house—she used to live here.'

'Oh.'

'We're living together now. Mary and I, that is.'

'Oh,' I repeated, utterly staggered by her directness. 'That's nice.' I looked at her and added, without considering, 'Cleo would never live with me.'

'Why not?' she asked quietly.

'She thinks she has to follow the rules. She knows, or she did know, that they're crazy, but her parents forced her first and she goes along with it still. She wants to find a man and get married.'

'And lead a normal happy life?'

'Yeah. Cleo's always believed in the weight of numbers.'

Jody smiled. 'The thing about numbers is that they weigh exactly what you think they weigh, no more, no less.'

'What do you mean?'

'Just that. They only have the power you think they have.'

'Well,' I said. 'I don't know about that—it always seemed to me that there was real power, you know objectively, with people like Cleo's mother and girls in college. They could force normal expectations on us.'

'You believed they could, didn't you?'

'Sure.'

'That's the point. While you're scared, they can force anything.'

'Well,' I said, feeling piqued that she made it all sound so easy, 'aren't you ever scared?'

Jody grinned at me. 'Sure. Fear is every woman's middle name. But it's my fear and it's not immutable. Courage needs practice, too, and it's not easy to begin at the age of twenty-something, when all your habits lead you to give in and accept.'

'Yeah,' I agreed, meaningfully.

Her face broke into a conspiratorial grin. 'It helps,' she said, 'If you don't sleep with the enemy.'

I didn't quite know how to take Jody. I wondered if all this was an elaborate con, but there was nothing to suggest that. Thoughts pounded through my head. Was she really so certain? Must be. How could her advice possibly be a joke? And how could it not? But she looked me in the eye, smiled and stood up. 'I must go now—take care, Maureen. And be strong.'

'Oh I will,' I replied, without thinking. 'Good luck.'

I watched her walk across the room. At the door she turned, flickered a benign wink and disappeared.

I rubbed my eyes and found myself muttering, what an amazing person, was she really sitting here? But I could not, in a million years, have invented her. I had never met anyone like her. You could say that she had turned lesbian after two broken marriages—but she was obviously impervious to external descriptions. Nothing seemed to take her unawares, nothing seemed to surprise or divert her from her knowledge. I found myself wondering how she would have handled the college scandal, the academic environment, friends she couldn't be open with—but then it seemed clear that she would have no friends she couldn't be open with, and I did not doubt that she was capable of handling anything. She's over twenty-five, though, I thought, hoping that time might be on my side, too. I had never had a conversation like it. I poured myself a glass of whisky and sat down again, no longer concerned with appearing to be excluded, no longer obsessed with joining in. After a while I got up, found Alvin and thanked him for his party.

'Going so soon,' he complained. 'I trust you had a marvellous time.'

'Well, yes. I sure did. Bye.'

'Bye bye and be good.' He waved and fluttered away.

I drove home.

When Inga left again for good, Max could think of no strategy adequate to the situation. We bought a dozen therapeutic bottles and collected Steve and Erif before heading home from the Alfred.

'How you feeling, Max-baby?' Steve asked him.

'Fucking awful, thanks. How's yourself?'

Steve laughed. 'Not so bad.'

'Half your luck.'

'And how's the lizards?'

'Goannas. Bloody nice creatures, goannas. Thought I'd lost the savage one yesterday—must've crawled under the concrete. But I teased him out with cat-meat.'

'They go for it, do they?' Erif asked.

'Too right,' he replied with enthusiasm. 'Amazing, isn't it?'

'How's it been since she left?' Erif looked concerned.

'Oh, the bottle's a man's eternal boon. Can't remember much of the last five days, really. Maureen seems to get me back from the pub all right and into bed, and I chunder off to the bridge every morning.'

'Ch ... chunder under it, I s-s-suppose?' Steve managed.

'No fear. Stomach must have a steel interior by now. Never feel that bad. Life! What a drag!' Max knocked back a glass of beer and filled it up again. 'I bet the new victim is some sort of big intellectual. She always thought I was stupid.'

'Her m-m-m-mistake, Max.'

'Maybe. Anyway, it doesn't add up. It's not as if I expected her to stay home and do all the housework and cooking and washing. I never asked her to do anything like that.'

'But she used to do it just the same,' Erif said.

'I suppose she did. But why?'

'Things like that have to be done. It depends who moves first.

I have to starve for hours sometimes before Steve gets off his arse. It's easier to do it yourself. But it doesn't mean you like doing it.'

Steve objected with a grunt. Erif grinned at him. 'It's true just the same.'

'It's s-s-s-so bloody trivial, though,' he said.

'It's only small if you're sitting back. If you're doing it, it's triviality that goes on and on and on, and no chance of getting out of it without getting petty and mean.'

'Shit, Erif. I was a model of willingness that week she was here. Water off a duck's back—she ended up going off and staying with a friend of Maureen's. Couldn't bear to be in the same house as me.'

Erif leaned over and smoothed back his hair. 'I'm sorry, Max, really sorry.'

Max smiled a tight wan smile and looked up at her. 'Can't be helped, can it?'

We filled our glasses and sat back, listening to Dylan wheezing that there must be some way out of here.

'Hey,' I said, remembering. 'I didn't tell you. I'm leaving.'

'Leaving Max?' Steve asked.

'Well yeah. That's involved, but I've decided it's time I left Australia altogether.'

'Jesus. When?'

'Pretty soon. I'll go down to Mallacoota for a while when term finishes, but I won't stay long. Reckon I'll be out of here by New Year.'

'That's all a bit sudden,' Erif said.

'Oh I don't know. I've thought of it for ages—going to London for a breath of real culture. Just made my mind up to do it.'

'Off to s-s-s-swinging London, eh, Craigie?'

'Well, I'll end up in England. I'm going to Afghanistan first.' I smiled enigmatically.

'What's there?'

'I don't really know. Mountains, deserts—seems a good enough place to avoid the parking fines.'

Erif laughed, then looked concerned. 'Have you got anyone to go with?' she asked. 'It could be dangerous.'

'Well,' I said, 'I tried to persuade Max, but he reckons it'd be too hot or too cold, too much dust, too many flies, and he'd rather go to Mombasa, he reckons, if he has to go anywhere. So I'm going by myself—should do me the world of good.'

'You'll probably get raped and mur ... murdered.'

'Steve—I've been raped and murdered all me life—it won't be new.'

Steve grinned.

'At least you could fight if you got attacked. You can't fight what they do to you in this godforsaken desert of a country.'

'Come on, Maureen. Australia's not that bad.'

'Bullshit,' I said goodnaturedly, 'it's worse. I'll never be free while I stay here. They're inside my mind.'

'Who?'

'The ordinary, normal, complacent bastards who populate this country. There's always a voice that says I'm out of my head, weak, stupid, just plain wrong. I'm going where they can't touch me.'

'You h-h-hope.'

'I hope. But I'll never hope anything while I stay. I'm sick of frustration, sick of fear, sick of hiding myself away in case I offend some bastard.'

'So you wave a m-m-magic Af-f-fghan wand and presto, Maureen Craig s-s-s-steps forward, naked and fearless.'

'Oh fuck off, Steve. I'll never get anywhere here, that's for sure.'

'No. I do agree. But you should really take Max along too.'

'Bet the beer's awful in Afghanistan,' he said, and sealed the subject.

I had decided to leave and, if there had been any doubts before I met Jody, they had now melted away. I resigned my tutorship, bought a ticket to Calcutta, and spent my spare time poring over maps. I thought often of Jody and how she had said that I would not leave myself behind. I was not absolutely certain what she meant—it seemed to me that, with my parents and all the people who had ever known me on the other side of the world, I would be free to do as I wanted. Of course I would meet people, and maybe they would have the same preconceptions about life—and me—as everyone here in Melbourne did. But I would move on when I chose, on and on. One of the abalone divers, a Belgian, had told me that women often lived together freely in his country. I wondered. And, at the back of my mind, I hoped that I would meet a man unlike any other on my travels, a man who would want me as I was, who would be as gentle and understanding as any woman, a quiet European perhaps, who would offer me an easy way out of all this struggle and uncertainty. Jody, I knew, would not have liked this fantasy, but I could not part company with my own version of Mr Right. Whatever happened, I would be far from Cleo and far from home. If I was going to learn to act for myself, I would have a fairer chance than ever before.

The year was over but for the exam-marking. I loaded the papers into the boot and set off for Maffra. See Cleo and tell her the news.

Her flatmate, Rhonda, opened the door and led me down the passage to their neat, clean kitchen. Cleo looked up from her teacup and offered an ambivalent smile. 'Didn't know *you* were coming.'

'Nice surprise for you all, eh?' I answered. Rhonda and Josie, another teacher, chorused yes and Cleo said she supposed so. The others looked faintly askance at her blasé attitude to a friend arriving from afar; Rhonda muttered tea and boiled a new kettle.

'Couldn't get the marking done back in Carlton,' I said, falling back on the age-old ploy of excusing myself, 'Too much drinking and pontoon, not to mention Ken torturing his girlfriend. Wondered if I might stay a few days—should get a lot done in dead old Maffra—especially with everyone at school all day.'

'Sure,' Cleo, answered indifferently. She appeared to be in the withdrawal stage where she made me fight for recognition.

'OK,' I said, relaxed and easy. 'That's fine.'

'You're cocky today, Maureen,' she said, when the others had gone off to play squash. I grinned.

'You won't believe me, Cleo, but I came down really because I've made up my mind at last and I wanted to tell you.'

'Tell me?'

'I'm leaving Australia. Getting the fuck out of here at last. Come January and Craig'll be gone.'

'You're kidding yourself again,' she replied, sceptical.

'I've already resigned from the tutorship.'

'Maureen. Really?'

I jumped up and danced around the table to hug her. 'Really,' I said. 'Isn't that great?' Hoping that it might not, after all, be such great news for her.

'I'm glad you're going,' she said stiffly. 'It's best. But I'll miss you.'

'Miss me? You haven't bothered with me much for years now.'

'I know.' She looked grave, the old solemn Cleo showing her vulnerable face, hidden lately under a schoolteacherly façade. 'I suppose I took you for granted, these last years. Knew you would be there for me. Knew you loved me.'

'It's good that you knew that,' I said, astonished at how well Cleo must have understood our long unsteady relationship.

'I suppose I always knew you'd go in the end. I never gave you much to stay for.'

I smiled wryly. 'No,' I said. 'I always wanted you to.'

'I know.'

'And that's one of the things I'm going away from. It's never been easy—not since your mother found out. I've pursued you, I suppose, and I hated to have to do that.'

'Poor Maureen.'

'No,' I said firmly. 'Poor Maureen's finished. Maureen's actually decided what to do for a change. I certainly don't feel poor.'

'I hope it'll be good. Really I do.'

'Yeah.'

Eagerly she asked me where I was going and how, grew worried at the vagueness of my plans, wondered if there really were buses in Afghanistan. I thumbed the atlas and pointed to the occasional place that sounded familiar—the Khyber Pass, Mount Ararat, the Himalayas.

'You are such a romantic, aren't you?' she said.

'I guess so. I always liked that awful poem *He Fell Among Thieves*. "Blood for our blood," they said, but they let him watch the night out and he saw the dawn over the Afghan snows. That's all I'm going on really.' I smiled happily. 'But it is like that. I want to be out of it, completely alone. I'd never do it by regular day-to-day choice. So I'm going to catapult myself into nowhere and start living.'

'You'll be the same.'

'And in the end I'll be different. I intend to learn how to act for myself, I intend to be free.'

'Ah, Maureen, you'd be laughable if you didn't sound so sure.'

I grinned. 'Oh, I am laughable. What've I ever been? Everybody's cabin-boy. Loyal to the last and willing. Fuck. And always, always without fail, I'd do anything for anyone if they'd like me for it. Terribly untenable for someone who usually wanted to do the things people never like. It doesn't look too bloody hopeful. But I've been thinking and I've hit on a strategy. If I get the hell out to the other side of the world, somewhere where I won't even meet anybody to please, I'll just have to please myself, even if it *is* an effort. It's foolproof.'

'Good luck,' she said, half-smiling, and kissed my cheek. 'Do you want to listen to some music—or are you going to start marking immediately?' She raised a quizzical eyebrow. In a whole year of visiting her she had rarely invited me to her room without my angling for hours.

'When'll Rhonda and Josie be back then?'

'Not for hours. They have tea with the others after squash.'

'You mean we've got the place to ourselves?'

'Yes.'

We went into her room, strewn with third form French corrections and geography text-books. 'Ugh,' she grunted, and stacked them deftly into a corner. 'I'll give them something and mark this lot in class.' She flicked through her records and came to *Blonde on Blonde*. 'This always reminds me of you and Carlton—Gunning Street that summer.'

'Yeah. Me too.'

She sat near me on the floor, head dropped onto hunched knees. Dylan and harmonica howled out I want you so bad. I dared to stroke her hair, moved closer to throw an arm around her, wanted to kiss her hidden face. 'Ah, Cleo,' I said, 'I wish it had worked. There's never been anyone to come near you these last years. Men or women.'

'I do love you,' she said without raising her head. 'I always did love you.' *Then why? oh why did you give me up?*

232

'It wasn't because of anything in you or in us. It wasn't that we lacked anything.' She looked up, regretful or ashamed, or both, eyes round and sad.

'No?'

'No. It was them. I was always afraid they'd reject me, condemn me. I'm not defiant by nature. It's always easier to accept and turn another way. And it wasn't just my parents—it was college again after I went back. It was everything I'd lose if I went back to you—no more comfortable easy getting along with everyone. I saw it happen to Libby. And the future. I could never see us with a future. I could never think beyond the University to any kind of life with you. I couldn't face a life of secrecy and I couldn't be defiant. And that's what you've got to choose between. I could never have done it in the end, even if my mother hadn't stepped in.'

'Even if you thought it right?'

'Even though I thought it right.'

'Isn't that a poor way to live?' I asked, without malice.

'I can only live as I'm able,' she replied, without injury.

'That's the worst of being me,' I said, smiling again. 'I could've lived with it—but no one else has seemed willing to.'

'But even if you did, my dearest, it would still make the same awful strain on the relationship—I am not enough for you, nor you for me. Two people together in a ghetto that's a prison. That could never last long.'

'But that's what marriages are like.'

'Except they have approval, they have sanction and they have the possibility of being at ease in the world. We had none of that.'

'Australia is worse than other places.'

'Maybe. But in the end it's bound to be much the same anywhere.'

'Well, it'd solve everything if I could fall in love with a bloke somewhere along the line—like that woman in *The Fox*. But I easily might not, knowing what they're like. I'd much rather have you, Cleo. You respected me, you liked me, you understood me—even if I did have to deal with a hostile world. But then I shouldn't have to hide, either, I shouldn't have to feel ashamed. I know I never did anything bad and still I act guilty. We were just people loving each other, not monsters.' Cleo nodded. 'It's a poor bloody world where such positive feelings have to be destroyed.'

'What a romantic you are.'

'What do you mean romantic? I don't see what's romantic about wanting to express your feelings honestly and freely.'

'Well, it's hardly realistic.'

'No doubt. The way things are. So they have to change. Not me.'

'Pipe dreams.'

'I met a woman a few weeks back who said that if you stop accepting, you start choosing.'

'What's that supposed to mean?'

'She reckons you don't have to put up with people's judgements, you don't have to behave as they expect you to.'

Cleo looked at me pityingly. 'Lovely in theory,' she said. 'Who was this person?'

'She's American—I met her at a camp party in Box Hill.'

'You are getting adventurous in your old age.'

'And what's more, she's living with another woman in a house full of women.'

'And what do they think?'

'She didn't say, but the way she talked they must all be friends. Anyway there's no bullshit about her—she wouldn't be hiding herself away.'

'When are you moving in?'

'Oh, Cleo, don't be so bloody cynical.'

'So you're going to start off by leaving Australia, are you?'

'Seems like the best course of action ...'

'Good luck,' she repeated, and, kissing me, asked me to come to bed quickly before Rhonda and Josie came back. 'We've got an hour at least.'

'And then you'll be transformed back into decent, clean-living Cleo.'

'I have to live the way I have to live.'

'Such stoicism.'

'I love you, Maureen. Please don't be hard on me. I love you, my darling.'

I stayed for days, until the papers were marked. Each evening after school she manoeuvred us away from the others, guarding me more jealously than she had ever done before. We went for drinks in the the old pub by the river, drove to the weir at Glenmaggie and the pine-forests at Stradbroke, walked together under the moon nearing full, arm-in-arm in the darkness. One day she came home at lunch-time and kissed me in the sacrosanct kitchen.

'Miss Atkin,' I said severely, lengthening my face and craning over Rhonda's spare spectacles. 'This is very serious, you know—this flirtation with life in which you are so brazenly indulging.'

A wry grin. 'I dreamed about you last night. You were in London and a tall man carried my suitcases up the flights and flights of narrow stairs. I was coming back to you.'

'Yeah?'

'Just a dream.'

'Did you feel good?'

'Trepidated, mostly.'

'What did I do?'

'It stopped before I got there.'

'Oh.'

'And yes there was another dream.' She frowned, bringing it back. 'Desolate. What a desolate dream.'

'Yeah?'

'There was this man, tall again. He came to the room where we were and he told me to come with him. I looked at you and you shook your head, saying no. But I went. He was very sexy—alluring. And I followed him down the corridors. And then ... and then. I must've realised I shouldn't leave you, because I turned around in the corridor and fled like lightning. And when I got back ... you were gone. Completely gone. I cried.'

'Poor Cleo. I wouldn't've gone, though.'

'Ah, but you would.'

'D'you want to come to Afghanistan with me?'

She laughed. 'Oh dear me, no. Burnt bridges are burnt bridges, aren't they?'

'And now is easy because tomorrow rubs me out.'

'Something like that. Oh, Maureen.' She hugged me so tightly I felt her ribs crunch mine.

'My darling,' I said softly.

I visited Cobb Swamp rarely now. There was little enough of myself that I could still share with impunity—songs, a beer, an afternoon in the garden. Mother's old prohibitions on Communism, atheism and abnormality (widely defined) left me with little to say and an ideological row always in the offing. Worse still, although I no longer accepted it, the shadow of an amorphous guilt still fell like a shroud whenever I walked up the back steps. Will she still be grinding her axes?

This morning, though, I was on top of the world, if a bit ashamed to be so. In a little while the family at Cobb Swamp would be powerless to force my hand any further, unable to demand obedience, unable to exact the penalties of our blood relationship. I whistled a bit, hitched up my jeans and walked in. Father was standing by the sink clattering the dishes and Mother, still in her dressing-gown, sat with her feet in the oven. She turned her worried head as the door slapped shut behind me, and smiled welcome through the mist of her disaffection.

'Hullo, Mum. How are you?' I said and bent down to peck her on the cheek. 'Hullo, Dad.'

'Hullo,' Dad grunted and smiled wanly.

'I'd be all bloody right if your father'd have a bit more common sense and consideration.'

'What've y'done wrong this time, Dad?' I asked, tone of mateship and alliance.

'What's he done wrong? Every bloody thing. I've been asking him to get more wood for a week in case we had another cool spell ...'

'It's bloody November,' he cut in.

'November or not, the mornings are cool. *He* doesn't feel it so he thinks nobody else will. And your poor old Granny's in there freezing to death.'

'How is she?'

'She'd be a bloody sight better if there was a fire for her to sit beside.'

'Jesus, Lotty,' he said, remonstrating. 'I've been working till after dark on the gravel-truck. I can't find wood for you in the dark.'

'Always some excuse,' she growled with an acid bitterness which would never forgive.

'All right,' he said with grit in the teeth which always meant explosions. 'I get up. I see you're feeling off-colour. I start washing up to give you a hand and what do I get? Abuse as usual. You can never do the right thing. If I'd been out getting wood, you'd want to know why I didn't wash the dishes.'

'No initiative,' she muttered, turning up the gas.

I stood and watched, like a film you'd seen hundreds of times before, the interminable reels repeating into oblivion. Father chucked out the last pot and swilled the water down. 'Wood, is it, then?'

'I've been asking you for weeks.'

'Whatever you do, it's never the right thing. It's always been the same.' He strode out, wrenching the door. Amazing that bloody thing was still on its hinges.

'Will we have some tea, Ma?'

'Oh yes dear, that'd be nice. You'd never believe the things I have to take from that man, always pretending he's helping out and always leaving the important things undone. He's obstinate and he's stupid. I don't know how I've put up with him all these years, and as if I didn't have enough on my hands with Granny so ill now and me not so bloody rosy meself ... he's worse than useless, spends all his time trying to make things harder for everyone else, I just can't ...'

'Oh shut up, Mum,' I said goodnaturedly.

'Taking his part again, aren't you?' Her eyes narrowed and she rubbed her hands on her warming feet as if for comfort.

'It's just that he's always trying to do what you want, but never seems to manage. It's just that I understand how he feels.'

'Oh you would, wouldn't you?'

'And really—you don't ever ask him pleasantly for anything. It's just nag, nag, nag until he's half-crazy trying to work out what you really want him to do.'

'There's no way of being pleasant to your father. You'd know if you'd lived with him all these years.'

'Well I grew up here, didn't I? I watched it all.'

'Oh, Maureen,' she groaned. 'Oh, Maureen, you don't know. You couldn't know.' Her head sagged and the tears started to come. 'The brutality. The sheer brutality of him.'

'When he loses his temper, you mean?' I asked.

'At night ...' She stopped, embarrassed, then went on. 'It's brutal; it's mean; it's horrible. There's no feeling, no talk, no communication. Nothing. He never talks to me anyway, not at any time. I can't stand it. I never could stand it. Oh God.' She sobbed—long racking groans, as if she saw clearly before her the vision of an ugly hostile world loaded inexorably against her, a world in which she had been helplessly thrown to suffer.

'Mother,' I said and put my arms around her.

'You don't know. You don't know.'

Perhaps I do, I thought, but decided not to say it, since I saw that she wouldn't get any comfort out of knowing her daughter shared her lot. I might as easily have sat like you, confused and injured, with my feet in a comfortless gas oven, if I had not had the good fortune of my woman-lovers, if I had not had a Cleo to show me a way to live at peace with my body; if I had married a good-natured bastard of a Jack; if Bony's assertions had seemed, however terribly and unjustly, to be true ... Perhaps I would have been like Mother, whose life was blunted, whose well-wrought moral trap had sealed her up from every alternative and kept her ungraciously resigned to a fate she must have thought inevitable.

'Poor Mother,' I said gently.

'Oh dear,' she said, blowing her nose and trying to smile, 'I must get up and get on. I haven't given Granny any breakfast yet.'

I stayed for the day, helped her with the chores and put off telling her I was leaving.

'Oh, I forgot to tell you,' I said finally after dinner, 'I've decided to go off to see the world at last.'

'When?' Mother asked swiftly.

'After Christmas.'

'So soon,' she said. 'But you'll have Christmas with us.'

'Of course.'

'England is it, Maureen?' Dad asked.

'Yes ... I ... er ... think I'll get there slowly, though. See something on the way. No point in flying over places.'

'Like where?' Mother looked worried.

'Oh, Afghanistan.'

Dad burst out laughing. 'Mad as a snake.'

'What's Afghanistan like, Joe?' she asked him.

'All bloody desert as far as I know.'

'You'll get killed, most likely,' she said.

'I'll be taking good care of myself, don't you worry.'

'But you'll be going on to do something in London, won't you?'

'Oh, I suppose so.'

'You have to think of your career.'

'Oh yeah. I'll be looking after that too.'

'Well, if there's anything we can do to help you get away, now, you let us know.' Mother spoke sadly.

The night before I left, Cleo had dinner with me—plenty of wine, good steak. I was full of leaving, full of preparation, full of gaiety. I racked my brains for a place to take her to make love a last time. Oddly, no-one was home when we drove back to the house. We turned no lights on, went quietly into my room cluttered with shadowy trunks and boxes, the desk and tables bare, luggage for the trip scattered around my rucksack.

A kind of ritual. I take her warm naked body into my arms, a tenderness which melts me. I will never kiss this soft mouth again, because we are celebrating the end. I tangle amongst Cleo's freckled limbs and she bends over me kissing my breasts, stroking my hair. I remember how often she has said to me: we fit. I remember her fantasy of the film that ought to have been made of us two, so close, to tender, so compatible. 'People like my parents would understand, then,' she used to say. How could they, any more than we, resist this compelling complete union?

'I will miss you, my Maureen,' she says, mouth flickering with the familiar wry smile.

'And me. You've been the centre of my life for years.'

'Too long. Anyway, you'll be in strange places, new places. You won't think of me.'

'Don't believe it, my darling.'

'It will be true in the end.'

'I suppose that's why I'm going.'

'Yes.' Her mouth is puckering. I want to protect her, to swear fidelities. The edges and surfaces of my skin shade off into hers. We are two candles burning side by side, wax fusing. I have known nothing else like this.

'No-one has ever made me feel like this,' she says, mirroring my thought. 'It's a lot to lose.'

'You've been trying to get rid of me for long enough.' I laugh.

'That's true. But it's strange. With men I'm always sitting on the ceiling watching, cynically almost.'

'You've always been a bit of a self-watcher, though.'

'And that's what I've loved about you. You take away the watcher. With you I forget, I'm whole.'

She moves against me, brushing her open moist lips across my mouth, cupping my hair with her small palm, exploring layers and lips of cunt with her fingertips. Our foreheads rest together, our minds flow into one another. There is no gap. Tonight perhaps no gap at all; because we both know that I'm leaving and there is nothing we cannot give. She, for the first time maybe, is free of all her manifold fears of me. So we lie together passionate tranquil hours, embraced as if forever.

'Will you come to me in England?' I ask her. 'I will wait for you. Until you've served your time here and can come.'

'No,' she says quickly, eyes puzzled and warm. 'No my dearest, this time you've got to go free. No promises.'

I seem to swoon. Relief and piquant regret. Leaving Cleo is final. I am glad I have the guts for it. I am enchanted that we part in such peace.

She went out to her car, kissed me gently, wished me luck. I stood in the warm night street and waved until the car disappeared around the corner. I stood in the warm night street, gathering my strength, and hoped for the best.

Afterword

I began writing *All That False Instruction* in Berlin in the European summer of 1970, as described in this letter to Sandy and Dave Fitts back in Carlton:

> A novel is perhaps being born: one exercise book is already bulging with scenes, fragments: most of it is alive, though large chunks wd. never get past your old guardian Rylah, who (I take it) has been returned along with Henry. Didn't you slobs vote hard enough? ... I have an attic here and am writing and thinking ... In Australia I could never write honestly about my necessarily secret "illicit" life, fears of condemnation, fears of opinion, the illusion of unending whispering behind me. I only see how intolerable was the pressure in retrospective freedom from it. There simply isn't a place for me in our land of surf and sunshine.

A letter to another Carlton friend, Denis Murphy, also spoke of the novel's beginnings:

> (Here, I'm) ... freed from the compulsion to continue my celebrated impersonation of the Australian male ... what a man-trap Australia turns out to be! I was so busy avoiding falling into a woman's role ... simply reacting against it, that I didn't realise, back there, that I was caught as squarely as anyone else. I honestly feel as if I've been let out of prison, freed from pretending I'm someone I'm not in order to avoid being something I can't be ... Writing this novel is, often, great fun, though certain (characters) turn into monsters ...

I left Melbourne in January 1970, heading for London via India and Europe. At that time, Henry Bolte had been Premier of the State of Victoria for fifteen years and his Chief Secretary, Arthur G. Rylah, was still vigorously enforcing Australia's censorship laws—which kept books by authors such as Barry Humphries, Henry Miller, William Burroughs, Norman Mailer, Philip Roth and Simone de Beauvoir on the banned list. At the national level, the conservative Liberal and Country Party coalition had ruled Australia for twenty-one years.

Germaine Greer's *Female Eunuch* would not be published until later in 1970 and writing by women was sparse. Helen Garner (her first novel, *Monkey Grip*, was published in 1977), Elizabeth Jolley (*Palomino* came out in 1980) and Kate Grenville had not yet appeared. In the Australia of 1970, women were banned from the public bars of hotels, were not allowed to work in managerial positions in the public service, were ineligible for bank loans without a male guarantor and were obliged to surrender their permanent status as teachers once they married. As elsewhere, acceptable roles for women were mainly domestic and subservient, career horizons were limited and stereotypical femininity was the rewarded personal style. A poll conducted in 1971 showed seventy per cent of Australians over thirty-five thought homosexuality was wrong and/or dangerous (*Age*, 19 April 1971).

Most of *All That False Instruction* was written in London during 1971 and 1972. The Australia to which I returned at the beginning of 1973, soon after completing the book, was on the verge of enormous social and political change.

More than two decades later, at a 1995 conference called Women Writing: Views and Prospects 1975–1995, Bronwen Levy remarked, in her keynote address:

> Elizabeth Riley's *All That False Instruction* represents what is, I think, the first second-wave feminist novel in Australia ... It is often seen as the first lesbian novel in Australia. I claim this as an early feminist novel because I think the narrative viewpoint of pre-women's and pre-gay liberation days, which is in part the topic and the point of the book, is explicitly lesbian feminist. *All That False Instruction* can be read as being written out of and perhaps written into (in terms of audience) a specifically feminist and lesbian feminist context.

While I don't disagree with the categorisations, the book was in fact written without exposure to a lesbian feminist context and without any prospect of a feminist audience—though such an audience did materialise by the time it was published and I was exposed to lesbian feminism before the text finally went to press. I wrote the novel in 1971–72. For me at least, these were very much pre-women's and pre-gay liberation days. It's true that the character Jody (who was probably too heavy-handed and even a mistake from an artistic point of view) arrives near the end and spouts feminist rhetoric. What she had to say drew on what radical lesbians were saying in Melbourne in 1973 (and a little earlier in London, though I was unaware of it); but she was an add-in who had not appeared in any of the original drafts.

Although I finished the book in 1972, publication was delayed until 1975. The major cause was extended printers' strikes in London; but trouble with my family—which led to the pseudonym and a raft of changes to the geography of the text—also contributed. In the three years of the delay, second wave feminism took off in Australia. *All That False Instruction* sits on the cusp of the pre-feminist world it was written out of and the feminist world that was emerging by the time it was printed. In the last chapter, the insertion of Jody and the scene where Maureen experiences a certain understanding for her mother were the two major adjustments I made at the editorial phase—carried on during 1973 in the new era of consciouness-raising. Although relatively small—and although Jody still feels undigested and didactic—they signal that the world in which the story takes place is on the brink of change. (In this new edition I have revised the scene and lessened, I hope, its implausible edge.)

It's also true that the second wave women's movement arose from exactly the same social conditions as *All That False Instruction*. And it is from this perspective that one could approach Bronwen Levy's view that the book was written out of a context that was specifically feminist—perhaps in the same sense as Germaine Greer's *Female Eunuch* (first published in London in 1970), which I read sometime in 1972. I was struck by the similarities between her themes and mine. But Germaine Greer was aware of her context ('this book is part of the second feminist wave' she wrote on page one), and I was not.

The women who came together in the Women's Liberation Movement in the early seventies were overwhelmingly (though not exclusively) people who had grown up in the same post-war decades as I had—and as Maureen Craig and her friends had. Even the women in our generation who were not involved in the political activism of the women's movement and would never have described themselves as feminists were affected by the same forces that made some of us take to the streets, the CR groups and the collective endeavours for social change.

In her review of new women's fiction (*Meanjin*, Summer 1975), Sue Higgins (Sheridan) wrote that the emerging female protagonists in books like mine and Vicki Viidikas' *Wrappings* were:

> ... outsiders in a world that seems to offer ... room to move and yet ... brings them up against barriers, material and psychological, that contradict their apparent freedom ... these women are ... not heroically invincible, but persistent ... Sensuous passionate beings. The freedom to be so was offered to our generation and we grabbed it—defied our parents, hid our Pills if necessary and began to discover our sexuality—only to find ourselves in a male

world which insisted that we had sexual autonomy while denying us autonomy as individuals, and as female individuals at that.

Suzanne Bellamy's review 'Fucking Men is for Saints' (*Refractory Girl*, June 1976) also remarked on the double-edged nature of 'freedom' for the generation that emerged in the sixties. While the protest movement against the Vietnam War mobilised dissent across the social spectrum, women were challenged by 'the publicly asserted (though privately feared) new open sexuality'. For her, *All That False Instruction* '... lays bare the tentativeness of those new sexual mores and the repressiveness with which women's sexuality was still confronted', and is '... one woman's creative evocation of that tentative growth in consciousness which formed part of the new women's liberation movement.'

Tentative indeed. Suzanne Bellamy points out that the 'radical' generation of the sixties in Australian cities and universities—which cohered in the Vietnam War protests—seemed radical only 'by comparison with other social groups and other periods and by self-definition'. Within the peer group, uniformity was 'as structured and enforced as in any other generation' (*Refractory Girl*, June 1976).

In her Introduction to *The Female Eunuch*, Germaine Greer speculates on the causes of the second wave of feminism. She too mentions the possiblity that 'the sexual sell was oversell' (Greer p.3). But she also suggests that the gains which had ultimately flowed from the first wave—such as education and a relative freedom from unwilling childbearing and heavy domestic labour—had led women 'to a position from which they could at last see the whole perspective and begin to understand the rationale of their situation' (p.3). She refers to the tension which arose from a woman's attempt to 'reconcile her schooling along masculine lines with her feminine conditioning' (p.5). In Australia, Maureen Craig's was the first generation where women went to university in large numbers, and where working-class people did it at all. While Maureen did begin to see and understand her situation as a woman, resolutions to its contradictions were not available to her.

All That False Instruction was first conceived in India, where I met Jan Rottamer in 1970. Jan was a German writer who had published a volume of short stories. We became close friends, exchanging stories constantly as we made our way from Delhi to Greece. He had been born before the Second World War and was seven years old in 1945. His tales of his youth—the end of the war seen through a child's eyes—were as riveting to me as mine were to him. According to Jan, the parochialism and prejudice I described were not to be found in

Europe, nor was sexism rife there. He was both fascinated and shocked by my stories of life in Australia in the 1950s and '60s. There's a terrific novel in this, he insisted. Among Jan's pantheon of great writers was Henry Miller, whose novels I went on to read. His passion for Miller's semi-autobiographical style, with no holds barred as to subject matter or the appropriation of elements of real life, certainly shaped my concept of what kind of narrative was possible.

On the train to Peshawar, through the northwest frontier country of Pakistan, Jan recounted tales of the British Empire's failed attempts to conquer Afghanistan and the defence of the Khyber Pass by the Patan tribesmen, heroic proud men whom he frankly idolised. Here was someone who took it for granted that the British were a scourge, at least in south Asia. In the Australia from which I'd come, the 'cultural cringe' still held sway. It was assumed that the British were the well-spring of true culture. Australians (only white anglo-saxon Australians were included in this category), while not totally alien, were nevertheless a cut below the English, producing an inferior colonial version of the great tradition. Real literature, real history, I was always led to believe, were produced in Europe, and especially in Britain. These beliefs were widespread in the halls of Melbourne University and were lodged in my mind with the force of natural truth. (This even despite the fact that my family had some Irish heritage and had always supported Irish nationalism.) Jan's easy-going contempt for things British was an unexpected antidote to the way we Australians educated in the sixties and before automatically deferred to the English. Setting out for London, I had thought I was on my way to Mecca and that I might never return.

I began writing as soon as I got to Europe, during my visit to Berlin, then went on to London, where I moved into a small upstairs flat in Crouch End with a couple of Australians I had met in India. One of my flatmates, Toni, had a job as Angus and Robertson's expert in Indonesian language—at a time when A&R, then one of Australia's most prominent publishers, with offices in Sydney and London, was expanding into Asia. I doubt if I would ever have been aware of the Angus and Robertson Fellowship if Toni had not brought the details home one afternoon in 1971 and encouraged me to put in an entry. A&R was after a work-in-progress, which was exactly what I had.

Later that year, I submitted my first two chapters, quite similar in form to the final published version, and went to Morocco to escape the miserable London winter. The previous winter, I had written to my Carlton friends lamenting the approach of a New Year without sun. My trip to Morocco, with its midwinter detour to the Ruhr and back, showed me great swathes of Europe which put the continent I had idealised in a different light. The truckie who gave my friend and me a lift had disgorged Spanish oranges in London and, in search of a new cargo somewhere near Cologne, drove us through the endless sprawling industrial landscapes of northern France, where there seemed to be no proper countryside at all. When I had first arrived in Berlin, I had been impressed with how many trees lined the city streets and, by contrast, I had felt Australian urban development to be in a much uglier mode. That trip across France put the earlier judgement in context. In fact, in Australia—where the soils are leached and infertile and the climate is arid or semi-arid, with little to support a dense population, even on the wetter eastern coastal strip—vast open spaces with little development still persist, even into the twenty-first century.

Though I'm now aware that the Tasmanian bluegum is an exotic in Spain and Morocco, and not necessarily desirable there at all, the sight of it that winter gave me a powerful pleasure. I wrote to Denis Murphy of a beach near Essaouira, an Atlantic town west of Marrakesh:

> We came through from the sand dunes and the red river-mouth across hills covered in gum trees and yellow wattle and a feathery bush in white flower. Flaked out in the sun under gum trees. Strangely, very like the feel of the Australian bush. Nice to be there.

In the middle of February 1972, when I picked up my mail at Agadir Post Office, I found a telegram from England which read:

> Community Chest. Proceed directly to telephone. Do not pass go. You collect A&R Fellowship Award. Congratulations. Please ring London collect. Love—John Ferguson, Toni Pollard.

Attempts to phone were frustrated, but a letter which arrived soon afterwards made clear that this was not a joke. John was staggered and thrilled that, out of over two hundred entries (some from well-known Australian writers), one of only two manuscripts sent from A&R's London Office had won the fellowship. It was exciting to read that the judges had said I'd won by 'a small margin of brilliance and boldness' and that, at the literary dinner in Sydney where the award had been announced, Germaine Greer had been guest of honour.

The outline I sent with the two chapters in my submission had stated in general terms that the book would be about a young woman's struggle to come to terms with her role as a woman under pressures from family and society. The man in the car at the end of the second chapter does ask Maureen Craig if she's a lesbian. But there's no other mention, to that point, of a lesbian theme. Within a few days of the news, I wrote home to my friends:

245

> I guess you might have heard by now that I got some money from Angus & Robertson for writing the novel and they're going to publish the goddam thing ... Always reckoned on Aussie censorship keeping it out of the homeland, but no. It's a staggering thing really, getting this ...

The book was developing as a frank and explicit story of a young woman's adventures with both men and women in pursuit of a world where she could be herself and still find pleasure and love. There was no doubt that, by the end of the novel, women would seem a far more promising prospect. To win the prize meant that, when the book got published, I would have to front up and be a public lesbian. In early 1972 it felt like a very high price to pay for the kudos and the cash. My letters reflect this:

> ... just as well I've been in Morocco away from the Literary Dinners, interviews and all that bullshit. Much better out of the way of it—maybe I should stay in the desert.

After winning the fellowship, I moved to Hackney with two men who worked fulltime and I spent the rest of 1972 writing longhand in the kitchen at 5 Powerscroft Road. I wrote from nine to five, at least five days a week, and completed the novel in little more than six months. I hardly ever took a break except on Sundays, when I caught the tube to visit Penny and Rob Gay at Montrose Road, with the next section or chapter hot from the nib. There we drank copious quantities of tea while they read the drafts and offered suggestions and editorial tips. Penny had been a friend back in Melbourne and Rob proved to be equally dedicated to the job of assessing, criticising and encouraging. We laughed our way through a great many afternoons and their contribution to the successful completion of *All That False Instruction* was incalculable.

Near the end of that year, with the first draft of the book complete, I struggled to find a title. Neither I nor any of my friends could come up with anything suitable. Then, one day, I sat down at the kitchen table with my friend Jenny and her friend, Ruth, having put *Music at Big Pink* on the stereo as we often did. The Band's haunting version of *Tears of Rage* (written by Bob Dylan and Richard Manuel) cranked up and the words leapt out at us: 'All that false instruction which we never could believe ... Tears of rage ...' There it was. Perfect. A phrase which (whatever Dylan might have meant by it), to me distilled the notion of prescriptive social conditioning into a punchy and mocking line.

Ironically perhaps, it was during that year that I slowly decided to go home to Australia. My three years away, just over two of these spent in London, had wrought significant changes in my feelings about the place. In 1970, not long after I had arrived in Berlin, I had written to Denis:

> It strikes me ... since I left, that most of the people I knew back home, excluding a few Carlton immortals, will live and die in steady jobs, triple-fronted brick-veneer villas and bored disintegrating marriages (like our own parents). The men are so busy playing at being men and the women at being women that they tend to forget they're humans ... As long as you drink your head off, fuck your head off and marry a virgin, as long as I talk trivialities, never say fuck, be a good mother to me kids, and as long as both of us prefer footy to Beethoven, and never show too much warmth or tenderness, it'll be alright Jack ...

Eighteen months later, writing to Denis again, my sense of London as the perfect escape had shifted:

> Can't honestly depict London as enticing at the moment though I think it'd be a pity if you didn't travel a bit outside Aust. before resigning to life amidst the Fascists ... In fact I am sick to death of the city, the noise, the crowds, the interminable streets and terraces—it's such an enormous bloody place.

Despite my conviction in July 1970 that there 'isn't a place for me in our land of surf and sunshine', I had begun to recognise that I was connected to Australia in a visceral way. I missed the trees, the food, the fresh air and the vast open spaces. I had grown up in the Australian countryside and I found that being away from it for years on end was almost beyond endurance. When I went to see the Ned Kelly film, the gumtrees brought me near to tears. I even missed the culture I had accepted as second-rate—the laconic humour, the stoicism, the sardonic edge. Far from longing to remain forever in the grey mists of Mecca, I realised that Australia attracted me more than Europe's galleries and theatres. I wondered if the great British Tradition had any relevance for me, after all. My time in London, where I had written a book that was anchored in an Aussie tradition that I had yet to discover, was a time of acknowledging a loyalty and sense of belonging to Australian culture. In later years, it has struck me that the implicit sense of colonial inferiority we imbibed as youngsters, and took to be natural, was not unlike the implicit sense of inferiority internalised by women.

I had also come to understand that, contrary to Jan's assertions, even if part of the trouble lay in conditions specific to Australia, the situation of women in general and lesbians in particular was problematic everywhere. By 1972, I had had an affair with a man who was both very different from the 'ockers' I'd known (he was sensitive, honest, and genuinely wanted intimacy), and very similar to them when it came to a certain automatic assumption of control and authority. I had also attempted an affair with a woman who was just as timid and tortured about having a lesbian relationship as anyone Maureen Craig had encountered.

Then, towards the end of 1972, I became friends with Jenny Pausacker from Melbourne. She was living in London with some other Australian women who were already involved in the English women's movement and all of them intended to return to Melbourne over the next few months. This, too, made a difference. While I found feminism a bit weird at this time ('women's dances' seemed pretty strange and I couldn't see why they wouldn't let men who wanted to help come to their meetings), I nevertheless sensed that, back in Melbourne, I might now find a community which would give me a sense of belonging on my own terms. I had no idea of course of the magnitude of the community that would emerge.

I delivered the manuscript to A&R and went home to Melbourne, where I moved in with Jenny, her sister and one of Jenny's feminist friends from London. The new friends to whom I showed *All That False Instruction* subjected it to a feminist fine toothcomb, where any reference that might be interpreted as anti-woman was identified and pointed out to me. It was in this period that the Jody sequence in the last chapter was written and the word 'queer' virtually removed from the text. Looking at the book now, it is interesting to reflect on the history of this word, which had been the denigrating term of description and self-description for gay people before the Liberation movements. The 'out-and-proud' Radicalesbian edit of 1973 replaced 'queer' with 'lesbian' but, oddly, retained 'homosexual' for gay men, in keeping perhaps with the gender-separatist spirit of the times. In the nineties, with the advent of queer theory, the word underwent a kind of reclamation and, had I stuck with my politically incorrect terminology, might by now have been seen as historically authentic.

Meanwhile, by May 1973, A&R and I were having trouble over their promotion of the book. An early press release had the heroine '... joining the abalone fishermen in an attempt to escape her obsessions.' I wrote a sharp letter objecting to the description of Maureen Craig's lesbianism as 'an obsession'. I got a reply agreeing to avoid this sort of approach in future. However, in August of the following year I was informed that '... what we intend doing is a plain-lettered jacket with the sub-title: A Novel of Lesbian Love ... we could also make the two Ls in ALL the outline of two women.' I rejected the subtitle in the strongest terms—I didn't want to sell my book via a titillating title in hot pink. It smacked of sensationalism—'a more than faintly salacious label' in the words of Sue Higgins in *Meanjin*, who echoed the suspicions of other reviewers that the subtitle was a clumsy marketing ploy concocted by the publisher. Worse still, it narrowed what I saw as a much broader canvas. While there is no doubt that I wanted to tell a story of the intolerance endured by lesbians, I was equally concerned to tell the story of a working-class woman growing up in post-war Australia. And even more generally, to tell a story about coming to adulthood as a reluctant outsider. In reply, I got a letter from the London office with the reassurance: 'we will not be using any sub-title'.

Nonetheless the subtitle was used for the hardback edition. Whether A&R's promises might have been honoured, had we not run into other difficulties, I cannot guess at. In September 1974, I took the proofs to show Mum and Dad. This was, I admit, very late in the piece and an honest appraisal of their likely reaction could—and perhaps should—have been made a lot sooner. My book provoked terrible pain and panic for them, especially my mother. Dad, though he remained basically homophobic all his life, seemed able to split his feelings for me away from his general judgements. Right up to his final years in the 1990s, he spoke of the Sydney Mardi Gras with utter disgust, but his loyalty to me somehow allowed me to escape these rather extreme sentiments. He even showed *All That False Instruction*, with obvious pride, to new friends he met after my mother died.

Mum, of course, had to deal with several very difficult things. The centrality of lesbian themes and experiences was as unwelcome to her as to Dad; but for her, there was also the collapse of her intense pleasure at my having won the prize and achieved publication. Although restricted in her own creative pursuits by the poverty and limited ambitions of her rural family, she was a gifted watercolour painter and a prizewinning amateur director and actress, with a very real passion for the arts; her excitement about her daughter's artistic success had been both sincere and shared with everyone she knew. Then there was the explicit nature of the language and material, which offended her in a way it did not offend my dad. Most disturbing of all was the fact that she saw herself in Lotty Craig. The day she read the novel, she cried without a break for twenty-four hours and her face aged about twenty years. (I did reconcile with my parents at the end of 1975, soon after publication and, when Mum died in 1993, I felt that we had gradually come to understand each other as adults with a fair degree of mutual acceptance.)

Looking back, I have no idea if my mother would have actually launched the libel suit she threatened. In fact, *All That False Instruction* IS a novel, not a memoir, and though it draws in part on real life, it is not a literal rendition of it and the characters are not faithful portraits of actual people. A&R and I might well have won the suit if one had been brought.

I left my parents' house in turmoil and rang A&R in Sydney immediately, where I spoke to someone in the marketing division. He told me there were two alternatives: either the book could be withheld until changes were made (I didn't want it delayed any further and didn't want to change it) or the author's name could be changed. I wrote to the London office, apologising for waiting till the eleventh hour to show the book to my family and suggesting the latter course of action. This would perhaps be sufficient to spare my mother the shame she anticipated in the town where she had lived all her life. Later, however, A&R's legal staff decided that the risk of a libel suit succeeding was serious enough that not only should I use a pseudonym, but the novel should also be re-sited to Sydney. The publisher changed all the locations and I abandoned my own name for Elizabeth Riley. ('Riley' I found in a phone book. 'Elizabeth' was chosen as an unimpeachable 'girl's name'.)

While A&R's decision hinged on the possiblity of a lawsuit, my own feelings centred on the implications for my mother and a very real desire to spare her unhappiness. However, her extreme reaction produced an unexpected fringe benefit: it gave me a way out of having to be the author in public, something about which I had always felt ambivalent. I had been imprinted, as was Maureen Craig, with the torture of other people's ostracism and scorn. It's true that by 1975 there were already women's and gay liberation movements in Australia and a certain amount of social and attitudinal change was underway. Lesbians who emerged as adults in this new set of circumstances had sometimes experienced exactly the same pressures as Maureen Craig, but often they had not. I had friends I greatly admired who came out on national prime-time television, but the thought of this kind of exposure for myself filled me with dread. It has taken me most of a lifetime to throw off caution sufficiently to claim the novel in my own name. I'm very glad, though, to have finally shed at least part of my old fear and reluctance. When you're over fifty, life is short and there's not much point in hiding. What the hell!

As it turned out, the decision to issue the book under a pseudonym proved unfortunate for A&R, as well as for me. The judges who gave my proposal the fellowship back in 1972 had probably made a canny choice—the novel was not only in line with that classic 'coming-of-age' tradition of Australian women's writing that includes *My Brilliant Career* and *The Getting of Wisdom*, but the arrival of the women's liberation movement made the early seventies an auspicious moment for a new book of this kind. Now, however, without any possibility of marketing the novel as that of their fellowship winner—or even having an author to promote the book!—A&R lost the investment they'd made in giving me the award. An offer from an American publisher evaporated.

I am very pleased that, for this second editon, the story has been relocated to its original setting in Victoria. However, I do want to apologise to any fans from New South Wales who might feel cheated at seeing Sydney, and especially Newtown, removed from the text. Someone who had been to Sydney University in the sixties once remarked to me on the excellence of the portrait of Newtown at that time. One must assume that it shared an essence with Carlton—though not, of course, the weather. Readers from Victoria have always suspected that the city in the book was not Sydney, but Melbourne with the trams turned into buses. A phrase like: 'The Melbourne winter as usual' never rang true for Sydney, where winter is rather sunny and, to those from the south at least, unbelievably benign.

In the late autumn of 1999, my brother and I drove to Perth to be with our dad while he was dying. Somewhere between Morgan and Port Augusta, as we streaked through the stark arid hills east of the Flinders Ranges, Shane asked me whether I had ever thought of re-printing *All That False Instruction* under my own name and describing how I came to publish my book as Riley. He felt the novel deserved much wider attention than it had received and that the story of how it had been relegated to relative obscurity was worth telling in itself.

In February 2000, I got a letter from an American writer and academic, Harriet Malinowitz, asking me if I would agree to an interview with her for the US monthly *The Women's Review of Books*. She had found my book in New York eleven years earlier and had wanted to locate me ever since. On the day her letter came, I wrote to Harper Collins (which had taken over Angus and Robertson) and commenced the process of recovering my rights and getting the novel reprinted. Though Shane planted the seeds of action, it was Harriet who gently propelled me into it.

Kerryn Higgs
May, 2001

References

Bellamy, Suzanne, 'Fucking Men is for Saints', *Refractory Girl*, June 1976

Greer, Germaine, *The Female Eunuch*, McGraw-Hill 1971

Higgins (Sheridan), Sue, 'Breaking the Rules: New Fiction by Australian Women' in *Meanjin*, Summer 1975

Levy, Bronwen, 'Different Views, Longer Prospects', Keynote Address at *Women Writing: Views and Prospects 1975–1995*

Murray-Smith, Stephen, 'Censorship and Literary Studies' in Dutton, G. and Harris, M. (Eds.), *Australia's Censorship Crisis*, Sun Books, 1970